HIGH-CALIBER
CONCEALER

a novel

BETHANY MAINES

Blue Zephyr Press
2661 N. Pearl, #360
Tacoma WA 98407

Cover art by **LILT**.

ISBN-10: 0692513825
ISBN-13: 978-0692513828

Q: What do you get when you cross Avon Ladies with Charlie's Angels?

A: A world-class intelligence organization run by women who really know their foundation. You get CARRIE MAE.

In *Bulletproof Mascara* Nikki landed unexpectedly in a world of international intrigue and learned to navigate the treacherous waters of her first professional job where it was learn fast or literally die trying. In *Compact with the Devil* the internal politics of Carrie Mae nearly got Nikki killed as she raced to protect the devilishly handsome pop star Kit Masters. Nikki's first two adventures were complicated by her attempts to hide Carrie Mae's real purpose from her family and her boyfriend/CIA agent, Z'ev Coralles. Juggling her work, her love life, and her family might be difficult, but Nikki never thought that a vacation at home on her grandmother's farm could lead to anything disasterous. But drug dealers, a girl in trouble, and an ex-boyfriend who broke her heart might just be her undoing. Now Nikki's personal and professional life are heading for a collision and even her Carrie Mae teammates-—Jenny, Ellen, & Jane— might not be able to save the day. Nikki may be a *High-Caliber Concealer*, but this time it might not be enough.

To Zoe

BRUNCH

Mexico

"I hate this," said Jane. "I can't believe you let Darla split us up."

Nikki wanted to adjust her earpiece, so that Jane's complaints wouldn't be coming in so loudly, but she was in full view out on a city street. Talking to herself and adjusting equipment would be a total giveaway to the mark. So instead, she grimaced behind her sunglasses and sucked it up.

"And Jenny's all by herself back in LA. What if she needs us?"

Nikki wanted to reply that between Jenny's bombshell blonde looks, Southern charm, and weapons proficiency that included everything from tanks to derringers, Jenny could look after herself. Nikki walked a few more feet, pretending to window shop while following her mark, an unassuming bank manager, who was about to have a bad day.

"And what are we doing? Scut work. We're half of the premier Carrie Mae covert action team and we're out on a Robin Hood job that a couple of newbs could handle. It's like having Batman and Robin go after shoplifters. You're Batman, by the way. In case you were concerned by that analogy."

"I'm Batman?" Nikki was startled enough to speak out loud, drawing a stare from a passing blonde, probably a tourist, with a toddler. The toddler looked up and grinned.

"I am Batman!" he yelled and began to run, pulling his mother with him.

"Of course," said Jane. "I would never suggest that you would wear red, yellow, and green all together with your coloring. That would be wrong."

Nikki glanced at her reflection in the shop window—pale skin, gray eyes, red hair. Red, yellow and green would indeed be an atrocity on her. The real question was: did they ever look good on anyone?

"And what about Ellen? Sent off alone to Canada to work for that racist wench. How could you let Darla send her away like that? For one thing, you know Ellen. What if she loses her temper? I mean, she doesn't usually. But what if she goes off on one of her tangents without us there to bring her back down?"

Nikki, had she been able to respond, would have agreed on that point. Ellen had started out life as a professor's wife and mother of two lovely young women who were now mothers themselves. Nikki suspected that she must have lived a Walter Mitty-esque existence prior to joining Carrie Mae. But somehow, between losing fifty pounds and becoming a military-level sniper, Ellen had begun to embrace all of the impulses she had previously kept inside. Unfortunately, not all of her impulses needed to be let out. When Ellen got mad, protocol had a tendency to go out the window.

"Meanwhile," Jane continued, " as your tech officer, I have to say that I'm going to register a complaint when I get back. Half the crap we got in our package is like five years old. I'm not saying we haven't worked with worse, but if Darla would have fully briefed us before we left, maybe I could have packed to compensate. This really is ridiculous. Sub-par gear like this could put your life at risk. I really am going to complain."

Nikki smiled, picturing Jane's Betty Page bangs bouncing in anger. Goth in style, nerd at heart, Jane had a rather black and white view of the world. She frequently missed the nuances of politics—hence her current rant against Darla, the temporary West Coast division manager.

They were a block away from the bank. Time to make a decision. Stick to the plan? Or deviate?

"OK, I've got eyes on the target," said Jane. "You are approaching go time. Phase One, implant the recording device. I'll handle Phase Two."

Nikki pulled the bank manager's wallet out of her skirt pocket and picked up speed. "Excuse me! Excuse me, Sir!" She waved the wallet in the air. The bank manager finally turned around as he reached the corner. "*Hola*," she said putting as much of an American accent on the word as she could. "You dropped your—" she hesitated, pretending to look for the right word. "*Billetera?*"

The bank manager patted his pockets, looking for the wallet that they had removed from his person as he'd left the bank for lunch. He looked surprised and then stepped forward to accept the wallet.

"Ah, *gracias*. I'm not sure how that happened." His English, as was to be expected from someone working in international finance, was flawless. She held out the wallet and waited until his fingers made contact with the leather.

"There's a bank account number inside. You will transfer all of the funds from Jirair Sarkassian's account into it."

"I can't do that! Who are you?" He pulled at the wallet wanting to leave.

"You will do it, Raul." Nikki held onto the wallet, and with her right hand she flicked out a deadly sharp little pocket-knife. The blade clicked as it locked into place and Raul's eyes widened at the sound. She took a step closer, pushing the knife against his groin, hiding the movement with her full skirt.

Raul's face went white under his tan. "I can't just transfer a client's funds!" He gasped, sweating. "He'll notice. You don't know who he is. He has associates who are… not nice people. And I've heard his girlfriend is psychotic. What you're asking is suicide."

"Trust me, Raul. He won't notice. He's dead. And as for his girlfriend—who do you think I am?"

Raul gulped.

"Just transfer the money like a good boy Raul, and I won't have to cut off any appendages." Nikki smiled and released the wallet. "You have until the close of business, understand?" He nodded and Nikki removed the knife, smiled and patted his cheek. "Good boy." Nikki proceeded up the street, leaving Raul sweating through his suit on the corner.

For the first time in an hour there was quiet in her earpiece. She made it nearly two blocks in blissful silence before Jane cleared her throat.

"Nikki, I'm fairly certain that was not what we were supposed to do. Darla had a whole plan."

"Two things," said Nikki, continuing toward the rendezvous point. "One, that plan was overly complicated and ridiculous. Two, Darla's not here. I took a short-cut and the job got done."

"If he complies," said Jane, sounding nervous.

"He'll comply," said Nikki.

"Probably, but it might have been nice if you'd let me know."

Nikki's stride slowed. There was an undercurrent to Jane's tone. "I was trying to give you plausible deniability."

"Well, I was kind of looking forward to getting to do… Never mind. It doesn't matter."

There was static as Jane's line went dead. Nikki saw her friend walk out of the alleyway in front of her. Even in sunny Mexico, Jane was dressed in all black. This week the tips of her hair were dyed purple.

"Also, I'm not comfortable with you pretending to be Val Robinson. It gives me the creeps."

"What are you talking about?"

"You told that guy you were Sarkassian's girlfriend. At her time of death, I'm pretty sure that was Val. Don't pretend to be her; it's bad mojo."

Nikki shrugged. "I didn't have time to go through the six degrees of separation. It was faster this way."

Jane looked skeptical, before her focus switched to a point a few inches above Nikki's head, her expression blank. Probably observing the internet through the screen of her Google-glass type eyewear, one of Carrie Mae's more recent innovations.

"He just logged in, and is transferring the money. That was fast. I guess you were right. Anyway, I'm all for speed and efficiancy, but this doesn't make you a little uncomfortable? I mean, you kind of robbed a guy on the street. You're a mugger!"

"When you take fifty dollars, you're a mugger. When you take five million dollars, you're a businesswoman."

"And if you use that five million to fund an organization dedicated to fighting for the rights of women?"

"Then I say that makes me a Goddamned hero," said Nikki. "Now let's get out of here. I have a date tonight."

JULY II
MIDNIGHT SNACK

Los Angeles

Nikki and Z'ev walked out of the salsa club laughing and holding hands. Date night with Z'ev Coralles, her half Afro-cuban, half-Jewish, all CIA agent boyfriend, had started out with dinner and moved on to dancing. She loved it when he planned date night—everything was always perfect.

"I guess we should practice that a bit more," said Z'ev ruefully. "That was bad. I didn't remember half the turn patterns."

"We weren't the worst couple on the dance floor," protested Nikki.

"We were rusty at best. You had a couple of good shines though."

"Whatever," said Nikki, secretly pleased. Three years into their relationship and his compliments still made her smile, his rich, bass voice still gave her shivers, and the smile in his brown eyes made a bad day seem pretty good. Date night was just what the doctor ordered. A body-glitter covered nymph snaked by them wearing a loin-cloth that sort of passed for a skirt, spiked platform heels, and mile-long blonde hair extensions. Her partner was wearing a skintight black Lycra shirt and pleather pants.

"See? If we keep practicing, some day we could be just like them," said Z'ev, leaning over to whisper in her ear.

"Oh, yeah, I can really picture you in those pants," said Nikki, biting her lip to keep from laughing.

"Well, I can't say I'd be entirely unhappy with those shoes," he said, taking on a speculative tone as he watched the glitter girl walk away.

"Oh, honey, I've got some of those—you can try them on when we get home."

Z'ev laughed and separated from her to go key-fishing in his pocket. They stopped at the Impala, Z'ev moving to unlock her door first. She stared at the car feeling a swell of sadness. Val Robinson, Nikki's first partner in Carrie Mae, and previous owner of the Impala, had abandoned Carrie Mae principles for money and a hot guy. Only her boyfriend, Jirair Sarkassian wasn't just an arms dealer, he'd been selling Thai girls into a world-wide sex slave ring. Nikki had stopped Sarkassian and Val—permanently—on her first mission with Carrie Mae. And this morning's little jaunt to Tijuana meant that they had finally rooted out the last of Sarkassian's little stashes. She hadn't wanted to tell Jane that half the reason she'd skipped the elaborate hacking scheme to simply threaten poor Raul is that she had wanted the matter done. She wanted to close the case files on Val Robinson once and for all. Which meant that she probably should consider selling the car.

She brushed her finger along the chrome detail of the door panel. Around her, Nikki listened to the babble of voices, mostly in Spanish. There was a rise in the volume of voices behind them and Nikki looked over her shoulder. A group of tough looking hombres were working their way through the crowd, all wife-beaters, gold and tattoos. They didn't appear to be doing anything more than laughing and joking with some of the other exiting club-goers, but mentally Nikki put them into the 'threat' category.

"I'm hungry," Z'ev said. "Want to get something to eat?" Nikki knew then that he'd also spotted the threat as he paused to take off his jacket. Biceps that size were usually a deterrent.

"We've got stuff at home. Besides the only thing that's open right now are more bars or Taco Bell." Nikki kept her tone light and watched the crowd part. The three men had almost passed them when one of them looked directly at Nikki and Nikki felt a jolt of recognition.

"Nikki?" he said, sounding almost as stunned as she felt.

"Donny?" asked Nikki.

That brought the attention of his friends and all three stopped—the two friends fanning out behind Donny in a spear shape pointed at Nikki. One of them had a gun tucked in the front of his pants. The other was casually rattling something in a film canister. Z'ev moved to her side of the car, making his presence noticeable.

"Nikki, how long has it been?" exclaimed Donny, reaching to embrace her and Nikki reciprocated.

"Forever! How are you? How's the family?"

"Good! You should call Mom. I know she'd love to hear from you. Do you have a piece of paper? I'll give you her number."

"Yeah, all right." Nikki fished in her purse and found a receipt and a pen, puzzled, but feeling that she was doing what he wanted. Z'ev hadn't moved, but the two amigos had relaxed and one was flirting with a girl.

"Have you seen Jackson lately?" asked Donny, as he scribbled the number on the back of the receipt. Nikki looked away from the number he was writing and into his face, annoyed. Z'ev was standing right there. Why did he have to bring up Jackson?

"Oh, you know, not since freshman year of college," she said, carefully casual.

"Not since then, huh? Never understood why you guys

couldn't make it work." He handed the receipt and pen back. "Anyway, give Mom a call. Tell her I'm doing fine and I'll call her in a couple of days."

"Yo, dawg, let's go," said one of the friends. "We gotta hook up with Billy."

"Yeah, yeah," agreed Donny, waving him away. "I gotta go," he said turning back to Nikki. "Hey, you gonna be OK with this foo'?" he asked, stepping back and taking his first real look at Z'ev. Nikki glanced over her shoulder at Z'ev, her eyes twinkling.

"With him? Yeah, I think so." She grinned at Donny's suddenly raised eyebrow.

"Well, you better take care of her then, *esé*," said Donny, suddenly going all tough and sort of flexing his shoulders in the way that only men seemed to be able to do.

"*Siempre*," said Z'ev calmly and not moving a muscle.

"Always is a long time," Donny said, backing off a bit.

Z'ev shrugged. Donny's friends had walked a little further down the sidewalk and Donny looked after them and suddenly sighed, looking a little tired.

"*Buenas noches*, Nicole," he said again and Nikki smiled. He started to jog after his friends. "And call that number," he called back over his shoulder and Nikki waved. Nikki held the receipt up to the neon glow of the bar signs. It had MEYERS and a 253 area code written on it.

Z'ev opened her car door and she got in, reaching across to unlock the driver's side before he got to it.

"You have a lot of friends who are drug dealers?" he asked, sliding into the seat and slamming the door.

"Drug dealers?" asked Nikki, startled.

"The film canister," said Z'ev, miming the shaking motion

she had seen Donny's friend using. "It's got crack in it. They give it a rattle and the sound let's you know they're dealing."

"Oh," said Nikki, punching in the number on her phone. "I guess that explains it."

"Explains what?" he asked, starting the car.

"Why he was wearing a wire - felt it when I hugged him," said Nikki. A Tacoma Police Department operator answered the phone.

"Yes, I need to speak to someone named Meyers regarding Donny Fernandez," she said to the operator. The operator immediately put her on hold.

"And this number goes to a police station," Nikki said turning back to Z'ev. She held up the receipt and he scrutinized it as they pulled up to a stoplight.

"This is Meyers," said a woman, abruptly answering the phone. She sounded as if she'd been hurrying.

"Hi, I just spoke with Donny," said Nikki.

"Where?" asked the woman, interrupting.

"Excuse me?"

"You saw him? You saw Don Fernandez?"

"Yes." Nikki noticed the shortening of Donny's name and realized that, as a fully-grown man, Donny might not appreciate being called by something that ended in a Y.

"Where?" demanded the woman. "When?"

"LA, about five minutes ago," answered Nikki, copying the woman's staccato pacing.

"LA? Damn it! What's he doing down there?"

"I don't know," said Nikki. "But he told me to say that he was fine and he'd call you in a couple of days."

"A couple of days? He's not supposed to disappear like this!"

Nikki heard the wail of confusion and worry hiding behind the woman's gruff tone.

"I'm sure he'll be fine," said Nikki soothingly.

"Who are you?" asked the woman, her tone suddenly becoming suspicious.

"Just a friend he bumped into," said Nikki. "Nice chatting with you. I'm sure he'll call. Bye now."

"But," began the woman, as Nikki cut her off, flipping the phone shut.

"Why didn't you give him your name?" asked Z'ev.

"Her," corrected Nikki. "And I have enough women yelling at me during the day. I refuse to give my name to one at night just so she can yell at me on my phone."

"You don't think she had caller id?"

"It went through a switch board. I don't think it'll be that easy."

"Aren't you worried about him?"

"Who, Donny?" Nikki scoffed. "He can take care of himself. Besides, he seemed fine." She wanted to say that she'd get Jane to run a check on Monday when she went into work, but didn't.

"So where do you know Donny from?" asked Z'ev, changing the subject.

"We went to school together in Kaniksu Falls and his mom used to babysit me."

"Kaniksu Falls? I thought you went to school in Seattle? Where's Kaniksu Falls?"

"It's a postage stamp of a logging town in Washington, About as far north as you can get without being in Canada, and as far East as you can get without being in Idaho. My grandparents live—lived there. Now it's just my grandma. Mom and Dad moved in with them before I was born. So I went to elementary school there, spent most of my summers with Dad's mom in Canada. Donny's mom used to baby-sit us; we were the Three Musketeers. Then, in sixth grade, when my dad split, Mom and I moved to Seattle."

"Who was the third?"

"What?"

"You said three musketeers. That usually implies three."

Nikki kicked herself for her slip up. All she had to do was stick to Donny, but no, she had to go mention the three of them.

"Oh. Uh, our friend Jackson. We kind of ran around like wild monkey-children." Nikki chuckled a little, remembering their eight-year-old selves.

"Jackson? Is that the guy Donny asked about? Guy you used to go out with?"

"Uh, yeah, we dated for about a second and a half. I think that's the restaurant Jenny recommended," said Nikki pointing out the window.

"In Junior High?" Z'ev sounded skeptical.

"No, his family moved to Seattle when we were in high school. We went out for a bit during senior year. Jenny said that restaurant was really good. We should try it sometime."

"But you broke up?"

"Yeah, we did." Nikki looked out the window. She didn't want to talk about Jackson. She didn't want to think about Jackson. For years now, she had been avoiding the topic in her head the way a person with a cavity will avoid chewing on that side. Why did he have to bring this up?

"It was just one of those things, you know? Stupid high school boyfriends." That hurt a little to say, but she could see that

Z'ev believed it and that was what mattered. "I haven't seen him since college." That at least was true.

"That's too bad," said Z'ev and Nikki glanced over at him nervously, waiting for the other shoe to drop. "You hate to lose touch with someone you grew up with over something like that."

"Yeah," agreed Nikki. "I guess I should have asked Donny how he was or something." She waited a beat. "Oh well, too late," she said cheerfully and Z'ev laughed again.

"Nice to know you're not bitter."

"No, really, I'm not," denied Nikki. "It's just been so long, you know? Why go there? What would we have to say to each other?"

"Yeah, I guess," he agreed with a shrug.

"Anyway, why do you care about some old boyfriend? You're not suspicious I've been secretly corresponding with Jackson for nine years, are you?"

"No, I'm just impressed that once again your entire history is one big grey area."

"What do you mean?" asked Nikki, startled.

"Well, you're Canadian, but not."

"I was born in Canada and my father's Canadian."

"You're from Seattle, but not."

"I lived in Seattle from high school on, and everyone knows where Seattle is. It's easier to say Seattle."

"You work for a make-up company, but you don't sell make-up."

"The Carrie Mae Foundation does a lot of good work."

"I'm not saying there aren't good reasons. I'm saying, is anything ever an absolute with you?" He spoke with a smile, but Nikki sensed he was serious. He didn't like surprises.

"My life is… complex." It was the best explanation she could come with.

"Baby, I work for the CIA and my life is less complex," he said dryly. "And with your tendency to get into gun battles and what-not, forgive me if I'm suspicious."

"There's nothing to be suspicious of," said Nikki, firmly.

He parked the car in her slot and turned off the engine. "Yeah," he said pausing, hand still on the ignition. "Maybe." He turned his head and smiled at her, his sleepy brown eyes twinkling and his mouth curving into the smile that made her heart do backflips. "Now about those shoes…"

JULY III
BREAKFAST

Nikki's eyelids popped open as if they were on springs. California sunshine filtered through the shades, dragging her from dreams about Kaniksu Falls. The image of her grandparent's farm still floated before her eyes. She rolled over to check the time and realized Z'ev was in the way. Sitting up with a smile, she leaned over to kiss him awake, but hesitated when she saw the clock. The red LED display claimed it was 6:45. Nikki yawned and stretched. It was too early to be awake on a Sunday.

Thinking of home reminded her of Donny, and she frowned as she went into the bathroom. Last night, she'd been certain that Donny could handle whatever came up, but this morning it seemed worrisome that he was so far away from any back up or support. Spitting out toothpaste, she came to a decision. If Donny was in trouble, it wasn't going to wait until Monday.

Nikki got dressed quietly and slipped out of the apartment, pausing to leave Z'ev a note that included a whole string of x's and o's. She never knew when he was going to be called into work, so she figured it was important to make sure all written communications included a quantity of hugs and kisses.

Gliding into LA proper with the top down on the sky-blue Chevy Impala, Nikki enjoyed the sunny Sunday morning and lack of traffic. She thought again about selling the car. It was a gas-guzzler, had a turning radius of a city block, and still smelled faintly of Val's cigarettes and perfume. It was damaging, old-fashioned, and unnecessarily flashy. Basically, it was the car version of Valerie Robinson. But she loved that Z'ev had laughed out loud when he'd seen it for the first time and then wanted to drive. She loved that she got nods from the homeboys when she was out. To be perfectly honest, she loved the car. Nikki cranked the radio loud enough to be heard over the rushing wind and put her foot down on the gas.

"I'm just not ready to let you go," said Nikki and patted the dash, so she could pretend she was talking to the car.

Nikki pulled up in front of a towering, glass-faced office building that was the west-coast headquarters of the Carrie Mae Foundation, and then turned down into the parking garage underneath the building. Even on a Sunday morning, there were a few cars in the parking garage but Nikki recognized Rachel White's new, red, VW bug with the Ben Hur style rims. Rachel ran the research and development department, more commonly known as Wonderland, in the basement of Carrie Mae. Nikki made a mental note to pop down and thank her for the acetylene torch / hairspray can. It had worked really well in the field.

Nikki walked into the front lobby and flashed her ID badge at the security guard, who smiled and waved in recognition. She walked past the honor wall. Discreet brass plaques with the names of fallen agents were stacked in an even grid from the floor to mid-way up the wall. As usual, Nikki reached out and touched Val's plaque. She'd accrued a lot of debt when she'd asked to have Val's name put on the wall, but she didn't think that twenty years of service, of being the biggest badass in the company, should be wiped out by a couple of months of stupid decisions. She'd learned a few things about Val when she'd taken possession of the car—things she hadn't told anyone—and so she touched the plaque to remind herself not be that stupid and to strive to be that great. And to make sure no one removed the plaque.

Nikki was reaching for the elevator button when she heard the traditional ding and the elevator doors opened. Rachel and Jane were standing in the elevator laughing. They both had the rumpled, slightly bleary look of people who'd been up all night, but they were laughing hysterically.

"Nikki!" exclaimed Jane. "Redhead!" That sent Rachel into a fresh gust of laughter.

"Yes," agreed Nikki, trying to fathom what was so funny. "I've been that way for awhile now." Jane giggled again, but Rachel made an effort to pull herself together.

"Sorry, Nikki, I think," Rachel paused to chuckle at Jane's laughter. "I think," she continued, "that we may have gotten a bit of laughing gas off Experiment-217. What are you doing here on a Sunday?"

"I was about to ask you guys the same thing," said Nikki, stepping into the elevator. "But I'm glad you are. I need to find someone, fast." Nikki pushed the button for the seventh floor and Jane groaned.

"No, Nikki. We've just finished and were going out to breakfast," wailed Jane.

"It'll only take a minute," soothed Nikki. Jane crossed her arms and leaned dejectedly against the elevator wall.

"It had better be only a minute," she muttered. "I'm hungry."

"Well, I haven't had breakfast yet either," said Nikki. "And besides, I've got Z'ev at home. I can't take too long."

"Yeah?" said Rachel perking up. "You're still seeing Mr. CIA?"

Nikki nodded.

"You gonna tell him about Carrie Mae?"

"She can't!" said Jane, shocked. "She wouldn't! You won't, will you?"

Nikki shook her head.

"You can't trust boys. Remember that."

Nikki chuckled. "You sound like my mother."

"Well," interjected Rachel, "then they're both paranoid. It's the CIA part of him I'd be worrying about."

"Can we keep it down?" asked Nikki, looking pained. "Darla hasn't figured out I'm dating a CIA agent yet, and I'm not really looking to explain it to her, if you know what I mean."

Rachel rolled her eyes. "Yeah, I hear you. Fortunately, Miss Utah isn't in the building. I swear, I cannot wait for Mrs. Merrivel to get back. The girls down in research were thinking about sending Mr. Merrivel a get-well-soon card, but I was wondering if maybe we couldn't maybe come up with something a little more useful. He had heart surgery, right? Was it a pacemaker thing? We could probably come up with a really great pacemaker if I had the girls think about it seriously."

"Mrs. Merrivel will be back when Mr. Merrivel gets better—and no, you cannot put an experimental pacemaker in his chest." Nikki tried to sound calm. Sometimes Rachel was a little too certain that her gadgets were awesome. "Meanwhile, can you give Darla a chance? She's actually got some good ideas."

Rachel rolled her eyes. "All of her ideas seem to involve cutting my budget."

"If all of Darla's ideas are so great, why are you sneaking into the building for illicit use of resources," said Jane. "You wouldn't have to do that with Mrs. M."

"I've had several years to build up a rapport with Mrs. M,"

said Nikki. "I want to work with Darla, but I also want to save lives. So, we'll just not mention this little excursion, OK?"

Jane laughed, as the elevator slowed to a halt. "OK. So, who are we trying to find?"

"An old friend of mine I bumped into last night," answered Nikki, reaching for the emergency phone.

"Speak roughly to your little boy, and beat him when he sneezes," said Nikki into the red phone and she heard the faint click that told her that the password was being processed. The weekly passwords were always quotes from Alice in Wonderland and Nikki's copy of Alice had begun to look rather well-thumbed as she had taken on the habit of looking up the quotes.

"I think he's in trouble," Nikki continued, returning to her conversation with Jane.

As they navigated the maze of cubicles toward Nikki's desk, Nikki told Jane and Rachel about her encounter with Donny.

"Hmm," said Jane, seating herself at Nikki's desk and logging on to the computer. "Give me a second." Jane's fingers flew across the keyboard and Rachel lounged in the cubicle entrance, watching with interest.

"Wow," said Jane, frowning at the computer screen, "Tacoma's police computer system is complete crap. I don't know why police departments insist on hiring former officers in their tech departments. Give me a minute while I break down this firewall." Jane typed a bit more, her eyebrows going up in a sharp "V" of concentration.

"OK, it should be printing out now," said Jane, hitting the enter button. Rachel walked away and then came out with a printout with Donny's picture on it.

"He looks nice," said Rachel, looking at the picture. Nikki

leaned over Rachel's shoulder and read the paper. Donny did look nice. His picture was a crisp, clean-cut, by the book, police department photo.

"He's investigating someone named Emmanuel Ruiz," said Nikki, reading from the print out, and Jane nodded.

"I'm looking him up now," said Jane, pointing at the screen. "Drug runner. I-5 corridor. Not a nice man."

"Current address?" asked Nikki.

"Last known was here in LA, but it says it's no longer active," said Jane and Nikki sighed in frustration.

"Donny probably is fine, but I'd feel better if I could go and ask him myself. You know?"

"Well," said Jane, "do you want me to leave this on the watch list for the next shift? They can call you if anything pops up on the grid or if they get anything on the police scanners. It's probably a misuse of company resources, but I doubt Darla will notice." Jane typed in a work order and emailed it. "So," said Jane, slapping her hands together and rubbing them together. "Where we going for breakfast?"

"Some place that serves Bloody Marys," said Rachel, leading the way back toward the elevator.

"I'm with you there," answered Jane, "but I want pancakes too. How about you, Nikki?"

"Pancakes and alcohol - it's working for me. There's an IHOP around here somewhere, isn't there? Or a Denny's. They have a bar, right?"

"I think so, but wherever you want to go is fine, 'cause I figure you're buying."

"I'm buying?" asked Nikki in mocking disbelief.

"You held up my breakfast for a whole twenty minutes," said

Jane. "And you made me work on a Sunday. You owe us."

"Oh, fine." Nikki shook her head as though the entire affair was a huge trial. "The things I do for my friends." Just then, Nikki's cell phone began to trumpet the *William Tell Overture*.

"High-ho, Silver, and away!" yelled Jane, as Nikki reached for her phone.

"It must be Z'ev," said Rachel.

"How could you tell?" asked Nikki startled, pausing with her finger over the answer button.

"Nobody gets that moony over a Lone Ranger song if it isn't their boyfriend," Rachel said. And Nikki finished answering the phone with a chuckle in her voice.

"Hey!" she said cheerfully.

"Hey, yourself," said Z'ev, and Nikki could hear the smile in his voice. "I thought you weren't working this weekend."

"I had a thought," said Nikki. "And I couldn't fall back asleep."

He laughed. "A thought, huh? You couldn't just write it down and wait till Monday?"

"Hey, I have to act on these things before they go away."

"Well, how about having the thought of coming home for breakfast?"

"Oh. Breakfast." Nikki looked guiltily at Rachel and Jane, who were maintaining carefully neutral expressions. "Um…"

"Um…" repeated Z'ev.

"I kind of promised to buy Jane and Rachel pancakes. I kind of owe them for helping me out this morning."

"I'll make pancakes," volunteered Z'ev. "Bring them over."

"Really?" asked Nikki surprised. He usually wasn't huge in the meet and greet department.

"Yeah, sure. I mean, I'll have to put on pants, but for your friends I'll make the effort."

Nikki laughed out loud. "Well that makes me feel special," she said. "But the real question is, do we have anything to make Bloody Marys out of?"

"Um…" she could hear him opening cupboards in the background and the slight unsuctioning sound as the fridge door opened. "We will if you stop at the store for the vegetables and tomato juice on the way home."

"So, in fact that would be a no?" asked Nikki and gestured Rachel and Jane into the elevator as it arrived.

"Well, you have vodka, so I say it's a yes."

"Right, so I'll stop at the store and be home in a bit."

"Cool. I'll start on the pancakes."

"'Kay. Bye."

"Love you. Bye," he answered and Nikki flipped her phone shut.

"New plan, ladies," said Nikki. "Pancakes and Bloody Marys are going to be served at the International House of Nikki."

"IHON?" asked Jane. "Doesn't have the same ring."

"You could go with IHOZ," said Rachel.

"International House of Z'ev?" asked Jane. "Yeah, that does sound better."

Nikki's phone rang again and Nikki sighed as Patsy Cline's *Crazy* filled the air.

"Isn't that your mom's new ring tone?" asked Jane. "Are you going to answer that?"

"Yes," said Nikki reluctantly picking up the phone. "Hi Mom."

"Oh, you're up," said her mom, sounding surprised. "I was

going to leave you a message."

"Well, now you can tell me," said Nikki trying not to be annoyed.

"Well, first of all," her mom's voice switched tones slightly veering into the planning voice, "we need to talk about the holidays."

"The holidays? Mom, it's the middle of summer."

"The perfect time to start watching those holiday air fares. Plus, I talked to your grandmother and she really wants us to come home this year. And I thought you might want to invite Z'ev."

"Uh…" said Nikki. She hadn't been expecting the conversation to go straight to the dating side. "I'm not sure we're there yet."

"You're twenty-six, Nicole. You'd better start thinking about being there. Besides, you've been living together for over a year."

"Uh, I'll think about it," said Nikki. Thinking about that was about the last thing she wanted to do, but a flat refusal would only make the nagging worse. "Is that all you were going to leave a message about?"

"Oh, no, I was going to tell you about your grandmother."

"You already said, Mom. She wants us to come home."

"Yeah, that. No, I was going to tell you what she said about Donny Fernandez. You remember your friend from elementary school?"

Nikki felt her heart freeze.

"What about Donny, Mom?"

"Apparently, he joined the police force down in Tacoma. Can't think why anyone lives there. Only now, he's missing!"

"Missing?" repeated Nikki.

"Oh yes," said Nell, relishing the details. "Apparently, a policewoman came out to see his mom last week to explain that Donny is missing. Has been missing for weeks. He went undercover in a combined police DEA operation and they lost track of him."

"Are you supposed to know about the thing with the DEA?"

"Well, they had to tell his mother. And Grandma said it was top secret and I wasn't to tell anyone, but who are you going to tell? Anyway," Nell continued, sounding blasé on the subject, "if he doesn't turn up soon, the department's going to hold a funeral. It's a tragedy."

"His mom and sisters must be freaking out," said Nikki.

"Pretty much. It's really terrible," said Nell, sounding sad in the distant way of someone totally unrelated. "Anyway, that was it. You should really think about the holidays."

"Yeah, I'll do that, Mom," mumbled Nikki, still thinking about Donny. How was she going to get him out of this mess?

JULY IV
LUNCH

Ice cream and the beach. It was a great Sunday routine. Although, considering how rarely either of them was in town for successive weeks, it wasn't much of a routine. Nikki considered every Sunday a luxury. When her phone rang, Z'ev groaned, and flipped it over.

"It's work," he said, handing it to her.

"I'm ignoring it," she said. He held the phone out, surprise clear on his face.

"I'll go get the ice cream," he said, a subtle thank you. They usually argued about who had to leave the safety of the blanket to trek across the sand for ice cream. "Vanilla and sprinkles?" he asked reaching into her bag for his wallet.

"Yes, please," said Nikki. She admired his calves as they walked past her field of vision, then rolled over to check out his butt as he walked away.

As soon as he was out of view, Nikki grabbed her phone and hit call back.

"This is the Carrie Mae Foundation," said the polite female voice that answered on the first ring. "How can we help you help the world?" It was the Foundation's newest tagline and they were repeating it into irritation.

"This is Nikki Lanier. You just called me?" said Nikki, hoping they had something on Donny for her.

"Just one moment," said the voice and then Nikki heard the

cheerful tones of *Blame it on the Bossanova*, until a second voice picked up the phone.

"Voice identification, please."

"He only does it to annoy, because he knows it teases," quoted Nikki.

"Thank you, Nicole." Nikki knew that her file must have popped up on the info tech's computer screen. It was the only time anyone called her Nicole. "You put a Don Fernandez and Emmanuel Ruiz on the watch list?"

"Yes," said Nikki.

"We have an agent removing an informant from a dangerous situation. This person does have information about Emmanuel Ruiz and is willing to talk to you, but briefly. They can be at your location in two minutes, do you want a meeting?"

"Yes," answered Nikki firmly. She stood up and slipped into her flip-flops. Pinching the phone between her ear and her shoulder, she tied her wrap around her waist and grabbed the pink straw bag, heading for the parking lot.

"Transferring your call to Melissa now."

"The GPS says I'm right on top of you, but I could use a few more landmarks," said a brisk voice almost immediately.

"The parking lot south of the Ferris Wheel. Redhead next to the blue Impala," said Nikki, jogging to make her statement true. She had barely arrived at the car when a low riding, black-windowed, acid green two-door Honda Civic pulled to a stop.

"Hey, you Nicole?" asked the driver, getting out. She was about Nikki's age and wore sagged Dickies and a white tank top over a black bra.

"Melissa?" The girl nodded.

"That your car?" she asked, jerking her head toward the Impala as she walked around to the passenger side of her car.

"Yeah," said Nikki, feeling the familiar twinge of car guilt.

"Nice."

"Thanks. Yours too."

"What do you want to know about Emmanuel Ruiz?" asked Melissa, pausing with her hand on the door handle.

"I don't actually, but I have a friend who's an undercover cop. I think he's in trouble and I know he's going after Ruiz. I need to find my friend before something happens to him." Melissa nodded and opened the passenger door. Sitting in the passenger seat was a little girl of about nine or ten. She had big dark eyes and clutched a purple backpack nervously.

"This is Elly Ruiz," said Melissa. "She's going to stay with her grandparents." The little girl nodded.

"Hi, Elly," said Nikki softly, kneeling down to look Elly in the eye.

"*Hola,*" whispered Elly.

"Do you know where your father is?"

"She doesn't speak a lot of English," said Melissa.

"*Donde està su padre, hoy?*" asked Nikki switching languages.

"*Èl va al parque.*"

"Park?" repeated Nikki. "Which park? *Que parque?*"

"MacArthur," said Elly. "*Por el carmelo grande.*"

"By the big candy?" asked Nikki, looking up at Melissa in confusion. Melissa shook her head.

"*Caramelo rojo grande,*" repeated Elly, nodding. She let go of her backpack and gestured with both hands up above her head. Suddenly Melissa laughed.

"The Big Candy. It's a sculpture in MacArthur Park. Big red thing with white blobs on it. Sits up on these stilt things. On the

6th Street side of the park." Nikki nodded.

"Do you know when, Elly?" asked Nikki. "*Cuando?*"

Elly held up one hand, her fingers spread.

"*Cinco?*" asked Nikki, and Elly nodded.

"*Gracias,*" said Nikki, leaning into the car to hug the little girl. "You were a big help."

"Is she going to be safe with her grandparents?" asked Nikki, as Melissa shut the car door.

"Should be," said Melissa. "I'll have someone keep tabs on her."

"Thanks Melissa, I owe you one."

"No sweat. I'll call in the favor someday."

Melissa got back into the Honda and drove off, the neon green car sliding along the road like a slot car, cornering evenly and weaving in and out of traffic.

Nikki shook her head, and patted the Impala affectionately. Walking back toward their spot on the beach, Nikki scanned the sand, looking for Z'ev. She was nearly to the blanket when she spotted him talking to a middle-aged guy in a straw hat, who was almost certainly not the ice cream vendor. Nikki could tell by the lack of an ice cream cart.

As she watched, Straw Hat handed a slip of paper to Z'ev, who scrutinized it and then put it away in his pocket. They shook hands and Straw Hat moved away at an easy amble, heading in Nikki's general direction. Nikki frowned. Z'ev was working. She knew what working looked like and Z'ev was doing it. He was working on their only weekend together this month! The CIA weren't even supposed to work inside the country.

Nikki flopped down on the blanket, fuming. She kicked off her flip-flops and placed her bag in the original indent it had left in the sand before her trip to the car. Stripping off her wrap, she shoved it back into the bag, only then noticing that Z'ev's gun wasn't inside. If there was any doubt before, there wasn't now. No one took a gun to get ice cream. He must have gotten it when he reached in for his wallet. The fact that she hadn't noticed irritated Nikki even further. And now he was going to come back and wonder why she was mad and then he would know that she knew and then he would wonder how she knew when she was supposed to be being lazy on the blanket.

Nikki took a deep breath and let it out slowly. Maybe there was another explanation. She had to get over this in a hurry. He always knew when she was mad. She just wasn't very good at acting. Maybe he had taken the gun out of habit. Nikki knew that lately she felt a little defenseless when she went out without some weaponry, and he had been in the business a lot longer than she had. Maybe that was it. And maybe Straw Hat had been just some guy, handing Z'ev a business card. It could happen. Nikki took another deep breath and settled herself in a relaxed position on the blanket. She was concentrating so hard on being calm that she didn't realize Z'ev was back until he dripped ice cream on her stomach.

Nikki sat up with a small gasp as the cold ice cream made contact with her skin.

"Oh, not funny, mister," said Nikki reaching for her towel.

"I didn't do it on purpose," protested Z'ev, but laughing while he did so.

"Sure, you didn't," said Nikki shooting him an angry look over the top of her sunglasses.

"It was an accident, I swear," said Z'ev sitting down and handing her a vanilla cone with sprinkles and a cherry. He was working on something with chocolate and covered in whip cream.

Nikki bit back an angry retort and accepted the ice cream cone.

"What do you want to do about dinner?" asked Nikki when the soothing balm of ice cream had been applied to her tongue.

"It's not even two yet and you're worried about dinner?"

"I like to plan ahead."

"I don't know. What do you want to do about dinner?"

"There's this cute little Indian place over on West Sixth I've been wanting to try."

"West Sixth, where's that at?"

"LA proper, over by MacArthur Park."

"Oh. Sure, sounds good."

Nikki congratulated herself on the ease of her maneuvering and finished off her ice cream, saving the cherry for last.

JULY V

DINNER

Nikki checked her watch. She had thirty minutes before she had to meet Z'ev. She'd lucked out when he'd gone off to meet an old friend for "drinks." Nikki had nodded and pretended she believed him. Z'ev did not have old friends. Or if he did, they certainly didn't have his phone number or know where he lived. He was totally, totally working. Nikki knew it shouldn't bother her as much as it did. After all, she was working. Why shouldn't he? But it grated. It grated on her that she was lying. It grated on her that he was lying. She wondered how long they could keep this up. She loved him, she thought he loved her, but really… how long until their relationship became an impediment to their jobs?

Nikki peeked through her binoculars. She was parked across the street from the park on Alvarado. MacArthur Park was split in two by Wilshire Boulevard and the southern half of the park was mostly taken up by a small lake, while the northern portion had play areas, a band stand, and a soccer field. The Red Candy sculpture protruded from the tree line like a pink UFO. Installed in 1987, the original bright red had faded in the sun over the years. The park had a history of gang violence, but stepped up police patrols in recent years had put a damper on the violence and currently the park was filled with families, roller skaters and dog walkers for L.A.'s lazier dog owners. The closest group to the sculpture was a child's birthday. One child, who appeared to be about six, whacked away at a piñata that was almost the same size as the little girl was and shaped like Snow White. The family cheered her on, their claps punctuated by the sound of the boombox pumping out Ariana Grande's latest single.

Nikki got out of the car and began her approach. The restaurant Z'ev had picked for dinner was only a few blocks away. With any luck she could scoop up Donny, or at least make sure he was all right, and be having appetizers with Z'ev in thirty minutes.

She walked past the drinks table of the birthday party and scooped up a six pack of soda—just in case, then spotted Donny's group through the trees. They were loud and boisterous. Apex predators of the human world didn't need to wear camouflage, in fact it paid to advertise. They quieted down as they approached the candy sculpture. Another group was already waiting for them. Nikki couldn't say for sure, but from the tattoos she suspected they were Crazy Town Locos. She slipped a little closer, comforted by the heavy weight of the Sig Sauer on her hip.

The gangs were squaring off when she saw Z'ev approaching from the opposite direction. Nikki wanted to react to that, but Donny was already moving. He approached the front man of the Crazy Town Locos, a tough looking guy with a buzz cut, a neck tattoo, and a black duffle bag. Donny carried a matching bag.

Z'ev caught sight of her and glared. He made go away gestures and Nikki shook her head. He made more emphatic gestures and Nikki shook her head again. The silent argument might have kept going, but they both saw the surreptitious movement at the back of the pack of Crazy Town Locos. Guns were coming out. Instinctively Nikki reached for her gun, then realized Z'ev was going to see whatever she did. Time for the back-up plan.

Nikki ran out into the circle of men just as the first gun man stepped forward. Breaking off one of the soda cans, she hurled it through the air, where it impacted against his forehead in a spray of dark brown soda. She continued running as the man talking to Donny reached toward his waistband. Swinging the remaining five cans on their plastic tether she smashed them into his face. The gang member crumpled to the ground, as they connected with his temple before bouncing off in all directions.

"Move your ass, Donny!" she yelled, continuing across the clearing toward Z'ev. Donny snatched up the other man's duffle bag and ran after her.

Z'ev had his gun out, covering their exit. He pointed emphatically toward the right and Nikki did as directed; taking an erratic course through the underbrush, looping back toward the play area.

"Gun! Gun! Gun!" she screamed, running at the child's birthday party. There were screams as people took up her refrain. Parents snatched up children and began to run from the park. There was a blare of sirens from behind them on Wilshire, but Nikki kept running. Scooping up the Snow White *piñata*, she turned to Z'ev who was already taking off his jacket and wrapping it around the piñata. Nikki huddled closer to him as they ran; blending in among the other parents hauling children away from the park. Once they were across the street and it seemed clear that no one was following them, Nikki dropped the piñata in the nearest trashcan.

"I should really –" Donny began looking as if he would go a different way. Z'ev grabbed him by the elbow and forced him to keep walking in the direction they were going. Nikki did the same with the other arm.

"Nikki, I cannot believe you did that," Z'ev snapped.

"I know, right?" said Donny. "You nailed that guy smack in the forehead! Last time I saw you, you could not hit the broad side of a barn. How'd you do that?"

"I joined the company softball team," said Nikki, looking around nervously as they stopped at a crosswalk.

"That was awe—" He glanced at Z'ev. "Totally irresponsible."

"Shut. Up. Nikki, that was dangerous and stupid. You should not have been there. And then you should have left when I told you to."

"Oh, come on. No one even shot at us. They were too stunned to figure out what was happening."

Donny snorted. "Jackson and I used to call it the I Love Lucy effect."

"Shut up, Donny," said Nikki.

"I had it under control, Nikki," growled Z'ev.

"Well, how was I supposed to know?" Nikki snapped back, "You didn't tell me."

Donny's head bounced back and forth between them like a ping-pong ball.

"It was a DEA investigation—I couldn't tell you. I contacted a friend of mine. He was doing me a favor and no one was supposed to know."

"Well, Donny is my friend. I wasn't going to leave him out there with his closest back-up in Tacoma, Washington."

"That isn't your responsibility. And again, I had it under control. I talked to my friend, Joe. Joe knew about Donny. It would have been fine." Z'ev spoke through clenched teeth.

"And again, you could have told me!"

"I didn't think Joe would want it blabbed all over LA."

"Suddenly I'm all of LA? Oh, thanks. Nice to know I have your trust."

"I didn't want you involved!" shouted Z'ev, as they stopped

in front of a restaurant.

"He's my friend!" Nikki shouted, yanking Donny closer to her.

"He's dangerous!" Z'ev yelled back and yanked Donny toward him.

Down the street more police cars arrived and there was the sound of distant gunfire; all three ducked slightly.

"Guys, can you keep it together for the kid here, please?" asked Donny.

A police car whizzed by and, taking their cue, Nikki, Donny, and Z'ev stepped into the restaurant.

"Three for dinner?" asked the host.

"Yes, please," said Donny, shaking himself free.

"We can't stay for dinner," said Z'ev.

"Dude, I've had nothing but tacos for the last week," said Donny. "Don't be a Mexi-can't; be a Mexi-can."

Nikki tried to turn her laugh into a cough under Z'ev's disapproving stare.

"I'm Jewish," said Z'ev.

"Nobody's perfect," said Donny, with a shrug.

"This way," said the host. Another cop car drove by and Z'ev allowed himself to be led toward a back booth.

"I don't mean to be a pain," said Donny, as the host left them to be seated. "But I do have a slight problem."

"What?" growled Z'ev.

Donny hoisted his hands, lifting two black duffle bags into view above the table.

"Oh, crap on a cracker, Donny." It was one of Ellen's favorites 'swears' and Nikki found it creeping into her vocabulary. "You've got the drugs and the money? I'm assuming that's drugs and money?"

"I hope so," said Donny. "Otherwise there wasn't any point to that little party."

"I'll call Joe," said Z'ev standing back up, he dialed his phone as he walked away from the table.

"He seems like he's wound a little tight," said Donny sitting down across from Nikki.

"He doesn't like me getting shot at."

"No one was going to get shot at," said Donny dismissively.

"Yeah, they were. Those Crazy Town Locos were busting out the heavy weaponry. I don't believe they were planning on handing over the money. They were going to shoot you."

"Noooo," said Donny, but hesitantly, as if he were reviewing the last few minutes in his mind and starting to doubt that he was in the right. "They weren't going to shoot me."

"Yeah, they were," said Z'ev and Nikki at the same time.

"We had the long view on the situation," said Z'ev sitting down next to Nikki and waving to the waiter. "The guys at the back were packing Beretta Model 12's. They came to play."

"I could have handled it," said Donny with a shrug. "I'll have the Saag Gosht, please," he said to the waiter. Nikki could tell Z'ev wanted to argue and she could tell that he was annoyed that Donny was using the waiter to prevent arguments. But she knew that neither Donny or the waiter could tell. Z'ev, after all, was a professional.

It was a talent that infuriated Nikki. She always felt out-classed when he went into agent mode. Soon, the waiters were calling him Mr. Z'ev and Donny was telling them 'this one time in college…' stories and comparing notes on this year's potential match-ups for the World Cup.

Nikki made it through dinner, but she didn't remember how. Modern fusion gastro Indian was not her idea of a good meal. The food all came in tiny weird bites that tasted like freeze dried air and she never seemed to be able to catch up with the conversation. Throughout dinner, police cars drove up and down the street, and once, they saw the SWAT van lumber by.

"Joe wants to pick you up," said Z'ev to Donny, when they were standing out on the sidewalk again. He handed Donny a business card. "He said to call him at 6:00 P.M. and he'd have a pickup time and location figured out by then.

"Great," said Donny, chewing his toothpick. "Can I crash at your place until then, Nik? I should call my LT and get stuff figured out."

"Yeah, of course, Donny. Not a problem." She could almost hear Z'ev gritting his teeth.

She loaded them both in the Impala and drove home, where Donny locked himself in the office to make some phone calls.

"This is what I'm talking about, Nikki," Z'ev said when the silence had stretched on for about an infinity.

"What you were talking about when?" asked Nikki bewildered.

"Last night. You want to know why I'm so suspicious—it's because you do stuff like this. You dove right into the middle of a gun battle."

"I did not dive. I just ran out there and got Donny."

"They were pointing weapons."

"Yeah, at my friend. I needed him out of there."

"You could have let the DEA and police figure it out."

"They were going to figure it out after he was dead."

"I told them he was a cop. They had it under control."

"Well, you didn't tell me. There could be a little more information sharing."

"Yeah, there sure as hell could be."

"What's that supposed to mean?"

"It means I'm not Lois Lane. I know that you put a romance novel dust jacket on *Bullseye's Don't Shoot Back*. I know what eye shadow you use to cover up black eyes. I know you're…" He hesitated, unwilling to actually say it. "I know something isn't –" His phone began to ring. He had ringtones assigned to almost everyone in his contact list and they both instantly recognized the old telephone sound that indicated that it was a work call.

They both stared at the phone, abandoned on the kitchen counter with the car keys.

"You'd better get that," said Nikki, glumly.

"We're not through talking about this," said Z'ev, picking up the phone and walking into the bedroom. A minute later, he came back out. "I have to go."

"You said they wouldn't call you for at least another month."

"I said it was unlikely. Apparently, something came up."

They stared at each other, Z'ev in the kitchen and Nikki in the living room and one hundred million miles apart.

"I love you," said Nikki, because she couldn't think of anything else to say.

"I love you, too," he said, walking into the living room. She put her arms around him and buried her face into his chest—into that perfect little hollow below his shoulder that seemed meant for her.

"How long are you going to be gone?"

"I don't know. It sounded like a couple of weeks."

"I worry about you," she said, looking up. "I know you can

take care of yourself, but I worry."

"The feeling is extremely mutual," he said, laughing with just a hint of bitterness.

Nikki wanted to tell him he was imagining things and that everything in her life was normal. She wanted to lie, lie, lie. But she couldn't. Maybe if she was a better liar, he wouldn't get that look, that sad one that said he didn't trust her. Impulsively, she kissed him. Hard. Wanting to imprint herself on his brain and body.

"Not to bust up the party or anything," said Donny, clearing his throat. Nikki stepped back and Z'ev immediately dropped his mask back into place. "But I've got a meet location and they want to pick me up now."

Nikki nodded. "I'll get my keys."

"You'll have to go without me," said Z'ev, reaching for his jacket. "Sorry." He picked up his watch from the tray by the door and slid it on his wrist. There was a honk from the parking lot. "I'll call you when I can," he said, kissing her unresponsive mouth. "And don't get her shot." He pointed at Donny, who gave a half head jerk, half nod. The door slammed shut and Nikki twitched slightly, buffeted by the impact.

"Well," she said after a moment. "I guess we should go."

The door opened back up, Z'ev stepped in again and Nikki smiled.

"We need to try that again," he said. He grabbed her and kissed her into a huge dip. "Right," he said, setting her upright. "That's better. I'll call you." And then he was gone again. Nikki giggled and caught site of Donny who was wearing a wide grin.

"Shut up," she said.

"I didn't say a word."

"Yeah, well, keep it that way," she said, grabbing her purse.

The 'meet' turned out to be held in the parking lot of Pinky's Hot Dogs. Nikki was a bit disappointed. She was getting used to a Carrie Mae rendezvous being boring, without any glamour or mystery or atmospheric fog, but she'd been hoping that other agencies had things better planned. The Impala cruised down the freeway and Nikki was keeping an eye out for her exit when Donny finally spoke up.

"So what does he do for a living?"

"Um," Nikki paused. Z'ev had told her the cover story to use if this question ever came up, but all of her friends were Carrie Mae and they all knew. It had never really come up before. "He works for the State Department."

"The State Department?" repeated Donny skeptically.

"Yeah," said Nikki, aiming for cheerful.

"Uh-huh," grunted Donny. "And what do you do?"

"I work for the Carrie Mae Foundation, helping women on a world-wide level," said Nikki glibly.

"Yeah, right," said Donny sarcastically.

"No, really. I do." He held eye contact for a second, and he frowned when Nikki didn't look away.

"You know," said Donny conversationally, after a few moments of silence. "I'm good at being an undercover cop. I say it's because I'm good at spotting liars. My ex-girlfriend says that's because I am a liar. That may be true. I choose not to speculate. But you, on the other hand, could never lie at all. You'd try, but it was never any good, anyone who really knew you, could spot the lie in a heartbeat."

"I'm not lying, Donny," said Nikki, laughing. "I really do work for the Carrie Mae Foundation."

"Yeah, I know," said Donny. "That's why I'm worried."

They pulled into the parking lot of Pinky's and Nikki backed into a spot so she could see the whole parking lot.

"I think we're early," said Donny, checking his watch. "You want a hot dog?"

She looked at Donny in disbelief.

"We had dinner, like an hour ago."

"Yeah, but Pinky's hot dogs are supposed to be really good, and what with the adrenaline and wanting to get out of there, I didn't eat what I could."

"You are a bottomless pit." It was a childhood refrain and Nikki found it easy to fall back on.

"So, you want one?" he asked getting out of the car. The smell of frying meat and French fries wafted from the diner.

"I'll just have some of yours."

"No, you won't. Get your own damn dog."

Nikki waffled and got out with him. It was true what he'd said about dinner and the food did smell good. They ordered dogs and stood waiting for their order to come up.

"So you and this Z'ev guy, huh?" Donny asked, taking a seat on the curb. Nikki sat down next to him, trying to keep her knees together in her skirt.

"Yeah," she said.

"You're pretty stuck on him?"

"Yeah," agreed Nikki.

"It's funny, but I really always thought you and Jackson would make a go of it."

"Well, I thought so too, until he broke up with me," said Nikki with a shrug.

Two cars pulled into the lot, one green, one dirty white. A black guy in a doo-rag got out of one and into the other. After a minute, he got out again and went back to the original car and they both drove off.

"Drug deal?" asked Nikki, jerking her head at the cars.

"Probably a gun, since he actually got in the car," said Donny. He sighed and rubbed his face. "Today was supposed to be like that, you know? We go in, do what we do, fast and casual, and then we leave. Nobody makes a fuss. Nobody gets hurt. I wasn't even supposed to leave Washington. But I had a shot at getting tape on Ruiz. I figured I should take it."

"Dogs are up," said the waiter from the order window.

Donny and Nikki stood up and retrieved their hot dogs, chewing as they walked back to the Impala.

"I like your car," said Donny, as Nikki perched on the hood.

"Mmm," said Nikki around a mouthful of hot dog. "I got it from my first partner at Carrie Mae."

"Man, you would have had to pry the keys to that baby out of my cold dead fingers," he said cheerfully.

"I dropped her off a bridge in Thailand," said Nikki, swallowing a suddenly dry chunk of hot dog. Donny started to laugh and then took a second look at her face.

"Damn it, Nikki. I think I'd feel better if you would lie."

"Sorry," said Nikki, forcing a laugh. "I'll try lying next time."

"You and this Z'ev guy are going to have problems," Donny blurted out, and then laughed guiltily.

"No!" lied Nikki, "we're fine. Mostly, anyway."

"Yeah... right now, but Nikki... Well, I've worked undercover stuff for a while now. Like I was saying earlier about lying and being a liar."

Nikki quietly eyed him over her hot dog. She didn't like where this was going.

"It's really hard to maintain a relationship when you're hiding parts of your life from your significant other. Even if you think it's for their own good, you're still hiding yourself from a person that you should be the most open to. I'm not trying to bring trouble on you guys and I don't really know what you've got going on with your Carrie Mae stuff there, I'm just trying to tell you from my own experience."

Nikki shrugged awkwardly. "How do you manage it then?"

"At the moment, I don't," he said, with a shrug. "Sorry, I know that's not very helpful. I think the thing that my ex kept asking for that I wasn't able to wrap my head around was that she didn't want details of what I'd been out doing. She didn't need to know all the horrible stuff I'd seen. She wanted to know how I felt about it, where I was going, who I was, what I wanted. And I kept saying that everything was fine. Fine isn't a real answer, you know?"

"Yeah, but if you say something else, they might get mad or leave," said Nikki.

"She left anyway," said Donny. "I should have taken the chance."

A black Ford Explorer rolled into the parking lot and stopped in front of the Impala.

"I think this is my ride," said Donny.

"It better be," said Nikki, "I'm not packing and they're blocking the exit."

The door opened and a man in a Hawaiian shirt stepped out. Nikki slid off the hood and landed on the pavement with the solid click of her heels hitting ground. She recognized him as the man Z'ev met at the beach.

"You must be Joe," she said, and he grinned.

"Nice to meet you. And believe me, I'd love to stay and chat about how you managed to get our friend Coralles wrapped around your finger, but I'm working on a bit of a timeline. I need Fernandez. Now," he turned to Donny, "If you're done with dinner and a date, do you think we could get this show on the road?"

"Thanks for the ride, Nik," he said, leaning over for a hug and kissing her cheek.

Nikki hugged back. "Tell everybody hi for me," she said.

"You bet," said Donny. He jogged over to the Explorer and got in. Joe followed Donny into the interior, shutting the door after them. Nikki waved as the Explorer left the parking lot.

AUGUST I
PRE-FLIGHT CHECK

Tijuana • Friday

"Nicole Lanier!" Nikki pulled the phone a few inches away from the overly loud greeting.

"Donald Fernandez!" She barked back and Donny laughed.

"Hey Nik, where you at?"

"Tijuana airport."

"For reals? Cool, I guess. You and the big brah take a little vacay?"

"No, he's still away on assignment. I'm helping out the Tijuana Branch."

"Still? He's not following the budiquette of how to treat your best chick very well."

"Donny, have you been undercover with stoners?"

"Sorry, it's a hazard of the job. I busted some total bro brahs last week and I can't seem to lose the surfer-dude patois."

"Well, keep using words like *patois* and you'll ditch it in no time."

Donny laughed again. "Well, I'll definitely ditch it soon. I'm on my way home for a couple of weeks. Mom demanded I come home after scaring the crap out of her with my disappearing act last month. Of course, when I go back to work, I'll be all Spanglish, all the time. Which is unfortunate because the guys already call me *Telemundo*."

"What is it with cops and nicknames?"

"We're stunted emotionally," said Donny. "Anyway, the reason I'm calling is that I wanted to see if you were possibly thinking about taking a little trip to the old stomping grounds, too?"

"Did my mother call you?" Nikki demanded.

"No, I swear," said Donny laughing. "Why, has she been after you?"

"Yes, I've been dodging her calls for weeks. She keeps saying that my grandmother would love to see me."

"She probably would," said Donny.

"I don't need the guilt from you, too," said Nikki. "I would love to go visit Kaniksu Falls. I haven't been back in years. But it's not feasible with work right now."

"What, you never get to take a vacation?"

"Yeah, I can take a vacation. But my boss's husband had open heart surgery and now she's out on sabbatical to take care of him and her temporary replacement is kind of having a rocky time of it. I need to stick around and make sure things go OK."

"Except that you're in TJ," objected Donny.

"Only for a few days. There was a situation." Nikki didn't add that she thought Darla, Mrs. M's replacement, had sent her to Tijuana simply to get rid of her, and she didn't add that it had been over a month since she'd heard from Z'ev. She also didn't add that it had been almost the same amount of time since the team had officially been together. Darla had sent her to Mexico a lot lately. Not that the Tijuana Branch couldn't use the help, but even they were starting to think it was more than a bit ridiculous. To be perfectly honest, she was about one more trip to Mexico away from telling Darla where to get off. She didn't add these things because, while Donny was her friend, this was an open phone line, and well, he wasn't one of the girls. "Anyway, don't get me wrong, I'd love to fly home and keep you from freaking out over the fact that the nearest Starbucks is two hours away."

"I get weird when I'm too far from the mother ship, man. *Por qué, no?*"

"*Porque tengo un trabajo.*"

"Ah, man. Sad face."

"Seriously, did you just speak an emoticon? Stop hanging with stoners."

"Well, I also have a job. And periodically it requires me to assume the guise of a hapless youth devoted to the pursuit of narcotics. I am what I am. I'm a yam. *Que será, que será.*"

Nikki laughed.

"Oh, wow, dude. Are you watching the news? Someone killed an RCMP?"

"What?" Nikki picked up her carry-on and moved closer to one of the lounge TV's. The closed captions were scrolling in English on the bottom of the screen with a one second lag time behind the announcer.

"The car chase ended with one man, who may have been a member of the Canadian Mounted Police, dead at the scene. The RCMP have refused to comment at this time," said the announcer. "But they have confirmed that one officer is dead and that they are working an ongoing murder investigation. Although, they would not confirm that the car chase, which ended near the Canadian US border, and may have involved the woman shown here –" The video footage flipped to a frozen and blurry photo of a fifty-something woman leaving a gas station.

"Oh crap," said Nikki. The footage was blurry, but she still recognized her co-workers when she saw them on the TV.

"...was directly related to the investigation currently being conducted at the residence of Officer Douglas Pearson." The video feed switched to an aerial shot of a suburban house that had been cordoned off with crime scene tape. Officers in windbreakers were carrying boxes out to a large police van.

"What did I say? I said, don't do anything stupid," said Nikki. "Why don't they ever listen to me?"

"Uh, Nik? You're kind of losing your nut over there. What's going on?"

Nikki pulled the phone away from her face and looked at it blankly. She'd forgotten she was still on the phone with Donny.

"I have to go, Donny. I think I need to get on an earlier flight."

AUGUST II
SOMETHING STUPID

It really was a damn international incident. Nikki read through the report with the deliberate pace of a turtle, all the while Darla's red nails tapped on Mrs. Merrivel's desk.

Nikki's team was behind her, sitting in the row of chairs against the wall. They looked rather like a gang of unruly Catholic school girls who had been called into the principal's office. Ellen sat with stone-faced stoicism, her eyes fixed at a point somewhere near the ceiling above Darla's head, refusing to acknowledge her accuser. Jenny fixed Darla with an eye-burning stare of hatred, blinking at a reptilian rate. And Jane was playing Fruit Ninja on her phone. Leave it to Jane to protest through sound effects.

Nikki knew she could skip the rest of the report, save them all some time and start the dialogue. She should really be the grown-up in the room. Mrs. Merrivel was counting on her, after all. But it had been a long two months and Darla had been hell-bent on putting Nikki and the team in their place. So instead, Nikki counted to ten, pondered her grocery list, and tried to remember if she'd bought toilet paper on her last trip to the store. Then she turned the page with infinite slowness and read every single word.

Eventually, Nikki finished the report and tucked the pages back into their manila folder, tamping the edge to align the papers neatly. She wanted to turn around and yell at Ellen and the girls. She'd been away for two lousy days. The last thing she said was, "Don't let Darla goad you into doing something stupid." And what did they do? The high-speed chase—not that bright. Illegally extracting Ellen from Canada—kind of dumb. And last, but not least, running over a fricking mountie—definitely something stupid.

"So?" demanded Darla. She was a forty-five-ish reddish-brown brunette, short and stocky, with a sensible haircut and sensible shoes. The only real Carrie Mae thing about her was her manicure. Her nails were bright red and perfectly rounded in a gel manicure and a tiny incongruous flower had been painted on the pinky. It seemed out of character, but the look had been carefully maintained for the entire time Darla had been in LA. Nikki clung to the idea of that flower as an indicator that Darla was more interesting than her plain exterior would indicate.

"Sorry, what was the question?"

"Were you, or were you not, aware of their activities." Darla pointed an accusing letter opener at the women behind Nikki.

"I'm not going to answer that question," said Nikki. "If I say yes, then you'll blame me for the entire incident. If I say no, then you'll say that I'm an incompetent team leader." Darla's lips pinched tightly and her eyes, smoldering with fury, showed that Nikki's assessment was accurate. "Here's a question for you: do you know why you have this job?"

Darla blinked.

"You have this job because I saw you speak at the Leaders in the Field conference last May." The sword swooping noise from Jane's phone stopped mid-swoop.

"I went to that conference," said Jane. "I don't remember her."

Nikki addressed Jane without turning her head, keeping her eyes locked on Darla. "Well, that's possibly because only ten peo-

ple showed up to listen to her speak." Nikki saw Darla wince.
"And I think you went to the symposium on mass hypnosis instead. Ellen was sitting on the Future of Weaponry panel."

"Where was I?" asked Jenny.

"I think you were in the bar," said Nikki.

"Oh, right! That dentist conference was in the same hotel. That was hilarious."

"What's your point?" said Darla.

"My point is: do you think I couldn't do this job? And more to the point, do you think it wasn't offered to me?" Darla looked uncertain and Nikki continued. "I was running the division while Mrs. M was in Turkey, so why wouldn't I continue to run it while she helps her husband recover from heart surgery?"

Darla looked uncertain and wary, but didn't speak as Nikki continued.

"Because if I've learned anything from Mrs. M, it's that we have to think of more than just the immediate problem. If we want Carrie Mae to move into the future we have to put women with new ideas in positions of power. I heard you speak at the conference and I knew that you'd been buried. You were never going to get any higher than being a city branch leader in Utah."

Darla's lips twitched angrily.

"But I thought your ideas were big. I thought they had promise. I thought if you could prove yourself here in LA, you might have a shot at moving up the food chain. Instead, you moved into the big desk and started acting like you're strictly Utah."

For a moment, it looked like Darla might explode and then her shoulders sagged.

"What's the point?" she muttered, her eyes drifting to the window. "Everyone hates me here. They all think I stole your job.

How am I supposed to get anything done, when for every order I give they just look to you to approve it?"

"I didn't realize it would be this much of a problem," said Nikki.

"And none of that changes the fact that your team killed a cop," said Darla snapping back to angry.

"From a certain point of view," said Nikki with a shrug. "Another way of looking at it is that they stopped a serial killer who was preying on First Nations women because he knew their deaths were less likely to be fully investigated."

"The evidence on that is… it's not definitive. They killed a Canadian police officer!"

"The skeletons in his basement are pretty definitive. What you really mean is that I embarrassed you in front of your Canadian friend," said Ellen, through clenched teeth.

"What's that supposed to mean?" demanded Darla.

"It was pretty clear you were real cozy with the Alberta Branch leader," said Jenny. "Of course you'd cover up for her."

"You're the ones with something to cover up," bellowed Darla. "Maybe if you'd actually filed a report or followed the chain of command, I could have done something, but no… you're Nikki's team, you don't have to follow the rules!" She threw up her hands in outrage, and sat breathing heavily into the silence that followed.

"I did file a report," said Ellen icily. "You buried it."

"I did no such thing!" Darla's eyes widened in outrage. "I do not bury reports." She stabbed a finger into the desk with each word.

"Somebody did," said Ellen, glaring.

"Well, it wasn't me," Darla shot back.

"Actually," said Jane, clearing her throat nervously. "There might be a way to check that."

"Talk to me, Jane," said Nikki.

"Well, every time a report is generated it's given a unique file number. Even if the file is deleted that file number is never repeated. Sometimes files get deleted for perfectly legit reasons, but the person who deletes it has to put in their ID number. That number and the ID number of the report originator get stored in a computer somewhere. They're still retrievable."

"I filed it when I was in Canada," said Ellen, looking worried. "The first time I saw Officer Pearson, when I was in the middle of that other mission, I came back and I filed a report, but no one did anything. Can you access Canadian files?"

"I don't have clearance," said Jane. The unspoken thought clear on her face was that she could probably hack into the Canadian system, but a nervous glance at Darla showed that she didn't want to say it.

"But I do," said Darla waking up the computer. "How do I do it?"

Jane dropped her phone and moved to the other side of the desk. Talking quickly, she walked Darla through the process. Nikki watched as Jane's jet-black head bobbed next to Darla's cinnamon-colored one. Darla was right about one thing, as long as Nikki and her team were in LA, the branch was never going to follow Darla. Darla ought to be able to have support from the women in her command. This incident would never have gotten this far if everyone had been talking to each other. For the good of the company, she was probably going to have to do something. The question was, what?

"That bitch!" growled Darla, slamming her palm down on the desk, then looking at Nikki. "I sent your team to Alberta as a personal favor—and this is how she repays me? I knew I couldn't trust her."

"I thought you and the Alberta Branch leader were friends," said Ellen, exchanging looks of confusion with Jenny.

"She saved my life once," said Darla shaking her head. "I owed her. She said she needed a sniper, and I figured if I sent you we'd be square. She's the one who deleted your report."

"Oh," said Ellen. "I thought it was weird for you to be friends considering that she was such a racist and you seem fine with…" Ellen paused and blushed.

"And I'm married to a black guy?" finished Darla. "Yeah, that's one of the reasons I wanted to get clear of the debt I owed her. I don't like being around her."

"Check this out," said Jane, pointing at the screen. "Ellen's report isn't the only one she deleted."

"I'm going to file a formal complaint," said Darla, her eyes sparkling. "Threaten me, will she? Can you print out a report on this?" she asked Jane, pointing at the screen, and Jane nodded. "And then I need you to start tracking down the agents who originated the reports. I need more ammunition."

"Give me a minute," said Jane, already reaching for the desk phone.

"It won't be enough," said Nikki, perching on the windowsill, and leaning back against the glass, warm in the afternoon sunshine.

"What do you mean?" asked Darla, looking as if she'd just remembered Nikki were in the room.

"It's an international incident, right? If it had stayed between you and what's-her-name in Alberta, it'd be fine. But she's already filed a formal complaint against us, hasn't she? It's going before the Council." The Council was the international ruling body of

Carrie Mae. From there the organization forked into smaller and smaller units: divisions, branches, units, teams, and finally the lowly agent.

"It doesn't matter. Not with this information. I can fight back." Darla's eyes sparkled with the prospect of holy battle.

"We'll still be a liability," said Nikki. "I told you. We've got to think about the future."

"I'm not going to fire you. That cop was killing girls and one of our own people ignored it."

"The Council is old school," said Nikki, shaking her head. "They already think Mrs. M and 'her girls' are troublemakers."

"Do they?" asked Jenny, looking surprised. "You never told us that."

Nikki shrugged. "Mrs. M never considered you, or your actions, a liability. She didn't want you to behave any differently."

"I can put you on two weeks unpaid leave," said Darla slowly. "That way I'm punishing you—addressing the infraction inhouse—but during the course of my investigation into your actions I've discovered several breaches in protocol on the part of the Alberta Branch. Breaches that The Council should address. It'll change the focus of the investigation." She sat back in her chair, and eyed Nikki. "I should have come to you before now. I misinterpreted your intentions."

Nikki shrugged. "I don't really want the job."

"I don't know why not. The big chair is kind of cushy." She bounced up and down for emphasis, and Nikki laughed.

"Too cushy. It sucks you in."

"I've got the girls running down the missing reports," said Jane, hanging up the phone. "It may be that we can find duplicate copies that weren't deleted because they weren't connected to the same server. We're also looking for the agents who filed the reports. Once we've got a list of names I can send some people out on interviews."

"Good. Make sure you update someone on the case before you leave."

"I'm leaving?" Jane looked at Nikki, panic stricken.

"You're not fired," said Nikki, and Jane sighed in relief. "We're on unpaid leave."

"And you should probably leave the state," said Darla matter-of-factly.

Jane looked horrified. "No, no, no. Remember what happened last time you tried to make me take time off?"

"I remember you disobeyed orders, hacked into the computer of an international arms dealer, and got stuck in a German hotel eating sausages," said Jenny. "You obviously don't know how to vacation, and require my assistance."

"Do I really have to go on vacation with Jenny?" demanded Jane, turning back to Darla.

"Frankly, I don't really care," said Darla. "But I want you out of reach of any council investigators. Outside of Nikki, you're not exactly political animals. I can't trust you to say the right thing. Leave town, and stay out of sight for at least two weeks. I'll call you if I need it to be longer."

"Sweet," said Jenny.

"I wouldn't mind seeing the girls. And didn't you say your mother's been bugging you to come visit?" asked Ellen, turning to Nikki. Nikki made a face. She didn't need reminding.

"But," said Jane, looking distressed. "I can't leave the state. My computers… my research… my giant crossword puzzle…" Her eyes bounced to each of her teammates in turn, looking for help.

"Honey," said Jenny, standing up. "You clearly need Cancun more than I do. Come on, Nikki, help me get her outta here before she chains herself to the desk in protest."

AUGUST III
EMPTY BED BLUES

"Hey," said Nikki, picking up the phone as she fumbled for her keys.

"How'd it go?" asked Mr. M.

"We're on unpaid leave for two weeks while she handles the political stuff. Does your wife know you're asking about her work?"

"I'm asking about my friend's life. It's a clear distinction," said Mr. M primly. "I can't help it if your life happens to involve her work."

"You argue like a lawyer," she said affectionately.

"How fortunate that I am one," he said, and she could hear his smile over the phone. "Look, it's not my fault that the two of you have decided to work for an international corporation who take its motto, 'helping women everywhere' a little too seriously. If you would just work for the CIA like I did, we wouldn't have this problem."

Nikki laughed. "Actually, I was thinking about your wife's edict to avoid anything stressful." She climbed the stairs to her apartment, pausing to check the mail.

"I don't find you stressful," said Mr. M. "What I don't understand is why she's not checking in on you herself."

"She called while I was in the car," said Nikki.

"Ah! That explains her mysterious, sudden trip to the grocery store."

"I think it's taking all she has not to call Darla and meddle," said Nikki.

"I really wouldn't mind if she worked," said Mr. M. "She doesn't have to be home every minute to take care of me. I had surgery. I'm not incapacitated."

"You had open heart surgery," said Nikki. "With complications. And let's face it, left to your own devices, you'd probably be chowing down on bacon and trying to run a 5k or something."

"I would not," said Mr. M. "I dislike running."

"I notice you didn't comment on the bacon."

"I try not to lie," he said, as she unlocked the door, letting it swing open with a bang, waiting for a welcoming yell from further inside. "Any word from Z'ev?" he asked as if anticipating her next thoughts. The apartment remained echoingly empty.

"No," said Nikki. "I got a letter last week. Forwarded from work, which meant it had half the letter blacked out. I suppose it's better than nothing. At least I know he's alive."

"Still thinking of breaking up with him?"

When Nikki thought of her boyfriend the last thing she wanted to think about was breaking up. On the other hand, it was becoming increasingly difficult to lie to him about what she really did for a living.

"Mr. M, you've got to stop bringing this up. I don't know what I'm going to do."

"I know, I'm sorry. I'm not trying to pester you. I just think it's a shame to throw away a good relationship."

"I appreciate the sentiment, but I'm pretty sure your wife, my boss, thinks I should break up with him."

"Miranda is not as romantic as I am," he said matter-of-factly. "She doesn't trust Z'ev not to expose Carrie Mae to the CIA and I, as a romantic, think that you should take the risk."

"If it were just me, I'd probably chance it," said Nikki with a sigh. "But it's not just me. A lot of women could be arrested, or worse, if Carrie Mae gets exposed. The CIA doesn't take too kindly to others playing in their sandbox. At best, they'd probably call what we do 'industrial espionage,' at worst they'd call us traitors. And what about all the women we help? I'd be risking a lot on the chance that Z'ev loves me enough not to blab."

"I fully understand what's at stake," said Mr. M. "But as someone who was in the CIA and loves a Carrie Mae agent, I think that maybe Z'ev could be trusted and that breaking up with him seems unnecessary."

Nikki sighed. She didn't want to have this argument again. She didn't want to point out that Mr. M had been retired from the CIA by the time he'd married Miranda. And she didn't want to point out that he was assuming an awful lot about how much Z'ev cared about her. "Well, don't worry, I'm not throwing anything away. And seriously, he has to be home for more than forty-eight hours before I think we can consider it a relationship—good or otherwise."

"I see your point," said Mr. M. "What are you going to do with your time off?"

"I was thinking about going to see my grandma. Mom's been pestering me about going, which means Grandma's been pestering her."

"I thought you got along with your grandma?"

"I do! I've been meaning to go. It's just that all the holidays end up being with my mom too, and you know my mom."

"Drives you nuttier than a Christmas fruitcake," agreed Mr. M.

"And getting vacation time hasn't exactly been easy. Clearly, I should have thought of unpaid leave earlier."

"And how would you have arranged that?"

"I would have told Jane she had to go on vacation, which would obviously have resulted in a fistfight in the front lobby."

Mr. M laughed. "Obviously." There was a tiny, far away noise from Mr. M's side of the call. "OK, that sounds like Miranda. I'd better go pretend I've been in the recliner the whole time."

"Mr. M! You should be in the recliner."

"Miranda took my phone," he protested. "I had to go get a burner out of the garage. Gotta go, bye."

Nikki set down her phone and purse and looked around the kitchen. There had been a time, between college and this job, when she had lived with her mother and an empty house sounded like heaven. Now, she missed having someone to talk to. She thought about calling her mother, realized that she wasn't that lonely, and dialed her grandmother while reaching up into the back of the freezer for some ice cream.

"Connelly residence," said her grandmother on the third ring.

"Hi, Grandma. It's Nikki."

"Ah, Nikki, my favorite grandchild."

"I'm your only grandchild, so that better be true," said Nikki laughing.

"Don't check the fine print, honey, just accept the compliment," said her grandmother, not quite laughing.

Nikki pictured her grandmother, Peg Connelly, standing in the kitchen of her farmhouse, short, gray hair fluffing out around her ears, probably barefoot and wearing jeans with some heinously pastel plaid shirt from Wal-Mart. It made her nostalgic and it made her feel the emptiness of the apartment even more. She yanked out the ice cream and shut the freezer door with a round house kick.

"I'm glad you called, honey," said Peg. "It's been so long since I've seen you. I feel like I've hardly spoken to you in the last year."

Nikki ignored the shooting stab of guilt. "It's been a really busy year. But it turns out I've got some time off and I was thinking about coming up for a visit."

"A visit? Well, that would be great. When do you think you'll be here? I'll have to clean up your room."

Nikki ignored that comment, since her grandmother's idea of horrible filth barely registered on Nikki's scale of unclean. "I was thinking I would drive up, so…" Nikki stared at the calendar, trying to math out miles to days. "Maybe, Wednesday?"

"Wednesday is fine, but I don't think you should drive up," said Peg. "Not by yourself. I don't think that would be safe."

"Mmm," said Nikki. "You make a point." She flipped the lid off the ice cream.

"You should check the flights and let me know when you'll arrive. I'll come pick you up in Spokane."

"I'll have to think about that," said Nikki, opening the cupboard to look for a bowl and then realizing that they were all in the dishwasher.

"OK," said Peg. "You can email me when you've got some flight numbers and let me know when you arrive."

"I think we can still say that I'll be arriving on Wednesday," said Nikki.

"Great. I can get your room clean by then. Or, you know, you can call me when you land at Seatac because I'll leave for Spokane when you leave Seattle. There aren't any direct flights from LAX to Spokane are there?"

"I don't know if there are or not," replied Nikki. She pulled out a large spoon and levered out a chunk of ice cream.

"You'll have to look into that."

There was a pause as Nikki said nothing and tried to juggle the phone while bracing the ice cream against the toaster for better leverage.

"Well, honey, I'm so excited that you're coming to visit!" said Peg. "It's really good because I've been wanting to talk to you about something kind of important."

Nikki paused with the spoon half-way to her mouth. Her mother had been hinting that Peg might be looking into selling the farm, and the idea of selling the family home made Nikki want to cry. She did not think she could face talking about it right now. Her mind flipped through a rolodex of responses. Then the doorbell rang.

"Is that your doorbell?"

"Yes," said Nikki.

"Well, you'd better go. I'll see you on Wednesday. Bye, honey!"

"Bye, Grandma." Nikki hung up the phone, set down the spoon, and reached for her gun. She flipped open the app on her phone that was tied to the web cam that watched her door. Jane waved up at it.

"Hey, Jane," said Nikki opening the door.

"Hey," said Jane, breezing into the apartment with take-out bags. "I bought Chinese and then I thought maybe you would want some too." She set the bags down on the kitchen counter next to the ice cream. "But we can always start with dessert."

"I'll take the Chinese first," said Nikki. "It'll give the ice cream time to soften. Where are the girls?"

"Ellen's at her kickboxing class and Jenny went to the range to blow off steam. They said they would be by later."

Nikki pulled some chopsticks out of the drawer and opened a container that turned out to be Mongolian Beef. "Jane, do you ever think that we ought to get out and meet other people? Maybe associate with someone who isn't Carrie Mae?"

"We do. We go to the gym, and you go to the linguistics group, and I have my Comic-Con friends. We see other people." Jane's hand paused over the Moo Shu Pork. "Why?"

"I'm not trying to break up with you, Jane. I've just been thinking a lot about my life lately."

"You mean you've been thinking about breaking up with Z'ev again," said Jane rolling her eyes. "You're not going to do it. I don't know why you keep talking about it. You look into his big brown eyes and you go all gooey and you don't do it."

"Yeah, but I should," said Nikki. "He's kind of incompatible with this job. He's a real danger to Carrie Mae."

Jane shrugged. "He is. But you're making it work."

"I'm making it work," Nikki repeated. "But my bigger question is: for how long? I keep thinking life would be easier without him. And then I start to ponder what else life would be easier without."

Jane stared at her, a worried crease forming between her eyebrows. "And, um, when you have these thoughts, do any particular names spring to mind? Do you have any ideas about how you would like to get rid of the names on said list?"

"I'm not going on a killing rampage," said Nikki.

"OK, but if you decide to go all Val Robinson on us, I'd like some prior warning."

Nikki thought about saying that sometimes she thought Val

Robinson's lone wolf approach had some real merits, but she knew Jane would blow a gasket if she so much as suggested it. Also, Val hadn't been an indiscriminate killer. She simply got rid of the people in her way. It was just that at one point, Nikki had unfortunately been in the way.

"So have you decided what you're going to do with your two weeks off?" she asked changing the topic.

"Jenny keeps saying we're going to Cancun," said Jane, looking doubtful.

"Won't the tan interfere with your preferred Goth lifestyle?"

"It would, if all of my Goth friends hadn't moved to San Diego and started having babies. Plus, I do carry sunscreen at all times."

Both their phones chirped and Nikki leaned over to check the message.

Coming in—don't shoot me.

"I wish Jenny wouldn't text that every time," said Jane, sighing. "The mobile companies can look at those texts if they want."

"They should get in line with the NSA," said Nikki with a shrug. "It reads like a joke."

Jane looked unconvinced.

"Hey, y'all," said Jenny, breezing in, smelling faintly of Dolce and cordite. "I brought some really fresh berries for dessert." She plunked the bag down on the counter next to the ice cream. "In case you want to try something healthy for a change."

"Yeah, we probably don't," said Nikki. "But they'll go good on the ice cream."

Jenny shook her head and investigated the Chinese food containers, selecting the grilled vegetables and chicken option. "So what are we talking about?"

"Breaking up with Z'ev and what to do on our unpaid leave," said Jane, making a sour face.

Jenny wrinkled her nose. "Honey, I don't want to be mean, but it's time to shit or get off the pot." Then she pointed her chopsticks at Jane. "Cancun."

"The problem is," said Nikki. "that I don't know whether to… Can we use a different metaphor while we're eating?"

"You had a perfect opportunity with Kit Masters," said Jenny. Being the son of an agent, he was covered under the immediate-danger-family-clause. Z'ev had cancelled your vacation plans at the last second, and you were even mostly broken up due to that phone issue. It was the perfect opportunity. It would have been like the break-up win of the century—dump Z'ev, find someone new in a week, and have that someone new be a European rock star. I'm telling you, it was the break-up trifecta and you blew it." Jenny shook her head sadly. "Anyway, my point is that the problem isn't knowing what to do. You know what you should do. You just don't want to do it."

"You really think I should break up with him?" asked Nikki and watched Jenny and Jane exchange glances filled with the telepathy of previous conversations.

"Yes," said Jenny, taking a deep breath. "I do. He's a threat to Carrie Mae and to you, and the only way that you're making this work is because he's never around, which is making you miserable."

Nikki looked at Jane, who nodded and then smiled apologetically. "Ellen feels the same way, I suppose?"

"I'm sure I couldn't answer that," said Jenny, who had clearly been spending time with Mr. Merrivel, "as we do not speak about you behind your back."

Nikki laughed and threw one of the fortune cookies at her. "Yes, you do. Behind my back, in front of my back, beside my back."

"Well, there's more of us," said Jane, practically. "We have you surrounded. What are you going to do on your leave?"

"I'm going to drive up and see my grandmother in Kaniksu Falls," said Nikki.

"That should be fun. You've been saying you need to visit her," said Jenny scooping some white rice out of her dish and into Jane's container.

"It's rice," said Jane rolling her eyes. "You can eat rice."

"It's white rice. It's devoid of nutrients."

"It should be nice to visit," said Nikki, ignoring the dietary squabble. "But I think she's going to ask if I want to buy the farm."

"She's going to ask if you want to die?" Jenny looked up, startled.

"What?" They stared at each other trying to figure out where the conversation had gone wrong. "No, she owns a farm. I think she's starting to feel too old to take care of it, and she's thinking about selling."

"Oh, right. Yeah, we had to work that out with my Granny. We were all so sad the day we had to take her cows away."

"I don't know what you have to do to get your cow license revoked," said Jane. "And it's possible, considering how deeply Southern you are, that I don't want to know."

"That is a slander on my heritage and my Granny," said Jenny. "You'd better watch yourself young lady or I will not teach you how to get free drinks in Cancun."

"I know how to get free drinks," said Jane. "I just have higher standards for my breasts."

"Ladies," said Nikki, "before this turns into a fistfight, can we focus on the really important question?"

"Sure," said Jenny, "What is the really important question? Is Z'ev getting suspicious?"

"What?" Nikki laughed casually. "No, I was going to say, chocolate syrup or berries on the ice cream?"

Jane's phone let out a chirp and she picked it up to read the incoming text.

"Can I have all of them?" asked Jane, setting the phone down. "That was the office letting me know that my mainframe access has been suspended for the next two weeks. This sucks, guys! I don't want to be on unpaid leave. It goes on our permanent record. It's not fair."

Jenny leaned over to give her a hug. "I had to turn in Freddy."

Nikki winced in sympathy. "I'm sorry, Jenny."

"It's OK," said Jenny, straightening her spine and putting on an obviously brave face. "We did the crime; I can do the time. Besides, I couldn't take an M-16 to Cancun anyway."

AUGUST IV

THE CANTINA BAND

Kaniksu Falls • Tuesday

Nikki paused at the four-way stop, considering her options. The problem with taking a road trip to find oneself was that she wasn't really lost and now she had arrived in Kaniksu Falls and was heartily sick of the company, but still no closer to any decisions. It was 7:30 P.M. on a Tuesday, which meant that her grandmother would be firmly ensconced at the Bingo hall for at least another hour. A flash of headlights behind her indicated that she'd taken too much time even by polite Washington standards. She took a left and headed for the tavern sign she could see cycling through a pattern of lights that formed an arrow pointing at a dark building barely visible in the dusk. She could get a drink and a burger and then go home to her grandmother, who was almost certain to have pie.

The bar was called the Kessel Run and it was decorated in a plethora of twelfth man football flags and kitschy alien crap.

She thought about calling Donny. Theoretically, he would also be in town somewhere. After their brief rendezvous in LA, she figured they had a lot of catching up to do. And she really did want to talk to him, but not on the phone. Phones were never secure these days. Nikki scanned the parking lot. There was only one car, a boring blue four-door. Nikki shook her head. She couldn't understand why anyone would drive a car so devoid of personality. She couldn't even tell what kind it was—Oldsmobile? Buick? It was the equivalent of the high-school wallflower, going out of its way to not be noticed. Volvos were like the AV club, full of weird boxy angles that no one understood, but were beloved by the in-crowd. Sports cars were the popular kids. SUV's and trucks were the jocks. This car was so blah, Nikki wanted to key it just because it would be character building for the car.

"That car was me in high-school—totally forgettable." Shaking her head again, she went inside. Nikki pushed aside a cardboard cutout of Harrison Ford, listing into the doorway, and sat down at the bar. Aside from a trio sitting in the back near the jukebox, she was the only one in the place.

"What can I get you?" asked the bartender, putting down the sports section and placing a menu in front of her.

Nikki considered ordering a glass of wine, but thought that she already stood out enough as it was. She glanced at the bar menu. It was heavy on the fried substances and beer. "Um ... How about a gin and tonic and a," She shifted a grease spot on the menu with her thumb, "Wookie burger? You know, as long as it's ethically farmed Wookie."

"Curly fries or wedges?" asked the bartender, ignoring her attempt at humor.

"Has to be wedges, doesn't it? Wedge to Red Leader and all that?" The bartender stared at her blankly. "Curly fries are fine," she said.

"Back in a second with your drink," he said, tucking the pencil behind his ear and then ambled toward the kitchen. Nikki surveyed the bar in the reflection of the ornate Budweiser mirror behind the taps. Grimy would have been doing the place a kindness. Everything seemed slightly sticky, like the concept of occasionally washing the bar rag that washed everything else had never been properly explained to the employees. On the other hand, if the three patrons at the back of the bar were anything to be judged by, then this place was a fancy night out for most of the clientele. The first man wore a grubby John Deere hat without a trace of Ashton Kutcher irony, a scraggly goatee, and a pair of Carhartt's so filthy the only clean space was behind the knees. Which she could see because he had one leg angled out from his chair and he was bouncing it with the kind of nervous energy usually seen on those with a severe caffeine addiction. The second man was clearly in his Sunday best of acid-wash black jeans and a blue button-up work shirt with a collar that must have been a hair too tight, because he kept tugging at it after every sip of his beer. How either of them had managed to scrape up an association with the girl who perched uncomfortably on the third chair, her arms crossed over a green cardigan and white blouse, was probably one of the mysteries of the universe. She looked to be in her early twenties, Hispanic, with thick, shoulder-length black hair, and big dark eyes that Nikki could tell had been crying recently. In Nikki's opinion, she was far too pretty, too well-dressed, and too young to be with either of the men. The two men seemed to be arguing quietly, but the more they spoke, the further away the girl leaned and the more she seemed to hunch in on herself, as if trying to become invisible in her chair.

The bartender returned with Nikki's drink. He set it down with the air of one doing his duty in the face of adversity. "It's going to be wedges after all," he said. "Those guys ordered the last of the curly fries." He jerked his head at the occupied table, with an expression that said he'd take the fries back if he could.

"Wedges are fine," she said, with a shrug.

The bartender shrugged back, as if to say that he couldn't be bothered with people who didn't understand the important things in life.

Her burger and wedges arrived a few moments later and both were surprisingly tasty. Fattening as hell, but not the greasy bomb of disgustingness that she was expecting. In fact, the burger was downright good, bordering on awesome. Perhaps cuisine was how the Kessel Run stayed in business. If that was the case, they should double the cook's salary.

She was savoring the crisp snap of the pickle on her fifth bite of burger when it happened. The hairs on the back of her arms stood up as the discussion at the back table rose in acrimony. The volume didn't go up, just the intensity of the whispering. Nikki shifted her eyes to the mirror and saw that the body language on the girl had moved from hunched to cowering.

"It's not my fault," said the girl, her voice wavering. She stood up to go, but Carhartt snaked out a hand and grabbed her by the upper arm.

"Let me go," pleaded the girl, sounding on the verge of tears. "It's not my fault." She tugged ineffectually at his hand.

Nikki took a deep breath and let it out again slowly. She'd really been enjoying the burger. Reaching into her purse, she dropped some cash on the bar.

Back at the table, Carhartt forcefully shoved the girl back into her chair and stood up, towering over her.

"I just want to go home," said the girl, tears sliding down her cheek.

"You'll go when I'm damn good and ready for you to go," snapped Carhartt.

Nikki stood up, blotted her mouth with the napkin, and turned to face the three at the table.

"Gentlemen, I think you should let the girl go." She used a loud, calm voice, so there would be no mistaking her intentions. The bartender, coming out of the kitchen, froze in the doorway, his eyes flicking between the table and Nikki, his expression akin to a deer in the proverbial headlights.

"Nobody asked you what you think, bitch," said the man in the button-up. Carhartt blinked at her.

"Let me rephrase that," said Nikki. "You're going to let the girl go."

"Or what?" asked Carhartt smirking.

"That wasn't an either or statement," said Nikki. "That was a fact."

"It's OK," said the girl, looking panicked. "It's OK. I don't want to start any trouble." She licked her lips and stood up. "Everything's fine, really."

Carhartt released the girl's arm and shoved her back into her chair. "This is none of your business," he said, trying to loom over Nikki. "Go away."

"I'm making it my business," said Nikki. "Now I suggest you sit down while she and I leave."

"Ain't going to happen," he said. "Go away." And then he pushed her, a one-handed shove on the shoulder, meant to send her toward the door.

Instead, Nikki side-stepped, seized his arm, pivoted and, with a quick twist of the hips, flipped him over her back and onto the floor. He landed with a hard crack, but promptly tried to sit up. She dropped her body weight through her knee onto his head and then bounced back to her feet. His head made a double clunk as it smacked into her knee and into the floor a split second later. Button-up was rounding the table at this point, aiming to tackle her, but instead she spun and drove her fist into his gut. He doubled over, gaping like a fish, and she seized his head and drove her knee up into his face. He staggered back, blood streaming from his face, and collapsed into a table, which tipped over on top of him. The fight was over.

"Clyde," said someone from the entrance of the bar, "you should probably call the sheriff."

"Yeah," said the bartender, his hand fumbling for the phone on the wall, his eyes still stuck on Nikki.

"It's OK," said Nikki to the girl who was still sitting where Carhartt had left her. "What's your name?"

"Ylina," said the girl.

"Hey, Merv," said the bartender into the phone. "It's Clyde over at the Kessel Run. Yeah, I've got a couple of drunks here who picked on the wrong girl. Can you send someone around to collect them?" He peered over the bar at unconscious Carhartt's body. "No, no rush. It's under control. I'll put them on the porch for you. Thanks." Clyde hung up and stared around the room at those who were still conscious. "Okay," he said clapping his hands together and drawing out the word to multiple syllables. "The sheriff will be here shortly. In the meantime, can I interest any of you in another drink or dessert?"

"The sheriff?" squeaked Ylina.

"It'll be fine," said Nikki.

"No, it won't!" Ylina edged around Button-Up's legs and started to fumble in Carhartt's pockets. "You don't know what you've done."

"It will be fine," said Nikki. "The sheriff will handle it."

But Ylina shook her head, ignoring them, and pulled out a set of car keys.

"Ylina," said Nikki. "Calm down. It's going to be fine."

"No, not fine," said Ylina, backing toward the door as if Nikki might try and stop her. "The sheriff's coming. Not fine!" Then she turned and sprinted out into the parking lot. A few moments later, the roar of a car engine could be heard, and tires on gravel as Ylina floored it.

"Some people got no gratitude," said Clyde, picking up Carhartt's legs. "Jackson, you want to give me a hand?"

"Nikki did it," said the man by the door. "Make her lift them."

Nikki looked up from Clyde to the man by the door and for the first time realized who it was. Jackson Tyrell. She felt her heart skip a beat and suddenly the juke box music seemed far away. This evening had definitely taken a turn and gone right off the rails.

"I only wanted a burger," she said.

"It is a tasty burger," agreed Jackson.

AUGUST V
THE WOUNDS HAVE ALMOST HEALED

Clyde looked from Nikki's frozen expression back to Jackson. "Well, Nikki did all the hard work," he said, picking up her name from Jackson. "So grab his feet. I don't like having bodies cluttering up the place."

"Statements like that make me worry about you, Clyde," said Jackson and walked forward to pick up Carhartt's feet.

"You go back to your burger, Miss," said Clyde.

Nikki sat down on the barstool and stared at her burger. She took a bite because it wouldn't do to have Jackson think she was upset. She chewed mechanically while they moved Button-Up to the porch as well. She took a gulp of her drink as Jackson sat down next to her.

"The usual," said Jackson to Clyde, who nodded and went back into the kitchen.

He was bigger than she remembered. Or maybe he wasn't. In high school, he had been small, only a few inches taller than Nikki—just enough so that when she wore heels for a dance he was still an inch or two taller. Everyone knew that he was small. They had been the cute little couple. No one could change his height, so why did he look bigger? Nikki squinted at him, trying to place the difference.

Dark blue T-shirt, naturally faded jeans, shit-kicker working cowboy boots, and dark hair that stood up at the cowlick in back.

Same as forever. He hadn't changed the uniform much since they were twelve. The scar on his face was new. It started below his left ear and cut to the mid-point on his jawbone. It looked like someone had taken a razor blade and sliced it down his face. He was tan and his hazel eyes had a few early wrinkles around them from squinting into the sun. Always strong for his size, his forearms now looked as if they had been carved from oak. His hands, large and callused, curled loosely around a glass of beer. He was leaner than she remembered. He had taken on the compact, wiry look of a Thai boxer. There was nothing but muscle to the man. All the excess had been trimmed away. And at last, Nikki nodded. This was what the difference was. She was seeing Jackson for the first time with nothing in the way.

"Were you planning on just sitting there?" she asked.

"You had it under control," said Jackson, looking around the room, as if surveying her work.

"I meant, were you going to sit there, without saying hello or anything?"

"Oh." He looked sheepish. "Hi."

There was a silence after that and Nikki stared at Jackson. Jackson stared back. For years, she'd been carrying around a speech in her head, a litany of the pain he had caused, and now faced with the chance to speak, she found the words wouldn't come. The person she was sitting next to wasn't the same person who had hurt her. The Jackson she remembered could never sit still. He had been a chair swiveling, toe-tapping, paper tearing, bundle of energy. This Jackson never twitched. He didn't even twist the bar stool back and forth.

"So what have you been doing with yourself?" asked Nikki. "You broke up with me, dropped out of college, then what?"

Jackson blinked. Whatever he had been expecting her to say, it hadn't been that.

"Short story or long?"

"Short," answered Nikki decidedly. She wasn't sure how much she wanted to torture herself. If he turned out to be happily married to a blonde with tits the size of pumpkins and three doe-eyed children she might have to go back home and slit her wrists.

"I ran away and joined the rodeo."

Nikki nodded. That fit.

"I won a few things, but it got to the point where I could see I wasn't going to be the best."

"And that would never do for you," said Nikki.

He grinned. "But I was hard-headed and I found I'd developed a taste for blood and bullshit, so I became a rodeo clown."

"How's that working out for you?"

"Not too bad," he said in his old, understated way.

"Are you the best at it?" prodded Nikki.

"I do all right," he said and took a sip of his beer.

"Meaning you are or close enough to the best," said Nikki. Jackson shrugged again, which Nikki took to be an agreement with her statement.

"How about you?" asked Jackson, setting down his beer. "I talked to Donny earlier this week. Said he ran into you down in LA and that you looked good." Nikki kept her body language relaxed, but she felt a nervous tingle in the base of her spine, and wondered what else Donny had told Jackson. And if any of the things he had mentioned were Z'ev.

"He didn't say much more than that," said Jackson, "but I got the impression that he was worried about you."

"About me?" said Nikki with a disarming smile. "Can't think

why."

Jackson looked pointedly at the table that Button-Up had crashed through. It was still laying on its side. the chairs pushed away at awkward angles.

"Neither can I," he answered. There was a glimmer in his eye that Nikki remembered, and it occurred to her to wonder what he was seeing in her for the first time.

Nikki took a quick stock of herself. Red hair, grey eyes, maybe a few more muscles. There reached a point in a girl's life where the metabolism of high school turns to the ass of college and she must either hit the gym or buy larger pants. Nikki had gone for the workout and although her pants size had remained virtually unchanged, the soft quality that characterized Nikki's appearance in high school and college had disappeared. Nothing else had changed. Had it?

"So…" said Nikki.

"So," agreed Jackson and that annoyed her.

"That's all you have to say to me?" she asked, feeling a flare of the old anger. "That really is it?"

"It?" repeated Jackson warily, and Nikki rolled her eyes.

"I think your last words to me were, let me see if I can get this right… Oh yeah… 'I can't see you anymore. I just can't talk to you.' End quote. I begged to see you and you said no. And then I went over to your apartment and you had moved out the night before. You broke up with me over the phone and said we could no longer speak. And now we're just gonna sit here and shoot the breeze?"

"And another country. Not only did I break up with you over the phone, I was calling from Canada. They had an open call for bronc riders at a rodeo up there." She could see by his smile that he was hoping she'd laugh, but Nikki didn't laugh.

"But we can talk now? Or should I move to the other end of the bar?"

"It's been nine years, Nikki." She continued to stare, not sure what to say. "Come on, I can't change my mind in nine years?"

She remembered a far-away day. It had been sunny with a sky like an upturned blue bowl over their heads. Jackson and Donny had found two oversized sets of boxing gloves in the shed and were wailing away at each other.

"It's my turn!" Nikki yelled.

"Girls don't box," said Donny, the enormous gloves dangling at the end of his skinny arms.

"You let me play or I'm telling your mom!" she said, hands on her hips.

"Better let her," said Jackson.

Nikki pulled the gloves off Donny and started jamming her fists into them. He helped her with the second one. "Now tell me what to do," she said to Donny, squaring off with Jackson.

"You just try and hit Jackson in the face," said Donny with a shrug.

"I'm the bell," said Jackson. "When you hear me yell 'ding', that's the start or end of the round. Ding!" Then he swung for her head. Nikki felt the entire glove along the side of her face, and automatically kicked Jackson in the shin."

"You're supposed to punch!" yelled Donny.

Nikki swung her left and then her right. It was hard to land the gloves where she wanted. Especially with Jackson swinging back. She finally started making progress—first her left glove hit him in the eye and then her right hit him in the mouth. She was lining up for another punch when –

"Ding!"

"Ding," she said. "You always were the bell."

"What?"

"When we were ten, you and Donny were boxing in the backyard, but we didn't have a bell or anything to signal the end of rounds, so you would yell ding. Took me years to realize that every time I started to win, you'd yell ding."

He laughed. "I don't remember that, but it makes sense. If I'd beat you up, your mother would have beat me senseless and you were probably too good."

"But you're doing it again. You always do. You don't like the game, so you cheat."

"You're going to hold me to something I said when I was twenty? And be mad at me for something I did when I was ten?"

"Yes!" exclaimed Nikki. "It's not what you said or when. It's you and me. I know you, Jackson. Everyone gets a fair deal from you. Everyone but me. I loved you. And beyond that, we were friends and I want to know why the hell some stranger gets better from you than me?"

"You only hurt the ones you love?" he asked with his idiot grin.

Nikki growled. She'd been aiming for a Marge Simpson murmur, but it came out more like a pissed off Z'ev.

"Because I couldn't ever win," he said at last.

"What?"

"Nikki, I hated college. I hated the pretentious neo-hippies living off daddy's money and thinking they were so much better than the blue-collar slob working in the paper mill. I hated the professors. I hated all of that and I didn't fit in. You, on the other hand, fit like a glove. You knew what the teachers wanted to hear.

You could have dated any guy on campus. You were where you belonged and I wasn't."

"You could have told me that!"

"No, I couldn't. I could barely explain it to myself. I've barely got it figured out now. But even if I'd been able to put it into words, it wouldn't have mattered. If I'd stayed to talk to you, you would have talked me into staying. You always got your way with me, and I needed things to be my way for a while. There was too much you and not enough me. I didn't even talk to Donny for a couple of years. I only came home at Christmas for three years in a row. My mom kept asking what she'd done wrong. And there wasn't anything. I just needed to be on my own."

Nikki opened her mouth to say something hurtful and then closed it again.

"Yeah, OK," she said. She drank the last of her gin and tonic and stared at the neon signs above the bar for a while. Alison Krauss was playing on the jukebox. The bartender came back in followed by the Sheriff.

"Jackson," said the sheriff with a sigh, "I thought you'd given up picking on things that didn't outweigh you by at least a ton."

"Wasn't me," said Jackson.

"It was the girl," said the bartender.

The sheriff looked speculatively at Nikki.

"Hello. I'm Sheriff Mervin Smalls. Is there a reason you took such a violent dislike to our friends Milt and Pedro, young lady?"

"I felt threatened," said Nikki. It probably would have sounded more convincing if she had actually looked scared.

"Right," said Merv.

"They were drunk," said the bartender.

"Thank you, Clyde. I would never have guessed."

"They came in with a girl and when she got up to leave, one of them grabbed her, so then Nikki said they should let the girl go, but they didn't want to and one of them took a swing at Nikki, so she defended herself."

"Again, thank you, Clyde, for that stirring narrative. Now, how about we let the young lady tell it?" Merv was a little over fifty and, while not exactly in fighting trim, had a comfortable beefy look that said he could toss a few drunks or small cows around without any problems. He was looking at Nikki with a set of hard, dark brown eyes, from under a set of bushy eyebrows, and Nikki wasn't sure that he was at all pleased with her.

"They wouldn't let the girl they were with leave, so I said they should let her go and one of them took a swing at me, so I defended myself," said Nikki. "The one in the Carhartts," she added, since the sheriff seemed to want specifics.

"Milt," said the sheriff, shaking his head.

"And the other one tried to jump her from behind," said Clyde.

The sheriff raised an eyebrow at Clyde, who smiled awkwardly and looked at Nikki.

"The other one attacked me while I was dealing with Milt," said Nikki, confirming Clyde's story.

"That sounds like our Pedro, tsk. And where is the other young lady now?" The sheriff looked around the room, as if she might suddenly appear.

"She took off," said Nikki.

"To be honest," said Clyde, "I think she might have stolen their car."

"We don't know that," said Nikki. "It might have been her car."

"The keys were in his pocket," argued Clyde.

"Well, considering how abusive he was, that would be in keeping with his personality." Clyde shrugged as if to say he did not agree, but wasn't planning on arguing further. "Anyway," she said turning back to the sheriff, "they attacked me. I defended myself."

Merv collected a handful of bar peanuts from the dish on the bar and thoughtfully chewed a few. "You paint a moving picture of fear. I feel that you were indeed threatened and acting in defense of your person. But just so the paperwork is tidy can I have your name and where you can be reached?" Merv pulled a pen and small notebook out of his breast pocket and clicked the pen at Nikki expectantly.

"Nicole Lanier," she said. "L-A-N-I-E-R."

"Ah," said Merv, flipping his notebook closed, without writing anything. "I should have recognized the hair. Just like your father's. Up visiting, are you? I had heard that you were living down in Los Angeles these days."

"Uh, yes," said Nikki. She'd forgotten how much people knew about each other in small towns.

"Good, I'm sure Peg will be happy to have you around." Nikki couldn't think of anything to say to that, so she said nothing. "Staying very long?"

"Just a week or so," said Nikki, frowning.

"Mm-hmm. Good. Thanks, Clyde," said Merv, taking another handful of peanuts. Clyde waved his dish-towel in Merv's general direction as acknowledgement. "Jackson, I can assume you'll make sure the young lady gets home without further incident?" Jackson nodded and Nikki fumed.

"Without further incident?" repeated Nikki, when Merv had

ambled out the door. "What did he mean by that?"

"I think he meant that he didn't want to arrest anyone else tonight and I should keep you out of trouble."

"I can keep myself out of trouble," snapped Nikki.

"Really?" asked Jackson.

"This wasn't trouble," she said firmly.

Jackson shrugged. She could see he was trying not to smile.

"It wasn't!" she protested, trying not to laugh herself. "OK, it was a little trouble, but not a lot of trouble."

"Well, maybe your definition of trouble and mine are different," he allowed and Nikki did laugh.

"Was it worth it?" she asked, turning the subject back to where it had been.

"Was what worth it?" he asked, returning her smile easily.

"Leaving us. Donny, your family, everyone. Leaving me. Was the pain you caused worth it?"

"I didn't want to hurt anyone," he said.

"I believe that, but knowing that you did, and knowing how much—because believe me, it was no small amount—would you do it again?"

"Yes," he answered without hesitation. "I had to. I couldn't continue pretending to be what I wasn't."

Nikki hesitated and then nodded. "Yeah, I figured."

Jackson was staring at her, a bemused expression on his face. Nikki stared back, waiting for him to speak.

"Hi," he said at last, putting out his hand as if to shake, "I don't think we've met. I'm Jackson Tyrell."

"New and improved?" asked Nikki with a laugh.

"Old enough to know what can't be improved. Now who the hell are you?"

AUGUST VI
WAIT A MINUTE

"Funny," said Nikki, around her last mouthful of burger, ignoring his outstretched hand. "Anyway, I'm glad you turned out OK and didn't go weirdly axe-murderer or something."

"Me too," said Jackson. "Are you heading up to your grandmother's?"

"Yeah. Let's hope I can find it in the dark. I don't think I've actually driven up to the farm myself in about a decade, so hopefully the Pederson's haven't changed their mailbox."

"They did actually."

"What? No more creepy folk-art kid staring at me through binoculars? Now what am I supposed to use to navigate?"

"Giant shark eating a mailbox boat. Mr. Pederson got a new skill saw for Christmas and Mrs. Pederson found Pinterest."

"Do you even know what Pinterest is?" asked Nikki, her eyebrows going up.

"I've had the concept explained to me," he retorted. Clyde came out of the kitchen carrying Jackson's plate. "Can you put it in a to-go box, Clyde? I'm going to caravan up to the Connelly's with Nikki."

"Sure," said Clyde with a shrug.

"You don't have to do that," said Nikki. "Stay here and enjoy your dinner. I've got a phone; it can give me directions."

"Reception's not so good up there. It's no trouble." Jackson stood up, pulling out his wallet to pay Clyde. "Peg's place is on my way home. You can follow me."

Nikki looked at his dinner, already in a to-go box, and Clyde already tucking Jackson's cash into the register. "OK, thanks."

She paused out in the parking lot. The air smelled of wood smoke. A rather homey scent in the winter, but during late summer and the height of the fire season, it made her nervous.

"Colville Complex is kicking up," said Jackson, sniffing the air as he stepped outside. "The wind has shifted."

"How big is that fire now?" She hadn't been following the news, but the Colville Forest Fire Complex had been on the front of every newspaper in every small town she'd driven through.

"Over a hundred acres to the west and another fifty to the east."

"I don't understand; I thought it was one fire?"

"It's all the Colville Forest," he said shaking his head. "So instead of calling out the West Colville fire and the East Colville fire they call it a Complex. Of course, we're all worried that it'll jump the river and the two will merge—then it really will all be one fire."

"The river's pretty wide. It can't really do that, can it?"

"If the wind is strong enough," said Jackson with a shrug. "All it takes is one little spark. Everyone with half a brain has been clearing brush, but if it jumps the river, it could sweep through all the dry grass and hit the town. We're all on high fire alert. Anyway, just follow me up to Peg's place."

She was unsurprised to see that Jackson was driving a black F-150, covered in mud, with a gun rack in the back window.

"What? No rope on the gun rack?" she asked, pointing at his truck.

"Rope on the gun rack is for posers," he said. "You can't leave a good rope up there. It would get sun damaged and brittle.

Plus, I actually like to use my gun rack to hold my gun periodically."

Nikki laughed. "This is one of those, 'you know you're a cowboy when…' things, isn't it?"

"Yeah, and what about the pimp mobile you're driving?" he demanded, pointing to the sky-blue '53 Impala.

"You mean, what about it could be more awesome? The answer is nothing."

He shook his head. "Follow me, and stick to the speed limit. Merv and his deputies take speed limits seriously here."

"You mean they take their source of income seriously?" retorted Nikki, who had a dim view of things impeding the max velocity of any of her vehicles.

"Whatever. Just keep it at twenty-five, OK?" Jackson climbed into his truck and Nikki dropped down into the Impala.

Kaniksu Falls was in the northeastern most part of Washington State, nestled in one of the bends of the Columbia River and flanked on two sides by the Colville National Forest and the Colville Indian Reservation to the south. When it came to bigger towns to go to, Canada was closer than the nearest American neighbor. It was therefore not entirely surprising that Nikki's father had been Canadian. Nell, Nikki's mother, hadn't been the only Kaniksu Falls teenager to venture across the border, where the drinking age was still nineteen, and come home with a Canadian boyfriend.

The town itself was a typical small town layout—main street, with a grid system branching out on either side. The high school lay on the edge of town with tiny little suburbs even further out and then, like electrons circling the nucleus of an atom, the farms and ranches were the last sign of humans before the expanse of forest took over.

Nikki stared at the shops as she drove by, all closed by 8:00 P.M. Only bars and restaurants stayed open later than that, and most of the restaurants were closed by ten. There wasn't even a McDonalds in town. The burger joint was literally called "Fast Food" and it wasn't being ironically Americana in style, it had just existed in the same beat-up drive-in location since 1963.

Nothing seemed to have changed since Nell had packed them up and left for Seattle—since Nikki's father had abandoned them. The grocery store, the hair salon, the Beauty Belle (where all the girls got their prom dresses), the bookstore (with new and used books!)—it all looked the same. Maybe slightly smaller and dirtier. Jackson stopped at a stoplight, and they waited on the empty streets for the light to change. Nikki could hear the whisper of music from Jackson's stereo over the sound of their motors. She stared around the intersection at the Antique Mall (commonly referred to as "the garage sale place"), the Mexican restaurant— previously a Shari's, Nikki guessed by the octagonal shape—the gas station, and the auto-body shop, trying to drum up some feeling of nostalgia. When she had visited during college there had always been the twinge of what might have been, the life she might have lived if her father and Jackson hadn't left. Now she found herself pondering how anyone lived without a twenty-four hour grocery store and Chinese delivery on speed dial. Did no one ever need to eat at 2:00 A.M.? Did they just cook their own food? No one should cook at 2:00 A.M. You were either drunk, sleep deprived, or getting off work at that hour. None of those were fit states to be operating an appliance.

As Nikki contemplated the problems of late night noshing, a figure turned the corner down the street and walked along the sidewalk. Nikki squinted in disbelief. He wore the same filthy Carhartt's, the same disgusting ball cap. It really was Milt from the bar. But the sheriff had taken him to jail, hadn't he? As she watched, Milt opened the door to the darkened auto-body shop and went inside.

The light turned green and Jackson's truck was already trundling across the intersection. Nikki hesitated, uncertain. Should she honk? Let Jackson go while she… She did what? Went and beat up Milt again? Nikki bit her lip and pushed the gas pedal, following Jackson. It wasn't any of her business if the sheriff didn't want to arrest people. She should let it go.

But she found herself stewing on it as she followed Jackson's truck up into the foothills, past the shark eating a mailbox boat, and onto the Connelly farm.

Jackson turned the truck around in the circular driveway and waved, but didn't stop, as he headed back down to the road. Nikki turned off the Impala and sat frowning for a long moment in the car. Then she shook her head, grabbed her bag and headed to the front door. Her grandmother's Ford SUV was still warm to the touch, which meant she hadn't been home for very long. Nikki rang the door bell and waited.

"Who is it?" asked her grandmother, from the other side of the door.

"It's Nikki, Grandma," said Nikki, not quite yelling to project through the door.

"Oh, good," said Peg, and Nikki heard the clunk of the deadbolt and a rattle of a chain latch being undone. Nikki didn't remember there having been a chain latch previously.

"Sweetie!" exclaimed Peg throwing open the door. "You're here!" Nikki was promptly smothered in a hug, but was dimly aware that Peg was holding something heavy in one hand as it clunked against her back during the hug. "I didn't think you were flying in until tomorrow. How did you get here?" She peered out into the driveway.

"I drove a little faster than I thought I would," said Nikki. "Grandma, why do you have a gun?"

"Oh, this?" Peg looked in surprise at the .357 revolver in her hand. "Well, I'm old, dear, and I live all by myself. It pays to be on the safe side. You see all those crazies on the news these days. I'll take you down to the quarry tomorrow and teach you how to shoot it. I'm a firm believer that if there's a gun in the house, everyone should know how to use it. But you said you were flying! You didn't really drive all the way, did you?"

"You said I was flying," said Nikki, stepping inside and shutting the front door. Peg locked the deadbolt, the door handle, and slid the chain into place. "I said I was driving."

"I don't think that's safe."

"And yet, here I am, safe and sound," said Nikki. "Now where's the pie?"

Peg laughed. "It's in the kitchen. How did you know there would be pie?"

"It's peach season," said Nikki, with a shrug. "Of course there's pie."

"Well, come into the kitchen," said Peg. "And I'll cut you a slice, while I confess a little something."

"Grandma, you didn't shoot someone, did you? Because I'm not burying any bodies until after pie."

"Don't be ridiculous. I haven't shot anyone in years."

Peg led the way into the kitchen. The yellow and red tile counter and backsplash hadn't been changed since her grandfather built it, but the floor was new.

"You took out the linoleum!" exclaimed Nikki.

"Yeah, I had a raccoon under the house and when Jorge went to get it out, the little bugger knocked one of the water pipes loose and flooded the whole kitchen. I had to replace it. I like this floor," she tapped the new wooden boards with her house slipper, "but I kind of miss the linoleum. It was a lot warmer on the toes."

"So what did you need to confess?" asked Nikki as she pulled down two plates from the cupboard.

"Well," said Peg, tucking her gun into the kitchen junk drawer, and picking up a knife from the wooden block. "I didn't really think you were arriving until tomorrow afternoon. There's ice cream in the freezer or whip cream in the fridge, hon. Your pick." Peg deftly sliced the pie and levered it onto the plates. "So I didn't really get a chance to clean out your room."

"What, you didn't get a chance to dust?" asked Nikki, covering her pie with whip cream.

"It's a little bit more than dusty," said Peg, wiping peach off the knife and looking extremely guilty.

"How much is a little bit?" asked Nikki.

"Well…" said Peg.

Nikki grabbed a fork and her plate and marched up the stairs to the second door on the left and swung it open.

"Grandma! What is all this stuff?"

"It's the attic," said Peg. "When the pipe burst, we didn't know originally where it was coming from so I had to pull everything out of the attic for the plumber to crawl around in. And once I had all the boxes and trunks down I started going through everything. That rack on the left is my mother's clothes. There are also some of mine from when I was a girl and I cared about such things. The ones in the middle are your mother's. She always was a clothes horse. There's a few of your baby things in the back. And the ones on the right are my grandmother's. I've been cleaning them up and pressing them. Once I know what I've got, I plan to sell them on the internet."

Nikki blinked at the treasure trove of vintage clothing. She could barely see the bed, its crisp sheets and comfy quilt beckoning through the racks and boxes of clothes.

"It's probably a good thing you came alone," said Peg, looking into the room. "I don't think we could wedge anyone else in there with you. That boyfriend of yours isn't coming, is he?"

"No," said Nikki. "He's on an assignment for work. I'm on my own for awhile."

"Well, that's good, I guess."

Nikki couldn't tell if she was pleased or disappointed.

AUGUST VII

QUARRY

Wednesday

Nikki bounced down the stairs wearing tennis shoes, khaki shorts, and a short-sleeve, lightweight button-up that hid her gun nicely. She'd been tempted to try out a few of the vintage looks hanging around the room, but had realized they probably wouldn't conceal any firearms. She sat down at the breakfast table, making sure not to catch her holster on the chair. The first few months she'd worn a gun, she'd felt like it had knocked into everything and she'd had to severely adjust her wardrobe to shirts that would drape nicely. These days she barely noticed she had it on.

Her grandmother set a bowl of oatmeal down in front of her and pushed a Tupperware container of cut peaches at her. Nikki took both without a word, respecting her grandmother's preferred morning mode. After Jane's Czechoslovakian Incident, she had finally learned that nothing good ever came of speaking to a non-morning person before ten. Nikki finished her breakfast, washed her bowl and then went out on the porch to wait for Peg's brain to switch back on.

The farm looked mostly like she remembered. Donna, her grandmother's geriatric gray mare, dozed in the near paddock, one leg cocked, chewing reflexively on some grass. The barn needed painting. There was activity in the peach orchard beyond the paddock. A man on an ATV pulled a trailer full of picked peaches at a snail's pace through the trees and down toward the barn.

"That'll be Jorge," said Peg coming out onto the porch. "He is always so careful when he drives. He never bruises a single peach. His nephew, on the other hand, drives like a crazy man. Might as well make jam by the time he's done."

"Did Jorge ever get his work visa settled?" asked Nikki, remembering the drama from last Christmas.

"Sort of," said Peg pulling a face. "So much damn paperwork these days. This country is fed by the efforts of migrant workers. I fail to understand why we make it so difficult to get work visas." She waved at Jorge, who waved back.

"Because politicians aren't farmers and farmers are too busy to be politicians," said Nikki, repeating one of her grandfather's stock phrases, which made Peg laugh.

"He was so right. Well, what's your plan for the day? Are you up for shooting at the quarry?"

"Sure," said Nikki. "Sounds good."

"Good. We should get going before the sun gets too high. I'll get the gun and bullets, meet you at the car in ten."

Nikki nodded and went to add some extra bullets to her own purse before arriving at the car.

The quarry was an old gravel mine cut into the side of a hill, revealing the hard strata of geologic time. While the mine had been closed for years the road up to it showed that it was clearly still in use and the twinkle of shiny brass among the rocks showed that Peg wasn't the only one who used it for an informal gun range.

Nikki frowned as she kicked over a rock and dislodged a mid-sized casing. A few feet away, a discarded Wolf 39mm ammunition box fluttered in the breeze, pinned in place by a dead branch.

"Something the matter?" asked Peg, taking her gun bag out of the car.

"What kind of guns do people like to shoot up here? Assault rifles?"

"I suppose," said Peg, with a shrug. "People have all sorts of things in their gun safes. That's why home invasions aren't too much of a problem around here."

"Hmm," said Nikki, looking at the spray pattern of spent AK-47 ammo. "Yes, but I thought full-auto was illegal here."

"Just because it ain't legal, don't mean people don't do it," said Peg. "What are you looking at over there?"

"Nothing," said Nikki looking up with a smile. Peg looked unconvinced, but carried some tin cans out to a board that had been placed between two rocks. The board had the sad, chewed look of anything at the wrong end of a gun range. "OK," said Peg, coming back and opening the bag. "This is what is known as a revolver."

"Grandma," said Nikki, trying to stem the tide of "Guns for Dummies" that was flowing at her.

"And that's because it's got this little cylinder here that re-volves, and that is where you place the bullets."

"Grandma."

"Now you've got to pay attention," said Peg. "It's important to know this stuff if you're going to be in the house with a gun."

"Yes, but—" said Nikki.

"No buts," said Peg. "I hope California hasn't turned you into some sort of hippie, gun control idiot."

In response, Nikki flipped up the tail of her shirt and pulled out her SIG Sauer. Walking down the line, she capped the cans one after another. When the slide locked back she dropped the empty and inserted a fresh magazine from her pocket. She stepped back, made sure the situation was secure, and then re-holstered.

"Actually," she said, turning back to Peg, "I firmly believe in gun control, just, you know, for other people."

She could see that Peg was stunned, but true to her character, she simply sniffed and struggled to look unimpressed. "I guess you're not kidding," said Peg. "What are you carrying?"

Nikki pulled out her gun and handed it to her grandmother. "A SIG Sauer P239. It'll shoot 9mm or your .357 rounds."

"Your mother doesn't know you carry this, does she?"

"Does she know about yours?"

Peg looked guilty. "I think she believes I got rid of it. I just don't talk about it." She turned Nikki's gun over in her hand. "I don't know about these kind of guns. I like the revolver. Fewer parts. And I can take it apart and clean it and put it back together without screwing it up."

"I can take this one apart without screwing it up," said Nikki. "But I know what you mean. I'll show you how later if you want. Do you want to shoot it?"

"Heck, yeah!"

Peg fired off carefully aimed shots, while Nikki reloaded bullets into her empty magazine.

"It's kind of fun!" said Peg handing it back. "But more kicky than mine."

"Yours is heavier," said Nikki. "The lighter the gun, the more you have to rely on your hands to control the recoil."

"Huh. Where'd you learn to shoot?"

"Um, my work offers courses on shooting," said Nikki. Which was true. True-ish anyway. "We travel a lot and they want us to be safe and prepared for any situation."

"I thought you were a project coordinator for a make-up company," said Peg, looking puzzled.

"For the Carrie Mae Charity Foundation, yes," said Nikki.

"Need a lot of guns working for charity work, do you?" Peg looked skeptical.

"Charity goes to the people in need," said Nikki. "And frequently the people in need live in dangerous situations. Carrie Mae likes its ladies to be well-groomed, well-spoken, and well-prepared."

"Sort of a Boy Scout philosophy, I guess," said Peg. "Let's shoot some more. I want to see how you do with mine."

It was close to noon by the time they quit and Nikki sank into the cloth seats of her grandmother's Ford, happily cranking the air conditioning.

"I love the Impala," she said, flapping her hands into the breeze from the vent, trying to channel more air to her skin. "But I do miss modern air-conditioning."

"When did you get that car? I can't say that I would have picked it out for you."

"I wouldn't have picked it out for me either," said Nikki. "It belonged to a co-worker of mine who died. She really loved that car, and I didn't have the heart to let it go out to auction."

"Oh, that's too bad. How'd she die?"

The thumping blades of the helicopter were close and Nikki glanced over her shoulder. The helicopter was holding steady at road level, with Ellen leaning out the door, aiming her rifle past Nikki at Val. She didn't hear the gunshot, but she saw Val jerk and fall over the railing. Nikki ran forward, catching Val's hand as it slipped from the edge of the bridge.

"Val!" yelled Nikki.

Val's hand was sliding from her grasp, it was wet with blood. Nikki leaned further over the railing, feeling a precarious shift in balance. Val looked up, her naturally pale face even paler. Behind her, Nikki could hear the helicopter settling onto the bridge.

"I take it back, Nikki."

"What? Val, hold on!"

"I take it back. I'm not sorry I bought you shoes."

"I lost those shoes! It doesn't matter! None of it matters!" Nikki was screaming now. "Just hold on to my hand!"

Val looked down at the water. Nikki could hear the pounding of feet on the bridge behind her.

Val looked up into Nikki's face and smiled. Then she let go.

"Val!" screamed Nikki as her friend tumbled into the turgid water of Chao Phraya.

Nikki paused, absorbing the memory like a blow, before answering her grandmother. Talking about Val Robinson, her first partner at Carrie Mae, had gotten easier, but she still never quite knew what to say. *Ellen shot her, and then I dropped her off a bridge?* That wasn't going to go over well.

"She drowned," said Nikki. *You know, eventually, if the fall from the bridge or the bullet wound didn't kill her first.*

"Wow, that's too bad. Was it an accident?"

"Well, no one drowns on purpose," said Nikki.

"I don't know—could have been suicide."

"It wasn't," said Nikki. "She just got careless." She tried to smother the bitterness in her tone, but didn't succeed. Val's betrayal still stung and she couldn't quite shake the feeling that she should have been able to talk Val into coming back to Carrie Mae. No one else shared that view. They all said that killing Val had been the only solution, but on sleepless nights Nikki found herself replaying the incidents in Bangkok, trying to figure out what she could have done differently.

"So you keep her car to remind you not to be careless, too?" asked Peg, and Nikki froze in her seat. She could feel a trickle of sweat roll down into her cleavage.

"Shh," said Nikki. "No one's supposed to know that."

Peg laughed, then she put out her hand and patted Nikki's knee. "We all got secrets, honey. But believe me, they're never as big as we think they are. Because, and don't take this the wrong way, generally speaking, no one cares about us as much as we ourselves do. If you don't want to talk about this Val woman, that's fine. I won't push it. But really, whatever you're not saying probably isn't that big a deal. It's not like you killed her."

"Right," said Nikki. *It was really more of a joint effort.* "Speaking of things that weren't my fault, I should probably tell you something before you hear about it around town." Nikki briefly filled her grandmother in on the events at the Kessel Run. "And then less than an hour later, I saw one of the guys walking down the street!"

"That sounds like Merv," said Peg, shaking her head. "Thinks a sheriff's badge gives him the right to run things however he wants."

"You don't like him?" asked Nikki.

Peg shrugged. "Not really, and I trust him only about as far as I can throw him. He keeps offering to buy my farm. Frankly, I'd rather let the vultures at the bank have it than sell it to him."

"Is bankruptcy a possibility?" asked Nikki, startled.

"Eh, no more than any other year," said Peg. "It's farming. You know, you just get along and hope the crops come in and if they do, it all works out, and if they don't then you have to get creative. But my advice is to stay out of the sheriff's way. Nothing good can come from hanging around him."

"I didn't intend to hang around him last time," said Nikki.

"Well, then you'd better stay out of bar fights," said Peg, tartly.

"It wasn't a bar fight," protested Nikki. "At least not much of one. They were drunk and stupid."

"Well, it's a good thing Jackson was there then, in case things had gotten dangerous."

"Uh, yeah," said Nikki feeling annoyed. She had downplayed the bar fight quite a bit, but she didn't think she'd made it sound like she needed help.

"He's such a sweet boy. I don't know why your mother never liked him."

"He's from Kaniksu Falls," said Nikki with a shrug. "She never likes anyone from Kaniksu Falls."

Peg grunted, but didn't refute her statement.

AUGUST VIII
TOWN & COUNTRY

Nikki exited the shower, wrapped herself in a towel, and went back to her room. After her parents were married they had spent a year traveling the country in a VW microbus. When Nell had gotten pregnant, they had returned to her parents' house and lived there until her father's abrupt departure. In retrospect, Nikki wondered what her grandparents had thought of her free-spirited father. Peg generally avoided talking about him at all. Given her firm, "if you can't say anything nice, don't say anything at all," philosophy, that didn't bode well for her opinions on him. She didn't remember her grandfather saying anything other than "stupid" before stomping off to the barn.

Not much had changed in the years since Nikki had last visited. Her room was still painted the bright pink with purple butterflies that she had favored when she was nine. Given that the Carrie Mae logo was a purple butterfly, Nikki found the décor comforting.

She shuffled through the racks of clothes. Peg had labeled each piece according to its original owner, with a guess at the year. She pulled out a pair of blue shorts with a double row of buttons up the front. It was labeled, 1933? Mama Connelly? Mama Connelly was her grandfather's mother. The shorts were paired with a sleeveless satin shirt sporting a collar and a long looping bow. Nikki remembered seeing pictures of Mama Connelly. She'd been shaped like a potato and mostly wore an expression of stern disapproval. Nikki couldn't imagine her ever wearing short shorts and a sleeveless shirt. She glanced out the window. Her grandmother was still down in the orchard checking on the harvest. So she pulled on her underwear and bra and then slipped into Mama Connelly's outfit.

Then she strutted down the hall to the full-length mirror and did a turn. She pinned a damp curl down over her ear and pursed her lips in the closest approximation to a cupid's bow that she could get without make-up.

"I need Keds and a scarf for my hair," she said to her reflection, only to hear her grandmother's laugh on the stairs.

"Look at you!" exclaimed Peg. "So art deco."

"Hey, Grandma," said Nikki, blushing at being caught playing dress up. "Mama Connelly didn't really wear this, did she?"

"Well, I have a hard time imagining it," said Peg, "because the woman was shaped like a fireplug when I knew her. But it definitely wasn't my mother's—totally wrong size—and I can't think of who else it would have belonged to. Anyway, go grab your Keds and head scarf and let's go into town. I have an appointment at the beauty shop."

"I'll change," said Nikki.

"No, don't. We'll stop and take some pictures. I need them for when I sell the clothes and you're much better than the sewing dummy, which was my next option."

"Grandma, are you really going to sell the clothes on the internet? You do realize that's not as easy as it sounds, right?"

"Yeah, I know," said Peg. "But I got a Dreamer who's going to help me."

"A dreamer?" Nikki repeated, but Peg was already heading down the stairs.

"Where are we going to take pictures?" asked Nikki when they were in the car. Photography had been her grandmother's hobby for years and her nervous forays onto the internet were reserved for email and photography chat rooms.

"Bill Hanna has a model-A in his barn. I called while you were putting on your make-up and he said he'd leave it unlocked for us. I've shot there before. It's got good reflected light this time of day. We'll pick up a few shots and then head into town."

"Do you know anyone with a 1950s Buick? Maybe tomorrow, I can wear the striped sundress."

Peg looked at her with shining eyes. "I know someone with a 1956 Chevy truck. And you've got that crazy car. I bet we could do a whole batch of matching cars and outfits."

"Oh, Grandma, I don't know," said Nikki, doubtful of the elaborate plan Peg was forming.

"No, it's going to be great. I'm going to call my web kid, though. This may change the website design."

"Website design? There's a website?"

"I told you. I've got Eric to help me. He's going to build a website as part of a school project. He's one of the Dreamer kids. Jorge knows him."

"What's a dreamer?"

"One of the kids who qualifies for the Development, Relief, and Education for Alien Minors Act. Washington has a lot of them. He's going to Wazzu and is doing an independent study over the summer on website programming. I'm his project."

"Oh," said Nikki. "I had no idea."

"See what you miss by not visiting more often?"

"I guess so."

The photo shoot with the Model-A was indeed quick. Peg

clearly knew the location and the car and whipped through her shots with ease.

"Maybe I can round up a couple of more girls," mused Peg when they were back in the car. "That way you don't have to do all the outfits this week."

"Yes," agreed Nikki, perhaps with more force than necessary.

"I'll ask Leona down at the beauty shop. She'll have some good ideas of who to ask. What do you want for dinner, by the way? We should go to the grocery store after the beauty shop."

"I can do that while you get your hair cut," said Nikki, who didn't think she could face the gossip hounds at the salon, particularly not in her great-grandmother's athletic apparel.

"Get whatever you want," said Peg, as she hopped out in front of the salon. "We don't have anything but pie fixings." Nikki nodded as she climbed into the driver's seat. Her grandmother had been seeing Leona for as long as Nikki could remember, but then so had half the town. Of Scandinavian descent, Leona stood almost six feet tall in her stocking feet, but no one, possibly not even her husband, had ever seen her in stocking feet. She wore four-inch heels to every event. Between her natural height, the heels, and her trademark bouffant, going to the Curl Me Crazy was like having your hair cut by a Wagnerian Valkyrie. Nikki didn't like to admit that as a child she'd had more than one nightmare about getting her hair cut and now that she was old enough to make her own hair decisions, she didn't think that there was a force on earth that could drag her back in.

The grocery store was not quite as she remembered it. There had obviously been renovations. Just not very good ones. The cement floor still bore the scars of the previous aisle locations and Nikki wasn't sure if sky-blue paint counted as an improvement if you could still see the butter yellow in patches on the ceiling. Nikki pushed the ancient cart down an aisle, pondering if LA had really made her that snobby or if this grocery store really was that bad.

The cart's left front wheel didn't quite touch the ground and it made an annoying clicking noise as it swung freely to and fro. Then periodically it would touch down in a direction perpendicular to all the other wheels and bring the cart to a shuddering halt. Nikki was standing in the produce aisle staring at wilting lettuce and some sad, sad apples when she heard someone calling her name.

"Nicole, Nicole, Nikki, Nikki, *hola*!"

"*Hola*, Donny."

"You came! You said you couldn't make it."

"Last minute change of plans at work," said Nikki, smiling.

"Good. Because thank God there's someone normal here," said Donny, engulfing her in a hug, his words tumbling over themselves. "This place isn't right, right? We're surrounded by ten million farms and they've the most disgusting produce I've ever seen. And I'm considering driving into Spokane just to get a decent cup of coffee. God, I need a coffee."

"Are you sure, Donny? You kind of seem like you've had some already." Nikki disentangled herself from Donny's hug.

"Yeah, yeah, I've been drinking the diner coffee with my dad. I'm pretty sure it's Folger's made with one of the owner's old gym socks for a filter, but the waitress said it was decaf."

"I don't think it was decaf."

"I don't think it was decaf either," agreed Donny, nodding vehemently, "but we had like four cups before I noticed. You know the weird thing, though? My dad is not even twitching. I'm not wrong though, am I? This place is messed up."

"The produce aisle is not inspiring."

"It wasn't this bad when we were kids, was it? I don't think it was. Did we all just grow our own vegetables? Why are you dressed like you're going to play tennis with the Great Gatsby?"

"It's a photography project for my grandma."

"Yeah? I've been trying to remember where we bought veggies before. I think we went to the farm stand out on River Road."

"That might have been what we did. I really don't remember. Are you staying out with your folks?"

"Yeah, but never mind that. I'm glad you're here. I think something weird is going down. I'm going to call the LT and see what kind of jurisdiction I have here."

"Yeah, I had a weird incident last night," said Nikki, as Donny's phone buzzed.

"Crap, it's my Dad. He's already checked out. We should talk, but not here. We're doing a Fernandez Fiesta on Friday. You should come. We'll talk then."

"Oh, my God, look who it is. Little Nikki Lanier. Our resident celebrity. Or are you just our resident celebrity-kisser?" Nikki pivoted to see who was throwing down such passive-aggressive attitude this early in the day.

"Ugh. Kristine Pims. I gotta go."

"Chicken," muttered Nikki.

"Damn straight," he agreed, but without moving. He appeared mesmerized by Kristine's rather bountiful bosom that bounced gently as she walked toward them.

"Hi, Kristine," said Nikki. Kristine had been a soft, blonde fifth grader with a bullying streak and a pout when Nikki had known her. It appeared that fifteen years had only added a little height and weight. Well, to be honest, it was a lot of weight. Although, apparently the weight had been distributed correctly for Donny's tastes. "I hear you barely made it into town before causing trouble," said Kristine archly. "Being a troublemaker must be in the blood."

"Uh, yeah, whatever," said Nikki. "Donny, I'll talk to you later?"

"Sure, sure," said Donny, trying to edge away. "You're at your grandma's, right? I'll call you."

"Why are you dressed like a 1940s tramp?" demanded Kristine.

"It's 1920s," said Donny.

"Statement stands, no matter the decade," said Kristine smugly.

"You think it's trampy?" asked Nikki, glancing down at her outfit as if seeing it for the first time. "Hmm. Well, I guess some of us aren't embarrassed of our bodies." Then she tilted her head and stared at Kristine with a fake smile.

"Well!" said Kristine, huffing out a large breath.

"So nice to have seen you again, Kristine. Don't let us keep you." Nikki pulled her cart back, ostensibly to make room for Kristine. Unable to think of a retort, Kristine simply looked furious and pushed by, clanking into Nikki's cart with unnecessary force.

"Bitchcakes!" said Donny. "Get yer hot bitchcakes! Served fresh, right here."

"I shouldn't have gone with the body comment," said Nikki regretfully. "It was a cheap shot, but it was the fastest way to make her leave."

"She earned it," said Donny, and Nikki wrinkled her nose in disagreement—no one earned having their body shamed in public. "I've run into her a couple of times since being back in town. Huge chip on her shoulder." His phone began to ring. "Anyway, I'll call you later. Gotta go."

"Too much coffee," Nikki muttered to herself as he jogged toward the front of the store.

Nikki loaded her groceries into the back of the car, having turned down the perfunctory offer of help from the bag boy who looked too young to be that soulless, and tried to decide what to do about dinner. She'd bought stuff, but she wasn't sure any of it made a dinner. She knew they were going to get back to the house and Peg would take one look and say, "Should have made a list."

She shut the hatch-back of the SUV and turned to wheel the cart over to the cart corral. Of course, it didn't want to go in the corral and tried to make an unpredictable left turn at the last second. Nikki kicked the cart to correct its trajectory and then instantly regretted it as she felt every metal slat through her Keds and heard the protest of the ancient seams on her shorts. Apparently 1930s ladies didn't kick things.

She was turning back to the car when she saw Ylina, the girl from the Kessel Run, exiting the grocery store. She had changed into jean shorts and a T-shirt, but it was definitely her. She looked furtively both ways and began to cross the parking lot.

Nikki jogged over. "Hey, Ylina! It's Nikki - from the Kessel Run."

"Yeah, I remember," said Ylina, but without stopping.

"I wanted to make sure you were OK. You seemed pretty freaked last night."

"I'm fine," said Ylina, still walking. Nikki jogged a little to keep up.

"Hey, I think you should know. The Carhartt dude—Milt? I

saw him last night. I don't think he went to jail."

Ylina laughed once, abruptly and bitterly. "Like he was ever going to jail."

"OK, but look, if he told the sheriff you stole his car, then you could be in trouble. You need to ditch the car ASAP."

Ylina finally stopped walking and stared at Nikki as if she had sprouted horns. "What?"

"And you probably ought to detail it, have it wiped down for fingerprints. I mean, that's probably overkill, but the sheriff seemed like kind of a dick, so better safe than sorry."

"What are you talking about?"

"The car. You drove Milt's car away from the Kessel Run. If you still have it, you need to ditch it." Nikki scanned the parking lot, but didn't see the boring blue four-door. "Just clean it up and leave it in a parking lot somewhere with the keys in it. If there's no evidence you had possession of the car then the sheriff has nothing on you."

"The sheriff always has something on me," snapped Ylina. "He's got something on every illegal in town. Look, Daisy Buchanan, I know you think you're helping, but you're not. Just leave me alone."

Nikki glanced at Ylina's shopping bag. Apples, protein bars, snack packs of fig newtons, and a couple of bottles of water. "Nice collection of snack food," she said. "If someone didn't know better, they might think you were preparing for a road trip."

"Yeah, well, someone should mind her own business," snapped Ylina.

"Ylina, I really can help," said Nikki, she reached in her purse and pulled out a business card. "Whatever it is you're up against, I can help."

"Carrie Mae Foundation? What—you're going to save me through better blush?"

"We don't just do make-up," said Nikki. "Or do you think that what I did to Milt and Pedro was dumb luck?"

"You don't get it." For a moment, Ylina's face softened, and then she looked around the parking lot, and shook her head. "Leave me alone," she hissed, before turning and running towards the far side of the parking lot, and crossing the street, walking quickly without a backward glance.

"You sure have a way with people," said Kristine, her cart rattling across the pavement. "Maybe you should teach a class about how to win friends." Then she laughed at her own joke.

Nikki was suddenly very aware of the hot asphalt burning her feet through her shoes and the brutal sun beating down on her overly white skin. She wasn't wearing enough sunscreen for this. She felt impatient, angry, and above all hot.

"Kristine!" Several mean thoughts crossed her mind, but she counted to ten. "Go get a life!" She finished on the least offensive thing that had percolated to the top and stomped off toward the car.

AUGUST IX
ROADSIDE ASSISTANCE

Nikki pulled up in front of the Curl Me Crazy and waved dutifully at Leona who was standing in the doorway with a cigarette in one hand. Leona fished a lighter out of the wide expanse of her cleavage and sauntered over to the car.

"Well, don't you look like the perfect Clara Bow? What a fun project for you and Peg. I was telling her you should turn it into a calendar when you're all done."

"Oh, God, I hope not," Nikki blurted out. "I mean, I'm not sure I really want to hang on people's walls," she added. Leona laughed.

"I don't know. I think I'd get a kick out of it."

"Different strokes for different folks," said Nikki.

"True. Your grams will be out in a minute. She was going to go to the restroom, but I think she may have been waylaid by Amanda Harrison."

"Oh," said Nikki, and turned off the car. No sense in killing the polar bears with car exhaust. Peg wouldn't be out for another ten minutes. "How are the corgis?" Amanda Harrison carried corgi pictures the way other people carried photos of their grandkids.

"Rex is in a feud with the mailman. Alfie is having bladder surgery on Tuesday. And Sofia isn't doing well with the heat."

"It has been quite warm," said Nikki.

"Well, being dressed in a sweater, a hat, and three inches of fur probably isn't helping any," said Leona. "Say, what's going on with you and that rock star? I bought his album after that picture in the Daily Star. It's pretty good. Are those really his abs? They didn't Photoshop them or anything, did they?"

"Uh…" said Nikki, mentally cursing her grandmother. No one else in America knew Kit Masters. Her teeny little indiscretion should have remained safely on the other side of the Atlantic, but one Canadian tabloid runs a picture and suddenly everyone knows? Leave it to Peg to point it out to everyone in town.

Peg swung open the door and came bustling out. "Step on it, kiddo! Before Amanda gets her second wind. See ya, Leona. Thanks for the 'do!"

Leona waved affably and stepped away from the car as Peg climbed in. Nikki turned the car back on and pulled away, happy to escape.

"Grandma," she said when they were finally on the road out of town. "Have you told a lot of people about that picture in the Daily Star?"

"Didn't have to," said Peg. "You remember Kristine Pims? Her father, Bill, owns the auto-body shop, and she does all the ordering for the shop. So she pointed it out to everyone."

"Wait, what? What does ordering for the auto-body shop have to do with anything?"

"She stocks magazines and newspapers for the lobby area," said Peg. "Recognized you right off. Quite the outfit you had going on there."

"There were extenuating circumstances," said Nikki. "So how many people did she show it to?"

"Just Leona," Nikki groaned. "But you know, that's exactly like telling lots of people."

"So has everyone in town seen that picture?" demanded Nikki.

"Well, I would guess that most people have. Probably some of them don't care, but it was a real interesting topic of conversation there for awhile."

Nikki groaned again. "If you didn't want to get talked about, you probably shouldn't have gone around kissing British rock stars," said Peg.

"I don't go around kissing British rock stars! It was just Kit."

"Uh-huh," said Peg, looking unconvinced.

"It was New Year's! Stuff had happened."

"Sure, the extenuating circumstances," replied Peg.

"Yes, damn it. The circumstances extenuated."

"Gotcha. Well—pull over!" Peg's hand shot out, pointing at the truck in front of them. As Nikki watched, the truck screeched to a halt and a cowboy swung out, his movements smooth and fast, speed deriving from the economy of motion, and snatched a shovel from the truck bed. Then he was sprinting toward a small, spiral of smoke from the brush on the edge of the road. Nikki was already pulling in behind the truck when she realized the cowboy was Jackson.

"I've got water in the back. Go see if there's another shovel in his truck."

Nikki ran for the truck as instructed, and pulled out a rake, before running after Jackson. By the time she got there, the fire had already spread from a thin, flickering ghost of fire to a full-on blaze intent on devouring the scrubby bushes that lined the road. Jackson was heaping dirt on the flames and Nikki set to work pulling brush away from the path of the fire, trying to deprive it of fuel. An entire clump of Scotch broom had already gone up, its yellow flowers withering to black ash with an acrid stench, but as Jackson heaped more dirt on the fire the flames began to die down. Peg arrived and leaned in to dump an entire gallon of water on the bush, then stepped back as Jackson took a final shovel full of dirt and patted down the muddy mixture. They stood silently, waiting for the flames to attempt a rebirth, but nothing moved.

"Cigarette butt," said Jackson shaking his head. "Car in front of me, tossed it out the window."

"Did you get their license plate number?" asked Peg. "I'd call them in. They could have done a lot of damage."

"Didn't have time," said Jackson shaking his head, and wiping ash out of his face.

"Well, stop up at the house on your way home," said Peg. "I'll fix you some lemonade as a reward."

"I'd rather have pie," said Jackson grinning.

"I thought the pie went without saying," said Peg, patting him on the shoulder. "Now let's get home before the groceries melt."

The groceries hadn't melted and Jackson helped carry them into the house, then started to put things away without being asked. Nikki watched suspiciously as he moved around the kitchen, tucking away the canned goods, putting the meat in the right fridge drawer without being asked. Just how much time had Jackson been spending in this kitchen?

"Did Jackson tell you he bought the spread up on Torrence?" asked Peg, pulling out pie and lemonade.

"No, he didn't," said Nikki.

"We didn't have a lot of time to catch up," said Jackson. "What with Nikki getting into barroom brawls and what not."

"Barroom brawl," corrected Nikki. "Singular, not plural. And you had plenty of time afterward. You could have mentioned it."

"It didn't come up in conversation." Jackson didn't look the least bit repentant.

"That terrain's a bit hilly for farming up there, isn't it?" asked Nikki, as Jackson pulled out the lemonade and glasses.

Jackson rolled his eyes. "You sound like my dad. Not everything is about farming." He handed Nikki a glass and pushed one in Peg's direction, trading it for a plateful of pie.

"So what are you going to do?" asked Nikki.

"Raise rodeo bulls and make wine."

Nikki accepted a wide wedge of pie from Peg. "Grandma, I'm not going to fit any of those vintage clothes if you keep trying to fatten me up. Bulls and wine? They don't seem to go together."

"*Au contraire,*" he replied, butchering the accent on purpose and laughing when Nikki winced. "Bull dung is a great fertilizer and makes the grapes grow faster. Grape skins are full of vitamins and can be fed to the bulls. Interlocking system." He laced his fingers together to demonstrate.

"You've got it all figured out then," said Nikki.

"No, I really don't," he said shaking his head. "This year is my first real growing season. I'm still struggling to hone in on the right grape varietals. It's interesting terrain up here. If I get any decent wine at all this year, it'll be a miracle. And the cows are doing their thing. But my babies only turn two this summer. They need another three years or so before I can put them to work. Right now, I'm keeping my fingers crossed that my savings don't run out before the bulls are ready. I'm probably going to be doing a couple of 'special appearances' in the ring for the next few years while people still remember me enough to care. Keep the cash coming in for a little bit, instead of going out."

"Three years?" Nikki took a bite of pie. "So this is kind of a long term thing you've got going."

"Well, I'm currently working my five-year plan, but I put together a ten-year business model before I even made an offer on the ranch."

"I think my longest range plan right now currently includes breakfast," said Nikki, feeling the onset of existential angst.

Jackson shrugged. "This is where I am right now."

"Jackson is going to be a big success," said Peg, patting his shoulder. "Just you wait. It's going to work out perfectly."

"Your grandma has a lot of faith," said Jackson, sheepishly rubbing his ear. "Anyway," he finished his lemonade in a gulp, "I need to get back home before Captain Beaumont gets too annoyed."

"Wouldn't do to upset your number one farm hand," said Peg, shaking her head and Jackson laughed.

"Too true," he agreed.

"Nikki, walk him out," Peg commanded.

Nikki did as she was told, but promised herself to have a little talk with Peg later.

"Peg's not too subtle," said Jackson when they were out on the porch.

"I have a boyfriend," said Nikki. "I guess I'm going to have to remind her of that."

"She knows," said Jackson. "I've heard all about your 'government employee boyfriend.' I just don't think she cares. And by the way, I don't think she cares too much for government employees."

Nikki sighed. "Z'ev isn't really…" she trailed off.

"Isn't really what?"

"He's not like other government employees," she said. "He

works for the state department and travels a lot. He's not a cubicle dweller or anything boring."

"Hmm. Well, it might help if you actually let him meet your family," suggested Jackson.

"Yeah, the problem with that is I'd have to let him meet my family," said Nikki.

Jackson laughed.

"I'd love to say that your mom isn't that bad."

"But we both know that you hate to lie. Are you going to the Fernandez thing on Friday?"

"Yeah. I was hoping to catch up with Donny. I've barely gotten to see him since he's been in town. Are you going? Do you want me to pick you up on the way down?"

Nikki nodded, making the date without thinking. "Yeah, sounds good. I ran into Donny at the grocery store. He said something odd. I didn't have a chance to follow up at the time because Kristine Pims showed up. Is she just a mega-bitch or does she reserve that for me?"

Jackson shrugged. "I've seen her be nice to people."

"I also ran into Ylina—the girl from the bar. She seemed kind of freaked and she implied that the sheriff was kind of a hard ass about illegal immigrants."

"He's the sheriff. He gets paid to be a hard ass about illegal immigrants."

"Yeah, but last night, after he took those two goons away, I saw the one in the Carhartts out on the street."

"Well, Ylina did steal his car and pot is legal now, so he probably didn't have anything to hold him on."

"What's pot got to do with anything?"

"Didn't you notice? Well, maybe you didn't, since you didn't have to schlep him out to the porch. The guy reeked of pot. They both did."

"Huh. You would think that my statement about her being threatened and attacked would be enough to warrant an arrest, regardless of whether or not pot was legal or his car got stolen."

Jackson shrugged uncomfortably. "The sheriff is kind of a good ol' boy. I'm not saying he's a swell guy or anything, but people wouldn't keep voting him in if he didn't do his job."

"Arresting people who attack women in bars is his job," said Nikki.

"You didn't suffer any from getting attacked."

"Oh, so I have to lose in order for them to be arrested? That's a chunk of bullshit that would fertilize a whole vineyard. I was attacked. He didn't arrest them. Next time, I'd think about voting for someone else if I were you."

Nikki marched back inside and managed, barely, to not slam the door behind her. She took a moment to count to ten. It was something her grandfather had always recommended, but she had never followed the advice until she started working for Carrie Mae. When she didn't count to ten bad things happened, and when you carry a gun, bad things tend to be a little more permanent.

There was a knock on the door. Nikki swung it back open prepared to continue the argument with Jackson.

"So, pick you up around seven?"

"What?"

"The Fernandez Fiesta."

"Oh, yeah. OK."

"OK, see you then."

Jackson walked off the porch and climbed into his truck.

"I'm still mad at you!" she yelled after him.

"You bet!" he yelled back, which didn't mean anything. Nikki glared after the dust trail left by the truck. The problem with being back in Kaniksu Falls was that it was too easy to forget that she wasn't seventeen anymore. Old habits died hard, and Jackson was a habit that seemed particularly hard to break.

Walking back down the hall toward the kitchen, she could hear her grandmother talking to someone on the phone.

"No, Nell, it has to be done." Hearing her mother's name, Nikki paused outside the kitchen. "Well, I know you don't want to, but it's time. Look, she's out on the porch with Jackson, so I don't have a lot of time to discuss this. Jackson is a fine young man. I've never understood why you don't like him. Yes, I know she has a boyfriend. Nell! Stop arguing with me and start listening. I will do it myself and if you don't want me to, then I suggest you take a few days off work and get your fanny over here. Call me when you leave Seatac. I'll head down to Spokane and pick you up." Peg slammed the phone receiver, still attached to its rotary dial body by a long curling cord back into the cradle.

Nikki pursed her lips, thinking about what she'd heard. Pre-Carrie Mae she would have barged in and demanded an explanation. But if she had learned anything from Carrie Mae, it was that a full frontal assault was not always the best strategic decision. Instead, she waited a second longer and then sauntered into the kitchen.

"Did you have any thoughts about what you wanted to do for dinner?" she asked carrying the pie plates over to the sink. "I bought a few things, but I didn't know what you wanted."

"I usually just make a sandwich," said Peg, running a hand through her hair. "Cooking for one is always so difficult. So whatever you want is fine with me."

"I'll probably make some chicken then," said Nikki, her mouth on autopilot.

"I'll cook it," said Peg. "But after I get back from the orchard. I should go check on things."

"OK," said Nikki, with a smile that had been carefully crafted to look genuine. "I'll probably go take a dip in the pond."

"Sounds lovely, dear," said Peg, already moving toward the door.

Nikki watched the door shut and tried not to grit her teeth. She was so tired of secrets.

AUGUST X
WHAT A GIRL WANTS

Nikki waited for Peg to leave then went upstairs to change. Her vintage outfit was going to have to be washed again. It smelled like smoke. She left it soaking in the sink as she changed into a swimsuit and shorts, grabbed a towel and headed for the pond. Her flip-flops smacked her heels, clicking along like her mind as she flipped through the theories of what Peg would think Nell needed to tell her. None of her theories seemed worthwhile. She stopped at the shed to retrieve an inner tube and noticed that her grandfather's beat up old Ford truck was parked under a tarp. She lifted a corner and kicked the tires. It seemed functional. With a shrug, Nikki left it and booted her inner tube down the hill to the pond. It bounced in crazy arcs before entering the water with a splash.

It was a manmade pond, fed by a re-routed creek that kept the water flowing and fresh. It had been intended for the cattle to use, but these days Peg didn't keep more than the one horse and a grumpy goat. It was shaded on one half by a giant oak and was cold even on the hottest summer day. Nikki slathered herself in sunscreen, put on her sunglasses and lowered herself carefully into the inner tube, holding her phone high above the water. Then she kicked her way to the shady side of the pond and dialed Ellen.

"Oh, thank God," said Ellen picking up. Ellen always said that after spending more than three days with her daughters and their children. The daughters seemed like very nice people, but they had a very mistaken impression of what stage of life their mother was in. "You've got to help me, Nikki. They've started pointing out LifeAlert commercials to me."

"Did you tell them that they've got it backwards and that you're the one who causes other people to fall and not get up?"

"Martina actually said the words, 'I'm not as young as I once was.'" Martina was younger than Nikki and had a two-year-old daughter. "I wanted to smack her. And then she suggested that I should really consider end-of-life planning."

Nikki snorted and almost fell through the inner tube. "They do grow up quick," she said, her voice quavering with repressed laughter.

"No, they got old quick! How did I raise such fuddy-duddy daughters? It's like they're trying so hard to be adult and instead they're just old, grumpy people complaining about the neighbor boy who won't stay off their lawn."

"Oh, dear."

"So, tell me if this is too bad. I invited the neighborhood boy in for cookies and then I went and played catch with him on their lawn."

"How did that go over?"

"My son-in-law, George, joined in. I think I'm making a dent there. He seems to enjoy breaking a few rules. But I swear to God, I'm napalming the next set of khakis I see."

"I thought you liked khakis?"

"On me! Down here I feel like I'm living in a frigging Gap Outlet."

Nikki laughed. "Jane must be rubbing off on you."

"Or maybe she's on to something. Maybe it's a truth that we should universally acknowledge: the Gap should be fire-bombed."

"Did they try to make you go to the Community Center again?"

"They tried to sign me up for square dancing, with a lovely gentleman who is eighty if he's a day. Square dancing, Nikki. Square dancing! Who do they think I am?"

"You're grandma, and grandmas stay home and bake things and nap. And apparently like square dancing."

"Is your grandma napping?"

"She should be," said Nikki. "She got up at six to go supervise work in the peach orchard, baked a fresh pie, made me breakfast, tried to teach me to shoot, had her hair done, and is now back out at the orchard. That's a busy day. I want a nap."

"She tried to teach you to shoot?"

"It was kind of adorable. She has this ancient .357 and was hell bent on teaching me gun safety."

Ellen laughed. "What'd she think of your gun? Which one did you bring?"

"The SIG Sauer. She liked it, but she worries about cleaning and loading."

"It is harder to screw up a revolver. And if she's not worried about reloading speed, then it could be the right gun for her."

"The right gun is the gun you practice with. I'm not about to try and get her to switch guns. Stick with a system that works."

"She sounds like the kind of grandma I need to hang with. I mean, I love all you young people, but I wouldn't mind hanging out with a few more of my own cohort."

"What? Who would teach you what twerking was if you didn't have us?"

"I actually wish I could blot twerking from my brain," said Ellen.

"Some things you can't un-know."

"Sadly. But I'm assuming you didn't call to rub in your sweet vacation?"

"No, I called to ask for advice."

"Advice, I have. I am full of advice. This afternoon, I advised my five-year-old grandson to build a rubber band gun and shoot his mother in the rear."

"By advise, I assume you mean, 'helped build'?"

"So I prefer the CIA's interpretation of the word 'advise.' What's your point?"

"No point, that's just an example of why I love you. But that may be the kind of advice I need." She filled Ellen in on her adventures in Kaniksu Falls. "So what do you think?" she asked when she was done.

"I think that's weird. If he wasn't going to arrest them, then he should have said so at the time he took them away. Also, if your grandma doesn't like him, then I would trust her opinion more than Jackson's. She's lived in that town a long time, and what did you say? He's only been back a few years? Yeah, I wouldn't be swayed by that opinion. And then there's Donny. He's a cop. If he thinks something's up, then there's probably something up."

"That is probably totally unrelated," objected Nikki. "He's a narcotics cop. He probably spotted some sort of local drug dealer or something."

"OK, leaving out Donny," agreed Ellen. "But any which way you slice it, I find the situation suspicious."

"You think I should investigate?"

"Well, speaking as someone who just went rogue and helped the worldly exit of a serial killer, I think we can safely assume that my answer will be yes."

"Two days, Ellen," said Nikki. "I was gone for two days. You couldn't wait until I got back?"

"Lives were in danger and you were out of cell range. I thought Darla was covering for her Canadian friend, and the best thing to do was save the girl and worry about the paperwork later."

Nikki sighed. "Yes, of course, the answer is always save the girl. But you can't go out on your own like that."

"Oh, please," said Ellen. "You break rules all the time."

"I do," said Nikki. "And I know this is unfair, but the difference is that I don't get caught. You have to have an eye on the bigger situation. Mrs. M has a hard enough time wading through Carrie Mae politics without us handing weapons to her enemies."

"Are things really that tough?"

"Carrie Mae was founded with the idea of small actions making a difference. Tiny missions, usually performed by one to two agents. Mrs. M and a few others have pushed Carrie Mae into the twenty-first century by using larger weapons, bigger teams and going after major issues. Which means that we're leaving a more extensive footprint and costing more money than we used to, and it means that some of the older leadership people aren't really comfortable with what we're doing."

"They want to shut us down?"

"They want to refocus and recommit to our original ideals."

"They want to go back to the sixties," translated Ellen.

"Yeah. We have to be careful until we get women in positions of power who can help push our agenda forward."

"Like Darla," said Ellen.

"Right. And we have to at least look like we're trying to keep Carrie Mae flying under the radar. I'm not objecting to what you did. I'm saying that maybe there were better ways to do it, that didn't put our team, Mrs. M, and our branch in hot water."

It was Ellen's turn to sigh. "Sorry. Yeah. Sorry. I guess I got really focused on the mission, forgot there might be a big picture."

"Well, it's your job to get mission-focused and it's part of my job to worry about the big picture. But that's why next time you should make a bigger effort to call me."

"Right. Check. Note taken." She sighed again. "What are you going to do about the sheriff?"

"I have no clue. I'm not even sure what there is to do."

"Well, call Jenny and Jane. Maybe there is some sort of technological wizardry that Jane can come up with that might help. Jenny will probably say to kick his ass, but she might have more useful thoughts after she gets that out of her system. If nothing else, you should consider going to look at the auto-body shop. Seems kind of suspicious that Milt, or whatever you said his name was, walked into a closed store."

Nikki grunted. "Yeah, maybe. I'll think about it. You know, I really did just want a nice vacation."

"Hey, Mom, come on, we're about to play Jenga!"

"I'll be there as soon as I get off the phone," said Ellen brightly. Nikki could hear footsteps retreating in the background. "And I would like it if my daughters weren't so monumentally boring, but we can't always get what we want, now, can we?"

AUGUST XI
CAPTAIN BEAUMONT

Nikki checked the Indiglo on her watch: 11:05 P.M. Peg would have had enough time to enter REM sleep. She waited another ten minutes to be on the safe side and then swung the door to the old shed open. She opened the door to the Ford and began to push it out of the barn. About twelve feet later gravity caught up and the truck began to roll on its own. Nikki hopped in and steered it to a safe stop down by the gate to the property. She opened the gate and then went back to the truck. Time to practice those hotwiring skills.

She turned on the flashlight app on her phone and looked under the dash.

"What are you doing?" demanded a male voice.

Nikki immediately turned her phone toward the voice, blinding the speaker, and prepared to look helpless and cute.

"Oh, it's you. Jackson, what are you doing here?"

"Captain Beaumont and I are out for a run."

"Who's Captain Beaumont?"

In response, a black lab jumped up and put his paws on the window frame, panting in Nikki's face.

"He's Captain Beaumont. What are you doing?"

"I'm hotwiring grandpas' truck."

"OK, but why?

"Because it's a pre-90s vehicle. Cars post about 1994 have the automated key fobs, which are harder to hotwire."

"OK, but why not use the key?" He reached in and flipped down the visor. The truck key tumbled down into Nikki's lap.

"I think Captain Beaumont is laughing at me."

"Probably," agreed Jackson. "Seriously, though, what are you doing that you can't use your car or borrow Peg's?"

"My car is too easy to spot and Grandma always puts her keys in her purse and she puts her purse in her room. I think Mom used to steal the car when she was a teenager."

"Much like you appear to be doing now. Where are you going that you don't want your car remembered?"

"Jackson, this is really one of those times that you should ask yourself if you really want to know?"

"You're not stealing more pigs again, are you?" Captain Beaumont pushed away from the truck and began to sniff around the tires.

"Oh, my God, you steal one pig, one time, and no one lets you forget it."

"Hey, I was very helpful in the porcine theft department if you remember. It was Donny that got us caught. Just tell me what you're doing."

Nikki knew she should lie. But Jackson was staring at her with those blue eyes that knew right where all the skeletons were buried and where all the pigs had been set free and suddenly it was like she'd forgotten how.

"I'm going to go check out the body shop."

"Check it out for what? What are you going to do, break in? That's ridiculous."

There was a thump as Captain Beaumont jumped up into the tailgate-less truck bed.

"It's not ridiculous and get your dog out of my truck or he's coming with me," said Nikki, starting the truck.

"Nikki, you're being crazy!"

"Say goodbye, Captain," said Nikki, rolling the truck past Jackson. She expected him to yell, but instead there was a second thump as Jackson jumped up into the truck bed too. Seconds later, he was wiggling through the back window.

"This is crazy," he said, when he'd righted himself in the seat. He was wearing a zip-up hoodie over cut-off sweat pants and sneakers.

"Hey, I'm not the one out for a run in the middle of the night."

"Captain Beaumont is a black dog."

"What does that mean?"

"He gets too hot during the day, but he likes to run. Plus, I'm training for *American Ninja Warrior*."

"You're making this up."

"I'm not making this up. And you're the one stealing a truck!"

"It's not stealing if you return it."

There was a scrabbling as Captain Beaumont tried to climb in the window too. He stopped half-way through, either high-centered on the seat back or content to only mostly be with his person.

"What is your dog doing?" demanded Nikki as Captain Beaumont began to lick her ear.

"He was trained to be a police dog and this is how he indicates when he smells someone batshit crazy."

"I am not crazy."

"You're stealing a truck with the intention of breaking into a building."

"I told you—I'm not stealing the truck. I'm borrowing it quietly."

The argument continued as Nikki drove down into town. The Columbia River reflected the moonlight like a ribbon of polished steel and the lights of the houses glowed softly from behind closed curtains as they drove toward Main Street.

"I don't know why you think the auto body shop is going to have anything to look at," complained Jackson. "Even if, and I say if, you really saw that Milt guy go in there, what's that got to do with anything?"

"I did see him. Please stop second-guessing me. And it might seem like nothing, but you've got to follow your gut in these situations," said Nikki, checking the review mirror and pulling into a parking spot well away from the light of a street lamp. "You have to look for loose threads and then you pull them."

"And how often have you been in 'these situations'?" demanded Jackson, making air quotes.

"Oh, you know," said Nikki, cutting the motor and fishing in her bag for some binoculars.

"No," said Jackson, eyeing the binoculars. "I don't know."

"Tell your dog to move his butt." She pulled Captain Beaumont all the way into the cab, so she could look through the back window of the cab and scrutinize the body shop through the binoculars. It was a cement block building of an odd height, not quite two stories. One corner was a glass enclosed little lobby with uncomfortable looking chairs and a tall desk. The rest of the front was covered by two roll-up garage doors. The office was dark and a closed sign hung at a careless angle on the door, but a tiny ribbon of light could be seen around the edge of one of the garage doors.

"You can't just yadda yadda sex," said Jackson.

"What?"

"That episode of *Seinfeld*? 'And yadda yadda, one thing led to another…' You can't just wave your hands over the important parts and expect me to not question it."

"I don't have time for this," said Nikki. "Nobody invited you to this party, so stop being such a Debbie Downer."

"You were stealing my dog. And besides someone has to keep you out of trouble."

"Jackson." She stopped, trying to think of the right thing to say. This was ending up like every argument she'd ever had with Z'ev. "I don't need to be kept out of trouble."

Jackson stared at her, his forehead wrinkled, eyebrows pinched together in skepticism. "Are you sure?"

"Do you need to be kept from throwing yourself in front of giant cows?"

"Bulls. And no, because I'm good at it and I know what I'm doing."

"Yeah, exactly."

"Oh." He paused, the effort of shifting mental gears showing on his face. "OK."

"Now you can stay in the truck if you want. I'm going to go for a closer look. I'm just going to take a little poke around. I'll be back in about twenty minutes."

"I'm not staying in the truck. And –" He broke off and then pointed out the window at the body shop. Nikki ducked and then peeked over the edge of the seat with her binoculars. Milt and another man walked around the corner of the building. Milt was waving his arms and even most of a block away Nikki could hear his voice, if not the actual words. He sounded angry and defensive.

"Who's that with Milt?" she asked, passing the binoculars to Jackson.

"That's Bill Pims," said Jackson, without taking the binoculars. "He always wears that ratty, red ball cap."

"There must be a back door then," said Nikki, training the binoculars back at the building as Milt and Bill climbed into the body shop tow truck and pulled away.

"I don't know," said Jackson. "I take my car to Josie's."

"Well, they probably didn't climb out through a window, so I'm going to try behind the building first." Nikki picked up her bag, a brown leather messenger style bag that looked ordinary enough.

"How do you know there's no one else in there?" asked Jackson. Nikki swung the truck door open and hopped out.

"I don't," she said, shutting the door quietly.

She hadn't gone ten steps before she heard Jackson's door shut and the sound of his feet on the pavement behind her.

"Is the Captain going to be OK by himself?"

"Yeah, I left the window open. He'll be fine." He looked around, craning his neck to see if they had been spotted.

"Jackson, stop twisting your head like an owl. It makes you look guilty."

"But we are guilty," he hissed.

"Speak for yourself," said Nikki. "I don't feel any guilt."

The back door was locked, but it was a simple deadbolt that Nikki picked in under thirty seconds.

"You carry a set of lock-picks around with you?" he asked as she tucked them back in her bag.

Nikki shrugged. "They come in handy. I'm going to go in first. Give me a second to get my bearings and then come in after me."

Nikki stepped into the garage and looked around. In terms

of secret lairs, it was a severe disappointment. It was just a garage. A moment later Jackson stepped through the door; he looked around and gave a low whistle.

"Would you look at this equipment? Who knew Bill had the budget for this? I always got the impression he was barely making it."

"This stuff is expensive?" asked Nikki, waving at the collection of grease covered machines.

"Yeah! He could practically machine his own car with this setup. That, over there, is a-"

"I don't want to know," said Nikki, cutting him off. "That information is only going to fill up valuable hard drive space in my head. But would you say that the equipment is unusual for a body shop?"

"A little bit," said Jackson walking further into the garage. "I mean, for a shop this small."

There was a sharp bark and a scrabble of nails against the door that made them both jump. Nikki opened the door and Captain Beaumont leapt in, tail wagging.

"Left the window open, you said?"

Jackson sighed and hung his head. "I'll take him back to the truck."

"No, the last thing we need is for someone to spot us traipsing back and forth. Let's just finish searching this place and get out of here."

"But I don't know what I'm looking for."

"Anything unusual," said Nikki. Jackson grunted in dissatisfaction at her answer, but began to prowl around the machines.

The garage had space for two cars, which were currently occupied, one by a truck with the hood up and the other by a Honda four-door. The front driver's side area was primer gray and the trunk area had been stripped down to the metal frame. The garage was quite tall, probably designed to accommodate semi's and RV's, and at the back of the room a set of stairs led up to a small office perched improbably on stilts above everything. Nikki jogged up the stairs and opened the door. The floor was a grease stained industrial carpet, the file cabinets were that peculiar puke beige that never matched any office anywhere, and the desk was a particle board 1970s job laden with a greasy fingerprint-covered computer, a half-eaten burger, and three months worth of paperwork. Nikki began going through the filing cabinets. She wasn't expecting to find much. Bill might have kept incriminating paperwork around, but then again, he'd also kept a receipt from a 1991 trip to the gas station and a 1995 nudie calendar and a 2001 petrified cheese sandwich jammed between a parts catalog and a folder full of sales receipts.

"Find anything?" asked Jackson, poking his head through the door.

Nikki let a stack of paperwork drop in disgust. "It would take a forensic accountant and a maid a month to find anything in this mess. Did you find anything?"

"He's got some strange machines for a small town auto shop, but there's no law against having a machinists shop worth of stuff in your tiny business."

Nikki nodded and glanced out the window to the garage floor. "What's your dog doing?" Captain Beaumont was sitting perfectly still next to the Honda's primered fender, staring intently at it.

"Oh, crap," said Jackson. "Uh, I need a toy. I'm supposed to play with him when he does that." He began to look around for a toy, as if one would magically appear.

"What are you talking about?"

"I told you, he was trained as a police dog." Jackson was jogging back down the stairs and Nikki trailed after him. "That's his signal."

"I thought you were joking about that."

"No, he flunked out because he didn't like loud noises. Who's a good dog? You're the good dog!" Captain Beaumont looked thrilled to have his goodness recognized and leapt up to wrestle with his human.

"So what's that a signal for?" asked Nikki, bending over to inspect the Honda's side.

"Drugs!" said Jackson, still using his happy, good dog voice and leaping around the car with the Captain.

"I think," Nikki began, but was cut off as the far garage door began to rumble upwards. She looked toward the back entrance, directly visible from the slowly rising garage door and then back at Jackson, frozen in place with his arms full of dog. "Under the Honda," she commanded, and slid into the pit space beneath the car. Jackson shoved the surprised Captain Beaumont in next and then wriggled in after her.

"I asked you to do one thing," grumbled Bill stomping into the garage.

"I was distracted," complained Milt. "I just got my ass handed to me by the boss."

"And that prevented you from picking up the damn Slim Jim?" demanded Bill, collecting the thin piece of metal from a workbench and waving it at Milt. "I'm starting to think that red-head beat what was left of your brain into a pulp."

"She got a lucky shot in," whined Milt.

"Yeah, well maybe if you didn't smoke so much of your own product, she wouldn't have gotten so lucky."

"Like you don't smoke," said Milt.

"Not when I have a job to do," said Bill. "You know that's why Ylina got stopped, right? It was probably you sitting in the car that left all kinds of scent all over the place. I can smell you from here."

"Ylina got stopped because she's a dumb whore. This is not my fault. And if you tell the boss that, I will beat your head in."

"I'm not telling nothing to the boss," said Bill. "But you should stop crying to me about how it's not your fault and get Ylina and the car back before he decides to beat your head in."

The garage door rumbled closed and Captain Beaumont let out a soft woof.

"Not exactly the drugs I had pictured when the dog sat down," said Nikki, holding up a hand rolled spliff from where it had been carefully perched next to an array of tools.

"No, but check this out," said Jackson, pointing to the inside of the fender. Above the wheel, space had been hollowed out and a compartment welded in with a latching door. "There's one on each side. How much do you think would fit in there? Ten pounds per wheel?"

"Probably, and I'm sorry, what was that you were saying about me being crazy?"

"You are crazy. Apparently, you're also right. But it's still ridiculous to go around breaking into places like the Hardy Boys."

"You're a Hardy Boy. I'm clearly Nancy Drew."

"Whatever. Can we go now? I want to get out of here before the drug smugglers come back."

Nikki nodded and helped lead Captain Beaumont out from

under the car. Only when they were safely back in the truck and heading for home, did conversation resume.

"So what do we do now? Call the sheriff?"

Nikki hesitated, and then shook her head. "Even if he believed us which, considering he let Milt go the first time, seems unlikely, he's going to have a problem with how we found out."

"That's because breaking and entering is bad," said Jackson.

"I'll keep that in mind. Anyway, we don't have any proof. So I think the next step is to talk to Donny. Donny already thinks something weird is going down. He said so at the grocery store. He'll probably be able to use what we found out to bring in state police or something."

"OK, we'll talk to Donny on Friday night at the Fernandez shindig," said Jackson nodding. "But Nikki?"

"Yeah?"

"Can you warn me next time we're going to engage in illegal activity?"

"Well, there wasn't supposed to be a 'we' this time. You weren't invited, remember?"

"Yeah, who does usually get invited to these parties? That 'not boring' boyfriend of yours?"

"Oh, God no. He disapproves of my adventures even more than you do." She slowed down to make the turn onto Peg's property.

"Isn't that a little bit of a problem in your relationship?"

Nikki squinted out the cracked windshield. "A little bit," she admitted. "Get out and open the shed door for me, will you?"

Jackson flipped on the light in the shed and held the door while Nikki backed the truck in. She cut the motor and hopped out with Captain Beaumont close on her heels.

"This brings back memories," said Jackson hoisting one of the inner tubes. "How many hours did we waste floating in the pond?"

"They weren't wasted," said Nikki. "They were enjoyed and savored."

Nikki flipped off the light and stood waiting for her eyes to get accustomed to the moonlight. Jackson helped her wrestle the lock back in place and stood looking down at the peach orchard.

"Race you down to the pond," he said, looking over his shoulder at her. It was too dark to see his eyes, but she caught the grin.

"I don't know," she said, but he was already running, Captain Beaumont at his heels.

Nikki sprinted to catch up. Ahead of her Jackson slithered to a stop on the tiny dock, kicking off his shoes and pulling off his sweatshirt.

"That's not fair!" Nikki yelled, as he cannonballed off the end of the dock. "You have less clothes on than I do. And a head start." She yanked off her shirt and used the seconds Jackson was underwater to unclip her gun and hide it under her jeans.

"You're just mad because you're slow," he said, resurfacing.

Nikki stood on the dock in her underwear, one hand on her hip. "I am not slow. I will beat you to the tree." She pointed to overhanging oak on the far side of the pond.

"Not a chance," said Jackson, and dove underwater, starting to swim.

Nikki waited the fraction of a second until he was underwater and then sprinted along the water's edge. She arrived, gasping for air, but ahead of Jackson.

"Now, who's cheating?" demanded Jackson.

"I didn't say I would swim," said Nikki. "I said I would win. And I did. Although I paid a heavy price. I think I stepped on either a frog or a cow pie back there. I didn't stop to investigate."

"Some thing's are better left a mystery," agreed Jackson. "You coming in or not?"

In answer, Nikki dove off the bank in a shallow arc. The water was a cool shock and she popped back up with a gasp. There was a splash next to her and Captain Beaumont paddled by with a long stick.

"Never mind the Captain," said Jackson, swimming closer in a strong butterfly stroke. "He doesn't really understand that no one wants a giant slimy oak branch." He pushed against Captain Beaumont, who remained unconvinced and swung his head around, batting at Nikki with the stick.

"Hey," said Nikki, pushing back, but the branch pushed her against Jackson. The contact of their skin was electric and Nikki found herself staring into his eyes and remembering what it had been like to be in love with him. It had been easy. It seemed like everything had been easier then.

"Hey, yourself," murmured Jackson.

Nikki knew she shouldn't. She knew she was probably going to regret it. And she knew she wanted to anyway.

Their lips met and for a moment there was the familiar spark. His hands slid from her waist up her rib cage and for a moment she forgot to kick. The cold water splashed over head and Captain Beaumont jabbed her with his stick.

Jackson pushed Beaumont away, laughing. "We're not buoyant enough for this. We should head for shore."

He swam for the dock and Nikki followed more slowly. He let her climb the ladder first, but when they were on solid ground, he slid an arm around her waist and pulled her close.

"Um," said Nikki leaning back. "Uh, no, I think."

"Not the boyfriend?" Jackson seemed exasperated.

"Yes, the boyfriend. I love him!"

"But it's us."

"No, it's just you and me," said Nikki, sitting down on the end of the dock. "There is no us."

Jackson flopped down next to her, leaning back on his elbows. Captain Beaumont nosed in between them and laid down, panting.

"Sorry," said Nikki, awkwardly.

"Mmph," said Jackson, flapping a hand dismissively. "You're probably right. Moonlight and adrenalin aren't the most sane reasons for reviving a relationship."

"Well, I do want us to be friends again though," said Nikki and Jackson laughed.

"Are you actively putting me in the friend zone? I've read the internet—I should not let you put me on layaway. I should demand that you make a decision. You should respect me for the great catch that I am."

"You haven't been reading the internet. You've been reading *Marie Claire*."

"I think it was *GQ* at the barber shop actually. Besides we've got the time. I'm not going anywhere."

"What does that mean?" demanded Nikki, reaching out to pet Beaumont who leaned happily against her.

"Just that you're right. It is you and me. We've been friends since we could walk and I fully intend to keep being friends with you until we can't walk anymore. I'm just saying we've got time for… whatever." He flapped his hand at the water, consigning their future to the future.

Nikki knew she should probably argue and make things really extra clear, but in all honesty, she kind of liked the idea that she and Jackson would be in the same old folk's home. There was quiet for several minutes, but eventually Jackson sat up and began to look for his clothes.

"Peg and Jorge are getting old," he said. "They won't be able to run this farm forever."

"I know," said Nikki with a sigh. "But she doesn't want to move in with mom, not that I can blame her there. And it doesn't sound like she's ready to sell. So, we'll cross that bridge when we come to it, I guess."

He shrugged.

"Are you secretly trying to tell me that she needs to be moved to a nursing home or something?"

"What? No! But I'm here and I see how she needs help with stuff. And I know that she's never going to actually ask for help."

"Well, it's not your problem," snapped Nikki. "If she needs help, we'll hire someone to do chores around the farm. You're not obligated to help."

He turned to her, frustration clear on his face. "I'm happy to help. That isn't the point."

"Then what is the point?"

"What I'm trying to say," he paused, as if trying to formulate his words carefully, "is that in case you didn't know, because you haven't been around, that she needs help. Currently, I'm happy to help with odd jobs and heavy lifting. But I can see a time coming when there will be more than that."

"Oh." Nikki decelerated her temper out of warp factor four. "Yeah, I know. Mom knows too."

"I don't know that Peg knows that you know."

"Oh, dear God, I've had less confusing conversations with Kit and he's British and crazy. What are you trying to say, Jackson?"

"I think Peg is concerned that you and Nell aren't aware of the status of the farm because you aren't around enough. She feels like she tells you things but it doesn't sink in because you're not here to see it. You need to be here more."

Nikki tried to formulate a response to the suggestion and then laughed. "No."

Jackson looked confused and slightly hurt. "No? Just no? You didn't even think about it."

Nikki shrugged. "I can't. I'm out of the country for weeks at a stretch. I have my mail delivered to work so they can manage my bills for me. I would have my boyfriend do it, but he's in the same boat I am. I can't make new friends because I can't make plans more than twenty-four hours in advance, and I even break a lot of those. I've got exactly enough energy and space for the life I'm currently living. I love Grandma, but I can't fly up here once a month to reassure her that I know she's got it rough and check in on whether or not she needs a handyman or a lift to the doctor. I appreciate that you're looking after her best interests, but I've got responsibilities to a lot of other people. I have to consider more than just what she wants."

"Other people that are more important than your family?"

"Yes, actually. Grandma isn't in crisis. She's fully capable, and while I appreciate her emotional needs, and I wish I could be there for her, I can't. And furthermore, she hasn't asked me to. Given the current situation parameters, I need to stay where I'm at."

For a moment, Jackson looked like he was going to argue.

Like this was going to be a full-blown yelling match. Z'ev would have argued. The old Jackson would have left. Instead, he paused to consider matters, then spoke his mind. "A phone call every couple of weeks would probably do it. And I'm not sure I like the Nikki that thinks of her family as current situation parameters."

"I have to," said Nikki. "Someone has to be clear-headed and make decisions. It's my job."

He pulled on his sweatshirt, losing his face in the folds for a few moments. "That's one hell of a job you've got there, Nikki. It doesn't sound very nice."

"Nice is for people who have time," said Nikki.

"Uh huh. Your grandfather used to say that, didn't he?" Nikki shrugged. He pulled on his shoes and straightened up. Nikki folded her arms across her chest. "Anyway, come up to the ranch one night while you're here and we'll get shit-faced on really good wine and talk about the good old days and you can tell me about your not very nice job, and why you carry lock-picks and a gun."

"You're not supposed to notice the gun," said Nikki.

"Yeah, like I'm not supposed to notice that my ex-girlfriend has become a bad ass? So we're just going to pretend you're the shy, retiring type? Who's going to buy that?"

"Just about everyone," said Nikki with a grin. "You'd be surprised."

"But I don't know why you'd bother," said Jackson, turning to jog up the hill. "Come on, Captain." The Captain went by, a blur in the darkness.

Nikki gathered up her clothes and gun, and jammed her feet into her sneakers, walking on them like flip-flops, bending the heels down in a way her mother would have hated. She shuffled up to the house and then stopped, staring at her grandmother's SUV.

She could have sworn that it was pointed the other direction when she'd left the house. She placed a hand on the hood and pulled it back when she discovered the engine was still warm. She glanced up at the house, but all the lights appeared to be off. Where had her grandmother gone?

AUGUST XII
MOTHER & CHILD REUNION

Thursday

Nikki felt like her head had barely hit the pillow before she heard her grandmother get up. She rolled over, checked the clock and recoiled at the 5:15 time. Farmers were crazy. She heard Peg shower and clump down the stairs and then leave the house by six. After that, there was blessed silence and Nikki went back to sleep. She was still yawning at the breakfast table when Peg returned at ten.

"You sleep a lot," said Peg, pouring herself a cup of coffee.

"I have to make up for when I'm out on a job."

"What is it you do again?"

"I'm a project coordinator for the Carrie Mae Foundation."

"Uh-huh. And what's one of them do?"

"The Carrie Mae Foundation is a non-profit organization with the goal of helping women, and it has branches all over the world. My team and I travel to many of them and work with their personnel to help implement procedures and solve problems." Nikki rattled through her cover story with ease. She called it the 'airplane speech' since it was what she told to strangers on a plane.

"So you fly into some place and tell them what to do? People must love you."

"It's more like people have a problem and they send for us."

"Getting to ride in and save the day is lot better than swooping in and telling them how to do their jobs."

Nikki nodded her agreement and Peg sipped her coffee.

"Oh, I talked to George Parsons this morning. He's got a '53 Cadillac Le Mans—whatever that is. I think it's a convertible. I figured you could do that striped sundress with the matching hat. You'll look like a 1950s Vogue cover if I can get the angles right.

"OK," agreed Nikki.

"I'm still thinking about who's got what other cars. George said he'd ask some of his car friends."

Nikki nodded again and continued to eat her breakfast, letting Peg's meandering digression of cars, shooting styles, and camera equipment wash over her. She waited for a break in the conversation intending to bring up her grandmother's late night trip.

"Of course, we'll have to finish up by two because that's when you'll have to go pick up your mother at the airport."

Nikki paused, spoon halfway to her mouth. Peg was continuing on to discuss which outfits they might do later in the week, if they got the right cars.

"Grandma, you can't slip that in and pretend it didn't happen. I know you called Mom."

"Well, I don't know why you wouldn't want to see your mother," said Peg defensively.

"Because she's overbearing, tries to run my life, and has no sense of boundaries," said Nikki.

"She's not that bad," said Peg.

"Grandma, last time you came to visit us in Seattle, you left after three days."

"There was an emergency at the farm."

"Really? Because what I remember is that Mom kept trying to get you to look at Senior Living Homes and you threw a pile of brochures at her head and called her an ungrateful harpy."

"Yeah…" Peg trailed off and had the decency to blush. "It's my own fault really. We spoiled her when she was younger. She was our only daughter and most of the time there wasn't any reason for her not to get her way. I think she just got into the habit of thinking that she could arrange things the way she thinks is best. She forgets that other people might have differing views on what's best for them."

"That is a very kind way of describing her," said Nikki, going to the sink to rinse out her bowl.

"She's not a bad person," said Peg firmly.

"Nope," agreed Nikki, "she's just a monumental pain in the ass."

"Nikki! You can't talk about your mother like that." Peg looked genuinely disapproving.

"So we'll all just be thinking it then?"

"Nikki," Peg looked unhappy.

"It's fine. We'll just keep it between us," said Nikki, patting Peg's shoulder.

"That is not what I said," said Peg, her lips pinching unhappily.

"Right, because we're not saying it," agreed Nikki. "We're just thinking it."

"You are not funny, young lady."

"I'm a little funny," said Nikki, and Peg's lips twitched upward.

"Go get changed," said Peg throwing up her hands in exasperation. "Hopefully, we'll get this shoot done real quick and be back in time for lunch."

But they weren't. George Parsons wanted to chat. And then he wanted to polish every piece of dust off the Le Mans with a diaper. And then the light shifted. By two Nikki was hot and sweaty from trying to look effortless and breezy and she was starving.

"You don't mind, do you?" asked Peg, hopping out of the car. "I told Jorge I'd go over the numbers with him and someone needs to get your mom. We really should have left twenty minutes ago. You know how she hates to wait."

"It's fine," said Nikki. "But hurry up and close the door so I can crank the AC. You don't need me sweating through this frock."

"Thanks, sweetie!" Peg slammed the door and jogged off toward the operations shack on the edge of the orchard. Nikki watched her go with a smile. She was pushing seventy-one and didn't seem to have slowed down a bit.

The drive into Spokane along Highway 395 was a pretty one, taking her past the edge of the Colville National Forest and Nine Mile Falls before dropping her into the suburbs of Spokane. After wending her way through the center of the city and out the other side she finally arrived, very late, at the Spokane airport. The airport was a boring assortment of buildings, looking like the usual collection of forgotten moving boxes piled next to each other. The best she could say about it was that it had very tidy landscaping.

Nikki checked the charge on her cell phone and began to worry. Being this late should have made her mother begin a five-minute rotation of calls and texts. She pulled into the loading zone and scanned for her mother. She finally spotted Nell by her shirt, which was, of course, a loud paisley print with a neckline that was far too low. Nell was talking to a stylish blonde and behind her was a girl with jet black hair standing next to a slightly older woman dressed in khakis. Nikki groaned and dropped her head on to the steering wheel, which honked the horn. Her mother looked around and waved happily. Oh, so happily.

"Nikki, look who I found on the plane!" chirped Nell.

"All of my friends," replied Nikki, glaring at them.

"Yes! They're coming with us back to the farm!"

"Really? Because I was thinking about firing them off into space."

"Don't be a sour puss," said Nell, "and help us load our bags in the back."

"We've got it," said Jenny, taking Nell's suit case. "You go ahead and get in the car."

"We met your mom!" squeaked Jane thumping into the driver's window in a way that reminded Nikki strongly of Captain Beaumont.

"Why don't you eat this granola bar?" said Ellen taking an appraising look at Nikki.

Nikki thought about refusing, but decided it was a pointless gesture. "Thanks. What are you guys doing here?" She unwrapped the granola bar and began to take enormous bites, trying to eat as much of it as possible before her mother finished fussing with the luggage.

"I called the girls to talk about your situation and see what they thought. And it turned out no one was having much fun on their vacation. Jane wouldn't leave the room until after dark and Jenny got a sunburn on her boobs and my daughters tried to sign me up for a class on making bread."

"You don't enjoy baking," said Nikki, puzzled.

"No, I really don't," agreed Ellen. "There's too much flour all over the place. It annoys me. Anyway, we decided that your mystery and pie vacation sounded like more fun. So here we are, and as a bonus we got to meet your mom."

"Swell," said Nikki sourly as Nell climbed into the passenger seat.

"Nikki, you really shouldn't snack," said Nell, eyeing the granola bar. "You'll get fat."

"Studies show that snacking improves the metabolism," said Nikki, around a mouthful of granola bar.

"And don't talk with your mouth full. What will your friends think?"

"Justifiable homicide?"

"Why do you have to be weird? She's not always this weird," said Nell turning to reassure the girls in the back seat.

"Actually," said Jane, "I'm fairly certain that she's at least that weird all the time."

"I'm just trying to figure out why she's dressed like *A Long Hot Summer*," said Jenny. "That's a little outside the norm."

"I'm helping Grandma," said Nikki.

"What a fantastic dress. But what on earth are you helping her with?" asked Ellen, poking her head around the seat to inspect Nikki's dress.

"My mother fancies herself an amateur photographer," said Nell, sounding embarrassed. "I'm sure this is one of her projects."

"Yes," said Nikki. "Yesterday I was Clara Bow. You should see all the vintage clothes Grandma dug out of the attic."

"Really? Can we try them on?" Jane loved vintage almost as much as she loved goth.

"Sure," said Nikki. "I'm sure Grandma will be happy to have another model. Maybe we can find you some sort of 40s pinup thing to wear."

"This is so much better than Cancun!" Jane clapped her hands ecstatically and Jenny rolled her eyes.

"Oh, it's definitely not better than Cancun," said Nell, looking apprehensive. "It's really just a farm. Not very big or very exciting even."

"It's better than Cancun for Jane," said Nikki.

"She doesn't like happy places or drinks with umbrellas in them," said Jenny bitterly.

"Not even the ones with extra fruit?" Nell was confused.

"If I'm going to drink alcohol, I like it to taste like alcohol," said Jane. "Besides, Jenny, with your health kick lately, I can't figure out why you're drinking anyway."

"That's why you add the fruit," said Nell. "It's practically a health food!"

"Thank you, Nell. I'm glad someone understands. Nikki, she stayed in her room on her computer for most of the three days we were there."

"Jane, I'm not sure you're grasping how to properly Cancun," said Nikki.

"That's what Jenny said, but I don't think I'm obligated to Cancun the same way other people do. And it's not like I didn't do stuff. I did stuff. I went on a nighttime fishing cruise. I caught fish. I'm not entirely sure what kind of fish, but it was very exciting. I went to a museum about the Mayans. And I took a guitar lesson from a Mariachi musician."

"You see?" said Jenny. "She's hopelessly cultural."

Nikki clucked sympathetically. "Well, we've known that about her for years now. I really think you should stop trying to broaden her horizons at this point. Ellen, didn't your daughters mind that you left early?"

"Possibly," said Ellen, leaning forward against the car seat to make conversation. "But I think they may also have been a little glad. I overheard Martina tell George that I wasn't a very relaxing grandmother, and that she remembered me being a lot less strenuous when she was a child."

"That's a terrible thing to say," said Nell, her eyes widening. "What did you do?"

"Oh, nothing. There wasn't anything to do really, and besides it's true. I was about fifty pounds heavier when they were young. I feel bad actually. I was the mom who would buy a tub of icing and a bag of cookies and make 'homemade' Oreos. How any of us made it out of their formative years without diabetes is a miracle. It wasn't until my husband died that I took up exercise. But as a result, the girls are a bit soft and I think they find me rather tiring. The grandkids love me though, and really, sowing generational discord is what brings joy to a grandparent's heart."

"That sounds like something my mother would agree with," said Nell, glancing at Nikki. Nikki, who was concentrating on making a turn, couldn't tell if Nell's expression was angry or guilty.

"Probably," agreed Nikki. "Although, if I ever have kids, I expect you'll do the same thing. Probably with more bribery though."

"What do you mean if?" demanded Nell. "There better be grandkids in my future. Are things not going well with Z'ev? Where is he, by the way? When do I get to meet him?"

"Things are fine with Z'ev. He's on assignment. And never if I can help it."

"Your jokes aren't funny," said Nell. "What was that, Jenny?"

The conversation in the back of the car was already moving off of Z'ev and onto a local news story they'd seen at the airport.

"Hey Mom, can you call Grandma and tell her we're bringing the girls with us?"

"I already did while we were waiting for you," said Nell. "You really ought to make more of an effort to be on time, Nikki. Otherwise people will think you're rude."

Nikki ignored the comment, since on the scale of annoying things her mother was going to say today, sliding in one about being late was barely going to tip the meter.

The rest of the drive was peppered by observations of the countryside, embarrassing childhood stories, and a circular discussion over whether or not bartenders expected their patrons to actually eat the fruit in drinks. Nikki pulled to a stop in front of the house and breathed a sigh of relief. Peg came out to the car and welcomed everyone, except Nikki.

"Sorry, sweetie, but with this many people I need you to pop back to town and pick up a few more items for dinner."

"Jane wants to see the clothes from the attic. Jenny will want to go swimming in the pond. And Ellen will be happy to help with dinner as long as it's not baking," said Nikki, taking the grocery list with a sigh.

"Easiest house guests ever then," said Peg.

Nikki waved and got back in the car. An hour later, she finished loading the groceries in the car and slammed the back hatch, ready to finally be done with the day, when her phone rang. It was an unfamiliar number with a 360 area code and Nikki picked it up with a frown.

"Hello?"

"Babe? Awesome. I was afraid you wouldn't pick up."

"Z'ev?" Her heart rate went up and she couldn't keep the little squeal of excitement from her voice. "Are you back in the States?"

"Yeah. Actually," he paused to clear his throat and Nikki was instantly suspicious. "I checked my messages on the flight back over and I heard that you were going to be in Washington State."

"Yes?" Nikki couldn't figure out where this was going.

"Well, I was hitching a ride with the DEA and they had a flight that was already going to Washington. So I rented a car in Spokane and drove up. I'm in a motel near this weird little bar called the Kessel Run. Uh, I hope that's OK."

"I'm not going back into the grocery store. It depresses me."

"What?"

"Nothing. Forget it. I just have to call Grandma and make sure we can add another for dinner without me driving all the way back into town."

"Another?"

"My grandma called my mom and made her fly out. And apparently the girls weren't enjoying their vacations, so they decided to come crash mine."

Z'ev snorted in laughter.

"So there's a house full of people and Grandma made me drive back to the grocery store and I'm starting to really hate the grocery store. Let me call her and make sure we don't need to go back in and then I'll come get you."

"This is cool. I'm excited to meet your family."

"Yeah, you won't be as excited after you meet them."

"Stop being so down on your mom."

"Stop being so positive about my mom," snapped Nikki.

"Sorry. I didn't mean to like your mom without permission."

Nikki laughed and climbed in the car. "She drives me so crazy. I was in the car with her for an hour and a half and I already want to kill her. It's like she just looks for ways to undermine me."

"It's good the girls are there then. They'll keep you from stabbing her in the eye."

"I hope so. I'm glad you're here too. I really want to see you. Although, now that I'm thinking of it, there might not be any room for you at the house."

"I can't stay in your room?"

"Umm… no? I'm fairly certain Grandma would shit a brick rather than let unmarried people stay in the same room together."

"She does know we live together, right?"

"Yes, but that happens in another state. And the reality that exists in the State of California doesn't apply to the rest of the world. Also, you'd be a bit difficult to wedge in with all the clothes."

"I'm not even going to inquire about the last statement."

"Probably just as well. Give me about twenty minutes and I'll meet you at the hotel."

"I'm over at the bar actually. I bumped into your friend Donny Fernandez."

"Don't let him get you into trouble," said Nikki.

"You're going to be here in twenty minutes right? How much trouble can he get me into in twenty minutes?"

"You'd be surprised. Love you."

"Love you, too," he said.

AUGUST XIII
HOT DICE

Peg had been about as happy to have Z'ev visit as Nikki had expected. She could hear Nell jumping up and down in the background. But Peg had only said, "Hmm, sure, I guess."

Nikki pulled up at the Kessel Run and spotted Z'ev's rental car, a green four-door Camry, the world's most boring car. Clyde was behind the bar again. This time the place was busier and the Harrison Ford cut-out had been pushed up against the wall. Clyde was navigating the room with a tray full of food held high.

"Hey, Nikki," said Clyde, with a brief nod as he edged past her.

"Hey." She scanned the room looking for Z'ev.

"If you're looking for that big guy," Clyde said, coming back the other way, tray empty. "I think he went out back with Donny Fernandez."

"Thanks," said Nikki, walking further into the bar, past the restrooms and the open door to the sweltering kitchen. She could hear the sounds of men's voices, but couldn't tell if they were excited or angry. Nikki quickened her pace, the stiff cotton of her sundress making swishing noises against her skin, and pushed through the swinging wooden screen door out onto the back porch.

They were all off the porch, some kneeling, some standing over a flat spot in the grass. Most were Mexican and they all spoke Spanish. Nikki spotted Donny, and recognized Carlos and Rey-Rey

Vallejo. Z'ev was kneeling and there was a substantial pile of money on the ground. They were shooting craps and Nikki watched this entirely masculine form of entertainment with interest. Girls, as a group, just didn't go out back to shoot dice.

Nikki wound one arm around a porch post and leaned against it, pausing to admire Z'ev. He'd been someplace sunny. He was tanner than when he'd left LA. He was strutting a ghetto look in a white tank-top and jeans, too. His watch wasn't gold, but it did have the heavy expensive look that was required for any truly macho guy. To really pull it off, he should have had more jewelry, but Nikki knew that he didn't ever wear any. He probably wouldn't have worn the watch either, except that it was company issue. But it was his attitude that was putting the act over and Nikki could see that in the circle of men there wasn't a single person who doubted Z'ev's street cred. He really was good at this sort of thing.

It was Donny who acknowledged her first, although she wouldn't have bet that Z'ev didn't know she was there.

"*Hola*, Nikki," said Donny with a head jerk and a smile.

"*Hola*. I thought you liked me. Are you trying to get my boyfriend in trouble?" Nikki replied.

"Trouble? What trouble?" asked Donny spreading his hands upward in a too-innocent shrug.

"Aw, come on, baby," said Z'ev. "You worry too much." They held eye contact for a moment and Nikki found herself short of breath. He really had been away too long.

Nikki readjusted her position, leaning her elbows on the porch railing which she knew displayed her cleavage to an advantage.

"You'd better watch yourself," she replied. "I went to school with some of these guys and they'll take your lunch money faster than spit." She nodded toward Carlos and Rey-Rey. Z'ev gave them a questioning look and they both nodded unrepentantly.

"Well, you'd better give me some luck then," he said falling back and walking over to the porch. "Blow on my dice."

"Blow on your own dice," she replied tartly. That got a laugh and some comments from the other gamblers.

"You just don't like it when I gamble." He was whining for the audience.

"No," corrected Nikki. "I just don't like it when you lose."

"Well, if you don't give me any luck, what do you expect? Come on. You know you want to."

He held out his palm and rattled the purple dice around with clicking sound. Nikki didn't move, but her eyes twinkled.

"No? Well, OK."

He started to pull the dice away and Nikki's hand shot out, grabbing his wrist. Not taking her eyes off his face, she brought his hand to just below her mouth and blew gently over the dice. There was a silence from the men. No one thought that was funny. Z'ev grinned his all too charming smile that still made Nikki's stomach do back-flips, and knelt down. There was a flurry of betting. Z'ev took one more glance up at her and winked. Then he threw the dice.

The clear, purple cubes bounced across the money, reflecting sunlight from the golden rays of the setting sun. One rolled gently to a stop showing five dots. The other ricocheted off a shoe and spun to a halt, clearly displaying two small white dots. There was a groan from the men who had bet against Z'ev. Z'ev held his hands up and looked around triumphantly and began to gather up his winnings.

"*Te amo*," he said kissing his fingertips at Nikki.

"Oh, *te amo, te amo*," Nikki repeated mockingly. "Now that he wins the money."

The crowd laughed.

"Well, baby," said Z'ev plaintively and paused. They all turned to look at him, standing there in his muscles and money. "Of course."

Nikki laughed, she couldn't help it, and that set the men off too. Z'ev grinned and folded his money over into a wad.

"Another round?" someone suggested, but Z'ev shook his head.

"Sorry, I got better things to do."

"Yeah, like Nikki."

"Funny Rey-Rey, real funny," said Nikki. Donny smacked the back of Rey-Rey's head.

"What?" asked Rey-Rey.

The game began to break up, men disappearing back into the bar or out to their trucks. They all shook Z'ev's hand or gave him the shoulder-to-shoulder bump that was what Nikki mentally referred to as a man hug. Donny shook hands with Z'ev and waved to Nikki.

"*Buenas noches*, Donny."

"*Buenas noches*," Donny called back and headed toward the front parking lot.

"You really went to school with those hoodlums?" asked Z'ev when they were alone.

Nikki nodded as Z'ev walked the short distance to the porch rail where Nikki still leaned on her elbows. He traced one finger along her collarbone and then down across the top of her breast.

"Kindergarten through fifth grade." She lowered her head and leaned down to kiss him. "We should go. They can't make dinner without us," she said, after a moment.

"Are you sure?" he asked, kissing her again. "The hotel is right over there."

Nikki giggled, tempted. "Wait, no," she said pushing away. "Mom will totally know and that kills my mood."

He nodded. "Fine. I just need to run over to the hotel and grab my shirt."

"That's not yours?" asked Nikki pointing to a blue and white checked shirt on the railing. Z'ev shook his head.

"Not mine. Someone must have forgotten it."

"I'll bring it in to Clyde. The bartender," she added, when he frowned in puzzlement.

"I'll meet you back here in two minutes," he said, checking his watch and then stealing another kiss before he jogged around the corner toward the hotel across the street.

Nikki picked up the shirt and shook it out, folding it over her arm. The screen door slammed behind her and Kristine walked out onto the porch.

"Well, look whose gone washer-woman," drawled Kristine, slightly drunk. "Give me a minute and I'll give you my panties." She laughed loudly at her own joke.

Nikki said nothing.

"Geez Nikki, it's bad enough that you speak the language, but you really have gone native. You're even dating one of them—" Just as when she'd grabbed Z'ev's wrist, Nikki's arm shot out, but this time her hand clamped around Kristine's jaw. Kristine made a slight 'urk' sound and sloshed some of her beer.

"I just know that you're about to say spic or nigger or something else that I don't want to hear," said Nikki in a conversational tone. "You have a problem with me. I don't know why, but I don't really care why either. I can deal with it. But I will not tolerate insults to my friends." She gave Kristine's head a little shake. The sound of her teeth clicking together was audible on the empty porch. "So consider this your warning. There won't be another one. Now, I'm going to let go and you can say whatever it is you want to say and we'll go from there. We clear?" Nikki stared into Kristine's saucer-sized eyes and knew she ought to feel bad about this.

She let go and Kristine took a stumbling step backwards eyes fixed on Nikki.

"Got something to say?" asked Nikki, and her tone sounded hard even to her own ears.

Kristine shook her head back and forth.

"Then get back inside." She pointed to the door and Kristine did as she was told, tripping a little over own feet.

"She'll hate you for that."

Nikki turned her head and saw Donny at the foot of the porch stairs.

"Forgot my shirt," he said pointing to Nikki's arm. He walked around to the railing side and Nikki handed the shirt to him.

"She already hated me," she said as he pulled it on. "I don't know why."

"Jealousy," said Donny, buttoning his shirt.

"Jealous? Of what?"

"A glamorous job, glamorous boyfriend, in a glamorous town. You got out of Kaniksu Falls and she never did. Grass is always greener, and all that stuff." He put the last button through the proper buttonhole.

"OK, sure, I guess. But I don't know why she thinks that means it's all right to say such racist crap."

"You used to be shy," said Donny. "She probably thought she could get away with it. Trouble with you now is that you sneak up on people."

Donny leaned against the rail and Nikki backed up a step or two so she could see his face clearly.

"What do you mean?" she asked warily.

"Well, anyone with eyes looks at Z'ev and knows he's a dangerous man, but you, you sneak up on a person. You're the scorpion at the bottom of a man's sleeping bag. The copperhead in the underbrush. By the time they see you, they've already been bitten."

"*Latet anguis in herbe,*" murmured Nikki. Donny raised an eyebrow. "A snake lurks in the grass," she translated. "It's a Latin proverb." Donny nodded.

"That's you," he said.

"You're crazy," countered Nikki.

Z'ev came around the corner. He'd changed into slacks and a button-up shirt and he was wrapping a tie around his neck.

"Z'ev," said Donny. "Do you think your girlfriend's dangerous?"

"Every day," answered Z'ev, looking up from the tie.

"Does anyone else think that?"

"No, and I can't figure out why. I can't do this without a mirror."

"See?" said Donny, as if his point had been irrefutably proved.

"You're both crazy," said Nikki, untangling Z'ev's tie.

"Whatever." Donny grinned. He slapped the railing twice with an open palm, and glanced at Z'ev. then back at Nikki. "You're coming to the Fiesta, right? We still need to talk."

"Yes! I need to talk to you too. Jackson is planning on coming."

"Oh, good," said Donny looking pleased. "I keep meaning to call him, but the family's been keeping me busy. I'll see you guys later then—Friday around five. But you know the family. It won't really start kicking till about nine."

"Still out on Meyer?" asked Nikki looping the tie around Z'ev's neck and pulling it through.

"That's the place. See you then." Donny ambled off with a wave and Z'ev waved back without moving his head.

"What was all that about?" asked Z'ev, as Nikki stepped back to check her work.

"Oh, we bumped into a girl we used to go to school with and she was throwing some massive shade at me, so I told her where to go."

"Massive shade?" he repeated, mouthing the words as if they were an unfamiliar food.

"Let it go," said Nikki, shaking her head. "Anyway, then Donny said I used to be shy and that's why she thought she could get away with that. He says now I sneak up on people."

"I could see that," said Z'ev nodding. "Don't really see you being shy though."

"I was," she said with a shrug. "If it hadn't been for Donny and Jackson I wouldn't have had a friend. All the other kids seemed so with it. And Kristine, the girl who was here, she used to boss everyone around. One time, she told Becky Newmire that she couldn't wear blue, and she didn't, for like, three years. If I saw Kristine coming my way, I'd just go hide in the giant tires on the playground. I didn't ever speak up—not for Becky Newmire, not for myself. I think that's something I've learned from working at Carrie Mae."

"Now you take charge and get what you want," said Z'ev, miming a Rosie the Riveter pose.

Nikki laughed. "Yes, that's me. Come on, we might as well get this over with. Promise you'll still love me after you meet my mother?"

"*Te amo*," he said, kissing her. "A thousand mothers couldn't make me love you less."

"Yeah, you say that now," said Nikki.

AUGUST XIV

GREEN ACRES

As Z'ev and Nikki pulled up to the house, Nell and Jenny were returning from the pond, towels over their shoulders.

"Were they bathing in the water tower?" whispered Z'ev and Nikki slapped at him with her free hand.

"Now is not the time to start being funny," she hissed back.

"Well, you let me know when the time is. I've got more."

"You know, comparing a farming community to *Green Acres* is not going to endear you to people who actually live here."

"*Petticoat Junction. Green Acres* was later. You must be Nell," he said walking forward and holding out his hand. "It's so nice to finally meet you in person."

Nell looked at Z'ev's slacks and tie and beamed.

"It's lovely to meet you too! I'm very excited that you could make it. Nikki said you were away on assignment."

"I just got back."

"How'd you get here so fast?" asked Jenny, trying to work out flight times in her head.

"I hitched a ride with some friends who were heading this way," he said.

"Hitched a ride on what?" Jenny was giving him the suspicious eye.

"Jenny," admonished Nell. "You shouldn't be so pushy."

"If Jenny weren't pushy, I'd think she were ill," said Z'ev. "It's all right. One of the good parts of working for the government is having friends in other departments. I hitched a ride on a DEA flight. They dropped me off in Spokane."

"Well, that's exciting!" Nell seemed impressed. "You'll have to tell us all about it at dinner. Which Jenny and I should go change for."

"We'll meet you in there," said Nikki, "We have to unload the groceries before the ice melts."

"Didn't you put it in the cooler? She always has a cooler in the back of the car," said Nell.

"And now I know why," said Nikki opening the SUV and pulling out the bag of ice as Z'ev grabbed the entire lot of grocery bags.

"Already making yourself useful," said Nell, and Nikki rolled her eyes.

"I aim to please. Lead the way to the kitchen."

"This way." Nell led him inside. Jenny was making hilarious faces at Nikki. It was all Nikki could do to not laugh and she felt herself relaxing even as the ice dripped in cold rivulets down her arms. Maybe this dinner wouldn't be straight out of one of the seven rings of hell. Her grandmother was great, her mother was attempting to be nice, and Z'ev was doing his blend in thing. This really was going to be OK.

The screen door swung open and Nikki looked up, expecting to hear her grandmother's welcoming voice and light step. Nikki's own steps faltered as she saw Jackson stride out onto the porch. He had gussied up. He was wearing his good boots—shiny snakeskin. The outfit was complete with an enormous belt buckle, clean jeans, new button-up shirt, and a shave. He had obviously been invited for dinner.

"What are you doing here?" demanded Nell.

"He's holding open the door and letting all the cold air out, waiting for you to bring the ice in," said Grandma stepping out onto the porch.

"Clearly he's here for dinner," snapped Nikki. "Some people like him."

"I'm sure they do," answered her mother, looking offended. "I simply wasn't aware he had been invited." Nell swept past Nikki and onto the porch. "Jackson, it's nice to see you." She dropped an icily formal kiss on Jackson's cheek and proceeded into the kitchen. Jackson, used to such behavior from Nell, calmly let her.

"Nikki, aren't you going to introduce us?" asked Grandma, smiling at someone over Nikki's shoulder. Nikki remembered Z'ev and twitched guiltily.

"Z'ev Coralles," said Z'ev waggling a grocery bag at her.

"Grandma, Z'ev. Z'ev, Peg Connelly," completed Nikki a second too late. "And this is Jackson, Z'ev."

"Jackson Tyrell," said Jackson.

"That some people like," said Z'ev.

"Apparently," answered Jackson. "Can't imagine who."

They squared off. Z'ev loomed over the shorter man, but there was a wry sparkle in Jackson's eye that refused to be intimidated by size. Jackson, tan and freckled under a thatch of unruly brown hair that poked in all directions even when he'd combed it, should have looked puny next to Z'ev, but didn't. Z'ev, who wore his tie and slacks with the same ease that Jackson wore his snakeskin boots, should have looked like a jumped-up city slicker, but didn't. They looked oddly alike to Nikki, both possessed of a similar raw energy and tensile strength. It was puzzling Z'ev, she could tell. He wasn't used to people that could match his force of personality. Nikki found she was holding her breath.

"Nikki. Nikki, Nikki," gasped Jenny, hitting Nikki's arm with each repetition of her name. "You said your ex-boyfriend's name was Jackson. You didn't tell me he was The Jackson Tyrell." Jenny's Georgian accent redoubled in strength on Jackson's name.

"Um…" Nikki looked from Jenny to Jackson. "Yeah?"

"Oh, my God, I'm in my swimsuit. I'm meeting Jackson Tyrell in a swimsuit."

"I like your swimsuit," said Jackson, grinning.

And Jenny giggled. She actually giggled.

"The Jackson Tyrell, meet Jenny Baxter," said Z'ev.

"I was in the stands the day you went toe-to-toe with Devil Winder," gushed Jenny. "I thought I was going to bust a lung from screaming."

"Seems fair. I busted my arm."

"Yes, well, why don't we talk about who busted what inside," said Peg sourly. "So we can stop letting the AC out. Nikki, can you and the big fella carry the groceries into the kitchen?"

"Who is The Jackson Tyrell?" asked Z'ev as they walked toward the kitchen.

"He used to do bull-riding and rodeo-clowning. Or whatever the proper way to rodeo clown in past tense is," said Nikki. "I didn't realize he was that big a deal. But you know Jenny and the rodeo."

"And he's your ex-boyfriend," he added, stopping in front of their Senior Prom picture displayed in the line of family photos down the hall. "Nice hair."

"Oh, God, don't look at that." Nikki pulled him away from the wall and into the kitchen.

"Still better than my prom picture. I had a 'fro and a Colonel Sanders suit."

"Why haven't I seen that picture?" demanded Nikki.

"I don't know. Why haven't I met your mother until now?"

Nikki made a face and didn't reply.

"Oh, look how cute you are in this one." Z'ev stopped in front of a family portrait, one of the few photos with her dad that hadn't been removed. Three-year-old Nikki's high cuteness rating had saved the photo from the fireplace where the rest of the photos of Philippe had ended up. "Nice moustache on your dad."

Nikki laughed. "Yeah, he used to rotate his facial hair all the time. Moustache, goatee, clean-shaven. He liked to be creative with his hair."

"Makes sense," said Z'ev.

"I guess," said Nikki, puzzled that her father's rotating facial hair made sense to anyone. "Come on, I'm dripping on the carpet." She walked into the kitchen and dropped the ice into the sink.

"Oh good, you brought the ice," said Ellen, appearing from the basement. "I just got the ice cream machine all set up. Can you bring it down here?"

"You're making ice cream?" asked Z'ev. "This is the best vacation ever!"

"I know, right?" agreed Jane bouncing into the kitchen in a bright orange polyester jumpsuit.

"Oh, my God," said Nikki.

"I know," said Jane.

"Holy crap," said Jackson walking into the kitchen after her. "I think I need my sunglasses."

"I know!" Jane seemed ecstatic with the hideousness of her vintage outfit. "Isn't it awesome? I wish there were a roller rink nearby."

"Nikki, your mom and grandma are arguing in the office, so I thought I should come in here to make myself useful," said Jackson.

"And get out of firing range, you mean?"

"Yeah." He glanced at Jane. "Of course, I didn't realize the dress code for this evening was Staying Alive. Maybe I should go home and change."

Nikki laughed. "No, please don't. The belt buckle is scaring me enough as it is. I don't think I could take you in bellbottoms. Can you get the groceries put away? And Z'ev, if you take the ice down to Ellen, I'll go sort out whatever family drama is unfolding in the office."

"What should I do?" asked Jane, fluffing the points on her enormous collar proudly.

"I would say go change, but I don't want to make you cry. Can you go make sure Jenny doesn't overdress, or underdress, as the case may be."

"OK," said Jane with a shrug, floating toward the back stairs.

Nikki walked down the hall. She could feel the muscles between her shoulder blades tightening as she got closer to the office. She took a deep breath and told herself that everything was going to be fine. She was going to be fine. This extreme mash-up of family, personal life, professional life, and past life was all going to work out fine. No secrets were going to be revealed. Everyone was going to be happy. Everything was going to work out fine.

The office door slammed open and Nell stomped out. "Your grandmother always tries to ruin everything!"

"What is she trying to ruin, Mom?"

Nell hesitated. Had she been working, Nikki would have attacked that moment. That little tiny delay that told her that whatever Nell said next was a lie.

"She invited Jackson on purpose because she doesn't approve of Z'ev."

"I don't disapprove of Z'ev," said Peg. "I don't know Z'ev. I do know Jackson. And I know that he is a good boy. He's got plans, a future, and eighty-three acres. You shouldn't have broken up with him."

"He broke up with me, Grandma," said Nikki, wishing she'd stayed in the kitchen.

"Well, I bet he's sorry about it now," said Peg.

"That's kind of irrelevant," said Nikki. "I'm with Z'ev."

"But are you happy, dear?"

"Grandma!" Nikki floundered. "I'm not having this conversation. This is ridiculous. For once, I'm on Mom's side." Nell beamed smugly. "You two wonder why I moved to California? It's because of conversations like this."

"Nonsense," said Nell. "You moved for the job."

"And I was happy to do it. Now, we are going to go back to the kitchen and finish making dinner. Grandma, you are going to be nice to Z'ev. Mom, you are going to be nice to Jackson and we are all going to pretend that we are nice people. I know it's a stretch, but we are going to make it happen."

"I don't know what you're talking about," said Peg. "I'm nice to everyone." She walked down the hall, her back poker straight, and disapproval in every line.

"Really, Nikki, you're behaving so rudely." Nell swept after Peg and Nikki clunked her head against the office door, once, twice, three times.

"Well, I think you should stick by Z'ev," whispered Jenny, tip-toeing down the stairs. "Why would she try and break you two crazy kids up?"

"Really? A few days ago you said that we should break up."

"I didn't know what I was saying," said Jenny.

"Uh-huh. You mean you hadn't met Jackson yet."

"I don't know what you're talking about," said Jenny, flipping one long lock of hair over her shoulder.

Nikki stared pointedly at Jenny's boobs that were being prominently displayed in a low-cut blouse.

"Oh, fine. Jane said you were going to notice."

"How could I not?" asked Nikki. "I think a NASA space satellite would notice those."

"That's not fair," said Jenny, stomping up the stairs. "Those have really good resolution these days."

"I didn't say don't wear it," Nikki called after her. "I was just saying, you know, da-a-mn."

Jenny flipped her the bird before disappearing into the guest room.

"You shouldn't police another woman's apparel," said Jane, coming out of the room.

"No, that's what I sent you to do," said Nikki.

"I mean, it feeds into the concept that women need to be ashamed of their own bodies and that men aren't responsible for their actions if a woman dresses too provocatively."

"Thanks, Gloria Steinem, but can you whip me up a feminist argument that supports me not having to stare at Jenny's boobs over the mashed potatoes?"

"I like staring at Jenny's boobs," said Jane.

"That's because you're a little bit gay," said Nikki, and Jane shrugged.

"I'm in touch with my inner lesbian."

"Well, stop touching your inner lesbian and come help make sure that I don't stab my mother with a fork over the salad course."

"I don't see why you shouldn't," said Jane. "As long as you use the right fork."

"You're not helping," said Nikki.

"I'm not really even trying," agreed Jane.

Nikki sighed and went back to the kitchen. She had the feeling that it was going to be a very long dinner.

But by the time dinner was served, détente appeared to have been reached between Peg and Nell. Jenny had reined the boobs in and was being perfectly pleasant, but still flirty. Jane finally changed out of the polyester when she got too hot and Ellen and Z'ev were collaborating on the perfect way to stack ice and salt around the tub of the ice cream maker. They appeared satisfied with their work as they sat down to dinner.

"And now we pray," announced Peg in a tone that brooked no argument, and folded her hands. Jackson and Nell, who were used to it, had already followed suit, and the girls, startled, followed along as well. Z'ev, who was Catholic or Jewish depending on which grandparent he stood next to, took the unexpected dose of religion in stride.

"Dear Lord," began Peg. "Thank you for blessing this table with good food and good friends, and for bringing the family back together again. Family bonds are more important than anything and we thank you for strengthening them."

There was an odd sort of clunk that might have been Nell adjusting her feet under the table or it might have been Nell kicking Peg in the shin.

"Please bless the bounty that we are about to receive. Amen. Now pass the mashed potatoes. Those are my favorite."

"So, Jackson," said Jenny, when the plates had been filled. "I'd love to hear some stories about the rodeo bulls."

"Two tons of snot and shit," said Nell, picking over the roasted vegetables to avoid the cucumbers. "What's there to tell?"

"Helen!" said Peg, resorting to Nell's full name. "Mind your language."

"I'm fairly certain I learned that language from you, Mother."

"Maybe, but I don't use it at the dinner table," said Peg.

"Add in another ton of mean and she'd be right, though," said Jackson, earning a rare smile from Nell.

"I'd rather hear about Z'ev's flight up from California. You got a ride with some DEA agents, you say?" Nell switched her focus to Z'ev, who looked up from his slice of meatloaf to find all eyes on him.

"Really?" Jackson's eyes flicked to Nikki and then back to Z'ev. "What was the DEA doing up here?"

Z'ev cleared his throat, a tiny tic that revealed only to Nikki that he was uncomfortable with the topic. "Apparently, there's a major pot pipeline from here down through Idaho and heading south and east. Would you mind passing the salt?" He smiled casually at Ellen, and Nikki knew he was hoping for a change of topic.

"I thought pot was legal in Washington now? Why would anyone smuggle it?" asked Jane.

"And why go south?" mused Nikki. "If I were going to smuggle pot, I'd bring it in from Mexico." She happened to look at Nell, who seemed frozen with a bite halfway to her mouth.

"You've spent a lot of time considering your pot smuggling plans, have you?" demanded Peg, skewering her with a suspicious look.

"Virtually none," said Nikki, with a shrug.

"Canadian pot is better quality," said Z'ev. "The further south you can take Canadian pot, the more it's worth. Now that pot is legal here, there might be an import slowdown, but probably not a lot, since most of the pot smuggled in from Canada doesn't stay here."

"I'm sure there's no actual pot smuggling going on in Kaniksu Falls anymore," said Peg firmly, and Jackson glanced at Nikki again. She was going to have to talk to him about that. He was a dead giveaway. The girls continued eating calmly, like properly trained operatives.

"Did the DEA say they were looking at Kaniksu Falls specifically?" asked Nell, clearing her throat.

"No, they said they thought it was coming in through the Colville Forest, probably on ATVs. They were hoping that the forest fires would flush out some of the smugglers."

"Speaking of Canada," said Peg. "Does anyone want to go into Canada tomorrow for some shopping? Sometimes it's better there than in Spokane."

"Ellen can't go to Canada," said Jane. Nikki shot a disbelieving glare at Jane, who became flustered. "I mean, she didn't bring her passport. Not that she's wanted in Canada or anything. The Canadian borders have required passports since 9/11." Jane trailed off in an awkward laugh.

"That's Jane—our idiot savant," said Nikki.

"This is the last time I let you watch my *Due South* DVDs," said Ellen with a sigh. "It gives you weird ideas about Canada. She's right though. I didn't bring my passport. No Canadian shopping for me."

"No Canada, then," agreed Peg. "Maybe tomorrow, Nikki can show you around town and where she grew up."

"Uh, if I have to," said Nikki.

"I'd like the tour," said Z'ev grinning.

"Donny invited us to a Fernandez shin-dig," said Nikki.

"Well, all right. But don't stay too late. Those parties get out of control after ten," said Peg.

"I need to call him," said Jackson.

"I don't want to go," said Nell. "Lucia doesn't like me."

"You insulted her tamales, Mom," said Nikki for the hundredth time. The long saga of why Donny's mom didn't like Nikki's mom could have filled six months worth of programming on *Telemundo*.

"They were really dry," said Nell. "I can't help that."

"You can help saying it to her face."

"I'm honest," said Nell. "That's who I am."

"Well, then, don't come."

"I won't," said Nell.

Nikki sighed and rolled her head around on her neck. It was going to be fine. Everything was going to be fine.

AUGUST XV
REPUBLICAN PAMPHLETS

Nikki plunked a load of dishes into the sink and took a deep breath. It was times like this that she missed her dad. She remembered him as a gregarious charmer who always seemed to have the right thing to say. She remembered a lot more laughing at the dinner table when he had been around.

Nikki scrubbed extra hard a dish in the sink and wondered if Nell would have been a different kind of mother if Philippe had been a different kind of father.

"Well, this seems to be going well," said Jane carrying in a stack of plates.

Nikki stared at her in disbelief. Sometimes she thought Jane existed in a parallel universe. "My mother is offering to show my boyfriend my junior high photos. Jenny is draped over my ex-boyfriend, which would be a lot less annoying if he didn't look so happy about it. And Ellen and my grandmother are attempting to discuss ammunition using mime, since they don't want my mother to notice."

"I know! It was adorable."

"That part was adorable, but nothing else."

"I don't know why you're so uptight," said Jane. "We can all handle ourselves around Z'ev, and aside from my gaff about Canada at dinner—which, I guess is why I shouldn't be out in the field—I don't think we're in danger of exposing ourselves."

"You got too relaxed," said Nikki, tiptoeing to the kitchen

door and checked the hall. She could hear voices from the living room and the clatter of dishes from the dining room. "You'll do better next time. Besides, it's not you I'm worried about. It's Z'ev and Jackson. Jackson is a straight arrow and can't lie at all."

Jane paused in scraping the plates and stood up, putting one hand on her hip. "And what does he have to lie about?"

"Well, we may have kissed," whispered Nikki.

"Oh, my God. Seriously? Why didn't you tell us?"

"I was planning on calling everyone tomorrow, but then you all arrived."

"No wonder you're trying to keep Jenny's boobs in check. OK, well, I think –" Whatever Jane had been about to say was cut off by an angry squawk from Nikki.

"What the hell is he doing here?" Nikki ran to the kitchen window where she could see Milt scrutinizing the cars in the driveway. She ran to the junk drawer and yanked it open, but her grandmother's gun was no longer in residence. Storming into the dining room, she found Jackson gathering up the glasses.

"Do you know where Peg put her gun?"

"She told you about that thing, huh? I think she moved it somewhere before your mom arrived."

"What about you? You own a gun, right?"

"Yeah, but—"

"Where is it? In the truck? Give me the keys." Nikki held out her hand for the keys.

"All my guns are at home," answered Jackson, backing up a pace.

"What're they doing at home?"

"It's not hunting season and I didn't think I'd need to be packing heat at a family dinner party."

"But you've got something else, don't you? Knife, something. I know you. You're always packing something. Come on, fork it over." Nikki reached forward and grabbed the waistband of his jeans, feeling for the weapon she was certain was there.

"Nikki!" protested Jackson, laughing, as her hand dove into his back pocket.

There was the slightest sound of a throat clearing, more of a murmur than an actual cough—Nikki froze. Then ever so slowly turned her head to the living room doorway.

Z'ev raised an eyebrow. Nikki smiled manically.

"I think I got that spider," she said, straightening up and dusting Jackson off. "You should have seen it, honey," she added over her shoulder. "It was huge."

"I think I'll just go… somewhere else," said Jackson, squeezing past Z'ev who stood immovable in the doorway.

"Big spider," said Nikki, measuring how big with thumb and forefinger. "Big."

"Rrrrright," said Z'ev. "Your mom's looking for you."

"Nikki," said Nell, "Are we expecting anyone? I think there's someone outside." The doorbell rang. "Oh, well, there you go." Nell walked down the hall.

"Mom, wait!" Nikki ran after her, but Nell had already opened the door.

"Well, Nell Lanier," said Sheriff Smalls.

Nells back stiffened. "Mervin Smalls. What are you doing here?"

"My job, of course. I'm investigating a crime. I'm sheriff now, in case you hadn't heard."

"I heard. I donated $500 to your opponent's campaign."

Merv laughed. "A waste of your money I'm afraid."

"What crime could you possibly be investigating?" demanded Nell.

"Well, interestingly enough, your daughter was involved in an altercation at a local establishment on Tuesday night and a car was stolen. A car that has not yet turned up. I've brought the owner to verify that none of the cars on your property are his."

"Are you suggesting that my daughter stole a car?"

"Well, it seemed like it might be prudent to check," said Merv. "Reports say that she was friendly with the thief."

"What reports?" asked Nikki, although neither the sheriff or her mother showed any signs of hearing her.

"Mervin Smalls," said Peg, coming out of the living room and into the hall. "Get the hell off my property."

"Mrs. Connelly, you seem to have taken offense when I offered to buy your property. If there's some sort of mistake –"

"I didn't mistake nothin'. Now get the hell off my farm and don't come back without a warrant."

"If that's the way you want to play it," said Merv, tapping his fingers thoughtfully on his gun belt.

"Yes, I do. Nell, shut the door."

"Yes, mother," said Nell, in tone of unbelievable compliance and slammed the door in the sheriff's face.

"Uh," said Nikki.

"So, we don't like the sheriff?" asked Z'ev.

"That sheriff used out-of-state money to get elected," said Peg. "He's been pressuring farmers all over the county to turn in lists of their undocumented workers. And I heard Randall Cobb bought him off to keep from getting half his work force turned into Immigration."

"Randall Cobb is a known liar," said Jackson, leaning against the living room door.

Peg squinted unhappily. "That's true, but that doesn't mean he's lying about the sheriff."

"If people don't want to get harassed by the sheriff, then possibly people should stop using illegal aliens."

"Well, you tell me how easy it is when your grapes come in," snapped Peg. "We'll see if you don't change your tune then. I know you're all hopped up on how undocumented aliens are a drain on our economy, but you've got to stop reading those Republican pamphlets. I've told you before and I'll tell you again—nearly every dollar earned by an illegal immigrant stays in the US. There is no drain! And maybe I wouldn't complain so loud if Mervin Smalls applied the law evenly across the board, but he doesn't. Notice how his friends never have any troubles with their workers."

"I think you've got a little bit of a personal bias on the immigration issue," said Jackson.

"And I think, that…" said Peg, whirling around, her finger raised to wag under Jackson's nose. She held the finger a second, seeming to reconsider whatever she had been about to say. "You should know better than to talk politics at a family gathering."

Jackson's eyes flicked from Peg to Nell to Nikki. "You are absolutely right. My apologies."

Peg looked around at her guests. "I'm sure it's time for pie," she said with a forced smile. Nikki frowned at Peg and Jackson. Something had just happened, but she wasn't sure what. The question was, who was she going to interrogate first—Peg or Jackson?

AUGUST XVI

PETTICOAT JUNCTION

"Tell me again why I couldn't stay at the farm?" asked Z'ev as she drove toward his motel. From his sour expression, she could tell he felt insulted. He probably also felt like she should have stood up for him.

"Because Grandma wouldn't approve," said Nikki, feeling a stab of guilt. She really should have demanded that he stay.

"I didn't hear her say she didn't approve." His tone was flat and emotionless, the way it was when he was totally pissed.

"Look, I chickened out and froze, OK? I'll figure it out to-morrow, but right now we're already in the car and headed to the motel. Besides," she said, slowing down to make a turn, cranking the wheel hand over hand, "the motel probably has more insula-tion than my room at the farm. And less clothes. And less butter-flies."

"I think it's a given about the butterflies," said Z'ev. "I'm fairly certain the motel has zero butterflies. But why do we need insulation?"

Nikki gave him a look. "Because I haven't seen you in a month and I don't know what you had planned, but I wasn't think-ing I'd just drop you off and head home."

"Ohhhh," said Z'ev, moving his hand over to rest on her knee. "Sorry, I was being dense. Nope. The motel's fine. Let's go to the motel." His hand slid a little higher, pushing up the skirt of her dress. "We could even go to the motel a little faster. You know, if you wanted."

Nikk's foot involuntarily slammed down on the gas pedal. She forced it to ease up. "Jackson said they are very serious about the speeding tickets here. I don't think my insurance can take any more speeding tickets."

"It's not really the speeding ones that are killing you," said Z'ev. "It was those reckless driving ones that did it." His hand inched a little higher, getting lost under the yards of netting that made up her petticoat.

"That was total crap," said Nikki. "There was nothing reckless about my driving. I had everything under—" she gulped as his hand found the edge of her panties. "Control." "Control" came out in a wavering tone and she bit her lip.

"You probably shouldn't have gone over the middle of the traffic circle," he said, sliding a finger under the edge of her panties.

"Traffic circles impede speed."

"That is what they're designed to do," he agreed.

"And it was an emergency." She breathed out audibly. She was working very hard to keep track of the conversation.

"Definitely an emergency," he agreed. The motel was finally in sight and Nikki was flipping off the ignition practically before she had finished parking.

"You are a danger to the highways," she said, taking off her seatbelt.

"I wasn't the one driving," he said, pulling her out of the driver's seat and into his lap.

"You were causing reckless endangerment of pedestrians," she said between kisses and loosening his tie.

"You know it turns you on." He paused a few moments later. "Seriously, are you wearing a tutu? What is going on with this dress?"

Nikki giggled. "It's the petticoat for my 1950s photo shoot. So the dress is extra fluffy."

"Extra fluffy in all the wrong places. No wonder everyone in the fifties slept in separate beds. I can't actually find you under all this crap."

"Well, we could go into your room," said Nikki. "I'll show you how it comes off."

"A plan I can get behind." He opened the door and there was a tangle of limbs as they tried to exit the car gracefully. Finally upright, she leaned against the car, panting a little. "No more petticoats," he said, reaching back into the car for her purse and locking the door. "From now on, we stick to decades with less underwear. The seventies, for instance. I fully support the braless seventies."

"You say that now," said Nikki, taking her purse. "But I'm not sure how you'd look in bellbottoms." She surveyed his butt as he led the way to his motel room. "On the other hand, maybe it would be fine."

"No, it wouldn't," he said, unlocking the door, and snapping on the light. "I'd have to buy Chuck Norris Action Slacks."

Nikki laughed and turned to shut the door. "Z'ev? How much money did you take off those guys at craps?"

"Five hundred bucks or so. Nothing big, why?"

Nikki stared at the car parked across the street in the Kessel Run parking lot. Maybe it was nothing. Maybe she'd seen it in her rear view mirror on the drive.

"No reason," said Nikki, shutting the door. "I'm sure it's fine."

Z'ev looked at her and then flicked off the light and went to the window. The neon arrow from the Kessel Run illuminated the room in successive bursts of blue and green. "I don't recognize the car," he said, "But someone is definitely inside." There was the flare of a lighter and they could both see the glowing tip of the cigarette for a moment.

"It's probably someone smoking before they go into the Kessel Run," said Nikki.

"Is there any reason to think it isn't?" asked Z'ev looking at Nikki.

"No," she said smiling. "I'm just paranoid about motels ever since I saw that *Vacancy* movie."

A woman got out of the car, barely a silhouette in the light from the parking lot, snubbed out the cigarette on the ground and went into the Kessel Run.

"Uh-huh." He shut the curtain, locked the door, and turned on the bedside light before beginning his evening routine. As usual, his things were laid out with OCD precision and while Nikki watched, he removed his wallet and placed it on the bedside table, followed by his watch. His tie came off and was folded and placed next to his bag. Nikki picked up the tie and began rolling it. He fiddled with his phone, dialing up music and placed it on the table.

"What are you doing?" he asked removing the now rolled tie from her hands.

"If you fold a tie for packing it gets creases. It's better to roll it."

He'd set the station to 1940s pop and after setting down the tie with a shake of his head, he pulled her into a dreamy box waltz.

Nikki sighed as she relaxed into his shoulder. "Have I mentioned that I love that you dance?"

"Once or twice. You caused me to write my grandmother a

thank you note. My mother was annoyed."

"Why was your mom annoyed?"

"Well, apparently forcing me to go to those dance lessons was serious work for my mom, and she only stuck with it because Grandma insisted, but she thought it was sort of useless. And getting my note made Grandma so smug she was insufferable for a week."

Nikki giggled and then sighed again. "I missed you." His arm tightened around her waist, but he didn't reply. Instead, he kissed her neck, following along the curve until he got to the spot just behind her ear.

"You were going to show me how the dress comes off?" he murmured.

"Ah, yes, it's very complicated. There's a zipper at the back."

"Mm-hmm." His hands found the zipper and inched slowly downward, exposing one inch of skin to the air-conditioned room at a time. Nikki began to unbutton his shirt, returning the favor. "Does it go up or down?"

"The zipper goes both ways," said Nikki and was rewarded with a pinch to her butt, barely felt through the petticoat. She giggled. "The dress goes up." The dress was yanked over her head and as she laughed, he pushed her backwards onto the bed. "You still haven't dealt with the petticoat."

"What? Are you in a hurry?" He picked up her foot and gently removed her shoe before flinging it across the room.

"Yes! One month, Z'ev. It's been one month!"

"So what you're saying is that you want me to get closer?" The other shoe went spinning through the air.

"There's something wrong with you. Normal men—" Whatever Nikki had been about to say next was silenced by Z'ev's mouth.

The petticoat was brutally removed and her bra was popped off with a speed and efficiency that sent it flying across the room.

An hour later, as they lay in the darkness entangled in the sheets, Z'ev fumbled with his phone to turn off the music. In the silence that followed, Nikki snuggled against him and then pushed away.

"You're too warm," she complained.

"And you are like a tiny oven," he murmured back. "I could bake pizza on your stomach."

"We're not very sexy, are we?" she asked plaintively.

"What are you talking about?" he asked, disbelief coloring his tone. "How on earth was that not sexy? We are sexy as hell. We are so sexy, they probably have a photo of us in the dictionary under sexy."

"No, I'm not complaining about the sex. The sex was sexy. But you and I, we're not very… we should be snuggling and looking romantically at each other. Instead, we're complaining about the heat. I mean, we even waited until after dinner to tear each other's clothes off."

"Because you are a tiny furnace. And we had to wait until after dinner. It would have been rude otherwise. Seriously, it's hot. Did the air conditioning turn off? I hadn't realized that Washington was so hot. I thought it was supposed to rain all the time."

"West of the Cascades. East of the mountains it's a whole different weather system and it's hot, hot, hot."

"I think I can see a mirage in the heat waves coming off your thighs."

Nikki chuckled. "This is what I'm talking about. How is that sexy talk?"

"You've been watching too many movies," he said. "We're

real people sexy." He flipped over onto his stomach, a position that Nikki knew meant sleep was imminent. "Real people would feel like idiots if they talked like sexy people all the time. Besides, who's defining sexy? I'm not talking like some idiot *Fifty Shades of Grey* character. Here, I'll tell you what," he reached out and pulled her closer. "Your lips are a scarlet thread and your words enchanting. Your cheeks, behind your veil, are halves of pomegranate."

"What?"

"Song of Solomon. My love for you is like a gazelle, yadda yadda yadda."

Nikki wanted to laugh and make his quotes a joke, but she couldn't. There was something very serious about having a man quote the Bible at her, and besides, Z'ev was already unconscious on the last yadda. She lay next to him for a long time before falling asleep.

AUGUST XVII

PLANNING COMMISSION

Friday

"So," said Jenny, when Nikki had finished catching them up on her excursion to the body shop. "The DEA is right, there's definitely a smuggling pipeline coming through here. Bill Pims is using modified cars to get it across the border and they're doing it here because frequent trips across the border aren't unusual. So what's the problem? Let's tip off the DEA."

"Or better yet, your friend Donny," said Ellen, stroking by on an inner tube.

"Bill's not the boss," said Nikki. "And although I might be able to tell Donny I illegally searched the body shop, there's not much he or the DEA can do without evidence. But that's not really what I'm worried about."

"What's got you worried?" Jenny flicked water out of the pond with her feet and onto her inner tube.

"Ylina. We have the time to sit on the smuggling situation and consider what the best course of action is, but she's running scared. Whoever the boss is, she's scared of him. I think we need to find her and get her out of town."

"She didn't sound very receptive," said Jenny.

"She wasn't," agreed Nikki. "But that's hardly surprising. There's no Carrie Mae branch nearby, no Carrie Mae lady to lay the groundwork. All Ylina knows is that some crazy chick in a bar beat up her co-conspirators and now wants to 'help' her. I'd be suspicious too."

"Well, and not to violate the prime directive, but here's a question," said Ellen. "Just because she's a woman, are we obligated to help her? We don't know she was coerced. They could be co-conspirators. If she got herself mixed up in drug smuggling, maybe she should reap the consequences."

"And if the consequences were going to jail," said Nikki, applying more sunscreen and scooting further into the shade of a beach umbrella propped in the fork of a tree, "I'd agree with you, but the sheriff here seems more likely to deport her and a drug kingpin isn't likely to turn her over for a jury by law either. She's headed for trouble."

"So then we have two options," said Jenny, kicking back toward the shore of the pond. "Find the drug kingpin and eliminate him, either by having him arrested or something more permanent. Or find Ylina and get her out of town, then tip off the DEA."

"I think we should pursue both," said Ellen, stretching out on her inner tube.

"I also want to hear what Donny has to say tonight at the Fiesta," said Nikki. "He keeps saying that he needs to talk and he's hinted that it's work related. Maybe he's got a line on the drug smuggling that we don't know about."

"That would make it easier," agreed Jenny. "Although, that seems unlikely. I mean, when does anything go 'easier' for us?"

"Sometimes it does," protested Ellen, sounding closer and closer to being asleep. "By the way, has anyone seen Jane?"

"She's in my room, going through the clothes with Grandma," said Nikki. "I think she's picking out outfits for you and Jenny to wear."

"She'd better not be. I'm not involved in that pinup girl train wreck." Ellen lifted up her sunglasses to glare at Nikki as if the pinup girl train wreck was Nikki's fault. Which, upon reflection, it sort of was.

"What about Z'ev? Where's he at?" asked Jenny.

"Back at the hotel. I'm meeting him in town for lunch and then we're coming back here to hang out. You guys, what am I going to do? I can't have him staying at a hotel."

"You mean, you can't be staying at a hotel," said Ellen. "Don't think we didn't notice you sneaking in this morning at the crack of dawn."

"I did not sneak," said Nikki vehemently. "But staying at a hotel is ridiculous for all parties concerned."

"Yeah, but your grandma's eyes kind of bugged when Jane assumed he was going to stay with you," said Jenny. "It's her house. I think you have to respect her wishes."

"We already live together," said Nikki. "It's ridiculous!"

"Then you should have said something last night," said Ellen.

"I froze. It's not a conversation that I've ever had to have before. Maybe I can get Mom to talk to her," said Nikki with a sigh. "That went OK, right? She seemed to like Z'ev."

"Oh, yeah, she is definitely Team Z'ev," agreed Jenny.

"But your grandma is clearly Team Jackson," said Ellen. "What's that about?"

"He has eighty-three acres," said Nikki, as if that explained everything. "And he really is a nice guy. I think that's probably why I was so heartbroken up when we split up. We had always been friends and losing him wasn't just losing a boyfriend, it was like losing my best friend besides."

"I think he's dreamy," sighed Jenny, paddling by again.

"Yes, we all know," said Ellen.

Jenny sighed again. "I wish I really could date him," she said wistfully.

"Speaking of your mom and grandma," said Ellen, paddling over to the shore and arriving dripping on Nikki's blanket. "Was it just me or were they weirdly twitchy?"

"Yeah, they're fighting about something. I'm not sure yet what it is. They'll tell me eventually, or one of them will slip up. I'm not really in a hurry to involve myself in whatever drama they've cooked up."

"Yeah, but…" Ellen trailed off and then shrugged.

"Yeah, but what?"

"I don't know. I thought they seemed extra twitchy about the pot conversation."

"Do you think one of them is involved?" asked Ellen seriously and Nikki burst out laughing. "What? You've said before how farms always have financial troubles. Maybe Peg's farm is a stopover on the green underground."

This caused Nikki to laugh even harder.

"I don't think she's taking your slang seriously," said Jenny.

"Well, fine. Whatever you want to call it. Peg could be involved."

"Not a chance," said Nikki, finally recovering. "When my mom found out that I tried pot in college she about lost her nut. And then Grandma called and followed up Mom's rant with one of her own. They both voted against Initiative 502 and legalizing marijuana. I doubt you could find two people more opposed to marijuana and anything related to marijuana than those two."

"Could be a clever cover," said Ellen, leaning back on the blanket.

"Yes, a cover story they've been working on for over a decade." Nikki shook her head in disbelief. "That sounds highly unlikely. Anyway, I'm going to go talk to Mom, see if she can't convince Grandma to let Z'ev at least stay somewhere in the house."

Nell was easy to find. She stood on the porch, hands on her hips, the picture of angry womanhood.

"Have you seen your grandmother?"

"No, she probably went down to the orchard to check in."

"I don't know why. Jorge runs it all just fine without her."

"She likes to keep tabs on her farm. What's wrong with that?"

Nell flapped her hands in annoyance at Nikki's comment.

"But speaking of Grandma. Do you think you could talk to her about letting Z'ev stay at the house? Having him stay at a hotel is embarrassing."

"Sure. I mean, I'll try. But honestly, you should just pack him up and bring him here tonight. She can't kick him out and she'd never be rude to his face. That's how I got your father through the door."

Nikki laughed. "I'll do it."

"I'm sure you don't care what I think, but I really do like him."

"You like him because he's not a farmer."

"I like him because he can provide for you without both of you having to scrape and work all your lives. So yes, that means, not a farmer."

"I don't have to be provided for, Mom."

"And neither do I, but it would be nice to have the option to not be strong all the time."

Nikki bit back a sarcastic reply. There was something incredibly sad about that statement. On impulse she kissed her mother on the cheek. "You don't have to be strong all the time, Mom. I'll take care of you."

Nell look startled and clearly at a loss for words.

"Anyway, I'm going to go meet Z'ev for lunch and then I think you're right, I'll bring him back here."

"How are you going to meet him? Your grandmother has the car."

"I'm going to take my car."

"It doesn't have any air conditioning."

"So we'll roll down the windows. Is there some place you wanted to go, Mom?"

"Yes, I wanted to go into town and see Leona."

"You could take Grandpa's truck. It's in the shed."

"Does it still run?"

"Sure, I think Grandma keeps it for hauling stuff."

"It doesn't have any air either. If I go to the beauty parlor, my hair will be sweated out by the time I get home. Can you stop by the orchard and tell your grandmother to come back. I wanted to use her car."

"Sure," said Nikki wanting to leave before her mother came up with a laundry list of chores or messages to deliver.

Nikki made the short trip down to the orchard. The orchard, with its neatly placed rows of peach trees, should have seemed the picture of bucolic farminess, but it always reminded Nikki most strongly of a construction job site. It was organized and run from a rickety trailer that smelled of damp and still faintly of skunk from the time a skunk had crawled under the trailer and died. They had removed the skunk and relocated the trailer to a new site, but even bleaching the floorboards hadn't quite removed the stink. In front of the trailer, there was a tiny parking area, mostly for the four-wheel ATVs that pulled trailers full of peaches from the orchard to the barn.

Nikki parked the car next to Peg's SUV and Jorge's blue Toyota Tacoma and got out. A large whiteboard in front of the trailer showed a list of names and assignments. She could hear the rumble of ATVs further out in the orchard, but none were close to the trailer.

She walked up the stairs and reached out to open the door and then stopped. Something was wrong. She should have been able to hear voices through the paper thin walls. Feeling a little silly, she pressed her ear to the door. She could hear the soft rustle of movement, but no voices. Frowning, Nikki leaned off the stairs and peered through the window. She was able to hold the position for only a few seconds and then had to jump off or fall over.

Hurrying back to the truck, she climbed in and drove away. She had been right. She was not prepared to deal with her family's drama.

She pulled up at the Kessel Run and shoved her way past Harrison Ford. "Clyde, I need a shot of Yukon Jack stat!"

Z'ev looked up from his menu. "Yukon Jack?" he asked as Clyde poured. Nikki gulped it down and slammed the shot glass back on the bar.

"Thanks Clyde, now bring me a margarita, and don't spare the tequila."

She collapsed in a chair opposite Z'ev, and fanned herself with a napkin.

"Bad morning with your mom?"

"My mom was actually supportive and fine," said Nikki. And then leaned in closer to whisper. "I think we're in the matrix."

"If we were in the matrix then your mom being supportive and fine would be a dead giveaway, wouldn't it?"

"*Twilight Zone?*"

"Maybe. Why,,,,, what happened?"

"So I stopped by the orchard on my way here, to tell Grandma that Mom wanted to use the car and I happened to look in the window of the job trailer and..."

"And what?"

"I saw Grandma making out with Jorge, her foreman."

Z'ev grinned. "Yeah, he's her foreman."

"It's not funny! I may be scarred for life."

"Well, at least now you know what they were arguing about last night."

Nikki shrugged. "I can't believe they were arguing about that. So Grandma has a boyfriend. Why is that a big thing? You know, as long as I don't have to see it."

"Different generations think different stuff is a big deal," he said with a shrug.

"Well, the question is, do I tell them I know, or do I wait for them to tell me?"

"Wait," said Z'ev firmly. "Do you really want to get into a discussion of how you know?"

"Excellent point," said Nikki.

"Are you sure you want to eat here?" asked Z'ev, wiping off his menu with the corner of a napkin.

"Yeah, the food's fantastic. I just try not to touch anything. After lunch, I think we should check you out of the hotel."

"Your grandma changed her mind?" he asked, raising an eyebrow.

"Mom said she'd talk to Grandma," replied Nikki.

"Hmm," said Z'ev.

"Hmm, what?"

"Well, you know your family best. I don't want to cause an argument. Plus, last night you weren't exactly demanding that I stay with you."

"I told you, I froze," said Nikki.

"Nikki," he said.

Nikki felt the butterfly of panic start to flap in the pit of her stomach. He was going to say something serious. She couldn't do serious. Not in front of Clyde and Han Solo.

"Nothing. Let's just eat lunch."

Nikki wanted to argue, but she knew it wasn't in her best interest. They had been skating along the surface of their relationship for too long. There were cracks in the ice, but they just kept skating. Sooner or later the ice was going to break and that was going to be a bad day for everyone.

Returning to the farm, they parked next to Jackson's F-150. She could see Jackson out in the paddock, cleaning up Donna's area and fixing the hay bales to the goat's specifications. "Oh, shoot. He's making me look bad. I was going to do that later this afternoon."

"Your ex-boyfriend sure hangs around a lot," said Z'ev.

Nikki shrugged. "He and Grandma always got along. I think it's nice that he helps her. I wonder if he knows about Jorge?"

"Seems like something he would have told you, doesn't it?" Z'ev climbed out of the truck and pulled his single bag out of the truck bed.

Nikki shrugged again. "Jackson is not known to be verbose."

Z'ev laughed. "Did he sign up for the Louis L'Amour school of How to Be a Cowboy, or what?"

"Hey, there is nothing wrong with the Louis L'Amour school," said Nikki, feeling annoyed. "The world could use a few more straight-shooting white hats in it."

"White hats get dirty," said Z'ev.

"Stop being metaphorical," snapped Nikki, knowing she sounded like her mother and hating it.

"I wasn't actually. White hats collect dirt and sweat too easily."

Nikki showed Z'ev to her room and went back downstairs while he unpacked. She was still annoyed about his crack about Jackson. Still annoyed about everything, actually.

She grabbed a few sodas from the fridge and walked out to the paddock, then climbed up onto the fence rail and sat, watching Jackson. He had his shirt off and was rambling around in his jeans, cowboy hat and work gloves. He'd worked up a sweat and Nikki had to admire the sharp v-shape of his lat muscles as he hefted a bale of hay from the truck. He ignored her, reaching into his pocket and flicking his pocketknife open with a quick snap of the wrist. It made a sharp clicking noise and Nikki suspected that in a pinch it would be faster than a switchblade. He slit the twine on a bay of hale and reached for a pitchfork.

"I was going to get to it later today," she said. "I told you, you didn't have to help."

"And I told you that I didn't mind helping. Besides, you were gonna be out here in your snappy clothes and shovel the horse shit?"

"I was gonna change. I do have other clothes."

"I believe that you have lots of clothes," he commented with a half twitch of a smile.

"I brought you a soda pop," she said, holding up two cans still on their plastic leash. "But if you're going to insult my clothes I don't think I'll give it to you after all." He leaned the fork against the barn and walked over.

"I love your clothes," he said, putting one foot on the bottom rail and leaning his elbows on the top, facing Nikki. "I wouldn't dream of insulting them." His face was perfectly serious, but there was a twinkle in his eye. Nikki laughed and handed him a can, keeping the other for herself.

He smelled like hay and Nikki let her gaze run down the length of his torso. He had a scar that ran from his ribs to his back. It was wide and had the slightly shiny, stretched look of a cut that hadn't been sewn up properly.

"What'd you do?" she asked pointing at the ugly scar.

He glanced down at himself as if he'd forgotten there was something there.

"Got tagged by a bull," he said, popping open his soda. "Ugly son of a bitch snagged me in between the tabs on my vest and dug right in. Threw me like a slingshot. I've got it on my highlight tape if you want to see it." Nikki climbed up on the fence to sit on the top rail.

Nikki laughed and opened the other soda. "I think I would actually. That sounds worth seeing." Jackson shrugged. "What about that one?" she asked pointing to the scar on his face.

He shrugged again. "Who can remember anymore?" He turned around to lean his elbows on the fence and stare out into the orchard. "So, you've got this big fella with you."

"Z'ev," said Nikki. "His name is Z'ev."

"Yeah," he said and Nikki couldn't tell if he was agreeing or if there was some sort of subtext that she was supposed to be picking up on. "He seems pretty stuck on you."

"I'm pretty stuck on him."

"Yeah, but…"

"Yeah, but, what?"

Jackson turned around again, a sudden return to his old restless self.

"But he doesn't know, does he?"

"Doesn't know what?" asked Nikki, feeling her fingertips go icy on the soda can and her palms clammy.

"He doesn't really know you. He doesn't know about things like bar fights and how you keep yourself out of 'trouble.' Does he?"

"He suspects," said Nikki quietly.

"And that's got you worried."

"Yes," she whispered.

"You don't want to leave, but you're afraid you can't stay."

"Yes," she whispered again. She stared out past the barn, past the orchard and into the purple smudge of mountains. Jackson finished the can in one long drink and emptied out the last dribble into the hay before crushing the can between his hands. Behind her, she heard the screen door slam.

"He's coming our way," Jackson said. Nikki didn't look around, trying to compose her face into something presentable. Jackson swung around, heading for his hay bale.

"When the time comes, if you need a place to go," he said, looking back at her, "my door is always open."

"Thought I'd come and see if I could help," said Z'ev arriving and raising his voice to carry across to Jackson.

"No need," said Jackson, waving his hand. "I'm about done for the day." He finished scattering the hay and shouldered his pitchfork, carrying it into the barn.

Z'ev glanced up at Nikki and she looked back, seeing the sweetness in his face that he was so careful to hide most of the time.

"What's the matter?" he asked frowning and searching her face.

"Nothing," she answered. His eyes jumped to Jackson suspiciously and Nikki pulled herself together. She leaned down and kissed him. "Come on," she said jumping off the fence. "I'll show you the barn and you can meet Donna and Fidget the Goat."

They were on their way back to the house—being head butted by Fidget could only hold someone's interest for so long—when they heard Nell and Peg arguing.

"I didn't hear the car pull in," said Nikki.

"She's got to be told," said Peg.

"And I totally disagree," said Nell. Nikki could hear her feet on the wooden porch steps. She glanced at Z'ev who winked. Nikki smothered a laugh behind her hand.

"Don't you walk away from me, young lady," said Peg, hurrying after her if the quick shuffle Nikki heard was any indication.

"They really have their panties in a twist over this Jorge situation," said Z'ev.

"I know," said Nikki. "I feel bad. Maybe I should tell them that I know."

"You keep claiming that your mom has been a constant thorn in your side, and you're going to pass up the opportunity to let her suffer a little bit?" Z'ev sighed mockingly and hugged her. "You're too soft-hearted."

"I just like making you think that," said Nikki, only half-joking.

By the time they'd followed Nell and Peg into the house, the argument had either simmered down or been silenced by Nikki's Carrie Mae teammates, who were chattering and clearly dressed for a party. Jane was wearing a sleeveless 1970s polyester dress in a nude beige that, on her very pale skin, looked fantastic.

"Nikki, what do you think of this dress?" demanded Jenny upon their entry. "Jane, do a twirl for Nikki. I think tans like that always make a person look naked from a distance, but Ellen thinks it looks good."

"I think you're both right," said Nikki. "I think Jane looks great in that dress and from a distance someone will probably think she's naked."

Jane smirked at Jenny. "Is it appropriate for the party with Donny's family? I don't want to be overdressed for a family BBQ. And you know, I'm trying to wear less black."

"Ah, well, see here's the thing about the Fernandez BBQ's," said Nikki. "Donny has a very extensive family. And they all have a rather inclusive idea about what constitutes family. And their property is next to a junkyard and the river, so there's a lot of space. So when they say it's a family BBQ, what the really mean, is that half the town will be there and the other half will be calling the cops with a noise complaint."

"So am I over or underdressed?" asked Jane frowning.

"Perfectly dressed," said Nikki.

"OK, whew. I didn't want to have to wear any of my own clothes."

"God forbid," said Ellen. "Nikki, that's not what you're wearing, is it? She gave Nikki's shorts and T-shirt a disapproving frown.

"No, I'm going to change."

"Should I change? You guys make me fashion paranoid." Z'ev glanced at his jeans and T-shirt in the mirror nervously.

"No, you're fine," laughed Nikki. "I'll just be a minute."

But it was several minutes later and Z'ev had gone to change his shirt by the time they all climbed into Peg's SUV for the trip to the Fernandez house. Jane was carrying a pie because Peg didn't feel comfortable sending them to a BBQ without something to contribute.

The road followed the meandering curve of the Columbia and as Nikki drove, her mood alternated between fond reminiscence and annoyed surprise at each change in the landscape that she spotted. Everything seemed to be changing. More development, more houses, more people everywhere she looked. One thing had not changed however, the fat Studebaker standing on its trunk, the front wheels, or what was left of them reaching skyward to mark the entrance to the junkyard. When Nikki saw that, she knew it was time to turn at the next driveway. The Studebaker was more rusted than ever and she could see a bird's nest now resided in the driver's side wheel well, but it still stood, right where Crazy Cooter Johnson had planted it. The long gravel driveway led through a field studded with similarly planted cars, sticking up through the long grass, some tilted at drunken angles.

"What's with the cars?" demanded Ellen staring out the window.

"That's Crazy Cooter's Junkyard," said Nikki turning into the Fernandez driveway. "He calls them modern art. If you go further down he's got a regular junkyard operation, but he says it would be rude to have such ugliness next to the road where everyone can see it. So he puts the cars out for people to look at. Jackson, Donny, and I used to play out there all the time."

"That sounds totally unsafe," said Ellen. "What if a car fell on you?"

"Umm, I don't know," said Nikki, who was surprised that she had never considered that. "He's got them pretty well anchored.

We used to climb on them all the time. They never seemed tippy."

"We used to ride on top of the ATV when Grandpa would load it in the back of the truck," said Jenny. "It's funny the things you did as a kid that sort of horrify us now."

"Lawn darts," said Z'ev. "Tiny metal javelins for kids to throw at each other. What could go wrong with that?"

Nikki parked the SUV next to a low-rider El Camino, last in a string of cars that lined the long gravel drive down to a brown house hidden behind some aspen trees. "I forgot we were going to see Mexicans. I should have driven the Impala."

"Nikki!" protested Jane, but only halfheartedly as they began to walk toward the house.

"What? How is that racist?"

"It's stereotyping," said Jane. "Mexicans do not all like cars."

"I'm glad that we have our own personal PC police," said Nikki. "It makes us unique."

"Is that Jackson's truck?" said Jenny pointing.

"Yeah," said Nikki. "Although, how you can tell one jacked-up F-150 from another is beyond me. I think that's why so many of them have stickers on the bumpers. It's so they don't get into the wrong truck at WalMart."

"Nikki!" said Jane again.

"What?"

"Now you're redneck stereotyping."

"Jane," said Z'ev gently, "you know she does it on purpose, right?"

"Does what?"

"She says non-PC crap just to mess with you," said Jenny. "Although, that is totally true about the bumper stickers and WalMart."

"Nikki, do you do that? And Jenny, stop slandering citizens of rural areas."

"Of course I do that," said Nikki.

"Rednecks," said Jenny. "We're rednecks. And we like trucks, WalMart, and beer. Get over it."

"I don't think," began Jane, and then they rounded the corner to the back of the house and stopped. The patio of the Fernandez household was strung with party lights and held about two hundred people. In the gathering gloom of nightfall the looming hulks of the junkyard could be seen off to the left and the river glittered in the distance, reflecting the last few rays of sunset. "Oh," said Jane. "We didn't bring enough pie."

AUGUST XVIII

RUNNING IN THE DARK

"Nikki!" shouted one of the people in the crowd.

Nikki's head swiveled, trying to spot the source. A tall brunette made her way off the dance floor, swaying slightly. It was a little difficult to tell if Gloria Estefan had been right and the rhythm had gotten her or if it was the rum and coke in her hand.

"Hey, Jackie! Everyone, this is Donny's cousin, Jackie." She embraced the dark-haired girl in the sequined blue top.

"Donny said you were coming! I said I'd believe it when I saw it."

"Why wouldn't I show up?" asked Nikki.

"Because you're all 'big time, I make out with rock stars' now."

Next to her, she felt rather than heard Z'ev make an annoyed grunt.

"Yeah, that was kind of a misunderstanding," said Nikki.

"I don't think he misunderstood where his hands were. That guy is super hot."

"Jackie, I'd like you to meet my boyfriend, Z'ev Coralles," Nikki interjected, trying to divert the flow of conversation.

"Ha!" Jackie laughed and tipped a little of her drink out onto the ground. "Awesome. Donny and Jackson are over there somewhere." She waved in the general direction of the bar.

"Good," said Z'ev. "I could use a drink."

"I'm following him," said Jenny.

"Ditto," said Ellen.

"I brought pie," said Jane, looking star struck at Jackie.

"Jackie, this is Jane," said Nikki.

"I like pie," said Jackie.

"Jane's a little bit of a lesbian," said Nikki.

Jane looked horrified.

"So am I!" yelled Jackie, throwing up her hands, flinging more of her beverage around. "This will be awesome—later we can make out. But the real question is, do you know how to dance?"

Jane looked back as Jackie led her away, and Nikki waved goodbye. "I think we may need to go rescue Jane later," said Nikki, joining the group at the bar and fishing around in one of the ice buckets for a soda pop.

"There's beer on tap and margaritas in the pitcher," said Ellen, looking up from her conversation with Donny.

"What'd you do, send her off with Jackie?" asked Donny. "You're never going to see her again. There's real booze back here ,too. I found Z'ev some nice bourbon."

"I want to play tag later," said Nikki. "I don't want to get too drunk."

"We're not going to play tag," said Donny dismissively.

"You say that every time," said Nikki. "And then your dad brings out the flashlights."

"Yeah, but we're all too old and too drunk for that," said Donny.

"That's why I'm drinking soda."

"Tag?" asked Ellen.

"Flashlight tag or jailbreak," said Nikki. "Out in the car field. It's fun. We used to do it all the time when we were kids."

"No, seriously, we don't do it anymore," said Donny. "The

little kids aren't old enough, and the old kids are too old and fat."
He patted his stomach, which was far from fat.

"Oh," said Nikki, feeling a wave of nostalgic sadness. "I was looking forward to that."

"If you want, you can borrow some flashlights and walk out there though," said Donny. "I'm sure Dad still has them all prepped up and ready to go."

"Maybe. It's not the same if no one's chasing you."

"Isn't that the truth," said Donny, laughing.

"What are we talking about? Who's it for tag?" asked Jackson. "I came prepared. I wore tennis shoes instead of boots." He held up one foot to demonstrate.

"Are you sure you won't lose some sort of cowboy points for not wearing boots?" asked Nikki.

"Don't worry, I've got plenty in the bank," said Jackson, smirking.

"You guys, we're not playing tag," said Donny.

"What?" Jackson looked at Nikki for confirmation and Nikki shrugged.

"But I've been training for *American Ninja Warrior*. I was totally going to kick your ass tonight."

"That is literally my favorite show," said Jenny.

"I built a warped wall in my barn," said Jackson. "You can try it if you want." Jenny's eyes widened as if he had offered her a stack of gold.

"Yes, but her second favorite show is *The Bachlorette*," said Nikki.

"What? That show is terrible."

"I like to make fun of the contestants and throw things at the TV," Jenny said, glaring at Nikki.

"That could make it more fun," agreed Jackson. "But you'd still have to watch it."

"The three amigos! *Juntos otra vez!*"

"Nikki, Jackson, you remember my dad. Dad these are Nikki's friend's Ellen, and Jenny. Jane is somewhere with cousin Jackie."

"*Nunca podría volver a verla.*"

"*Hola*, Mr. Fernandez," said Nikki as he hugged her. "*Esta es mi novio, Z'ev Coralles.*"

"*Es grande*," he said, shaking hands with Z'ev.

"He also *habla espanol*," said Z'ev.

Mr. Fernandez laughed. "That's good. Jackson," he reached out to shake Jackson's hand. "Always so good to see you. Thank you for helping my nephew get that job in Calgary."

Jackson shrugged. "Any time." Donny looked from his father to Jackson. "Talented horse people are hard to come by. My friend was happy to have qualified help."

"When did you do that?" asked Donny.

Jackson shrugged again. "Couple of years ago, when your dad called."

"My dad called? Why does no one tell me these things?"

"Mr. Fernandez, Donny says we're not playing flashlight tag," said Jackson, ignoring Donny.

"You want to play tag? Of course, we can play! I will get the flashlights!"

"What'd you do that for?" demanded Donny. "Now he's going to try and roust the whole party."

"Good," said Jackson. "Nikki and I want to play."

"That's right," said Nikki. "Now pick whose team you're going to be on."

"Oh, come on," whined Donny. "This is why I hate playing with you guys. I always have to pick and then there's the running. I hate the running."

"You getting tubby in your old age?" Nikki poked him in the side.

"I think so," said Jackson. "Tubby and soft. He doesn't want to lose."

"This is ridiculous," said Donny, batting at their fingers. "I'm not choosing."

"OK," said Jackson. "We'll pick. I get Jenny and Ellen."

"That's my team! You can't have my team."

"They're my team now. You can have Donny and *Es Grande*," said Jackson.

Nikki looked doubtfully at Donny and Z'ev. "Fine, but I'm keeping Jane."

"That's cool with me because if you've got Jane you've also got Jackie."

"Damn it!"

"The tactical errors keep piling up. You are going down, Red."

"Why do I feel like we just got picked last in gym class?" asked Donny, turning to Z'ev.

"Because we just got picked last in gym class," said Z'ev. "Nikki, this isn't going to be another paintball situation, is it?"

"No, because Jackson's not a whiner like those stock brokers," said Nikki. "Come on, we need to find Jane. And Donny, you need to help me pick out your most athletic, least drunk relatives."

"What happened in paintball?" asked Donny.

"Some stock brokers got painted with extreme prejudice,"

said Z'ev.

By the time they were all gathered around the red Buick and Mr. Fernandez had set up the judge's lawn chair and the judge's margarita pitcher, the teams were fairly evenly divided. A few younger cousins and Donny's marathon-running uncle had migrated to Nikki's team, while Jackson had pulled the weight lifting auntie and the spin-class obsessed mother of twins who looked about as competitive as Nikki. Nikki made a mental note to put her down for Carrie Mae outreach. There was no reason not to have a Carrie Mae operative in Kaniksu Falls.

"OK," said Mr. Fernandez, passing out a flashlight and a strip of blue or red cloth to each player. "The red Buick here is jail. If you get caught you have to go to jail. You can escape from jail if someone on your team sneaks up, touches the Buick and yells 'jail break.' In order to get caught the other team must shine their flashlight on you, and yell your name. If you don't know the person's name you can yell 'Blue, I see you.' Once caught, you must be escorted back to the Buick. You must leave your flashlight on at all times. The boundaries are the road, the green Chevys, our property line, and the junkyard fence. The game ends in one hour. Nikki's team are the foxes, Jackson's team are the rabbits. Rabbits you get a two minute head start." Mr. Fernandez checked his watch.

"I don't have the appropriate gear for this," said Jane. "We need radios, night vision. Maybe some sonar."

"Hour starts now. Run, rabbits, run!" Mr. Fernandez threw his hand up in the air and Jackson's team scattered.

Nikki, turned and inspected her team. "Jane and Jackie are going to be the jailers. They're in charge of patrolling to make sure no one sneaks up and releases our prisoners. Jane, if you could figure out how to climb up into the Buick and yell directions if you spot anyone, that would be really helpful. Everyone else, pair up. If you catch someone, one of you escorts the prisoner, the other keeps looking. But agree on a meeting point before you separate. Remember, if Jane yells directions, they will all be based off the Buick. Three o'clock will be passenger side, six will be roof side, nine will be the driver's side, etc. Also, does every team have a watch or a phone? Good. Let's all meet back here in twenty-five minutes. We'll assess who we've caught and who's still missing."

"Two minutes is up!" yelled Mr. Fernandez settling into the lawn chair, carefully balancing his margarita and his iPhone. "Hurry up, Team Red. I'm live tweeting who gets caught!"

"You tweet? My father tweets. This is just great."

"You don't follow me?" demanded Mr. Fernandez. "I'm @ KingMoustache. I have three thousand followers."

"I'm following you now," said Jane, whipping out her phone. "I'm @BlackDeath." "Nikki," Donny said, shaking his head, "*Tío* Eli, and I are leaving now because I cannot have this conversation. But I want you to know that I blame you for making me run just when I was getting a good buzz on." The pair jogged off, Eli setting the pace, Donny following reluctantly after.

"Ready?" asked Nikki, turning to Z'ev with a smile.

"Honestly, no. Somehow I'm never quite ready for when you go rogue commando on me."

"I don't go rogue," said Nikki. "I just go commando."

"That's true," said Jane. "She doesn't like panty-lines."

"We're leaving now," said Nikki, sticking out her tongue at Jane. Jane waved, already scrutinizing the red Buick, trying to figure out the best way to climb it.

The air was hot and smelled of dried grass and the damp mud of the river. Nikki and Z'ev waded through the waist-high grass, their flashlights swinging in wide arcs. The hulking pillars of planted cars loomed around them in the darkness and above them the stars littered the sky untainted by the competing glow of city lights.

"It's nice out here," said Z'ev looking around and taking a deep breath.

"Yeah," said Nikki, reaching for his hand and leaning into his shoulder. "This is one of my favorite parts of being here." She looked up at the stars. "When you can see all the stars, you realize that it's not really dark. You can't see any stars in LA."

"We can see one or two," said Z'ev.

"You know what I mean."

"Yeah, I do." He put his arm around her and for a moment everything was perfect.

"Two flashlights, twelve o'clock!" bellowed from Jane behind them. Nikki took off at a sprint.

Forty minutes later, Nikki was gasping for air. Z'ev was escorting Jenny to the Buick. Flashlights bobbed in the field like fireflies. Still no sign of Ellen, but then she didn't really expect to find Ellen. She just wanted to get Jackson. Ahead of her, Jackson monkey-climbed over a tractor, bounced off some sort of Honda, and sprinted for the fence line. Nikki hesitated.

The field of cars was mostly rectangular, except for one part where the junkyard pushed out into the field. Jackson was following the fence line along the bulge, swinging back toward the Buick. It was clear that Jackson really had been training. He was definitely faster than her and his vertical leap was impressive. He'd cleared that loose cow without breaking stride, much to the cow's dismay.

Making a decision, Nikki hopped the fence and headed into the junkyard. She dodged freezers, leapt over a stove, and landed on the winding path formed by walls of junk that would lead straight across to the field. She stood up to run and stopped. Ahead of her, a flashlight glimmered.

"Ellen," breathed Nikki grinning. "Never trust a sniper to play by the rules."

She slipped quietly along the lane, stopping by a pile of sinks. A woman was rooting around inside the trunk of a compressed Toyota.

Nikki jumped around the corner, training her flashlight on the woman. "Ellen! Gotcha!"

Only, it wasn't Ellen. Ylina raised her hand against Nikki's flashlight. She had a gym bag in one hand.

"Jesus, Mary, and Joseph! Are you following me?"

"No! I'm playing tag."

"You're playing tag in a junkyard? What is wrong with you?"

"No, I'm cheating by cutting through—never mind that. What are you doing here?"

"None of your business," said Ylina, slamming the trunk of the car shut.

"Look, Ylina, I know about the smuggling. You and Milt and Bill Pims. You've been smuggling pot in from Canada, haven't you?"

"I don't know how you found that out, but if you know what's good for you, you'll keep your mouth shut."

"Ylina, I know you're in trouble. Why don't you let me help you?"

"Because I don't need help! I'm going to cash in my insurance policy and blow town."

"Why not blow the whistle? Turn state's evidence?" suggested Nikki.

Ylina's laugh was as surprised as it was genuine. "Yeah, right. Why don't I just sign my own death warrant? Leave me alone. I can take care of myself."

"Yeah, like you were taking care of yourself at the Kessel Run?"

"Just leave me –" Ylina abruptly cut off and turned toward the road. "Shit. This is your fault. I don't know how, but it's your fault."

The high-pitched wail of police sirens sounded from the road, like wolves howling in the distance. Ylina took off running toward the center of the junkyard. Out in the field, the flashlights began to all head for the Buick.

Nikki hesitated again, and then, cursing, she headed for the Buick, too.

AUGUST XIX
KICK MY ASS

Nikki arrived at the Buick at the same time as Ellen.

"Where is everyone?" she gasped, swinging her flashlight around.

"They all ran," said Ellen. "Most them went up to the house, but I saw Z'ev and Donny go this way."

"They must be going to the boat house," said Nikki. "Come on."

"Why the boathouse?" asked Ellen as they jogged.

"Noise complaints," said Nikki. "It looks better if they have less guests than they do. Mr. Fernandez has been stashing extra party guests at the boathouse for years."

The boathouse was a shack on the edge of the river built for storing inner tubes, canoes, and camping equipment, but also used as a woodshop and all-purpose escape from the bustle of the house. Nikki remembered it as a dusty hideaway from adults and sun. As they approached they could hear the raucous sound of male voices.

"What's going on in there?" Ellen asked.

"No clue."

They pushed through the crowd, illuminated by a single swinging bulb. Z'ev and Jackson were in the center of the crowd and as Nikki watched, Z'ev swung a punch at the smaller man. Jackson slipped a little sideways so the punch didn't land square. Z'ev came in for a body shot and Jackson let it hit, letting himself get shoved into the canoes strapped to the wall so he could rebound, coming back in double fast. He landed a flurry of blows and Z'ev staggered back, unprepared for this sudden onslaught. When he hit people, they usually stayed down. Recovering, he stayed up on the balls of his feet and swung again for his opponent. Jackson twisted sideways, aimed for the gut. Z'ev adapted to the move and flicked his elbow, landing it across Jackson's ear. The elbow shoved Jackson's head back in range for the other hand and Z'ev went for the punch. Jackson went down, but came back up like he was on strings. Then he went further up, jumping and came down with a punch on Z'ev's face that landed like a mule stomp. Z'ev went backwards, his nose bloody. Jackson followed him, allowing no quarter, putting in hooks to the gut with a staccato fury. Z'ev covered up, lowered his head, centering his weight and then shot for a tackle. Jackson spun him off with ease. But Z'ev showed no surprise at the side-slip and whirled faster than Jackson had been expecting, landing a heavy fist across the side of Jackson's face; he'd just wanted the distance.

Jackson backed up and they squared off again, staring at each other. They were both bloody now. Along the side of the room, Rey-Rey was hosting the betting pool.

"Fifty on Jackson. He never loses," called Louis.

"Nobody's lasted this long before," countered Rey-Rey. Whatever he would have said next was lost in the noise as Z'ev made another charge. The crowd moved in around them, obscuring them from Nikki's view.

"Nikki, you need to stop them!" demanded Donny, pushing through the crowd.

"Me? What the hell are they arguing about? I left them with you."

"Jackson said something. I don't know what. I think it was something about you. And then Z'ev got mad and the next thing I know, they're fighting. Are you going to stop them?"

"I'm thinking," replied Nikki, wincing as she heard the sharp sound of fist connecting with flesh.

"Thinking about what? They're going to kill each other!"

"I doubt it," answered Nikki. "I think they want to know who's top dog."

"And you go off with the winner? That's bullshit, Nikki."

"This isn't about me," snapped Nikki. "It's about who's tougher. They'd be doing this even if I wasn't involved."

"Bullshit!" repeated Donny. "And if you won't stop it, I will!" Donny began to push through the crowd.

"That's the hard way to do it," said Ellen.

"Agreed," said Nikki and then climbed up on a counter top. "Cops! Cops! Run!"

The effect was instantaneous. The crowd dissipated immediately, pushing past and in between Z'ev and Jackson, effectively blocking them from fighting further.

"Nikki, what is wrong with you?" demanded Donny, picking up Jackson. Jenny and Ellen sat Z'ev on a Seadoo. Jane ran in, panic in her eye, took in the scene, then stopped, and shrugged.

"How is this my fault?" demanded Nikki.

"How is it not?" snapped Donny. He opened up a cupboard under the workbench revealing a mini-fridge. He angrily pulled out ice packs and tossed them at Z'ev and Jackson. "Get the first aid kit out of the cupboard." He pointed to one by Nikki, and she randomly opened cupboards until she found the right one.

"It is not my fault," reiterated Nikki, inspecting the first-aid kit. "If they want to beat the crap out of each other, it's got nothing to do with me." Like most first-aid kits, it contained a smattering of bandages and nothing truly useful.

"Like hell it doesn't! They're fighting over you."

"Even if that were true, that would be their problem. I am neither a prize to be won nor responsible for their actions."

"That's right," affirmed Jane, picking straw out of her hair.

"Well, speaking for myself," began Z'ev.

"I suggest that you don't," said Nikki. She sorted through bandages and a crusty bottle of iodine before finally finding some more modern materials. "If I thought for a moment that the two of you were fighting over me, I'd kick both your asses. I do not date people based on their fighting ability."

Z'ev and Jackson exchanged glances.

"Uh, well, yeah, you do Nik. Always have," said Jackson. "Definitely an alpha male kind of girl." Nikki slammed down the bottle of hydrogen peroxide and glared at Jackson.

"You take that back! I like sensitive men."

Donny snorted in laughter.

"Yeah, men who sensitively hit hard," put in Z'ev. Nikki glared at both of them. Pouring hydrogen peroxide onto a cotton ball she jabbed it into a cut at the outside corner of Z'ev's eyebrow.

"Ow," he said flinching.

"See, he's sensitive," said Jackson.

"You shut up too," said Nikki, shoving the bottle of peroxide at Donny. Donny took it and began to clean up Jackson. Nikki was done first, and she angrily began to repack the first aid kit, gathering up the discarded band-aid wrappers.

"Your boyfriend hits hard," said Jackson, looking at Nikki as Donny taped a final butterfly bandage over a split on his cheek.

"Not hard enough," said Z'ev, creaking to his feet, and limping over to the refrigerator. He pulled out two beers and handed one to Jackson, who carefully applied the beer bottle to his eye.

"The two of you are making me crazy," said Nikki. "I wish I'd stayed in LA. I should know better than to try and go on vacation."

"Hey, we're not getting shot at, so you know, still better than work," said Z'ev.

Jenny, Ellen, and Jane all nodded.

"I wanted to have a nice quiet time with my grandma. I wanted to eat peach pie and float in the pond and have a nice time."

"We floated," said Jenny.

"There was pie," said Jane, looking around as if pie might appear. "It's probably all gone now though."

"You know where it went wrong? The Kessel Run. I should have just driven straight to Grandma's, but no, I had to stop for a burger."

"Well, Ylina's probably glad you stopped," said Jackson, shifting his beer to the other side of his ribs.

"No, she really isn't," said Nikki.

"What are you talking about?" asked Donny.

"Never mind," said Nikki, throwing up her hands. "It doesn't matter. Let's just go home."

"That's right," said Z'ev. "Because God forbid that we actually talk about anything. Just brush it under the covers. That's how the line goes isn't it?"

"Oh, my God. You're still mad about that? How are you still mad about that?"

"Man, I feel like I'm back at my parent's house," said Jackson to Donny, but looking from Nikki to Z'ev.

"I know what you mean." Donny nodded and reached in the

fridge for a beer.

"Should we do something?" asked Jackson.

"You talk to him all the time, Nikki!" yelled Z'ev.

"Nah," said Donny reassuringly. "As far as I can tell, this is what they do in between making out."

"Once a month is not all the time, Z'ev!"

"He wrote a song about you!"

"He also wrote a song about his coffee being cold and lighting his pubic hair on fire. Trust me, it's not the compliment you think it is."

"What are they talking about?" Donny staged whispered at Jenny, sitting down next to Jackson.

"I don't have to hear those on the radio." Z'ev waved his arms in huge gestures of frustration. "It's like the number two song in Brazil. It's on once an hour!"

"Kit Masters," hissed Jenny.

"Who's Kit Masters?" asked Donny, looking around the room for an explanation.

"Pop singer from England," explained Jackson. "There was a picture of him kissing Nikki on the front page of the *Star* awhile ago. It was big news around here."

"I haven't even seen Kit in four months and even then it was just dinner. What is your problem?" yelled Nikki.

"Never heard of him," answered Donny, twisting the top off his Bud Light.

"Neither had anyone else around here. Apparently he's big in Europe. Jake's Records did good business in importing his album after the picture came out. He's not bad. Catchy. If you like that kind of thing."

"My problem?" repeated Z'ev. "My problem? Well, apparently my problem is that I'm not your type."

"What the hell are you talking about?"

"I'm not your type."

"Not my… What the…" Nikki sputtered, unable to formulate words. "How are you not my type Z'ev?"

"You know," said Z'ev making gestures with hands as if squishing something down into a smaller size. "Compact and white!"

"Dude, I think he's talking about you," said Donny to Jackson.

"In case you hadn't noticed Nikki, I'm six foot two and brown!" yelled Z'ev.

"About me?" asked Jackson.

"I don't care how tall you are!" yelled Nikki, once again starting with the wrong thing first.

"Yeah, compact and white, that's you."

"Wait, I'm white?"

Donny laughed, trying not to snort beer through his nose.

"And I'm not dating your skin, I'm dating you. I don't give damn about your skin color!" She finished with the important thing.

"Everyone else around here seems to."

"You cannot blame me for their retarded attitudes."

Behind her, Nikki could hear Jane, the word police, make an annoyed noise over her use of the R word, but she could only argue with one person at a time.

"And if it comes to types, well, I'm not exactly your type either. I looked up your ex-girlfriend on Facebook. And let me tell you, next to her I look a little too compact and white."

"Then you shouldn't have snooped on Facebook. I don't ask

you about your ex-boyfriends. Although, clearly," Z'ev waved a hand at Jackson, "I should."

"I told you about Jackson," protested Nikki.

"You said he was one of those stupid high school boyfriends."

"Ouch," said Donny. "That's not right."

"It's fair. I'm not too anxious to explain Nikki to an outsider," answered Jackson with a shrug.

"That right there," yelled Z'ev, pointing at Jackson. "Why am I the outsider? I should be the insider. She's my damn girlfriend!"

"Yeah, man, I hear you. You want to know why the hell some stranger gets better from her than you?" asked Jackson, raising his beer to Z'ev.

"Stop misquoting me," snapped Nikki to Jackson. "Our situations are not at all the same."

"Ding," quoted Jackson, with a glint in his eye. "You always did like to be the bell."

"It isn't the same thing!" said Nikki, not sure who she was more mad at.

"Yes, it is," said Jackson. "You think I cheated? I had to, just to stay in the game. It's hard work keeping up with you and you were always the one who called the shots. Turns out, he's just a better fighter than I was. Don't you think you owe him the honesty you wanted from me?"

Nikki thought about punching him. She thought about punching Z'ev. She thought about dropkicking all of them out the door.

"You, shut-up," said Z'ev, pointing at Jackson. "You don't get to be on my side."

"I am leaving," Nikki announced. "I have had all the vacation fun I can handle for one night."

She stomped out of the boathouse and straight into Merv the Sheriff.

"Well, if it isn't little Nicole Lanier," said the Sheriff, overly stressing the French accents in her name. "What kind of trouble are you up to now?"

"Sheriff," began Nikki, when the boathouse door burst open and Jane and Jenny both ran out.

"Hiya, Sheriff," said Jenny. "Nikki, let's head up to the car, shall we?"

Nikki stared at her friends, puzzled. Jackson, Donny, Ellen and Z'ev came out more slowly.

"Hi, Sheriff," said Donny. "Is there a problem?"

"Well, Donald," said the Sheriff. "That depends. Are there any more of you in there?"

"No," said Donny, shaking his head. "Just us. We're on our way up to the house."

"You don't mind if I take a look do you?"

"Suit yourself," said Donny with a shrug.

"What happened to you two?" asked the sheriff, pointing at Jackson and Z'ev before opening the door to the boathouse and glancing around.

"We tripped," said Z'ev.

"Jackson, I've not known you to be the clumsy type," said the sheriff. He turned and looked at the group and smiled. Once again, the smile seemed delayed, as if the sheriff deployed it because it was the socially acceptable time to do so.

"These things happen," said Jackson.

"Hmm. Well, we've had some complaints about people trespassing out in Cooter's field. You all wouldn't know anything about that, would you?"

"We've been in the boathouse," said Jackson. "What would we know?"

"This is nonsense. I'm going to the car," announced Nikki, still annoyed. She turned around and began the long walk up to the car. Jenny and Jane kept pace.

"Well, that was a close one," said Jane.

"What are you talking about?"

"I thought for sure you were going to punch the sheriff."

"Why would I punch the sheriff?"

"Well, you know," Jane looked at Jenny, who shrugged. "Mispronouncing your name is kind of one of your pet peeves. And you were already annoyed."

"The sheriff is an ass hat," said Nikki. "And I am annoyed. But unlike some people," she turned slightly as Z'ev caught up, "I don't have to punch everyone who annoys me."

"That sheriff is an ass hat," said Z'ev. "Donny just tried to get a meeting with him to talk about some sort of drug smuggling thing and the sheriff totally blew him off. Donny's a decorated narcotics officer and that sheriff treated us all like delinquent kids. And that's putting it kindly. I think you're right. There's some really racist bastards around here."

"If it helps, he doesn't seem to like me much either. I try not to worry about it. In fifty years everyone will be sort of beige," said Nikki.

"I don't have fifty years," said Z'ev. "I'm brown today."

"Well, what do you want me to do about it? Jane and Jenny won't let me punch the sheriff." Jenny and Jane were trying to distance themselves by walking further ahead.

"I want you to acknowledge that it's a problem," said Z'ev

his voice rising.

Nikki turned around, sharply, prepared to make a very pithy point, and saw the sheriff coming up the path after them. "I don't really think that now is the time for this," she said and turned on her heel, walking more quickly toward the car.

"It never is," muttered Z'ev, but followed along.

They returned to the house in awkward silence punctuated in intermittent spasms of Jenny and Ellen trying to make small talk. It was nearly ten o'clock when she parked the SUV.

"My grandma's usually in bed by ten," said Nikki, looking at the living room windows that still glowed with light.

"Maybe she and your mom are staying up chatting," said Jane, which made Nikki laugh.

But Peg was alone in the living room, wrapped in a fluffy bathrobe and reading a romance novel.

"Oh, good, you're back," she said looking up. "What happened to you? You all look disheveled."

"We played tag," said Nikki.

"And the other team won?"

"Um… I think it was a bit of a draw."

"All right then. There's some cookies in the kitchen for everyone. Um, Nikki, I was hoping we could talk."

"You can talk to Nikki tomorrow, Mom," said Nell, coming down the stairs. "I'm sure everyone's tired." Nell and Peg exchanged angry stares.

Nikki thought about interrupting and simply saying that she knew about Jorge just to bring the whole farce to an end, but she discovered that she really was tired.

"Mom's right, Grandma. We can talk tomorrow. I want to go to bed."

"All right, dear," said Peg, looking annoyed and also somewhat relieved. "Goodnight, everyone."

Peg went upstairs, followed by Nell, who appeared to be shepherding her along. Nikki tried to fathom why her mom was so uptight about Jorge, but understanding her mother had never been a particularly worthwhile endeavor, so she gave up.

AUGUST XX
BLACK CURTAINS

Saturday

With Z'ev still asleep, Nikki tiptoed down the hall to the first guest room, where Jane and Jenny were sharing a king-size bed. Although sharing was a rather generous term to describe the way Jenny was starfished across the bed.

Jane cracked an eyelid as Nikki entered and unfurled from the tight little ball she had been forced into. She nodded to Nikki's head jerk in the direction of the kitchen and reached for her robe and computer.

"This Ylina situation is getting worse," said Nikki when they were downstairs. "I don't think we can afford to sit on it any longer."

"Well, we've been kind of busy," protested Jane.

"Yeah, busy with our vacation. Meanwhile, she's actually in trouble. I ran into her last night at Cooter's junkyard."

"Nikki! Did you cheat?"

"Of course, I cheated. We were never going to win because you know how well Ellen sneaks up on people. So I had to at least catch Jackson and he's too damn fast."

"He is surprisingly quick," agreed Jane.

"He's training for *American Ninja Warrior*."

"Ah. How is his salmon ladder?"

"No clue, but his vertical jump is impressive."

"That's good, but grip strength is key on that show."

"Can we focus on Ylina?" Nikki poured herself a glass of juice and Jane a cup of coffee from the pot her grandma had started. Jane began to root through the fridge looking for milk and creamer.

"OK, but do you think we're focusing on Ylina as a way to avoid your personal problems with Z'ev?"

"Of course we are," snapped Nikki. "That doesn't mean she's not actually in trouble."

"OK, but I want you to be aware that avoidance is not a healthy behavior."

"Jane, telling people about their unhealthy behaviors is not a healthy behavior."

"Jenny says that too. Fortunately, you all love me." Jane was focused on her coffee and didn't see Nikki's affectionate smile.

"That is true. And we couldn't get along without you. You're an extremely valuable asset and if you ever fell into the wrong hands I'd have to kill you."

"What? Wait a minute! Why couldn't you just kill the wrong hands? Why me?"

Nikki grinned. "That's just how it's done. Ask Z'ev. Can't let intelligence like yours get utilized by the enemy."

"You make this stuff up," said Jane, accusingly.

"Generally, yes. Anyway, can you help me find Ylina? I think she's staying somewhere in town within walking distance to the grocery store."

"Give me a second."

Jane began rapidly tapping on her computer and making thoughtful little clucking noises at her coffee.

Ellen stumbled into the kitchen, looked accusingly at the pair of them, and went directly to the coffee maker.

"What are we doing?" she demanded after a half cup.

"Jane's locating Ylina for me," said Nikki. "Then I'm going to see her and drag her back here if I have to. I ran into her at the junkyard and she was talking some smack about how she was going to cash in her insurance policy. I don't know what that means, but it can't be good. I'm going to bring her here and sit on her until I can get Donny over to talk to her. I think he must be onto something if he was trying to get a meeting with the sheriff. Maybe he can convince her to turn on Milt, Pedro and the rest."

"It's as good a plan as any," said Ellen with a shrug. "And it has the advantage of not doing anything overly clandestine."

"Right!" said Nikki. "I happened to bump into her at a bar, I saw that she was in trouble, so of course, I called on my friend, the cop. It's neat, it's tidy, it's mostly true."

"It doesn't bring up the breaking and entering or the bar fight," said Ellen, raising her mug.

"Extraneous details," said Nikki. "Why bring them up? It doesn't matter."

"Sounds like you've got it all worked out," said Ellen.

"Mmm," said Jane.

"I did have it worked out," said Nikki. "Right up until Jane went 'mmm.'"

"What?" Jane looked up, confused.

"You said, 'mmm.' That's not a good sign."

"Isn't it?"

"You say mmm when your little computer friend tells you something you don't like."

"Do I? Oh. Sorry?"

"We don't mind that you say it," said Nikki. "It just generally means bad news."

"It's not bad news," said Jane. "Not really. But it's not great news. Ylina has been working for Crazy Cooter's Junkyard as a secretary for three years. You know, I thought you were all being mean. I was going to suggest that maybe we could not use the crazy word just because he's maybe a little outside the norm or maybe had some mental health issues, but it turns out that is actually the name on his business license."

"Yeah, it's Crazy Cooter's Junkyard," said Nikki. "I don't know why you always assume that we're being racist, sexist, and anti-crazy people. He had ads on the radio when I was a kid. Trade your scrap metal for craaaaaazy good prices at Craaaaaazy Cooter's, home of Car-Henge."

"Car-Henge?"

"It was a Stonehenge made of Mini-Coopers. You know, because they're British. I think he had to take it down though. A couple of them fell over, and replacement Coopers were hard to get."

Ellen and Jane exchanged glances. "That's weird," said Ellen at last.

"Well, he's crazy," said Nikki. "I mean, it's on the business license. He has a reputation to maintain."

"Still weird," said Ellen. "Anyway, I guess Ylina working out at the junkyard could explain why she was there."

"Sort of," said Nikki. "What else did you turn up, Jane?"

"She's been living at a place on Elm Street, but she stopped paying rent there three months ago. Which in and of itself doesn't mean much, but she's got a decent amount of money in the bank. That means she probably moved out and wherever she moved to she's paying in cash. She's got a four hundred dollar withdrawal on the first of the month for the last three months."

"Four hundred dollars!" exclaimed Ellen. "I wish I could find somewhere to live for that. In LA you have to pay four hundred to live under the freeway."

"Well, even here that's not going to get you somewhere very nice," said Nikki. "Why the move?"

"I don't know, but lots of other bills cease at about that same time. The cable got cancelled and hasn't been renewed. No utilities bill. No Netflix. She never had a car payment, so it's hard to tell if that's changed. But her gas expenditure hasn't increased—or at least her stops at the Pettit Gas Station have remained the same."

"What about other cash withdrawals?" asked Ellen.

"Yes, her cash withdrawals have gone up. There's what's presumably rent on the first and then a couple hundred a week. By the end of the month she's pulled out most of her paycheck."

"She's been planning to run for awhile then," said Nikki.

"I'd say so," said Ellen. "And she thinks whoever is going to be looking for her would have the ability to hack her bank account and trace her. She's stockpiling cash."

"The question is, where is she staying now?" Nikki frowned. "Friends, relatives?"

"A motel," said Jane. "That's my best guess. There's one within walking distance to the grocery store. The website is in Spanish, so you'll have to look at it for me. But I think it's four hundred a month. It's trying to attract temporary workers. It's got a construction crew special. I think. My Spanish still isn't that good."

"Can you hack them? See if Ylina is registered?"

"Working on it," said Jane, nodding.

Nikki washed a few dishes from the night before while Ellen read the paper. It was wait on Jane time and it didn't pay to rush the her. Jane made angry noises and tapped the computer screen more violently. Nikki and Ellen exchanged looks, but said nothing.

Ellen got up and poured herself some cereal. Nikki made tea.

"Oh, my God," said Jane finally. "Worst hack ever."

"Really awesome security?" asked Ellen.

"No, really shitty technology from like 1996. It's so slow and glitchy. How do they even use this software? It's heinous." She poked angrily at her screen again.

"Hitting the computer harder won't make it go any faster," said Ellen.

"Are you sure? Because it feels like I could just—" Jane's finger hit the screen in a staccato burst of fury. "Gah!" She threw the tablet on the table.

"Room seventeen. Don't ask me to go back in there. It was horrible."

Nikki laughed. "Thanks. I won't. OK, I'm going to run out there before anybody gets up."

"Your grandma's already up," pointed out Jane. "I heard her head out to the orchard hours ago."

"Yes, thank you. Before anyone else gets up and comes downstairs."

"Do you want me to go with you?" asked Ellen.

"Mm, no. I don't want to freak her out or feel ganged up on. I just need her to get in the car and come with me."

"And if she won't get in the car?" asked Ellen.

"I'll knock her out and put her in the car. Problem solved." Nikki put down her juice and looked around for her keys and shoes. She thought longingly of her gun, but it was stashed in the bottom of her bag where Z'ev wouldn't see it.

"OK, wish me luck," she said collecting her purse and sliding into her running shoes.

"Good luck!" said Jane, rebounding back to her normal

cheery self.

Nikki started up the Impala and was about to pull away from the house when the passenger side door opened and her mother landed in the seat.

"Oh good, I caught you," she said smiling. "Ellen said you were going into town. I want to stop at the grocery store."

"I'm not really, uh ... I was going to pop in on a friend," said Nikki.

"That's fine. I can wait in the car."

"Uh." Nikki thought about aborting the mission. Then she thought about the scared look on Ylina's face the night before. "OK, we can make that work."

"Mm, it smells like Chanel in here. Did you start wearing Chanel? I thought you hated Chanel. Didn't you say it smelled like dead flowers?"

"It is Chanel," said Nikki. "The car used to belong to my old partner, Val. I think she spilled a bottle in here one time. The scent comes out every time I warm up the car."

"Your old partner? You sound like a cop. Do project managers really have partners?"

"Can you open the gate, Mom?" Nikki stopped the car, idling it in front of the gate to the road. Nell looked annoyed. Farm etiquette dictated that the passenger opened and closed the gate. Personal belief held that Nell didn't do that kind of work. Nikki could see the conflict in her face. Eventually, the years of farm living won out. She got out of the car and opened the gate. Nikki pulled through and waited while she closed the gate. She thought briefly about pushing on the gas pedal and leaving her mother behind, but she didn't follow through. Things with her mother were actually better than they had been in years. But for a moment, the urge to run had been overwhelming.

Nell got back in the car, slamming it closed with a loud bang.

"OK, can we go now?"

"Sure," said Nikki.

The ride into town was silent and awkward. Nell seemed constantly on the verge of saying something, but never did. It was the conversational equivalent of almost sneezing, but having the sneeze dissipate at the last moment.

Nikki pulled up in front of the motel. Run down seemed too polite a term for the mega-crap show that was this motel. It didn't even have a name—the neon sign out front just read "otel." The M was burnt out and didn't look likely to be replaced. There was a cop car in the parking lot, but that didn't seem like much of a surprise.

"What are we doing here?" asked Nell looking around.

"I have a friend who got into a little bit of trouble," said Nikki. "I'm going to pick her up and take her back to the farm."

"She needs to tell the guy to man up and marry her," said Nell.

"What? No, Mom. Not that kind of trouble. She just needs a place to stay for a day or so until Donny can help her straighten things out. Anyway, stay in the car. I'll be right back."

Nikki jogged up the stairs to the second floor landing, trying not to touch the rickety Rat Pack era railing that looked nearly rusted through. The motel was shaped like an "L" and as she counted down the numbers on the doors, she realized that room seventeen would be near the bend in the "L". She looked down the length of walkway and felt her stomach sink. The door straight ahead of her was already open. Nikki stretched out her stride, trying to hurry without running. She slowed down as she approached, missing her gun again. The room had been tossed, the mattress was off the bed and cut open, the picture with its sad, faded rural scene had been ripped from the wall. Clothes were scattered everywhere. And by the bed lay Ylina. Her hair was wet and lay in dark strands across her wide-open eyes. Nikki stopped and stared at the body, trying to decide what to do next. Her eyes flitted around the room, trying to avoid Ylina's accusing stare, but always returning to it. Her pants were dry, but her top was wet. There were bruises on her neck. She was missing a shoe. Nikki didn't see the shoe in the debris.

There was a sound from within the room and Nikki tensed, reaching for a gun that wasn't there. Then the sheriff stepped out of the bathroom. For a second he froze, clearly surprised to see her.

"Miss Lanier, what are you doing here?"

"I was looking for Ylina," said Nikki.

"Apparently, someone else found her first," said the sheriff, gesturing to the body. "Strangled her, and drowned her in the bathtub last night."

Nikki looked at the body again and then around the room. She didn't see the duffel bag that Ylina had been holding at the junkyard.

"How long have you been here?"

"I don't see how that is in any of your business. Just what's your interest here, Miss Lanier? You seem mighty interested in some girl you bumped into at a bar."

"Nikki, what's taking so long? Tell your friend not to pack anything, because we're only going to want to burn it after it's been here."

Nikki turned around, trying to block her mother from seeing

the body, but it was too late. Nell's hands flew to her mouth, holding in a scream, and her eyes went wide.

"Well, hello, Nell," said the sheriff.

Nikki watched her mother's eyes drift from the body up to the sheriff. She was surprised at how quickly their expression shifted from horror to hatred.

"This is a surprise. I'm investigating a crime," said Merv, his eyes flicking from Nell to Nikki and back. "That's my job, after all. But the question I'd like answered is: what are you and your daughter doing here?

"You stay away from my daughter," said Nell. "Or so help me I'll—"

"You'll what?" asked the sheriff quietly as he took a step closer.

Nell backed up.

"Maybe you should tell your daughter to go back to LA where she belongs. Now I suggest both of you leave before I arrest you for interfering in a police investigation."

The sheriff slammed the door in their faces and Nell immediately turned and headed for the car, pulling Nikki with her.

AUGUST XXI

TRUTHINESS

Nikki drove until her mother held up her hands as if signaling surrender. "Pull over. Pull over. Pull over."

Nikki did as she was told, and Nell dashed from the car into the long grass in the drainage ditch and upchucked her breakfast. Nikki sat on the hood and waited for Nell to finish. When Nell began to stagger back in her direction, Nikki fished in the glove compartment and pulled out the pack of wet wipes and the flask of vodka. The car had come to her that way, and Nikki had seen no reason to discontinue stocking Val's emergency kit.

Nell wiped her face and socked back a long gulp of vodka. "That girl was really dead."

"Yes."

"How can you be so calm about it?" demanded Nell, her fist crumpling the wet wipes.

"Well, as you used to say, crying won't fix the situation."

Nell gaped at her. "That's not what—I didn't mean it about things like this."

Nikki shrugged. "It's still true."

"No, no it's not. That girl—someone killed that girl. Someone snuffed out her life like it was nothing. You're supposed to get upset about things like that, Nikki!" Nell dropped the flask and wipes and grabbed Nikki's shoulders, shaking her.

Nikki removed her mother's hands, holding her by the wrists. "I don't get to be upset, Mom. I have to think of what to do next."

Nell stepped back, seemingly bereft for words. "Sometimes I don't think I even know you anymore."

Nikki let out an exasperated sigh. "Mom, I think the real question is, did you ever know me?"

"Yes, yes I did! We used to be close."

Nikki laughed. "When? When was this mythical time?"

"When you were younger. Before your father left. We used to be best friends."

"Yeah, you made it pretty clear to him that it was just the two of us and then surprise! He left."

"That isn't what happened!"

"Really? Then tell me what happened. What really happened to make Dad leave?" Nikki knew this wasn't the time for this conversation. Not that there had ever, in the history of her life, been a right time for this conversation, but anything was better than thinking about Ylina and her wide staring eyes.

Nell's lips pursed in a way that made her look surprisingly like Peg.

"Spit it out, Mom. Whatever it is you want to say, just spit it out. I don't really have time for this." Nikki waited, and Nell opened her mouth then closed it again. "Nothing? There's a shock." Nikki turned to get into the car.

"He went to prison," said Nell. Nikki rotated back to look at her mother.

"What?"

"When we got pregnant with you we were broke and his mother had disowned him for marrying me."

"Yeah, I know."

"So we moved in with my parents, and he liked it. But he knew I hated it. And we could never seem to save up money to move. Every time we got cash together something would happen—the car, the dentist, whatever. So he decided to do the one thing he was really good at." Nell's words were tumbling out rapidly now as if she was in a hurry to get them out and away from her. Her hands clasped to each other, clenching and unclenching.

"What was he really good at?" asked Nikki.

"Smuggling," said Nell. "He bought a car off Crazy Cooter. Then he fixed it up with some sort of secret compartment, drove it into Canada and picked up some pot. But after the first couple of times he started to worry that he was getting recognized. So then he started taking out some engine part and having a tow truck drive it back, so that if the car got stopped at the border he wouldn't be there, but also the tow-truck driver couldn't be held accountable. He sold the pot and the car to a biker gang in Oregon.

I wanted to move then. That was a lot of money. But he said it was easy, and that if he did it a few more times we could move without having to find jobs right away. And then he said if we saved a little longer we could move and buy a house straight away. And it was only pot, so I figured what harm could it do?"

"He got caught?"

"Sort of," said Nell, her nose wrinkling in unhappiness. "He was starting to have to get creative. He'd drive across the border in one location and have it brought back in another. And he'd change up his hair style. Anything to keep the border guards from noticing that he traveled back and forth a lot. And then Merv Smalls started sniffing around. He was a Sheriff's Deputy then. He was certain your father was smuggling, but he couldn't ever figure out how he was doing it."

"So what happened?" Nikki couldn't believe her ears. It was

as though her mother was rewriting history with every word, blotting out the past and redrafting it with a new and entirely unfamiliar plot. At the same time, the new version explained so many half-heard conversations and odd moments in her childhood.

"One day, Merv pulled him over and arrested him for having marijuana, just enough for intent to distribute and prison time."

"Merv planted the pot?" asked Nikki.

"He had to have," said Nell. "Your father never would have had that kind of crap pot on him."

"So Dad didn't leave. He went to prison. And you just told me he left?"

"Well, what was I supposed to say?" asked Nell, wringing her hands.

"I don't know. How about the truth?"

"I couldn't! Merv said I should leave town because your father's contacts might come looking for his money and their pot. And I told him to go to hell and that your father was innocent, but secretly I knew he was right. That gang he sold to—they were not nice people. So I took the money and moved us to Seattle and your father got extradited to a prison in Canada."

"Oh, my God," said Nikki. "How could you not tell me this?"

"Well, I knew that if I told you, you'd only want to go visit him and then you'd want to try to prove he was innocent, which you know, technically he was, but not exactly. But you would have wanted to solve the mystery. I let you read too much Trixie Belden as a child. I think it went to your head. But if you solved it, what would you have thought of your father then?"

"So instead you let me believe that dad left us? You couldn't say that he joined the Peace Corps or something?"

"Oh. Well, no. I didn't think of that."

"When did he get out? He was there for Grandma's funeral. He must have been out by then. Why didn't he tell me at the funeral?"

"He'd been out for several years, I think," said Nell with a shrug. "We got divorced while he was in prison. And after he got out, he just bummed around. I told him not to tell you because what was the point? He couldn't be bothered to show up and be a normal father, so what was the point of hurting you?"

Nikki wanted to shout or scream or punch something. She rubbed her hands through her hair and then threw them up in the air, slapping them down at her sides with a resounding smack. "I can't believe you never told me."

"Well, after we moved to Seattle –"

"And bought a house with his drug money."

"I thought I would tell you, but you were still young. And you had that habit of talking to people and telling them things. I didn't want anyone investigating us. It was just easier. And I kept meaning to tell you as you got older, but it never seemed like the right time."

"And now's the right time?"

"Well, my mother kept saying she was going to tell you if I didn't." Nell's lip pouted out in irritation.

"Wait, that's what you've been fighting about telling me? Not Grandma's boyfriend?"

"Yeah." Nell smiled awkwardly, then frowned. "What do you mean, 'Grandma's boyfriend'?"

"Oh, my God," repeated Nikki. She put her hands on top of her head and took a deep breath like she'd been running. "Oh, my God, Z'ev totally knows."

"He can't know," said Nell dismissively.

"Of course, he knows! I'm sure he ran a background check on me. No wonder he gives me that weird look every time I say 'Dad left.'"

"Your boyfriend ran a background check on you?" Nell look horrified.

"Of course he did! He works for the… government. He'd be an idiot not to make sure I wasn't a Russian spy or something."

She walked around the car, hands on her head. "This is so embarrassing. Jane probably knows. She must have looked me up at some point. How could she not tell me?"

"Why would Jane know?" demanded Nell. "Frankly, I wonder about that girl. She doesn't seem very bright."

"Jane is a Mensa member," said Nikki. "And she didn't just squeak in. She's smarter than the next twenty people you'll meet. Probably the next one hundred. The reason she's socially awkward is that she spends the majority of her time trying to figure out what's wrong with us Neanderthals. And Mother, I swear to God, if you say another word about one of my friends, I will slap you."

"I don't think I like your attitude," said Nell, folding her arms across her chest. "You constantly take their side. I am your mother. You are supposed to be on my side."

Nikki felt one of the tiny muscles in her eye twitch involuntarily.

"When you are on my side, maybe I will be," she said. Then she climbed into the car, slamming the door, and started the ignition.

"You are not going to—" began Nell, but Nikki had already hit the accelerator. The gas guzzling engine roared to life and launched her back onto the road, leaving Nell coughing on a cloud of dust.

AUGUST XXII

REGRETS, I HAVE A FEW

Nikki drove north for twenty minutes, ostensibly fleeing for Canada, but mostly just fleeing. As she left the farms and ranches behind, the Colville Forest closed in around her. The soothing monotony of pine merged with the hum of the road under the tires and the chug of the engine. She rolled down the window and let the wind buffet around the car, drowning out the sound of the radio and everything but her thoughts.

A few more pine trees passed and finally she pulled over in the barest scrap of shade caused by a straggly evergreen. The engine clicked as it cooled. She found that in times of stress her thoughts would turn to her old partner. Val Robinson had been forty-something, sophisticated, and easily the coolest person Nikki had ever met, but her take-no-prisoners, keep-no-friends philosophy had been a shock.

Nikki closed her eyes and leaned her head back, stretching out her neck. "I'm starting to think you weren't that crazy, Val," she said to the empty car. Talking to Val's ghost in her car was becoming a bad habit. Val's ghost never said anything useful in reply. Usually she smoked a cigarette at Nikki and said something useless, like "I told you so." Nikki took a few deep breaths and then reached for her phone.

"Hi," said Jane, picking up. "Did you get Ylina? Are you on your way back?"

"Jane, why didn't you tell me about my father?"

"What about your father?"

"Why didn't you tell me my father went to prison?"

"Your father's in prison?" Jane sounded shocked. Which meant, since Jane was an even worse liar than Nikki, that Jane was truly shocked.

"Jane, have you ever run a background check on my family?"

"No, why would I do that? It would be rude to do that to my own team. I have very clear ethical boundaries about data usage, you know."

Nikki sighed, and rubbed her temple with her free hand. She did know. This job was making her suspicious of everyone. Suspicious and cranky. And hungry.

"Nikki, what's going on?" asked Jane.

"I don't really want to cover it on the phone. I need you to do a few things for me."

"OK," said Jane.

"I need you to tell Grandma to go pick my mom up. I left her out on Old Kaniksu Road."

"You left your mom?"

"Yes. We're not going into it."

"OK, telling Peg to go get Nell. What else do you need?"

"I need you to borrow Z'ev's rental car and come meet me at the library."

"OK," said Jane, from the shift in her voice, Nikki could tell that Jane was already moving. "Should I get the girls?"

"No, just you, I think. The library only has two microfiche machines."

"No problem. What else?"

"Bring a sandwich. I'm starving."

"Got it. See you in a few."

The line went dead. "See, Val?" said Nikki to the resident ghost. "Friends are useful. I can rely on them."

The Kaniksu Falls Public Library looked like it had been designed by Mr. Brady from the Brady Bunch, clad in vertical wood siding, painted beige, and faced with a peculiar multi-colored slate. For the last decade, the library had been run by a series of dedicated librarians who attempted to lure the town's population of loggers and farmers into reading through events and community outreach. It was working. There were three separate book clubs, a movie club, and a youth garden, whatever that was. A bulletin board inside the lobby announced that this month's General Fiction Book Club was continuing their Banned Books series by reading *The Handmaid's Tale*.

"Have you read *The Handmaid's Tale?*" The librarian's nametag proclaimed her to be Bronwyn Tully. She was tiny, with a brown bun, a hemp skirt, and a pair of Birkenstocks.

"Yes," said Nikki. "I didn't like it. The main character was too passive. But it's very," she paused, and redirected her sentence. "Are you really getting any men to read it?"

"Oh, yes," said Bronwyn. "Our group is actually about fifty percent male. Besides next month we're reading a Raymond Chandler. The trick is to keep the reading list lively. And, of course, to serve cookies."

"Librarians—pushing feminism since 1897," said Nikki.

"Long before that, dear," said Bronwyn, her eyes twinkling. "Now, what can I help you with today?"

"I'm here, I'm here," said Jane, rushing through the sliding door, panting slightly.

Bronwyn looked amused, but her eyes narrowed slightly upon spotting Jane's computer. "You'll need to sign up for a library card if you want to use our wi-fi."

"No problem," said Jane, then looked to Nikki. "Do I need wi-fi?"

"Actually, I want to look up articles from the Kaniksu Tribune."

"How far back? And are you looking for a specific topic?" Bronwyn was already walking them toward the back of the library.

"About fifteen years. Topic was a drug bust of a local resident named Philippe Lanier, who was then extradited to Canada. It would also have involved a Sheriff's Deputy named Merv Smalls."

"Merv Smalls who's now our sheriff?" asked Bronwyn, glancing up at Nikki.

"Yes, that's right."

Bronwyn nodded and seemed to be thinking. "Any way to narrow it down to a specific month?"

"The arrest, I think, would have been in the spring."

"That's at least closer. Here are the microfiche machines. I'll be back with the film and show you how to load it."

Jane waited until Bronwyn disappeared into a back office, but Nikki could tell by the way she was practically hopping that it was a hard wait.

"Your dad was arrested?"

"Yes, for smuggling marijuana. Apparently, he didn't abandon his family. Apparently, he was actually sent to prison in Canada."

"Holy crap!"

"Pretty much, yeah."

"And your mom didn't tell you?"

"Not until today."

"And we're here to read the truth for ourselves?" Jane clasped her hands under her chin, her voice throbbing slightly. She had a very romantic view on the liberating power of research.

"Not exactly," said Nikki. "I believe that she told me what she thinks is the truth, but there were a couple of problems with her story. There's also the fact that Ylina is dead."

"What?" Jane's hands dropped. "Shouldn't we be doing something about that?"

"We are doing something about that," said Nikki. "I think the two events are related."

"Here we are," said Bronwyn returning a stack of dusty boxes. She extracted the tiny roll of film from the box and quickly and carefully inserted it into the machine. "Your best bet is to turn to section B where they used to keep the Police Beat. The editor used to enjoy making fun of 'filthy hippies' and the like. He would most likely have published a drug arrest." Bronwyn looked from Nikki to Jane's pent-up expression. "I'll leave you to it. Let me know if you need some other time frames."

"Thanks," said Nikki.

Bronwyn walked back to the front desk, her skirt swishing as she walked.

"I wonder if there's a course in discretion included in the librarian curriculum."

"Who cares about librarians?" demanded Jane. "Can we please get back to Ylina being dead, your father having been in jail, and how are those two possibly related?"

"My mother said that Dad bought cars at Crazy Cooter's, 'fixed them up' and then drove into Canada to pick up pot. When he started to do it multiple times he switched to having a tow truck driver tow it back across the border. The problem is that my Dad had zero car skills. My grandfather used to say that dad could talk a pig into bacon, but he had the mechanical aptitude of a donkey."

"Bill Pims! The owner of the auto body shop! You said he was converting cars to go across the border. You think he helped your dad?"

"I think he must have," said Nikki.

"And then he must have taken over the operation when your dad got arrested," said Jane, nodding, fixing the puzzle pieces in her mind.

"I don't think so," said Nikki. "When Jackson and I were in his shop, he talked about a boss."

""Well, then who's the boss? Besides Tony Danza."

"I have some theories, but I want to look through the old newspaper articles and see if Bill Pims or any of Dad's other associates ever got arrested or mentioned in the paper."

Nikki sometimes wondered, if things had been different, if she had gone left instead of right, if she had never met Z'ev or Mrs. Merrivel and joined Carrie Mae, if she would have been a decent linguist or made it in the world of academics. It was in moments like this that she realized the answer was a resounding no. Searching through old newspapers did not fascinate her. It made her bored and twitchy. Meanwhile, Jane giggled over the ads and pointed out "really interesting" articles on town politics. They found her father's arrest quickly enough and, after that, a smattering of mentions as the case wound its way through the court. But Bill Pims' name was absent from all records. In fact, nothing about the smuggling scheme was ever mentioned. It was limited strictly to Philippe's possession charge and his extradition.

After the last article, Nikki sat back in her chair, kicked her feet out, laced her hands behind her head, and stared at the ceiling. Her mother had always hated the pose. She said it wasn't feminine, but Nikki knew that it was because it reminded her of Philippe.

Jane, who knew what the thinking pose meant, began to tidy up by reboxing the microfilm and collecting their print-outs of the articles.

"It's the only way it all fits," said Nikki to the ceiling.

"Mmm," said Jane, who was used to this too.

"We need proof," said Nikki. "It's going to be a shock."

"Mm-hmm," agreed Jane.

"Someone to testify in court would be good too, but I think it's going to be a tough sell."

"Well, yes," said Jane.

"And Donny. I'll have to persuade Donny to cooperate, but I don't think that will be a problem."

"Not a problem." Jane kept her voice pitched at a soothing murmur.

"Right," said Nikki standing up. "We just might make it out of this without totally blowing our cover."

"That's nice," said Jane, who clearly hadn't been worried.

"But first we need to go see Bill Pims."

"OK!"

"Jane, are you doing that thing where you have no idea what I'm talking about, but you're going to be really supportive anyway?"

"You always explain eventually and it helps you to talk it out."

"Thanks. Also, did you bring that sandwich? I'm still starving."

"It's in the car," said Jane.

AUGUST XXIII
BAD GIRLS

Nikki sat in the car, finishing her sandwich, waiting for Jane to finish parking. She stared at the auto body shop. The open sign hung jauntily in the window but she couldn't see inside the office due to the glare of sun off the glass. She rolled down the window as Jane approached and sneezed, tasting the acrid tang of wildfire smoke in the air.

"So what's our plan?" asked Jane. "Go in there and rough them up?" she smacked a fist into her palm.

"We're going to go ask some questions," said Nikki. "Ninety percent of finding things out is having the balls to ask questions. People are usually so surprised that they answer."

"That's not as exciting as I was hoping for," said Jane.

"Well, this isn't exactly Al-Qaeda. It's a middle-aged body / fender guy."

"Who might have killed someone."

"I don't think he did. I think it was the boss."

"But you don't know for sure. We should beat the truth out of him."

Nikki sighed. "We'll keep that as a plan B." She stood, picked up her purse, and then decided against it, tucking it under the seat. Jane only ever carried a messenger bag that could fit her computer and a myriad of other gadgets. Functionally, it was exactly the same as a purse, but when it came to questioning people it had the advantage. It's hard to take someone as a serious threat when they walk in with an adorable little Kate Spade.

Nikki swung open the door to the shop and the bells tied to the handle didn't so much jingle as clank annoyingly against the door.

"Be with you in a second," someone yelled through the door from the garage side.

"This is awkward," said Jane. "I'm fairly certain that when coming to question people, you're not supposed to be kept waiting."

"You'll have to call ahead and make an appointment next time then," said Nikki.

"That doesn't seem practical," said Jane as Kristine Pims came into the office.

"What are you doing here?" demanded Kristine, and Nikki frowned. Kristine's eyes were red and her face was blotchy, and her blonde hair, usually curled and styled, had been shoved into a messy ponytail.

"I need to see your dad," said Nikki.

"Go to hell," said Kristine. "You're the last thing he needs to see."

"Oh, good grief! Kristine, I don't know what your problem is, but get over it. I have never done anything to you. Other than the little incident the other night, I don't know why you're mad at me. Frankly, I don't know why you even care about me at all."

"You don't know..." Kristine's face flushed red. "This is your fault. This is all your fault!"

"What is my fault? You living in Kaniksu Falls and working at your dad's shop? That is not my fault. If you're unhappy with your life, then leave. Nothing in your life is my fault!"

"It's your fault Ylina's dead. If it hadn't been for you interfering at the Kessel Run she probably would have just gotten beat up a little. But oh no, you had to swoop in like a big hero."

"That is not—" began Nikki, but once started Kristine couldn't seem to stop.

"You always swan around like you're so perfect and the rest of us are nothing, but your dad is the one that started this and it's your fault!" Kristine burst into tears and dropped onto the chair behind the desk as if her knees had given out.

"It's OK," said Jane, whipping a Kleenex out of her bag. "We all like to hate the way Nikki swans sometimes."

"What?"

"You do swan sometimes. I mean, not a lot. And usually it's for work. Also, not as much as Jenny. But sometimes there's swanning. It makes the rest of us ducklings feel ugly."

"Yes!" wailed Kristine from inside the Kleenex.

"I don't even know how to swan! And that's not the point. Jane, this is the last time I take you to question someone. You can't be on their side the moment they start to cry."

"But she's crying for a real reason," said Jane, patting Kristine soothingly. "Ylina's dead and her dad's in trouble."

"Yes," said Kristine. Well, it might have been 'yes.' It was hard to hear through the burbling sobs and snot noises.

"Stop crying," said Nikki. "Seriously. Nothing ever gets solved by crying and I don't have time for this."

"Nikki," said Jane, "be nicer."

"I don't want to be," said Nikki.

Jane frowned at her.

"OK, fine," said Nikki. "Kristine, I'm sorry I swanned. I didn't mean to swan. But for the record, using racial slurs is still not cool."

There was another sob and an emphatic hand wave.

"I don't know what that meant," said Jane, "But I think it was apologetic."

"I said, I didn't mean it," said Kristine surfacing, and sniffing fiercely. Jane offered her another tissue. "I just wanted to make you mad. It was the first thing I thought of."

"Well, the fact that you went first to a racial slur still shows an implicit bias," said Jane. "You may want to do some serious thinking about your own ingrained racism."

Kristine looked at Nikki in disbelief, who shrugged. "Sorry I called you fat," said Nikki. "I was embarrassed about my outfit and I wanted you to go away."

Kristine shrugged herself and blotted her face with the tissue. "I was being kind of bitchy."

The door from the garage banged open and Bill Pims came in with a spark plug in one hand. "Krissy, I'm going to need you to order - what the hell is going on in here? Bill looked at his daughter's red face and the crumpled tissues in her hand and a panic began to suffuse his face.

"You've been smuggling pot for the last decade, that's what's going on," said Nikki.

Bill's eyes widened. They went from Nikki to Jane to Kristine, then back to Nikki. "No, I haven't."

"Least convincing lie ever," said Jane.

"You started smuggling with my dad for a cut, right?"

"It was a straight fee," said Bill, his shoulders sagging. "We both had kids. It was a simple little plan. And it was just pot. I didn't think it would lead to all this." He sat down on the bench by the door, dropping the spark plug on a pile of magazines, and began to clean his fingers with a blue shop cloth.

"And then Merv Smalls arrested my dad, but the smuggling wasn't over, was it?"

Bill shook his head. "It quadrupled in the first five years. Doubled again after that. We had to cut back a bit when the century flipped. The DEA has been all over our ass."

"Because Merv started using illegal aliens to be the drivers."

"Wait, Merv? Isn't he the sheriff?" demanded Jane.

"He is now. Probably financed that campaign with drug money."

Bill nodded in confirmation.

"He took over my dad's operation."

"And expanded it," said Bill. "Once he figured out that he could use the Mexicans to drive, it was fat city. I'd modify a car every weekend in the nineties. If they got caught, he didn't care because they'd get deported."

"Wasn't he concerned that they'd talk?" Jane was reaching for her computer.

Bill shook his head. "He picked the ones who had family here. If they talked he'd make sure their family was dead by the time anyone came for him. But the DREAM act put a real crimp in his recruiting practices. Now it's a lot safer for them to admit they're illegal and go to the authorities. So he's shifting business models again."

"What do you mean? Shifting business models how?"

Bill mopped his forehead with the shop rag leaving streaks of black. "Well, with pot being legal in Washington now, he doesn't see any reason to keep smuggling from Canada. He's recruited one of the botanists from up there and he's planning on starting his own pot farm. I mean, he'll probably use someone else to run it because he has to be anti-drug when it comes to running for sheriff, but that's his plan."

"I thought the farms were going to be limited in size," said Jane. "How's he planning on growing enough to maintain his supply? Or is he really going straight?"

"That man is so crooked he could fit around a corkscrew without trying," said Kristine. "Besides out here, who do you think they're going to call to investigate the size of a farm?"

"That's a good point," said Jane, nodding.

"The problem is that if he's not smuggling out of Canada anymore, does he really need you?" asked Nikki. "Either of you."

"Why do you think I've been sweating it so hard," said Bill. "I keep telling Kristine we've got to get out of town."

"He'd only have his friends take care of us somewhere else," said Kristine. "What's the point?"

"Would you testify against him?" asked Nikki.

"Yeah, right. We're going to walk into the police station and someone is going to believe us," said Bill. "Don't be crazy."

"If he was arrested first," said Nikki. "Would you testify then?"

Bill and Kristine exchanged a long stare.

"I would," said Kristine quietly. "He killed Ylina. We may not have been best friends, but I always liked her. He shouldn't get away with it."

"I guess I would," said Bill after a long moment. "But I don't see how you're going to get him arrested with no evidence."

"We'll find something," said Jane, with confidence that Nikki thought was just slightly misplaced. "Let us worry about that."

"Ylina said she had an insurance policy that she was going to cash in," said Nikki. "Do either of you know what she meant?"

Bill shook his head, but Kristine bit her lip thoughtfully.

"Maybe."

"Maybe, what?"

"I don't know for sure, but one time I used her phone. She had an auto-record app open on it. One of those sound activated ones, so someone just had to start talking and it would start recording. She kind of flipped out when she saw me using her phone."

"Recordings of the sheriff? That's a worthwhile insurance policy. I didn't see a computer at her place though."

"I don't think she had one," said Kristine with a shrug.

"You think she kept the recordings on her phone then? That doesn't sound smart." Jane frowned at the sloppy technology use. "She should have made a back-up. What if her phone crashed?"

"I don't know," said Kristine with a shrug. "I don't even know that she actually made recordings."

"That's fine," said Nikki. "We can take it from here."

"We can?" Jane looked surprised.

"What are you going to do?" asked Bill. "Whatever it is, we can't be involved."

"Then you don't want to know what I'm going to do, do you? Just keep your heads down and don't say anything to anyone. Donny Fernandez will let you know when it's safe to talk."

"The little Fernandez kid?" Bill looked unconvinced.

"You mean, the three-times decorated, undercover narcotics cop? Yeah, that's who I mean."

"Oh. I guess I'm just used to thinking of him as a kid."

"Well, we all grow up sooner or later," said Nikki. "You probably ought to adjust your thinking."

AUGUST XXIV
I WAS ONLY ROBBING THE REGISTER

There was a dark cloud on the horizon, drifting steadily south. Nikki wondered if she'd even packed a rain jacket, but realized with a start that a rain jacket wasn't needed. Those weren't rain clouds in the sky, it was an immense and billowing nebula of smoke from the forest fire. Nikki rubbed her arm uneasily, discharging static electricity, and told herself that the Columbia was a wide river; there was no way the fire could span that distance. She checked the sky again and hoped she was right.

"So what's the next step?" asked Jane, settling her messenger bag on her hip. "Do you think the sheriff already found Ylina's insurance policy?"

"No, I think he was searching her room when we got to the hotel."

"How are we going to find it then? I mean, as a police officer he's got free rein to search anywhere."

"I don't think it's in her room," said Nikki.

"Then where?"

"Well, when I saw her last, she was fishing something out of a junker car on Crazy Cooter's back lot. And you said she actually worked for Crazy Cooter, right?"

"Yeah, as administrative assistant."

"I think she left it there. I think she went to get it, ran into me, saw the police cars coming to put the kibosh on Donny's party and panicked. I bet she left her insurance policy—whatever it is—at work and tried to take off."

"Why wouldn't she take it with her?" asked Jane.

"I don't know," said Nikki. "Maybe she did. Maybe I'm wrong. Maybe the sheriff has the recordings already and we're screwed. But I think it's worth taking a look, don't you?"

"Yeah, absolutely." Jane surveyed the street. "I have to say, I'm really enjoying this in-person investigation stuff. Usually I'm stuck behind a computer."

"Well, after you took the agent competency course, I thought you'd rotate out, honestly," said Nikki. "You seemed kind of into it."

"Yeah, so did I, but I talked to Mrs. Merrivel and in order to do more field work I'd have to leave the team."

Nikki's hand hovered over the car door handle. "I didn't know you'd talked to Mrs. Merrivel."

"Yeah, she thought it was great that I passed the competency course and that I'm a great back-up for you guys in case of emergency, but she said that the team needed a tech person. Which is true. You would be screwed without me. But if I really want more field work, I would have to get reassigned. So, you know ..." Jane shrugged to fill in the rest of the sentence.

"Jane," Nikki floundered for a moment, finding herself unexpectedly touched by her friends matter-of-fact acceptance of a dying dream. "I really appreciate your choice, because we do need you, but there's got to be a way to move ahead with your career."

Jane shrugged again. "Maybe. I just wish…" Jane trailed off awkwardly.

"You wish what?"

"Well, when I took the field competency course, I thought that maybe you guys would respect me more."

"Respect you more? Jane, we respect you!"

"Well, kind of. But kind of not. You guys kind of treat me like the junior partner. And I know I'm the youngest and I have the least field experience, but I thought once I took the course that everyone would let me do more stuff."

"I'm sorry," said Nikki. "I didn't know you felt that way. I didn't mean to make you feel like a junior partner. Whatever it is I've said, I swear I was only teasing. I really respect and rely on you."

"It's not just you. Ellen and Jenny do it, too. And not to sound dorky, but sometimes words hurt. It's hard to defend my decision to stay where I'm at when you guys call me your "idiot savant" or your "personal PC police" in public. I've had offers to go be on other teams, you know."

"I did not know that. Who offered you a spot?" asked Nikki.

Jane got the angry tone in Nikki's voice and shifted her weight nervously. "It's not a big deal. I like being with you guys more than I worry about my career. Besides, it's not like I'm the only one. I see team leaders trying to scalp Ellen all the time. That conference where you met Darla? I got done with my hypnosis seminar early and I went over to Ellen's Future of Weaponry panel. The Head of East Coast division was leading the panel and she practically offered Ellen whatever she wanted to move."

Nikki laughed. "Everyone wants Ellen. She gets offers all the time. It's because she looks the Carrie Mae part and she's quiet. They don't know that if they actually did manage to steal her they'd be getting a rebel and an insurrectionist. Why do you think her kids are always so surprised when she goes to visit? I guess that just leaves Jenny and me as the wallflowers without any invitations to dance."

Jane shrugged again. "I think they just assume she'll take over the team when you replace Mrs. M."

"Yeah, like that's going to happen. Anyway, Jane, I'm really sorry I made you feel like you weren't respected. I do respect you and honestly, we couldn't do without you."

Jane's bottom lip wobbled suspiciously, and she blinked and looked away. "I know, it's just nice to hear once in awhile. Anyway, we're going to Crazy Cooters? Should I return Z'ev's car? Should I ride with you? Follow you out there? Are we calling the girls? What are we doing?"

Nikki wanted to hug her, but Jane didn't like to hug in moments of emotional distress, so she tried to respect the boundary Jane was clearly drawing by clutching her bag in front of her.

"Umm, follow me out there, I guess. I don't want to return Z'ev's car yet. If we make him mobile, he'll only go poking around where I don't need him. I texted Jenny. She and Ellen will run interference with the family while we investigate because I don't think we need them. I think you and I can handle this investigation ourselves right now."

Jane beamed. "You're the boss." She headed for the rental car, her bouncing ponytail declaring happiness with each step.

Nikki waited until they were on the road before dialing Mrs. Merrivel.

"Nikki, help, I'm being held prisoner. Bring chocolate chip cookies soon," said Mr. Merrivel.

Nikki laugh-snorted in surprise.

"Very funny!" yelled Mrs. Merrivel in the background.

Mr. M chuckled, sounding pleased with himself. "Hey, kiddo. How's vacation going?"

"Umm, well, you know," said Nikki.

"That good, huh? Do you need to keep all the chocolate chip cookies for yourself?"

"Kind of, yeah. Actually, I really do need to talk to Mrs. M."

"Uh oh. That sounds like you may need to move straight to the bag of chocolate chips. I'll hand you over. Hon, Nikki's got a work thing.'"

"A work thing? I thought you were on vacation?" Mrs. Merrivel picked up the phone. Nikki could tell that she was smiling by the uplift in her voice.

"I'm on unpaid leave. Which is turning out to be unpaid working."

"Do you need back-up?"

"No, the girls flew in to help. Of course, they were on the same flight as my mother. And then Z'ev arrived, just in time for dinner at my grandma's with my ex-boyfriend."

"Ugh. John, pack up those chocolate chips for air mail. Nikki needs sugar stat."

Nikki laughed and she could hear Mr. M laughing too. She wondered just how much this sabbatical was going to be good for both the Merrivels.

"I do need sugar, but that's not why I'm calling. I've got a handle on the situation here, mostly. As much as I have a handle on any work situation, anyway."

"Then I won't worry. What's the reason for the call then?"

"How come you didn't tell me that you'd talked to Jane about field work?"

"I talk to everyone who passes the field competency course," said Mrs. Merrivel. "I assumed you knew that."

"I do know that, but I mean, why did you tell her that she couldn't do field work unless she left the team?"

"Because she can't. Her primary role on the team is technical support. She can assist with field work from time to time, but the team needs a tech person."

"But," said Nikki and then trailed off.

"Am I wrong? Do you not need that function?"

"No, we do, but, I mean, she really wants to do field work."

"Well, we discussed it and she said that what she really wanted to do was stay with the team. I said she could always change her mind."

Nikki sighed. "Is the East Coast Director trying to steal Ellen?"

"Everyone tries to steal Ellen," said Mrs. M. "They don't realize that if we left Ellen undirected we'd have a Canada situation every other week. Anyway, the one Susan has really been after is Jenny."

"What? Why?"

"Because she sees the success we've had with your team. She's read the profiles. She knows that you and Jenny have a pretty similar skill set. She thinks that if she can woo Jenny over, Jenny can start her own action team on the East Coast, and that probably if she could get Jenny, she could also get Ellen. Which really is a pretty good plan and would be good for Jenny's career. I'm very hopeful that, if we time it right, we can spin Jenny off in that direction. She could end up being head of her own division, which of course, would be good for all of us."

"Why haven't you talked about this before?"

"Well, you're not ready to move up," said Mrs. Merrivel matter of factly. "You're not even thirty yet, which I know makes The Council nervous. Give it a few more years and when you're ready for promotion this will all make a lot more sense."

"It makes sense now," said Nikki. And it did. All of it made sense. Mrs. Merrivel's plans always did, but, as usual, she was three steps ahead of Nikki. "But I like my life. I don't want to break up the team."

"No one's saying you have to," said Mrs. M soothingly. "This is for the future. Don't think about it. Put it on the back burner."

"You could have told me about it earlier."

"Why? So you could tie yourself up in knots over what might happen, on some unknown date, at some unknown time? You do best when you're dealing with the present."

"You know I don't want your job."

"I do know. You don't like it. It's not enough action and too much responsibility. But there may come a time when it's just going to be more convenient for you to have it, than not have it."

"That makes no sense," said Nikki, irritation coloring her tone. She hated it when Mrs. M Yoda'd out.

"I know. Like I said, don't worry about it. This is for the future."

"The problem is that the future has a way of sneaking up on me."

Mrs. Merrivel laughed. "It sneaks up on all of us, dear. Now I can tell you're driving, so you shouldn't be talking. I'll hang up and let you concentrate. I'll leave it to you on whether or not you should call Darla about whatever it is you're involved in. Be safe."

The line went dead and Nikki dropped the phone in the passenger seat in disgust.

"How am I supposed to concentrate with impending promotion hanging over my head?" she demanded of the empty car. The invisible Val Robinson that resided in the passenger seat pointed at her and laughed. And then because it was Val, flipped the bird to a passing truck on jacked-up wheels.

She really didn't want Mrs. M's job. There were too many moving pieces. The LA Branch was a sprawling mess that encompassed the greater Los Angeles area and all its municipalities. It had been leaderless for over two years. The Council kept throwing people at it, but no one could seem to stick in the job. And mostly that was because the LA Branch and the West Coast division were run out of the same building. With Mrs. Merrivel in the building, why would anyone bother to stop and ask a branch leader anything? Mrs. Merrivel had been hinting for the last year that Nikki might want the position. Nikki didn't. A new LA Branch leader, a smart one anyway, would relocate out of the fancy office building to one of the company owned warehouses downtown, out of Mrs. M's sphere of influence. And then she would have to start streamlining the reporting process, reorganize into teams and retrain some of the old guard. It was a ridiculous amount of work. And for what? So that eventually she could be considered for Mrs. M's job?

When she had filled in for Mrs. M while she'd been in Turkey it had been a last minute scramble with the understanding that the Council would replace her as soon as someone was available. That had dragged into weeks as Mrs. M's return was complicated by Mr. M's heart surgery. Nikki had hated every minute of it. There were too many pieces in motion, too many players on the board, too much politics, too much thinking about the future. She didn't want any of it. What she wanted was to stay with her team, sleep in the same bed as her boyfriend for more than three months of the year, and have her mom shut the hell up about pretty much everything and just be supportive for once. Those were not big goals. They were perfectly reasonable goals. Why did no one want her to achieve those goals?

She bumped down the long driveway to Crazy Cooter's, past the looming cars and under the archway made of deer antlers and bumpers, pulling to a stop outside a listing RV that had mated with a pre-fab shed. Cooter was sitting outside on a lawn chair, polishing a chrome hood ornament.

"That is the creepiest damn thing I have ever seen in my life," said Jane pulling up and exiting the car. "Who in the world builds a giant archway out of deer antlers and bumpers?"

"I call it the Roadkill Memorial," said Cooter, squinting up at Jane from under his straw cowboy hat. "It's in memory of those deer ones gone by."

"There is something wrong with you," said Jane.

"They don't call me Crazy Cooter for nothing," he said, grinning and displaying a gapped smile, missing the same amount of teeth as the average Canadian hockey player.

"Hi, Cooter," said Nikki. "Do you remember me?"

"Sure do. You're Nikki Lanier. You and Donny and the Tyrell kid used to jump out of refrigerators to try and scare me."

"It never worked," said Nikki smiling.

"Well, let's just say that three little kids weren't the scariest thing that ever popped out of a refrigerator at me."

"I don't want to know the scariest thing, do I?" asked Jane.

"Well, if you don't like the Memorial Archway then, no, probably not," agreed Cooter. "Well, Nikki Lanier, what can I do for you?"

"I'm here about Ylina," said Nikki, and Cooter stopped polishing for a moment.

"The sheriff was here earlier and I told him I didn't want to press charges and that he should get the hell off my property," said Cooter. "If you're here to persuade me otherwise you can go on and get too."

Nikki and Jane exchanged looks. "Press charges for what?"

"For robbing the till. But it was only a couple of hundred bucks. She probably needed the money. She's been a real help the last couple of years, so I'm just going to think of it as her bonus."

"When was the sheriff here?" asked Jane.

"About an hour ago, why?" Cooter looked from Jane to Nikki, looking worried.

"Um, well, did he say—what exactly did he say?"

"He said he'd caught her with some cash and wanted to look around to make sure she hadn't taken anything else."

Nikki and Jane exchanged another look.

"And he didn't say anything else about Ylina?"

"What else was there to say? Look, I know she's illegal. If I press charges the sheriff can send her back to Mexico. But she's been here since she was seven. What's she going to do in Mexico? I told him I hadn't noticed anything and that I knew she'd been saving up money, so it was probably her cash. He wanted to look around, but I told him to come back with a warrant. I don't hold with cops poking around."

"The thing is," said Nikki, then hesitated. "The thing is, I went to see Ylina at the, uh, place she's staying, about three hours ago and uh, well, there's no easy way to say this, but she's dead. She'd been killed."

Cooter started to stand and then sat back down, his face going white under his tan.

"That poor kid," he said after a minute. "I knew she was in trouble. I just knew it, but she wouldn't say anything. I should have made her tell me. I figured she'd come around in her own time. That poor kid." He fought back tears, and after a moment he blew his nose into a grimy red handkerchief pulled from the upper pocket of his overalls.

"Why didn't the sheriff tell me?" he asked looking up at Nikki, puzzled.

"That is an excellent question," said Jane. "Many of the sheriff's actions seem a little strange to me."

"That's because he's an arrogant prick who thinks he owns everything in the County," said Cooter. "But why wouldn't he tell me if Ylina was dead?"

"We think Ylina had something that the sheriff really wants, but that he didn't find in her room."

"Something bad?" Cooter still looked puzzled.

"Possibly something bad for the sheriff," said Nikki. She was trusting a lot on Cooter's innate distrust of law enforcement.

"Well, let's go look for it," said Cooter, standing up and dropping the hood ornament into the dust. "I never liked that guy," he said, yanking open the door to the shed. "If he had something to do with Ylina's," he hesitated, "with her not being here, then I want him to go down in a fiery ball of flames."

"We can help with that," said Jane.

"Good! I mean, I figured you would since he screwed Nikki's dad so royally, but you never know about people."

The shed-turned-office was filthy, except for the desk in the corner. A stray sunbeam sneaking through a grimy window illuminated the dust motes in the air. It smelled of grease and mildew.

"Ylina sat there," said Cooter, pointing to the desk that was organized in a grid of papers, computer, stapler, and pens that would have made an engineer happy.

"On it," said Jane.

"Cooter, what did happen with my dad and the sheriff?" asked Nikki, ignoring the desk in favor of the customer counter with the cash register on it.

"Bastard planted weed on your dad," said Cooter with a shrug. "Then he said a bunch of bullshit in court and got him extradited. Which, since your dad was one of my best customers at the time, hit me kind of hard. I'm sure it didn't do you any good either."

The cash register had been left open, the change and the small bills had been ignored.

"What did she take?" asked Nikki, poking at the cash register.

"Just the hundreds," said Cooter with a shrug. "About five hundred bucks. I'm not happy about it, but it's not the end of the world."

"Who's your best customer these days?" asked Nikki.

"Pedro Alavar," said Cooter. "Buys a lot of cars."

"Hangs out with a guy named Milt a lot? They both stink like weed?"

"Yeah, that's the guy. You know him?"

"We've met," said Nikki. "Jane what have you got?"

"Nothing, so far," said Jane, her fingers flying across the keyboard of the computer. "If there's something on here, then it's been wiped. It would help if I could take it into the office."

"You should probably stay away from Milt and Pedro," said Cooter, looking uncomfortable.

"They're the kind who wait for people outside of bars," said Nikki.

"If you mean that they don't believe in fighting fair and would sneak up on you in a parking lot, then yeah, that's them. Not nice guys."

Nikki stepped back and stared at the register. There was something odd about the whole thing. Ylina had gone out into the junkyard to get whatever it was out of that car. It had been a black bag. Then she'd heard the cops and gone running back in this direction. Nikki looked around the room, trying to put herself in Ylina's place. She'd been scared, rushed. She'd come back into the office. If the sheriff had found her here, what would she have done? Hidden the bag? Nikki glanced at the pristine desk. She wouldn't have hidden it in her area, she would have hidden it somewhere it could be overlooked. Nikki surveyed the room: two grimy chairs by the door, a deer head on the far wall, looking motheaten, one book case with a large collection of car owner manuals and National Geographics, and one table with an incomplete 375 piece puzzle on top. Nothing was out of place, just the register cash drawer hanging open.

"If she hadn't left the cash drawer open, would you have known anything was missing?"

"Not for most of the day," said Cooter. "I think she busted it. I tried to close it, but it just popped open again. That's actually the worst part. Cash registers ain't cheap."

Nikki pushed the drawer shut gently, but met resistance about an inch before the drawer closed. Frowning, she pulled the drawer back out and then lifted out the cash tray. Sliding her hand into the back of the till she felt along the back wall of the drawer inch by inch. On the far right corner she felt something hard and pulled it out.

"Yes!" said Jane, already reaching for the thumb drive in Nikki's hand.

"That's one of Ylina's doohickies," said Cooter. "I'm not supposed to touch them because I make technology die. That's what Ylina always says anyway. Said, I guess." Changing to the past tense brought up tears again and Cooter abruptly turned and went outside.

"I feel really bad for him," said Jane.

"I feel really bad for Ylina," said Nikki. "Now let's find out what's on the thumb drive."

AUGUST XXV

OVERDRIVE

Jane plugged the drive into Ylina's laptop and quickly tapped open the file. "It's audio files. All different dates. She seems to be organizing them by some sort of code. INC+5, INC+4, INC-2. I don't know what that means. Maybe she left some sort of key?"

"Hit the INC-2," said Nikki. "Let's try one while you're poking around."

Jane shrugged and opened up the file.

"I don't know," said a male voice. Nikki thought it was probably either Milt or Pedro's, but couldn't be sure. "I didn't think Jar Jar Binks was that bad."

"Not that bad? Not that bad?" The other voice sounded outraged.

"What? He was funny. I mean Jedi had Ewoks. I thought Jar Jar was the prequel version of Ewoks."

There was an inarticulate squawk and then the recording cut off.

"He makes a point," said Jane.

"Possibly if Jar Jar hadn't sounded so much like a 1920s black-face performer I might be able to go with that theory."

"I think that's unfair," said Jane. "He was an alien."

"But the cultural lens through which we view him is white America," said Nikki. Jane gaped up at her. "What? I do listen to you occasionally. Hit another one. Try that INC+5."

"I don't care," said Merv's voice. "I don't care if his grandmother is in the hospital. Go to the hospital and drag his sorry ass over here."

There was another voice, but Nikki couldn't quite make out the words.

"No," said Merv. "No more chances. He either gets the job done or I'm burying him out next to Luis. He's becoming a liability. I can't have him shooting his mouth off every time he gets drunk."

The second voice murmured something else, and then the recording shut off.

"Well," said Jane, "We'll probably need a larger sample size, but I'm going to guess that the plus and minus rating has to do with how serious the conversation is."

"The fact that Luis is buried somewhere is fairly serious," agreed Nikki. "Hit the one with the most recent date."

Jane did as she was told and there was a second of pause as the file loaded. The audio software displayed a sine wave of rising and falling bars that matched the voices.

"We just need a farm," said Merv.

"But it can't be too out in the open," said another voice. "We can't have people poking around."

"That's why I think the Connelly place is about perfect," said Merv. "It's an orchard. We leave the outside perimeter of trees and then we take out the middle sections. Lots of room to subdivide. Lots of good sunshine. Easy to keep nosy neighbors out of our business."

"You said she wasn't interested in selling."

"She's old," said Merv. "She's been talking about retiring and moving to the Westside with her daughter. We just have to find the right price. Plus, there's a nice symmetry considering her son-in-law started all this."

The other voice grunted. "I'm worried about certification." This time the voice was clearly recognizable as one of the voices from the previous conversation. Nikki thought it might be Milt.

"Don't be," said Merv. "I know the inspector for this region. I know whose table he's parking his feet under and I know his wife's phone number. We'll get the property. We'll set up a legal-size grow operation. We show it to George and get him to approve it. And then we expand, expand, expand. If he wants to come back and re-inspect I'll dissuade him. After the plants come in, we can cut off our Canadian friends and start shipping directly South."

"What about Pims? He's a liability."

"We'll see," said Merv. "It depends on how stop-happy the state patrol in Idaho and Oregon are. Now that pot's legal they'll be stopping every Washington license plate they see. Pims and his clever cars are still useful, for now. We'll re-evaluate next year."

"The Canadians won't be happy."

"Screw the Canadians," said the sheriff forcefully. "They've been nickel and diming me for years because they know I've got nowhere else to go. Meanwhile, I'm the one taking all the risks. Not anymore. Ylina, get your ass in here. It's time to hit the road." There was the sound of a door opening.

"I look like a soccer mom," said Ylina.

"A soccer mom with fifty pounds of weed in the under carriage of her minivan," said the sheriff. There was a chuckle from the other man in the room.

"I think it's the wig that really sells it," said Milt.

"That's easy for you to say. You don't have to wear it," said Ylina. They heard the sound of footsteps and then there was the rustle of cloth and the recording ended.

"Incriminating," said Jane.

"Yes, very," agreed Nikki.

"No, that's what INC stands for. I found a text doc with notes. That was an incriminating level of plus five. The Jar Jar Binks conversation was a negative two. She also makes the following statement:

I have been coerced into smuggling marijuana for the sheriff of Pend Oreille County, Mervin Smalls. I was brought to the United States as a small child. My mother died in 2010. I have no other family in the US, and I do not know my family in Colombia. The sheriff threatened to deport or kill me if I didn't work for him. I believe he is fully capable of carrying out either threat. Mervin Smalls imports marijuana from Canada inside cars modified by Bill Pims. He then sells it to gangs in Idaho. Using false passports and documentation, I drive the cars into Canada, put marijuana into a concealed compartment and drive them back into the US. I have made fourteen trips in the last year. The dates are noted below. I have made recordings of the Sheriff and his associates without their knowledge as proof of their crimes. I intend to—"
Jane stopped reading.

"Intend to what?" asked Nikki.

"I don't know," said Jane. "She didn't finish the sentence. Presumably she meant to give it to someone who could stop the sheriff."

"We need to get this to Donny," said Nikki. "Come on, let's take it next door and see if he's up yet."

Nikki tucked the thumb drive into her pocket and exited the junkyard office. Cooter was staring at the hood ornament he'd formerly been polishing as if it were a crystal ball.

"Do you think the sheriff had something to do with Ylina's death?" he asked looking up.

"Yes, I do," said Nikki.

"Are you going to stop him?"

"Yes, I am."

Cooter squinted at the sun as if checking the time of day and then back at Nikki. "That's not going to be easy. He's top of the food chain around here."

"Lions always think they're top of the food chain until they meet a crocodile," said Nikki. "I should have stopped him before he hurt Ylina, but I promise he's not going to hurt anyone else."

"You seem really confident," said Cooter frowning. "But you're an itty bitty thing and someone said you were a Carrie Mae lady. Are you sure you don't need help?"

"She has help," said Jane. "And you are underestimating Carrie Mae ladies."

Cooter scratched his head and then shrugged. "Just make it happen then, I guess."

Nikki nodded and got in the car. It felt anti-climactic to go out to the road and then one driveway to the left, but she needed Donny on board. He was the one who could take credit for all her investigating and keep Z'ev in the dark about her adventures here in Kaniksu Falls.

Mrs. Fernandez opened the door. "*Hola*, Nikki," she said smiling. "I'm so happy to see you. I didn't get to say hello at the party."

"I'm happy to see you, too," said Nikki, returning the proffered hug. "And I really want to catch up, but I need to see Donny about something."

"Oh." Mrs. Fernandez leaned out and inspected the row of

cars in the driveway.. "I'll check his room, but I'm pretty sure he spent the night at Jackson's. You know they haven't had much of a chance to catch up since Donny's been home."

Nikki threw her hands in the air in frustration. "They never tell me anything."

"That sounds like the boys," said Mrs. Fernandez nodding placidly. "Do you need his cell phone number?"

"No, I've got it in my phone. Thanks, Mrs. Fernandez. I'll go find him at Jackson's."

"OK, but when you talk to him, remind him that we're all going to Spokane tonight for his cousin's *Quinceañera* tonight. We're leaving at six, so he has to be home by then or drive himself."

"I'll let him know," said Nikki, backing toward the car. "Thanks." Nikki flipped through her contact list as she approached the car door and dialed, but Donny didn't pick up. Nikki tapped her nails on the roof of the car and waited for the beep.

"Donny, it's Nikki. I've got a serious situation. I need your help. Call me ASAP." She hung up the phone and went over to Jane's car. "He spent the night at Jackson's. Which means that they're probably ignoring their phones and playing video games. We'll have to go back up to Jackson's and roust them."

"Do you want to stop at your grandma's and um, make sure your mom got home OK?" asked Jane.

"No, not really," said Nikki. "But we probably ought to."

AUGUST XXVI
ROOTS, ROCK, REGGAE

Nikki pulled into the Connelly Farm and parked behind Jane. Her grandmother's SUV was already in front of the house. And for a moment nothing moved. Then the front door opened and Z'ev slid out, gingerly depressing the latch so as not to make any noise. He was wearing swim trunks and carrying a small cooler.

"What the hell did you do?" he whispered, tip-toeing over to the car. Jane handed him back his keys. "I haven't seen this much crying and door slamming since my sister was fourteen."

"So you have a sister," said Jane. "Interesting."

Z'ev spared a moment to give Jane a confused look. Jane smiled broadly and pointed back at Nikki.

"Yeah, Mom and I may have a had a bit of a moment." She dialed Donny again, and again it went to voicemail.

"We're all hiding down at the pond. I was sent on a snack retrieval mission." He hoisted the cooler as evidence.

Nikki hung up without leaving a message. "That's good," she said, feeling that he was expecting some sort of reply.

"So are you going inside? Or are you hiding with us?"

"I actually need to get a hold of Donny."

"Donny? Who cares about Donny? What did you and your mom argue about?"

"I don't know, how about the fact that neither of you ever told me that my dad went to prison?"

Z'ev's face twitched into an expression usually worn by small game upon catching site of a hawk. "Uh…"

"Seriously, how could you not tell me?"

"What makes you think—"

"Oh, please. I'm sure you did a background check on me."

Jane took the cooler out of Z'ev's hand and began to back slowly away.

"I had to for work," he said, in a measured tone, as if he had practiced this response.

"Of course you had to," snapped Nikki. "But once you found out my dad went to prison, why didn't you tell me?"

"I thought you knew."

"What? You thought I was lying about my dad leaving us?"

"Well, yeah!"

"Why would I even do that?"

"Do you really want to be discussing this now?"

"No, I want to call Jackson and tell him to wake Donny up!" She stared blankly at her phone, waiting for it to magically produce the information she wanted. "Jane! I need Jackson's number."

"I need to go into the house for the wi-fi to do that," said Jane who had made it all the way to the top of the path.

"Damn it!"

"I have Jackson's number," said Jenny, coming up the path with Ellen.

"Why do you have Jackson's number?" Nikki felt a sour twist in her stomach.

"He gave it to me," said Jenny with a shrug. "I was going to go over later and try out his warped wall."

"There's your choice, Nikki," said Z'ev. "You can discuss with Jenny how you don't want her to date your ex-boyfriend or you can discuss with me why I thought you were lying about your dad."

Everyone swiveled to look at Nikki.

"Oh, my God. There are firm work / life boundaries for a reason, people. This is exactly why I didn't want any of you here!"

"Not even me?" Jane looked hurt.

"Hey," said Ellen. "We're just here to help."

"Help? When are you guys helping? I can't leave the three of you alone without epic disaster striking! I am always on. You get to float in my damn pond, but I have to work. None of you ever stop to think about consequences because I am always there to clean up the mess. Once, just once, I'd like to not have to think about what happens next. But no, Nikki doesn't get Cancun because Cancuning is for people who don't have to be in charge."

"She's referring to herself in the third person," said Jenny in a hoarse whisper. "That is not a good sign."

"Gah!" Nikki threw her phone in the open window of her car. "I'm not dealing with any of you right now—I have a job to do. I'm going to go wake up Donny and make him arrest the sheriff. I will be back and maybe then I will be able to deal with all of your issues."

Nikki slammed the car door, revved the engine, and backed down the drive, ending with a burn out one-eighty to emphasize how annoyed she was. And because, let's face it, she enjoyed doing it.

She knew she needed to deal with the Jackson—Jenny situation, but every time she tried to think about it, her mind seemed to slide to some other thing to think about. There was no reason Jenny and Jackson shouldn't date. Other than the fact that it was weird, damn it! Weird, weird, weird. Damn weird. Jackson belonged to her. She was used to guarding his memory as something special in the past. She wasn't used to having him pop up and be a real person in the present with real opinions of his own. The real person he was now was well-suited to Jenny, she could see that, but at the end of the day it was still weird.

The road up to Jackson's ranch, or vineyard, or whatever he was calling it, was well graveled and freshly oiled and she slalomed up the road with a little bit of glee, putting the Impala through its paces. The house was a log cabin. Or at least one of the modern log cabins. Luxury living in a woodsy exterior, built on a grade so it appeared to be one story from the front, but opening into a daylight basement in the back.

Jackson and Captain Beaumont were sitting on the porch. Jackson was wrapped in a blanket and looked hung-over as a cliff, bleary-eyed and hair sticking straight up.

"It's weird!" said Nikki getting out of the car.

"OK," said Jackson. Captain Beaumont jumped the stairs to bounce around Nikki, interrupting her view of Jackson periodically with a flopping dog head. "Are we arguing about something that I don't remember? Can I get a definition of what 'it' is or am I guessing?"

"The idea of you dating Jenny is weird."

"It's a little weird," he agreed, nodding.

"Yes! Thank you. Why does no one else see it?"

"Well, I think we all see it. I'm just thinking about doing it anyway."

"Yes, Captain. Yes, I see you too." She paused to pat Captain Beaumont and then climbed onto the porch and flopped down in the chair next to Jackson. "That's probably fair. I mean, you guys do have a lot in common with your rodeo obsessions. But you know, it's weird. And besides, I thought you were going to try and win me back, etc."

"Yeah, but that was when I thought you were dating a douchebag IRS guy or something. Then I met Z'ev. You're right. He's definitely not a cubicle guy. And I may be stubborn, but I know when I'm beat. I don't stand a chance while he's around." There was a pause while they stared at the view.

"Except that I shouldn't let him be around," said Nikki sadly.

"He's not stupid," said Jackson. "He probably already knows that something isn't right. Why not tell him?"

"It's not just me," said Nikki, shaking her head. "I have the team to consider."

"Well, I don't know everything that's going on with you and your 'team,' but that doesn't seem fair to you."

Nikki sighed. "Since when is life fair? I need to ovary up, as Jane says, and just do it. He loves me and keeping him in a relationship based on lies is unfair to him. I love him, but I can't be a good partner to him and I should set him free to find someone who can."

"I understand that," said Jackson. "But I thought that about you and in retrospect it's pretty clear that I underestimated you. Don't underestimate Z'ev."

"You didn't underestimate me, though," said Nikki. "Everything you've said about that point in our lives was true. If you had stayed, I would have clung to you and insisted you stay in school. We would have moved in together after college and you'd be miserable in some nine-to-five job you hate and I would have probably made us move across the country so I could pursue a career in linguistics that I would have ended up hating, but would be too scared to leave. I never would have joined Carrie Mae or met the girls. That's what changed me. I'm a better human being because you left. You made the right decision."

Jackson shook his head, looking like he wanted to argue, but he didn't. When he finally met her eye, he smiled. "We really are OK, you and me?"

"Yeah," said Nikki. "We really are." He nodded and they were both silent for a long while. "The grapes look nice. I haven't been up here since I was a kid and who was it that lived here? The Kramer's?"

"Yeah. I won't ask Jenny out if you think it's too weird," he said.

"Nah. She's awesome, you're awesome. Why shouldn't the two of you at least go on a date?" Nikki scratched her head and then redid her pony tail. "It has been a long-ass day and it's barely three. I really thought this trip was going to be more of a vacation."

"There's coffee in the kitchen."

"No thanks. I need to wake Donny up and put him to work."

"I think," said Jackson and then squinted toward the road. "Are we expecting your boyfriend? I think that's his rental car."

"I wasn't expecting my boyfriend the first time, so sure, why not? He's full of surprises. Jackson, did you know my dad went to jail?"

"Your dad went to jail?" Jackson looked surprised. "When?"

"Apparently, that's why Mom moved us to Seattle. Dad didn't just up and leave us."

"That does make more sense," said Jackson. "He always seemed devoted to you guys. Or at least you, anyway. What did he get arrested for?"

"Holding with intent to distribute. Pot. He was extradited to Canada. But you didn't know before now?"

"No, my dad got transferred, remember? We left the year before you did. Although, now something Donny said makes way more sense. Something about undercover life running in the family. We were like twelve beers in, so I never circled back to that. You know, I have to say that having you guys back in town is the first time that it's felt like I moved home."

Nikki laughed. "I know what you mean. At some point last night while I was chasing you, and Donny was whining, it felt like we were twelve again. Living in LA is great, and of course, I have the girls, but there's that feeling that everyone in the whole city is from somewhere else. There're no roots. There's no one who's known me since I was five."

"You mean, there's no one who can call you on your bullshit?"

Z'ev's rental car bumped to a stop next to Val's Impala. Nikki wondered if the Impala would ever stop being Val's.

"Oh, I think I'm about to get called on my bullshit," said Nikki. "And look, you've got a front row seat."

But it wasn't just Z'ev. The entire team spilled out of the car.

"It's Beach Blanket Bingo," said Jackson, surveying the array of swimsuits.

"And I'm Annette Funicello," said Nikki.

"I am not Frankie Avalon," said Z'ev.

"Nikki, what the hell was that?" demanded Ellen, planting her feet and putting her hands on her hips. "Do you really think that we're not pulling our own weight and we're horning in on your vacation? We came to help you. If you need more help, you just have to ask. You know that."

"And I can date whoever I want!" said Jenny, who waved at Jackson.

"I'm here because everyone else was going," said Jane. "And I thought I should come and support you since we already settled our issue."

Nikki looked at her team with affection and wished she hadn't talked to Mrs. M. Looking at them now, it was as if they each had little Google location pins over their heads, giving off their future on the hover-over. Nikki wondered if Mrs. M was hoping that she and Jenny would end up as Division Leaders for the East and West Coasts at the same time. That would certainly make policy changes easier. Ellen and Jane, would they have their own teams? Would they go on to be branch leaders? Did they even want that? Or, like Nikki, were they dreading the day they'd be pushed out of the team? It occurred to Nikki to wonder if she was standing in the way of their ambitions.

"I know you're here to help," said Nikki, and Ellen looked surprised, while Z'ev looked suspicious. "But sometimes it feels like the decisions are always up to me. It's hard to relax when I always have to be keeping track of everyone, and today has been a bit of a hard day."

"She found out her dad didn't leave her and that, really, he went to prison for smuggling pot," interjected Jane.

"What?" said Ellen. "When did that happen? Honey, why didn't you say? That's terrible!"

"It's not that big a deal," said Jenny, kindly. "I've got, like, three cousins in prison for moonshining. Even the really good families have a few rats in the woodpile."

"It doesn't matter. I shouldn't have yelled at you. It's just, you know, Grandma and Jorge, Mom lying about my dad for years, and then Ylina and the sheriff on top of it. I snapped. I'm sorry. I feel like I've been wrong about everything since I got here."

"Peg finally told you about Jorge?" Jackson looked pleased. "I told her it wouldn't be that big of a deal."

"Well, I wouldn't say told, exactly," said Nikki. "But let's just say I know."

"Nikki," said Z'ev. He said it quietly, which is what made Nikki look at him. She hated it when he was quiet. It meant he had been thinking. He was far too smart to let him think. "Nikki, what about the sheriff? What's going on with him?"

"Ah. Yes, the sheriff. Jackson, where's Donny? I need to talk to him about the sheriff."

"He's not here," said Jackson. "The sheriff finally called him back and he went out to the sheriff's house to talk to him. Don't ask me how, because I'm kind of missing that portion of the evening in my memory, but Donny knows there's a smuggling ring in town and he wants to talk strategy with the sheriff. He even knows about Milt and Pedro and Bill Pims."

Nikki felt the blood drain from her face. She felt adrenaline hit her blood stream and her heart speed up. To compensate, she sat even more still. Adrenaline could make you panic, drive you into flight or fight. Now was not the time for either. Now was the time to make a careful plan.

"Oh, crap," said Jane, her hands flying up to cover her mouth. "He's going to be buried next to Luis."

AUGUST XXVII
UNRAVEL

"Who's Luis?" asked Ellen.

"I don't know," said Jane, "But Donny's going to end up buried next to him if we don't do something fast. Crap, crap, crap! Nikki, what do we do?"

Nikki felt the group's attention shift to her like a weight on her shoulders. What she wouldn't give for a real vacation where someone else was in charge and made all the decisions. She reached over and took Jackson's coffee cup to buy herself a little more time. "OK," she said, taking a sip. She needed to do a few things. She needed to find out if Donny was still alive. She needed to find out where he was being held. And she needed to get Jenny working on an extraction plan. But most of all she needed to get rid of Jackson and Z'ev.

"I think Jackson and Z'ev should –"

"No," said Z'ev, folding his arms across his chest.

"You haven't even heard what I was going to say."

"I don't need to hear what you're going to say," said Z'ev. "I've had enough. The rubber is meeting the road. Either I'm in or I call my friends at the DEA."

"How far away are your friends at the DEA?" asked Nikki, hoping for a life-line. Maybe the DEA could solve all her problems at once.

"About three hours," said Z'ev.

"Nikki, I don't think he has that long," said Jane quietly.

"He could already be dead," said Nikki. "We don't know."

"Nikki!" Jackson took his coffee cup back. "What the hell are you talking about? What is going on? And for the record, I'm with *Es Grande*; I'm not going anywhere."

Nikki sighed, weighing her options. Nikki looked from Jane to Jenny to Ellen. Ellen shrugged fatalistically and Jenny nodded. Whole truth, half-truth, quarter truth? Of course, the answer was never whole truth.

"You remember Ylina? The girl we met at the bar."

"Yes, what's she got to with anything?"

"I ran into her last night and—"

"When?" demanded Z'ev. "I was with you the whole night."

"When I was chasing Jackson. I cut through the junkyard and ran into her."

"That is cheating!" Jackson was outraged.

"Of course, it's cheating. How else was I going to catch you? Can we focus? Anyway, Ylina gave me a thumb drive. She said it was her insurance policy." Jane began to studiously study her nail polish, which for Jenny and Ellen was a dead giveaway that Nikki was lying. "When I went to return it to her today I found out that she'd been killed."

"Seriously?" Jackson looked shocked.

"Yes, and when Jane and I opened the thumb drive we found audio recordings that prove that Sheriff Merv Smalls is the head of the organization smuggling pot South out of Canada."

"Holy crap," said Jackson, unconsciously echoing Jane.

"And if Donny has gone to tell the Sheriff that he knows about half of the smuggling operation, how long do you think Donny's life expectancy is?"

"Not three hours," said Z'ev. "Will state police mobilize on a tip any faster?"

"Not from some random group of women. What about someone from the, uh, government?"

"Nikki, I'm fairly certain you've told Jenny, Ellen, and Jane I work for the CIA. I appreciate the pretense, but it would make the conversation a lot quicker if we skipped the ambiguity."

"You work for the CIA? Holy crap! Who are you people?"

"Jackson, you may not have picked the best morning for a hangover," said Nikki, patting him on the shoulder. "Sorry."

"Meanwhile, we need to come up with a plan." Z'ev paced from the car to the porch and back. Nikki watched him with affection. Jane and the girls seemed puzzled. "OK, I think you girls should stay here, while—"

Z'ev's comments were cut off by a hysterical laugh from Jenny. "I'm sorry, sweetie," she said, still laughing. "That was really funny right then. Nikki, what do you want to do?"

They were staring at her. More specifically, Z'ev was staring at her. She was stuck. Whatever she said next was going to reveal a lot to him. Her choices were to help Donny or preserve Carrie Mae's secret from her CIA agent boyfriend. And neither of those choice probably included an option for preserving her relationship. She was at the edge of the cliff and one way or another she was going down. Her only real choices were to see if she was going to slip and fall or go off in a swan dive. What had Jane said? Nikki likes to swan?

"Call the sheriff," said Nikki. "Offer a swap. The thumb drive for Donny."

"We can't give him the evidence!" said Jackson.

"Jane will upload it to the cloud or whatever and send it to Z'ev's DEA friends. I think we should still call them in for back-up. But I don't think we can wait for them. The cloud is a thing, right Jane?"

Z'ev wasn't saying anything. That probably wasn't a good sign.

"Well, it is a thing, sort of. It's a little more complicated than that." Jane had the uncomfortable look she wore when something Nikki said was a total misrepresentation of what she did.

"You know how I feel about complicated," said Nikki, and Jane sighed.

"You don't care as long as it gets done." Jane trudged up the stairs, past Jackson. "Jackson, what's your wi-fi password?"

"I don't have a wi-fi password," said Jackson. Jane looked slightly ill. "Who's going to steal my wi-fi? The cows?"

"OK, well, give me a few minutes, then, Z'ev, I'll need some contact info for your DEA friends."

"Before you do that, can you look up the sheriff's number?" asked Nikki.

"I can do that," said Jackson.

"You have the sheriff's number?"

"No, I have the Kaniksu Falls telephone book." Jackson reached down and removed a slim volume from under the leg of the table next to him. They all stared at the telephone book and Nikki poked it suspiciously with one finger.

"Is it really accurate? It has actual phone numbers?"

"Yeah. They update it every three years."

"That's weird."

"You're only saying that because you live in a city where it's weird to know your neighbors." Jackson flipped through until he found the page he was looking for. "There you go, Merv Smalls, address and home phone number."

"You know, even if he agrees to the trade, he's not going to let Donny live," said Ellen.

"Or anyone else he thinks might be a threat," said Z'ev.

"Yeah, I do know. But he only knows about me. He might suspect that I'll bring Jackson in, but the rest of you are going to be a complete surprise." Nikki dialed the number and waited. On the fourth ring, someone picked up.

"Yeah," said a male voice.

"This is Nikki Lanier. I need to speak to Merv Smalls about Ylina."

"He's busy."

"Is this Pedro? Pedro, put the sheriff on the phone or I'll drive out there and break your nose again."

There was a pause. "Give me a minute."

There was rustling and some distant, muffled yelling.

"Ms. Lanier, this is a surprise," said the sheriff. "I was under the impression that you would be headed back to LA by now."

"Sorry to disappoint," said Nikki. "But I had to stop by Crazy Cooter's and pick up a few of Ylina's things."

"I see," said Merv. "I didn't realize the two of you were that close."

"We weren't, but it's funny how no one in this town really likes you. Crazy Cooter didn't mind if I went through Ylina's computer or took the thumb drive she left. You know, the one with all the recordings she made of you and your friends."

The sheriff was silent for a long moment. "What do you want?"

"I want Donny Fernandez back in one piece."

"And are you suggesting that some sort of mutually beneficial arrangement could be made?"

"If Donny is still alive, then yes."

She heard the sound of dragging. "Say hello to your friend," said the Sheriff.

"Hi," said Donny. There was a smacking noise.

"A little bit more, please," said the Sheriff.

"Go to hell," said Donny, his tone was flat and angry, but still definitely Donny.

"Donny, hang in there. I'll get you out of this."

"Mr. Fernandez doesn't look too confident," said the sheriff.

"Mr. Fernandez just has to stay alive."

"And how do I know that you haven't made copies of the recordings?" asked the Sheriff reasonably.

"It's six gigs of data," said Nikki. "I don't have anything to copy it to or with and I certainly haven't had the time. The thumb drive is the only copy."

"And you're the only one who knows about it?"

"Did my father talk when you stole his operation out from under him?"

The sheriff laughed. "No, he didn't. Of course, he was worried that I'd go up to your grandma's house and discover a robbery gone wrong and all of you would end up dead. He didn't have much incentive to talk."

"I have the same amount of incentive," said Nikki. "Let's make a trade and then everybody can go back to their lives."

"Sounds fair to me. When and where?"

"Crazy Cooter's, tonight. 7:00 P.M."

"Too close to the Fernandez estate. I don't need a horde of crazy Mexican's butting in on my business."

"They'll all be in Spokane for his cousin's *Quinceañera*," said Nikki. "They leave at six."

"You seem so up to date on the comings and goings of our little town," said Merv. "I'd say you really seem to fit in here, except of course, you don't."

"Don't worry, I'll be heading out of town as soon as I have Donny."

"I'm counting on it," said the Sheriff. "See you at seven."

Nikki hung up the phone and considered throwing it across the lawn. "I want to punch that man in the throat. Jenny, how are you feeling about Crazy Cooter's strategically?"

"It's good," said Jenny, nodding. "River access, in case we want to get creative with a boat. Lots of good hidey-holes for Ellen, but also some good open spaces and lines of sight. I can start working on an exit strategy."

"Good. Ellen what have we got in the way of equipment?"

"Not a damn thing," said Ellen making a face.

"I brought my Borg cube!" yelled Jane from inside.

"You brought the whole basic kit?" Ellen yelled back. "Weren't you supposed to turn that in when we were put on leave?"

"Yeah, but I have two because I was doing some testing for Rachel. So I only turned in one."

"That's why we love you, Jane," yelled Jenny.

"Well, we've got Jane's make-up kit, so that should get us started. We're short on guns though. What did you pack—the 1911?" asked Ellen.

"The SIG."

"I've got a Glock and SIG P226," said Z'ev.

"Ooh, classic!" said Jenny. "Although, what is it with you and Nikki and the SIGs? Branch out, people."

"I didn't realize we both carried SIG's," said Z'ev quietly.

"It'd be nice to have a rifle," said Ellen wistfully.

"What I wouldn't give to have Freddy with us," said Jenny, sadly.

"I have a rifle I use for deer hunting," said Jackson. "I don't know if that's what you want."

"I'll take a look," said Ellen.

"Someone in town has an AK-47," said Nikki. "I saw the casings up at the quarry. I know it's not Freddy, but maybe we could find out who and borrow it."

"That seems like it might be over the top," said Z'ev.

"Over the top?" said Nikki, "Or really, just the right amount?"

"That's probably Bill Bartlby," said Jackson. "I can call him and see if he'll lend it to us."

"What does he do?" asked Nikki.

"Raises cows," said Jackson.

"Then what does he need an AK-47 for?" asked Ellen.

"So he can shoot it," said Jackson, with a shrug.

"I'm just not OK with that," said Ellen. "I really think those things should be more carefully licensed."

"They are carefully licensed," said Jenny. "Laws do not stop people from doing things they want to do."

"But the threat of punishment does," said Ellen. "And you can't punish someone without a law saying that something is wrong. And what are people doing with assault rifles that is totally reasonable?"

"Shooting targets is totally reasonable," said Jenny. "And only two percent of crimes are committed with assault rifles. I know lots of people who own assault rifles. Rifles are not the problem."

"You mean you're related to lots of people who own assault rifles. And having met some of your relatives, I don't think I'm comfortable with that."

"Hey, just because I happen to have some cracker, confederate flag-flying relatives that collectively have got the common sense of a single fruit fly and like to get drunk on Saturday night, does not mean that owning assault rifles is a bad idea. Because sadly, I don't think they can make a law that only excludes drunk jackasses and I don't think the rest of us want our civil liberties decided based on a survey of my relatives."

"Jenny's the one who steals my gun catalogs, isn't she?" asked Z'ev.

"Yes," lied Nikki.

"Besides," continued Jenny, "You're the one who just love, love, loves her Mauser."

"And my Barrett and my Dragunov. Doesn't mean I want other people to have them."

"Ellen has a Dragunov?" Z'ev looked impressed.

"Ladies," said Nikki, clearing her throat. Z'ev's commentary was making her nervous. "Let's resolve one of the thorny issues of the twenty-first century at a time when Donny's life is not on the line."

"Right." Ellen refocused and looked at Jackson and Z'ev, slightly embarrassed.

"I'm going inside to work on our exit plan," said Jenny, lifting her chin and heading for the house. Her dignified exit was somewhat spoiled as she caught her toe on the lip of the stairs and stumbled slightly. Jackson caught her by the arm and pulled her back to upright. "I'm fine, I'm fine," huffed Jenny, turning bright pink and hurrying into the house.

"So what I was saying," said Ellen. "was that we have Jane's kit. Three handguns, a deer hunting rifle, and possibly a AK-47 that we can borrow."

"My grandma has a Smith & Wesson revolver we can also probably borrow," said Nikki.

"OK," said Ellen with a shrug. "That's four hand guns and two rifles. There's six of us, so I guess that works out. How much ammo do we have?"

"How much ammo do we need?" asked Jackson. "Nikki, are you sure about this? Merv Smalls has been the sheriff here for five years. Do we really think he's going to kill Donny? I mean, Donny's a cop. You really think he's going to risk killing a cop?"

"Yes, I do," said Nikki. "I think he'll really kill Donny. Just like I think he really killed Ylina. Just like I think he really killed whoever Luis was. He's been using illegal immigrants to smuggle pot because he knows they're vulnerable and he knows that if they go missing no one will ask questions. Merv Smalls is not a nice man. He has over a decade invested in this scheme and if you think he's going to roll over and give in just because Donny is a cop, you're mistaken. Something needs to be done."

"OK," said Jackson nodding. "But are you the one to do it? Shouldn't we let someone else handle it? Someone with more…"

"Someone with more what?" asked Nikki. "Testicles?"

"I was thinking credentials," said Jackson.

"Relax, Jackson," said Ellen, climbing the stairs, and going into the house. "This is what we do."

"Is it?" said Z'ev. "Because honestly, that's what I've always wanted to know. Just what is it that the four of you do?"

"We work for Carrie Mae," said Nikki helplessly, knowing that he'd never believe the truth.

AUGUST XXVIII
GET READY

She could feel Z'ev carefully not talking to her as she loaded her gun and checked her extra magazine. She and Ellen had stolen a quick, whispered conference in the bathroom at Jackson's house.

"We'll tell him that we're private security for Carrie Mae because Carrie Mae has branches all over the world. That works, right? I mean, it's even sort of true. From a certain perspective."

Nikki had nodded. It might almost work. He was still going to ask why she hadn't told him.

She stole a glance at him through the racks of clothes in her bedroom. "Thanks for doing this," she said to Z'ev.

"Helping rescue Donny? What am I supposed to do—let him get killed and you get killed trying to stop it?"

"Nobody's getting killed," said Nikki. "It's going to be fine."

Z'ev finished strapping on the P226 and handed her his Glock and extra magazines. "You keep saying that, but I'm not sure what you're basing it on."

Nikki felt herself bristle. She was good at her job. If she could take down Val Robinson or keep Kit Masters from getting himself killed, she was pretty sure that she could put the kibosh on a small time sheriff in a small time town in the middle of nowhere. But she couldn't say any of that. She opened her mouth and shut again, swallowing her pride, and turning back to her gun.

"Nothing? Can you just say something?" demanded Z'ev. "Anything that makes this somewhat OK?"

Nikki took a deep breath. She needed to say something. She could see it in his face. She had to say something or she was going to lose him. This was it. She was going to do it. Now or never. Time to jump.

"Nikki?" Nell opened the door, her face tear-stained, and a Kleenex clutched in one hand. She looked from Z'ev, with his gun strapped to his leg, to Nikki with the Glock in one hand and the SIG on her waist, and froze.

"I cannot catch a break today," said Nikki.

"Nikki, what's going on?" asked Nell.

"I'm sorry, Mom," said Nikki, pushing her back into the hall. "We have to go help Donny right now."

"But, but," Nell trailed after them bubbling like a steam trolley. "I don't approve of guns."

"I picked up your grandma's gun," said Jane, from the foot of the stairs. "And the holster, speed loader, and a box of bullets. Do we need anything else?"

"But," said Nell staring at the gun in Jane's hand.

"Nope, a break cannot be caught," said Z'ev.

"I give up," said Nikki.

"Might as well," said Z'ev.

"Mom, I love you. We're leaving now. We'll talk when we get back. If you want to fight some more with Grandma while we're gone, you should ask her why she hasn't told us she's dating Jorge."

"Your grandmother is dating Jorge?" Nell's eyes snapped away from the gun and to Nikki's face.

"I saw them making out," said Nikki. "You should go ask her about it."

"Oh, you bet I will." Nell was already stomping back up the stairs.

"I can't believe that worked," said Z'ev, scratching his chin.

"She gets focused on the small stuff when she can't deal with big stuff," said Nikki.

"Are we leaving now?" asked Jane. She was carrying the gun in one hand and her case of Carrie Mae products in the other.

"We're leaving," agreed Nikki. "Where are the girls?"

"Jackson and Ellen are already on the road and I think Jenny's in the car."

"Great, let's go."

"That's a lot of make-up," said Z'ev.

"Well, you know, it always pays to look good," said Jane uncomfortably, hurrying to avoid eye contact.

The drive over to Crazy Cooter's was silent. Nikki wanted to say something, but couldn't find any words to say. She really didn't have anything that would make all of this in anyway 'OK'."

Crazy Cooter was driving a riding lawn mower with the mower removed through the compound when they arrived. He'd hitched a little wagon to it and stacked the wagon full of gallon jugs of water.

"You're back," he said frowning.

"We ran into a slight problem," said Nikki. "The sheriff kidnapped Donny Fernandez."

Cooter gaped. "But what do we do? We can't call the cops."

"I've arranged a trade," said Nikki, "but it would be better if you weren't here."

"I can't leave," said Cooter. "They've got a fire watch across the river. All it takes is one airborne spark and this place would go up like a can of napalm. I need to wet down the grass and clear the brush and…" He trailed off, looking at Nikki's face. "OK, I'll go." It took five minutes for Cooter to pack up and chug away down the road in a car that looked like it had been put together from junkyard rejects.

The dust had barely settled when Ellen and Jackson walked out of the freezer section. Ellen had Jackson's hunting rifle strapped to her back. Jackson was carrying Bill Bartlby's AK. Nikki liked it when Ellen went into shooting mode. She ditched her teacher's wife pose all together and the aviator sunglasses came out. The billowy skirts and scarves were removed, her hair got pulled back and suddenly it was like Ellen came into focus. She looked cool. Nikki tried not to say it, because she knew it made Ellen feel old, but she wanted to be like Ellen when she grew up.

"We look clear over here," said Ellen. "I think we've beat them here."

"Good," said Nikki.

"OK, Ladies," said Jane, opening the make-up case. "Here are your ear pieces." She held out her hand with what appeared to be two sets of butterfly earrings.

"Oh, no. Really?" Ellen made a disgusted face. "Those Mark-4's are so crappy!"

"I know, but I had to turn in the good kit," said Jane apologetically. "Sorry. This is what we have."

Ellen sighed and picked up an earring. "It's not your fault we got suspended. It's mine. We're extremely lucky you managed to keep any equipment at all. Thanks for looking after us."

Jane looked startled and pleased. "You're welcome," she said, then cleared her throat awkwardly. "Anyway, sync them to your phones." Nikki and Jenny each took an earring and Nikki moved one of the diamond studs Z'ev had given her up to the second hole in her ear and replaced it with the butterfly. Her phone took a second to sync, but then it went live.

"I give myself very good advice, but I very seldom follow it," quoted Jenny.

"Imagination is the only weapon in the war against reality," replied Jane.

"I knew who I was this morning, but I've changed a few times since then," said Ellen, which was her favorite quote to test with.

"We're all mad here," said Nikki, with a little more sincerity than usual.

"Loud and clear on all frequencies," said Jane, giving them the thumbs up.

"I get the feeling they've done this before," said Jackson.

"Mm," said Z'ev. "So do I."

Jane began to pull out the telescoping shelves of the make-up kit. "Jenny, the guns are in the bag in the back seat, if you want to take your pick."

Jenny opened the bag and then squealed in delight. "Oh, my God, is this your grandma's gun? It's so adorable." She held up the .357 Smith & Wesson. "Look at the engraving. I love it. It's a real live cowboy gun. And it has its own tooled leather holster." She hopped up and down a little in excitement. "Jackson, you can have the Glock."

"I'm not taking a handgun," said Jackson. "I don't know how to shoot."

Jenny looked as if Jackson had announced he was gay. "But, but, you have the rifle."

"Because I hunt deer that I later eat," said Jackson. "I'm not planning on eating any people, so I don't plan on shooting any people."

Ellen snorted. "Jackson, you're breaking her heart."

"I didn't say she couldn't shoot people, but I've never learned how to shoot handguns," he held up his hand as Jenny's face lit up. "And I'm not particularly interested in learning. I'm only here to get Donny out, remember? I'll be the wheelman, or the muscle, or whatever else you need, but I don't really think you should trust me with a gun."

"He's right," said Nikki. "If he doesn't already know, then it's too late to be teaching him. It'd be a waste of ammo."

"That's hardly a rousing vote of confidence for your friend," said Z'ev, looking offended on Jackson's behalf.

Nikki blinked. She'd forgotten he was there. He was doing his fly on the wall thing, which he was surprisingly good at for being so big. "I have every confidence in Jackson to do what he's good at. He's told me his limitations and I'd be an idiot not to respect that. We have limited resources and I need to put every bullet where I know it's going to count."

"People can't grow if you don't trust them outside their boundaries."

"If the stakes were lower or if Jackson were actually interested in learning, sure. But Donny doesn't have the luxury of finding out Jackson can't shoot straight."

"I'm with her," said Jackson, nodding. "That being said, who gets the AK?" He held up the gun and looked around the circle.

"Nikki," said Ellen, and Jane in unison.

"Oh, come on guys," said Nikki. "Be sensible. It can't be me. I can't show up to the exchange with an AK. Jenny, won't you feel better with a Freddy replacement?"

Jenny looked tempted, as she strapped on the ornate leather holster for the .357. "I would, but the exit plan calls for me to be in the junk section." She jerked her chin toward the maze of flattened cars. "It's close quarters; hand guns are more practical."

"Are you feeling OK?" asked Jane, reaching over to feel Jenny's forehead.

Jenny swatted Jane's hand away. "Situation dictates the strategy," she said, quoting their training officer, and the rest of the girls groaned.

"Don't start quoting Mrs. Boyer to us," said Ellen. "Or I'll have a PTSD flashback and punch you in the boobs."

"I'll take it," said Z'ev. "How did you talk him into loaning you an AK-47 anyway?"

Jackson shrugged. "I told him we were target shooting and he was happy to do it. Ever since that damn Initiative 594 went into effect, it's a crime to loan someone a gun without doing a background check, so this was his chance to have a tiny, political protest."

"And it never occurred to him that you might do something illegal with the gun?" asked Z'ev, looking perplexed by Bill Bartlby's careless gun safety attitude.

"He's known me since I was two—what trouble could I possibly get up to?"

Z'ev shrugged and took the gun. "OK, Chief," he said turning to Nikki, "What do we do next?"

"The goal is to get Donny, and us, out of here alive. Honestly, if he wants to make the exchange and drive off, then we let that happen. But let's be realistic, the odds are not good that he's going to do that. It's 4:30 now. I expect his ringers to arrive here in the next hour or so. We will let them get into position and then we will need to take them out prior to the exchange. Ellen, have you selected a location to watch their arrival?"

Ellen nodded.

"The red Buick. It's taller than most of the vehicles and it's got an unimpaired sightline from the top into the junkyard."

"Good. We'll be looking to you to direct us once the sheriff's men arrive. But while we're waiting for them, I want to plant a few surprises. Jenny, what are your recommendations?"

"I want to run a line of det cord across the driveway," said Jenny.

"Sure," said Z'ev. "If we had some det cord."

Jane pulled out the container of Super Silk Shaving Foam and popped open the bottom. "Here you go," she said, shaking the det cord out into Jenny's hand.

"Do we have remotes?" asked Nikki, peering over Jane's shoulder into the kit.

"I think so." Jane began rummaging in the kit.

"Good idea," said Jenny nodding. "Meanwhile, I think they'll be placing their shooters over in the crushed car section. I think Z'ev and I should be waiting in there, see if we can't flush them toward ya'll."

"It depends on how many people they bring with them," said Nikki. "And what kind of shape Donny is in. Even if you flush them toward me, I may not be much help if I'm dealing with too much fire power."

Jenny nodded. "I thought of that. Jane, do we have any of those Viper-12's?"

"We have three. And I also have three bottles of Rose Mist."

"I can work with that. We'll set up some pinch points, and hit them with the Rose Mist."

Z'ev cleared his throat. "Not to ask a foolish question, but we're going to hit them with a light, refreshing body spray?"

"That's 90% chloroform? Yes, we are," Jenny said.

"Works for me," said Z'ev.

"Where do you want me?" asked Jackson.

"You're going to be in charge of getting Donny out of harm's way. The sheriff will drive in. They'll be in one, maybe two cars. He'll pull Donny out, and there's going to be some smack talk. I'll hold up the thumb drive. He'll say throw me the thumb drive and I will. Hopefully, he'll let Donny go at that point. Once I extra, extra confirm that there are no other copies, he'll say something smart-ass, which will be a signal for his guys to show themselves. When they don't, there's going to be an awkward pause. That will be your moment, take Donny and head for the freezers."

"I would prefer it if there were some sort of signal," said Jackson.

"OK, I'll say 'eight seconds' and then you go."

"OK," said Jackson, nodding.

"After that, head for the Buick. Ellen can cover you from there."

"Sounds good," said Jackson.

"And what are you going to be doing while he's heading for the Buick?" asked Z'ev.

"I'll be hoping like hell that you and Jenny will be covering me as I run for the cars."

"I'm not sure I like this plan," he said.

"Do you have a better one?"

"Well, for one thing I can be the one to make the exchange."

"The sheriff doesn't know you. He's going to be suspicious and on his guard if I'm not there. This will work."

"You could get shot," said Z'ev.

"Meh," said Nikki with a shrug.

"Meh? What the hell is meh? Getting shot is not meh!"

"Well, no it's not. I just don't think I'll actually get shot. I mean, if Milt and Pedro are his right hand guys I feel fairly confident that we're not facing anyone who spends a lot of time figuring out how to shoot straight. You know what I'm saying?"

Z'ev opened his mouth to speak and then shut it again. "I cannot believe I'm even having this conversation right now. When this is over, you and I are going to have a long conversation about," he waved his hands in an all encompassing arc, "everything. Come on, Jenny, let's go sprinkle some damn Rose Mist around."

Jenny hid a laugh behind a cough, took an armful of equipment from Jane and hurried after him, shooting a Nikki a sympathetic look as she went.

"What about me?" asked Jane.

"You get the Glock," said Nikki. "Ellen's going to be our eye in the sky on this one, which means that we don't need you monitoring any computers or radios. You're going to be in the field."

Jane's eyes lit up. "OK, what do I do?"

"I want you to find a location out by the road. You're going to alert us to any cars that come, and once the sheriff arrives, I want you to pull back and help cover Jackson and Donny when they make a break for it."

"All right," said Jane, puffing up proudly. "You can count on me." She slid the make-up case closed with a resounding snap and grabbed up the Glock. "Should I go now?"

"Yeah, go now. Jackson and I are going to wait for your signal at the Fernandez house. Once you alert us that the sheriff's first team has arrived, we'll pull in and pretend like we don't know they're there."

"What if they don't send a first team?" asked Jane, and Nikki laughed.

"They'll send a first team. Don't worry."

"I'm off to the Buick," said Ellen. "Good luck, everyone."

Nikki nodded and gestured to Jackson to get in the car. Taking a last look around the junkyard, she felt the deep twist of fear in her gut. Their strategy was sound, they had taken as many precautions as they could and she had every faith in her team. Why was she so nervous? She watched as Z'ev and Jenny disappeared into the crushed car section and realized that her fear had nothing to do with the mission. Z'ev was an uncontrollable factor in her life—always had been from the moment she met him. Was she really ready to trust him?

AUGUST XXIX
SHOWDOWN

Nikki and Jackson parked behind the shed and watched the Fernandez clan pull away. The Impala didn't receive a second glance and Nikki couldn't tell if it was because they were so used to extra cars on their property or if they really hadn't noticed it. The sky across the river was dark with smoke and Jackson watched it nervously. She figured it was probably better to have him worry about that than it was to worry about Donny.

"So," said Jackson. "This really is what you do, isn't it?"

"Yeah," said Nikki.

"Huh. I always figured you'd get some sort of office job and marry a lawyer."

"Some sort of office job? I got a degree in linguistics, I speak four languages and you thought I'd turn out to be some sort of secretary? Wow. Thanks for believing in me."

"That's not what I meant," said Jackson. "And you hadn't even picked a major when I left. I just thought you were more of an office person than an out-in-the-field person."

"Guess you were wrong," said Nikki.

"What I mean is that I always thought I was holding you back," said Jackson. "My interests were more blue-collar and I wanted a job where I could be outside. I always thought that if we had stayed together, eventually you would have been embarrassed by me."

"I would never be embarrassed by you," said Nikki, shocked.

"Did you really think I was that shallow?"

"Not you, but the crowd you ran around with, yeah. And your mom always pushing you up the social ladder didn't help any."

"That is not fair. Judging me by Mom is a total low blow."

"Yeah, I know," said Jackson. "But it sort of creeps into your head."

Nikki's earpiece chirped. "Go ahead for Nikki," she said toggling the earpiece on.

"Sheriff's first team has arrived," said Jane, sounding breathless. "They're heading for the crushed car section, just like you said."

"Good. Jenny, are you and Z'ev good to go?"

"Five by five," said Jenny, her voice hushed.

"Ellen?"

"All set," said Ellen. "You are cleared to move."

"We'll give them a few minutes to get situated and then we'll go in." Nikki checked her watch. It was 6:15.

"How did you know that's what the sheriff was going to do?"

Nikki shrugged. "It's not my first dance."

"So you really think we can get us and Donny out of this alive?"

"Barring any unforeseen elements, yeah, I really do. What, did you think I was stringing all of you along and hoping it was going to work out?"

"Kind of."

"What the hell? Are you crazy? Why would you even go along with my plan if that's what you thought?"

"I couldn't think of a better plan," said Jackson with a shrug. "And your friends didn't seem worried. Besides, I figured I'd rather go down with you and Donny than a lot of other people."

"You're crazy," said Nikki.

It was Jackson's turn to shrug. "We all gotta die sometime."

"Well, it's not going to be today," said Nikki starting the car.

They pulled into Crazy Cooter's and Nikki pulled a u-turn, facing the car back up the drive. the rear end pointing toward the RV / shed / office.

"Sometimes, I can't believe that our parents let us play here," said Jackson. "It is like one giant tetanus shot waiting to happen."

"I don't think they knew we played here as much as we did," said Nikki. "OK, remember, talk loud and look confused and helpless. We're playing to the cheap seats."

"I don't know that confused and helpless is in my repertoire," said Jackson.

"Shoot for sad and stoic then. I'm pretty sure that's in your repertoire."

"What are you trying to say?" asked Jackson as they got out of the car.

"I don't know, how about the fact that you were Mopey Emo Cowboy our entire freshman year."

"I was not... There is no such thing as Emo Cowboy!"

"That is what you say now."

"Cowboy's cannot be Emo. Their very essence negates each other."

"Mopey Emo Cowboy," repeated Nikki.

"That's not cool."

"I call them like I see them," said Nikki laughing.

"I'm glad you came back," said Jackson, looking at her affectionately. "I didn't realize how much I'd missed you guys."

"I'm just glad we get to be friends again. Sometimes it feels like being an adult is all about losing people."

"Jeez, talk about Emo Cowboy. That's super depressing."

Nikki shrugged and sat on the trunk of the car. "I don't know. Sometimes I think Val was right. Maybe going it alone and looking out for number one really is the sensible way to live. Can't lose people if you don't have people."

"I don't know who Val is, but that's some depressing bullshit. Stop listening to her."

Nikki's earpiece beeped again, and she toggled it on. "Go for Nikki."

"Second team is in the driveway. I didn't see Donny in the car. I'm pulling back to my second location."

"Thanks, Jane." She kept her eyes on the driveway as she spoke to Jackson. "We're on."

"OK," said Jackson. He shifted nervously away from the car.

"You go when I say eight seconds."

"Got it."

"Stay calm. You'll be fine."

Jackson looked at her and she watched him breathe out, watched the nerves leave him.

"Yeah," she said, grinning. "You're going to be fine."

She watched as the Sheriff's car bumped down the drive in his county vehicle, followed by a black four-door, and pass under the archway of horns and bumpers. She paced out to the middle of the parking space and waited with her arms folded across her chest.

"Miss Lanier," Sheriff Smalls said, exiting the car. Milt got out of the passenger side, his eye still black from his fight with Nikki. The second car pulled to a stop and Pedro got out of the driver's seat.

"So nice to see you again," Merv said. "Mr. Tyrell, I see

you've decided to involve yourself in these high jinks. I can't say I think that was a smart decision."

"Where's Donny?" Nikki demanded.

"Mr. Fernandez was uncooperative. He got to ride in the back." He glanced at Milt, who sniggered. Milt snapped his fingers at Pedro. Pedro glared at one of the rent-a-henchmen he'd been riding with. Finally, one of them went to the trunk of the four-door and opened it. Donny was dragged out. His hands had been duct-taped together and he was sporting a black eye. He also looked pissed.

Nikki's earpiece beeped and she surreptitiously rubbed her ear to turn it on. "First team has been taken care of," said Jenny. "You are clear to move."

"You know, Miss Lanier," said the sheriff, "I don't know why I'm surprised at the way you turned out. You are Philippe's daughter after all. But I am surprised. You're a lot, well, harder than most women are. Are you sure you and I couldn't work together?"

Nikki's earpiece beeped.

"I'm not here for a job interview," said Nikki. "I just want to make the exchange and get the hell out of this town."

"Yes, but you see, what concerns me is that once you do leave this town, your friend is going to tell his other little cop friends and then I'll have problems. I don't like problems."

The earpiece beeped again.

"Donny is a narcotics cop," said Nikki, raising an eyebrow. So much could be said with facial expressions. "Do you really think this is the first... sticky situation he's been in? Or the first one that required a little discretion? Why do you think we're still friends after all these years? Don't worry about your little pot smuggling scheme. We've got our own plans to get back to." The wind was picking up. She could really hear it in the trees down by the river.

"Little? I smuggle tonnage, sweetheart. I am the direct Canadian pipeline from here to the heartland."

Beep.

"Yeah, and if Congress ever passes immigration reform your pipeline implodes."

"Well, fortunately, we all vote Republican out here, so that's not going to happen now, is it?"

"Can we make the trade?" said Jackson. "I hate talking politics."

"The man has a point," said Pedro.

Beep.

"Fine. You have the files?"

Nikki reached in her pocket and managed to hit her earpiece with the other hand. "Yeah," she said. "I've got it right here."

"Nikki! Get the hell out of there!" yelled Ellen. "The fire has jumped the river!"

Nikki held out the drive and watched a burning ember, drifting on the breeze, land on the ground at the foot of a radiator being used to hold up a potted plant. A small fire immediately started, licking up the sides of the radiator consuming old chemicals greedily.

"Jackson," she said, still holding out the thumb drive in one hand. "Eight seconds."

In the blink of an eye he had covered the distance between himself and Pedro. Events were moving in slow motion now. She saw the surprised expression on Pedro's face as Jackson upended him. She was dropping the thumb drive and pulling out her gun as Milt turned around to look at Pedro. Jackson and Donny were running. Milt was turning more, holding out his gun, and the sheriff was running at her. Worry about the far target. Worry about the far target. She squeezed the trigger and Milt went down, but the sheriff was already too close. She shifted her weight, preparing for the tackle, since she wasn't going to get her gun around in time. Embers were raining from the sky now. The RV was on fire.

She hit the ground and time sped up again. Everything was a mad scramble. Smalls had one hand out, trying to control the gun, blocking her arms, the other arm reaching for her throat. He was a large man, heavy, and quicker than he looked. But he'd landed off-center on her chest, so her legs were loose. She yanked one hand free and elbowed him in the ear. He pulled back slightly, easing the weight on her, which allowed her to get her hips out from under him. More elbows, repeat as necessary, until the sheriff changed tactics. He pushed back onto his knees, rearing back for a punch, and Nikki kicked downward into his knee, shoving him flat. His punch went wild, landing in the dirt. He grunted in anger and pain, then pulled back again, grinding all his weight onto the grounded gun with her hand pinned underneath it, once again reaching for her throat. She gave a sharp palm strike to his chin, and heard his teeth click together.

She aimed a punch at his throat.

He blocked it, but each movement was a backwards retreat that eased pressure on her gun hand, creating more space. Just a little farther and she'd have enough space to kick upward.

A little farther never happened.

The sheriff was lifted up into the air with the suddenness of a tsunami. He smashed back down again like a wave on rocks.

Nikki looked up at Z'ev. "Hey, babe." She looked at the sheriff, woozily attempting to sit up, gasping for air. "I was handling that."

"Well, I handled it for you."

"Thanks."

He reached out a hand to help her up as a bullet winged by her head and landed in the dirt. There was the chunka-chunka sound of the AK as Jenny responded. The sheriff scuttled backwards, wheezing, trying to get out of firing range.

"You gave Jenny the AK? You did remind her that Bill Bartlby is going to want it back, right?"

"We really ought to go now," he said ignoring her commentary. As if to emphasize his point, something exploded in the car section. A hubcap whizzed through the window of the office. "The car section is on fire."

"I gathered that," said Nikki, standing up. "What about them?" She gestured to the sheriff and his crew, all hiding from Jenny behind their cars.

"Let them burn," said Z'ev. "We've got the evidence. We've got Donny. What are they going to do?"

"I'll tell you what I'm going to do," yelled the sheriff, getting to his feet. His face was red, either from the heat or rage, Nikki couldn't tell. "I'm going to call my friends. the ones who smuggle my drugs for me, and I'm going to have them go up and pay your grandma a little visit. How fast do you think that peach orchard of hers will burn?"

The wind shifted, blowing smoke and ash into their faces.

"And if you've got evidence on me, then I've got evidence on you," he continued. "I'm sure the state police will be interested to know what you were doing here. Pretty young things running around with guns. That's not normal. I don't have to know what you're up to in LA, I just have to make enough people curious that they start investigating. And Donny? I just have to say that he was on my payroll and that we got into a dispute. Even if he proves otherwise, he'll still have a black mark on his record and trust me, it will follow him everywhere."

Nikki frowned. The sheriff read her expression as uncertainty and smiled.

"The best part about being bad is that you don't have to be tied down by rules and playing fair. If I'm going down in flames, you're going down with me."

Nikki could feel the fire at her back. Jenny was gesturing to her to get in the car. Z'ev was saying something, pointing at Jenny.

In the calm, cool part of her brain that was reserved for these moments, she did the calculations. He was absolutely right. He didn't have to have any proof. But the situation was weird enough that anything he said would get investigated. Investigations that would ruin Donny's career. Investigations that would cause Carrie Mae nothing but trouble. And then there was the threat against her grandmother.

"We can still all walk away from this," said the sheriff. "You got what you wanted. Let's just stick to the original agreement."

Z'ev was reaching for her, still saying something. But she couldn't hear him above the roar of the fire and the pounding in her ears.

He really shouldn't have threatened her grandmother.

"Come on," Merv Smalls said, smiling the smile that never touched his eyes, while his right hand reached for his gun. "Let's all just get out of here."

Her left hand hurt from where it had been ground into the dirt, but not so much that she couldn't pull the trigger. She felt Z'ev reaching for her, so she knew she didn't have a lot of time. Decisions had to be made.

She pulled the trigger. The Sheriff stumbled forward one step, gun halfway out of his holster, then dropped to the ground.

Z'ev picked her up like a football, tucking her under one arm and running for the car. There was another explosion from the car section and she could see the flames behind them, a wall of orange engulfing the junkyard.

Jenny revved the engine, as Nikki and Z'ev dove into the back seat, starting the car with the keys Nikki had left in the ignition. Val's Impala leapt forward throwing Nikki and Z'ev back against the cushions as Jenny floored the gas pedal.

AUGUST XXX

ENDINGS

"Slow down!" Nikki yelled as they hit the curve in the driveway. "We need to get Jane!"

Jenny slowed, but didn't stop. Jane ran out from behind a car and jumped in, throwing herself into the backseat across Nikki's lap.

"Hurry! We need to get out of here before the fire hits the det cord!" screamed Jane.

Jenny shoved her foot to the floor and the Impala streaked up the drive. The four-door sedan followed them. They weren't shooting. Instead, they looked equally as intent on getting the hell out of the junkyard. As they hit the road, the fire found the det cord buried under the dirt and the explosion shook the ground under the car. As Nikki watched, the archway of deer antlers and car parts began to topple down on itself.

"Jane, did you wire the Roadkill Memorial?" asked Nikki.

"Of course I did," snapped Jane, crawling over Nikki and Z'ev and into the front seat. "That was the creepiest damn thing I've ever seen in my life."

"Ditto to that," said Z'ev, gripping the door frame as Jenny took a corner faster than the recommended speed limit.

"It was in honor of the deerly departed. You know, deer," said Nikki, fully aware that she was focusing on the trivial, but feeling a deep, uncontrollable need to explain the pun.

"It was creepy as shit," said Z'ev.

Jenny jerked the Impala to a stop at the intersection to the main road. Ellen, Jackson and Donny were already waiting for them. The four-door sedan shot by them without stopping.

Donny was on the phone and they could hear the distant sound of sirens.

"Donny's calling the state cops," said Jackson. "But he wants to go back with the firefighters and try and save his parents' house."

Nikki nodded.

"What the hell?" demanded Ellen. "So it's OK when you shoot dirty cops, but when I do it it's an international incident?"

"I knew that looked like Ellen," muttered Z'ev.

"He was a threat to us."

"So was mine."

"No, yours was a threat to women in general. Mine was a threat to us. And I have someone who can work the cover up." She gestured to Donny. Ellen still looked unconvinced.

"You're assuming he'll cover it up," said Z'ev. "That's a big assumption."

"He owes us," said Nikki with a shrug. "And the fire should make it easier."

"You've covered all the angles then, haven't you?" Z'ev sounded bitter.

"I try," said Nikki. "Jenny, get out to the road and flag down the first fire truck."

"Yeah, yeah, yeah," said Donny walking back toward them. "I know, there's a lot more to cover, but come out here and do it in person. Right now, I have to go try to stop a wildfire." There was a pause. "Yes, sir, I do think I'm freaking Superman. I'm fairly certain it's on my birth certificate." Pause. "No sir, I do not think this is funny." Pause. "Yes, sir, I am aware that the State Patrol does not have a sense of humor. See you then."

He hung up the phone and looked at all of them. "OK, everyone. Thanks so much for helping, now you all need to leave."

"What about the fire?" asked Jenny.

"What are you going to do, carry buckets? I turned on the sprinklers before we left. I'm going to direct the firemen to skip Crazy Cooters and go straight to my parents' house. But, if my story that Jackson and Nikki are the only ones who came to make the exchange is going to hold water, I need the firemen to not see the lot of you. So, everybody climb back in Nikki's pimp-mobile and get the hell out of here."

"I don't want to leave you on your own," said Nikki, frowning. "Shouldn't Jackson and I stay?"

"Agreed," said Jackson. "I'm staying. Besides, I'm part of the volunteer fire crew."

"Then he can stay, but Nikki you need to go."

"I'm part of the cover story. I want to stay and help."

"And eventually the police will want to talk to you. But right now it's an emergency fire situation. Protocol says get civilians out. Plus, no offense, but you attract attention. And we want less attention, remember? You'll be more help if you leave."

"He's right," said Jenny and Ellen nodded.

"Fine," said Nikki frowning. "But I'm not happy about it." She hugged Jackson and then Donny. "Take care of each other. Don't do anything I wouldn't do."

"Although, it turns out that's a pretty low benchmark," said Z'ev. "So really, you probably ought to stick with using your own best judgment."

"Call us if you need help," said Jenny.

"Thanks," said Donny. "And I really do mean that. Without

you guys, I'd be dead. Now vamoose before you cause me even more of a headache than the sheriff."

Fitting four women and Z'ev into the Impala was a tight fit, but they managed, mostly due to the Impala's bench seating and Jane's skinny butt. They pulled out onto the highway, and Nikki rolled down the window. The post-mission crash was imminent, but she wanted to stave it off for as long as possible.

"INTERPOL sent out a B.O.L.O. on you," said Z'ev turning around in the front seat to look at Ellen. "What were you thinking?"

"I was thinking, 'Oh, look, someone should really crush this serial killer to death with his own car.' Although, really, that's a better death than he deserved after what he did to those women."

"Serial killer? I thought he was a cop."

"Turns out he was both," said Jane.

"And do you really think that was the best way to handle it?" asked Z'ev.

"Hey," said Nikki. "We don't second-guess the operator. We weren't there. Monday morning quarterbacking is counter-productive and besides, it's none of your business."

"None of my business," said Z'ev. "I'm in the damn CIA, Nikki! We're supposed to assess threats from foreign entities and protect the United States. Currently, you're the most foreign entity I know!"

"Yes," said Jenny, soothingly, "But we're not actually a threat, so really there's no problem."

"You just killed the sheriff," said Z'ev. "Ellen apparently ran over a mountie. Your body count for police personnel is looking suspiciously high."

"They were bad people," said Jane. "And you're not seeing all the bad guys we take down."

"No, clearly I'm not," said Z'ev. "But would you please explain who made you the decision-makers on who lives and who dies?"

Jane opened her mouth and Jenny poked her in the ribs.

Z'ev looked at all of them. "I'm going to stop talking now," he said. "I'm going to wait until we're not all armed and we're sitting in Peg's kitchen eating pie and the guns are all put away before we talk more. But when we do talk, I'm going to have questions, and there better damn well be answers."

He turned around, eyes facing front, walls up, ignoring all of them.

Nikki looked at the girls in the review mirror. Jane made a face, Jenny shrugged, Ellen spread her hands, palms up. Nikki nodded.

The drive was long, silent, and hot since the Impala cooling system couldn't push the air around fast enough to keep any of them from melting. Nikki pulled up in front of the house and saw a strange car in the driveway. Another rental car. Someone had sprung for the upgrades. It was a convertible with leather seats.

"Give me a second," said Nikki. "Let me make sure Mom and Grandma aren't having the pastor over for tea before we all go trooping in with our guns."

"We do look a little Not Suitable For Church," said Jenny, unstrapping Peg's six-shooter.

Nikki walked up to the front door and paused. There was something off, she could feel it, but she couldn't quite place what it was. She had one hand on the door knob and took a deep breath, then froze. Ever so slightly, there was the faintest scent of Chanel.

Nikki's skin felt clammy, and she reached for her gun as she opened the door. Her heart was racing.

"Do not move," she said.

"Ah, Nikki," said Valerie Robinson, "We've been waiting for you." Val looked suspiciously the same: hair cut in a sharp black bob, pale skin, blue eyes, crisp black shirt. She looked as she had always looked, effortlessly sophisticated and cool. The only difference was that there wasn't a cigarette in one hand.

"Where's Mom and Grandma?" Nikki demanded.

"I think Peg is getting baby pictures and Nell is fetching lemonade. Because I look like a lemonade kind of woman." Val paused, then continued when Nikki didn't comment or change position. "Relax, Red, I'm here about your father."

"Nicole Lanier," said her grandmother coming into the room and attempting to snatch the gun out of her hand, "we do not point guns at guests."

"But she shot me!" Nikki said, holding the gun further away.

"Twice," said Val holding up two fingers, with a lazy smile.

"What?" said her mother, coming into the room carrying a tray of lemonade. "Shot you? What is this? Nikki, please stop pointing guns at people. You can't carry guns around like that!"

Behind her, there was a slam of a car door and running feet.

"Nikki, what's going on? Why did you pull—" Ellen's sentence abruptly cut off.

"Oh, shit," said Jenny. Nikki heard the guns come out.

"Hey look," said Val, "the glee club has arrived."

"You are supposed to be dead," said Jenny, aiming steadily.

"Jenny, Ellen, Jane! What are you all doing with guns? You work for a make-up company!" Nell thumped the tray down on the coffee table. "You don't carry guns."

"These ones do," said Val.

"You want to shut up now?" asked Nikki.

"Actually, I think I'd like to hear more," said Z'ev, crossing the room and dropping into her grandfather's old armchair.

"Oh, please, it's not like you could ever keep a secret anyway," said Val. "You're a terrible liar."

"That is kind of true," agreed Z'ev.

"Nikki, who is this woman?" demanded her grandmother. "She said she worked with you."

"That is Valerie Robinson," said Jane, "and she's supposed to be dead."

"It's called Kevlar, sweetie," said Val, smugly. "Don't leave home without it."

"Next time, I'll make it a head shot, sweetie," said Ellen.

"Why— How are you here, Val?" demanded Nikki.

"We still haven't covered why you're carrying guns," protested Peg.

"I'm here about your father," said Val.

"Oh, God," said Nell. She picked up a glass of lemonade and emptied it into the ficus. Then she pulled out a bottle of Scotch from the sideboard.

"Actually, if you're pouring, I wouldn't mind some," said Val.

"You shot my daughter," said Nell, pouring out a generous measure. "Twice? The only way you're getting some of this is if I hit you up the side of your head with the bottle."

"Point taken," said Val shrugging.

"Actually," said Z'ev, "I'm with Peg. I want to know who Nikki and her friends work for." Nikki tried to read his expression, but couldn't.

"We work for the Carrie Mae Foundation," said Nikki defensively. This wasn't how she wanted to do this. She wanted to have a private, honest conversation with Z'ev where she could explain. Val, as usual, was ruining everything.

"The Carrie Mae Foundation carries a lot of heavy weaponry, do they?" asked Z'ev.

"Not a lot," said Jane. "Just the necessities."

"Just what does Carrie Mae do?" asked her grandmother.

"Carrie Mae uses a multi-disciplinary, local approach to solving the problems facing women on a global level," said Nikki, as if reciting a well-learned lesson, which thanks to Mrs. Boyer, it was.

"With extreme prejudice," added Val.

"Well, I appreciate that you want to help women," said Peg, "but that doesn't mean the four of you can form your own little vigilante group."

"What makes you think it's just the four of them?" asked Val, unwrapping a piece of gum and popping it into her mouth.

"Shut up!" Nikki yelled at Val. She could feel her breath coming in rapid gasps. This was her worst nightmare.

"That's impossible," said Z'ev.

"What?" asked Val, looking at Nikki's furious expression. "He's CIA. I'm sure he's figured it out by now."

"CIA?" repeated Peg. "Nell, be a dear and pour a glass for your mother."

"All of Carrie Mae?" He asked looking at her as if she were the only one in the room. Nikki felt herself flush bright red.

"Oh! He didn't know," exclaimed Val laughing. "That is so cute! You're like the Dumb and Dumber of espionage."

"All of Carrie Mae?" he repeated.

"Not all of it," said Nikki, blushing harder. "Just the non-profit portion."

"Most Carrie Mae ladies really do sell make-up," said Jane,

clearly trying to help.

"But not all of them," said Z'ev. "Most is not the same as all."

"Well, all of them do sell make-up. But some of them also do… other… stuff." She finished awkwardly, and glanced at Nikki apologetically.

"So what we have is a worldwide organization with advanced training in tactics, weapons, and explosives," said Z'ev. "That about sums it up, yes?"

"More or less," said Nikki.

"Only, it's an organization that no one knows about? How can no one know about it?"

"Because we're women," said Val, standing up, sounding suddenly bitter and tired. "And women are the invisible, alien others. The CIA doesn't know about us, not because we're so clever, but mostly because you're so dumb that it doesn't occur to you that women could do anything. Nikki, this has been fun. It's practically a Homecoming Dance and a ten-year high-school reunion all rolled into one. Now maybe we could get down to business?"

"What business could we possibly have?" demanded Nikki.

"I'll say it for the third time. I'm here about your father. He's in trouble. There isn't a lot of time and I need your help."

"Don't believe her," said Jenny.

"Actually," said Peg, clearing her throat. "I think she might be right." Everyone swiveled to look at Peg. "The reason I've been pushing your mom so hard to tell you about Philippe is that three weeks ago I got a letter in the mail. It was addressed to you, but I opened it because…" She paused, then shook her head. "Because I'm a snoop." She pulled a folded envelope out of her pocket and handed it to Nikki. "Once I read it, I knew it wouldn't make any sense if you didn't already know he'd gone to jail. I figured we had to tell you. I just thought we had more time."

Nikki read the letter. She read it again.

"Where is he?" she asked, looking up at Val.

"South Africa," said Val. "I can get him out, but I need someone I can trust."

"That's a laugh, coming from you."

Val shrugged and stood up. "Are you in or not? We have to leave now."

"Nikki, don't trust her," said Jane. "We have to bring her in. Mrs. Merrivel will want to know where she's been. Once we question her, we can put together a plan to go get your father."

"There isn't time," said Val. "And can you really be sure they would allow you to go? Helping your dad doesn't fall within mission parameters."

Nikki tucked the envelope in her pocket. Her jeans were covered in smoke and dirt. She couldn't even guess what her hair looked like. She knew her body was about to hit a wall—too much adrenaline, not enough food, not enough water, not enough time. There never seemed to be enough time. Everything she loved and wanted to cling to seemed to leave her behind. Everyone was always pushing her into something new. She didn't want something new. She wanted everything to be like it was. She could feel a rising tide of panic that seemed to sweep away feeling from her limbs and close her vision down to a tunnel.

She looked at Jane. Stuck behind a computer, when she wanted to do field work.

She looked at Jenny. Never going to be in command with Nikki around.

She looked at Ellen. Ellen, who'd buried her adventurous

side in mommyhood until she found Carrie Mae. Ellen smiled at her and tilted her head ever so slightly toward Val.

She couldn't look at Z'ev. If she looked at Z'ev, she'd know whether or not he still loved her, and the idea that the answer might be no was more than she could stand. She tucked her gun away in its holster, trying to hide the way her hands were shaking and pulled out the Impala keys.

"Fine. Let's go," said Nikki.

Val snatched the keys out of her hand. "I'll be driving," she said. "It is my car after all."

SEPTEMBER I
FINAL REPORT

Los Angeles • Monday

"What are we going to do?" asked Jenny.

Mrs. Merrivel picked a microscopic piece of lint off her skirt.

"Well, I guess we'll have to bump Jane up to field agent and request a new technology liaison."

"What are we going to do about Nikki?"

"I don't think there's anything we can do about Nikki."

"But she just left. With Valerie Robinson! We can't do nothing."

"Jenny," Mrs. M appeared to be picking her words carefully. "Your team garnered a great deal of political goodwill by dealing with Valerie Robinson, but the unfortunate Canadian incident with Ellen may have used up the last of it. Right now, Darla has made some very smart moves, one of which was putting your team on administrative leave. The current perception is that Darla is a hard-ass and that she is appropriately dealing with matters. If word gets out that not only is Valerie alive, but that Nikki has left with her, how well do you think that is going to go over? Darla will be forced to send teams to retrieve them. And if the three of you were to go and assist Nikki… I'm rather certain that you would also be added to the shoot-to-kill list."

Jenny gaped. "But, Val said it was about Nikki's father. It didn't sound like they were doing anything bad."

"Ah, yes, helping Nikki's father, the known smuggler? And

we believe Val Robinson, the traitor, do we?"

"Oh, crap," said Jenny, sinking down in her chair.

"Quite. No, the best thing we can do is nothing. The four of you are on leave currently and I think we can drag that out for a bit longer. Hopefully, Nikki will be back in a few weeks."

"And what if she isn't?"

"Then we'll come up with an alternative plan," said Mrs. M with a shrug.

"And what about Z'ev? He left right after Nikki. He wouldn't even talk to us."

"Well, thank goodness Jane kept her head and put a tracking device in his luggage. We know he simply returned here to LA."

"Yes, but he could be telling people about us right now. What should we do about him?"

"I've already taken care of it. I invited him here to the house for dinner. John is going to talk to him."

"Is that going to work?"

"It better. Nikki will probably be upset if I have to take measures regarding her boyfriend."

"If he is her boyfriend. She left at kind of sensitive moment regarding their relationship."

Mrs. M shrugged again.

"How can you take this so calmly?" said Jenny, jumping out of her chair and pacing the length of the office. "This is a serious problem!"

"Yes, it really, really is," said Mrs. Merrivel. "But it's not like I wasn't aware that this was a possibility. Admittedly, Val turning up again was a bit of a surprise. But Nikki's relationship with Z'ev was always leading in this direction."

"I just can't believe we're going to leave Nikki out there by herself."

"She's not by herself," said Mrs. Merrivel. "She has Val."

"I'm not sure which is worse," said Jenny. "Being alone, or being with Val."

"We'll have to wait and find out," said Mrs. M.

"Yeah," said Jenny, "if she survives."

A SNEAK PEEK AT
WHAT HAPPENS NEXT IN...

SOUTH AFRICA I
APPROACH VECTOR

Nikki looked out of the plane window at the distant ground. From the air, what had been a post-sunset world was now a twilight sphere of advancing shadows as the sun retreated beyond the curve of the earth. Below, the farm fields of South Africa unrolled like a patchwork quilt sewn by a half-rate seamstress. Somehow she hadn't pictured Africa having this much green.

"This is a terrible plan," said Nikki.

"I know," said Val, leaning over to look out the window with her.

"You say that now!" Nikki snapped around to look at Val.

Val popped a piece of nicotine gum in her mouth and grinned. "I said it when you came up with the plan."

"I can't believe I let you talk me into this," said Nikki.

"Hey, I just asked you to help rescue your father. I didn't say you had to jump out of plane without a parachute," said Val. "That was your idea."

"Coming up on the drop point," yelled the co-pilot coming into the cabin, and yanking open the exterior door. Nikki shuffled to the door, her wingsuit dragging behind her. The co-pilot checked his watch and held up three fingers, counting down. Val pulled her goggles down on her face.

"Yeah, but—" Whatever Nikki had been about to say was deliberately cut off as Val pushed past her and dove out of the plane.

Nikki rolled her eyes and checked her watch, marking the time. "Drama queen," she muttered. She pulled down her goggles and glanced at the co-pilot who gave her a thumbs up. Still shaking her head, Nikki stepped from the plane.

For a moment there was the delicious sensation of pure speed, unhampered by anything so mundane as a vehicle. Freedom, for Nikki, was going fast. All too soon, her watch flashed and with reluctance, Nikki widened her arms and spread her legs so that the fabric webbing between them could catch the air like sails. Val was below her already angling her body for the decent. Nikki squinted in the dim light trying to match her approach.

Nikki was buffeted by a gust of wind and found herself slipping off target. Battling back, Nikki corrected course, and blinked back tears from the cold air that blew in around the edge of her goggles. It was true; there were easier ways to get into the farm where her father was being held. But all of them would leave a footprint of some kind. Abandoned vehicles, changes of clothes, traces of hacking. Nikki wanted to drop in, collect Philippe Lanier from whatever hellhole he had been confined and disappear into the night. After that—Well, Nikki couldn't think about after that. Because after that meant thinking about what to do about Val and her... aliveness. Not to mention what to do about her job, the one she had unexpectedly quit, or her boyfriend, CIA Agent Z'ev

Coralles, who she had left sitting in her grandmother's living room with no explanation. The "after that" list on this mission was extensive and scary. Nikki avoided the thought and concentrated on not falling out of the sky like a rock.

The lights of the farmhouse, if you could call a sixteen bedroom mansion, with on-call chef, and a rooftop infinity swimming pool, a farmhouse, were ahead of them, forming a distinctive pattern in the darkness. The house, possibly in a nod to the Dutch owners, or possibly because even architects sometimes take drugs, was three stories, built in two long strips like a V. At the point of the *V* was a windmill. Their goal was the right wing of the house, which had a long narrow pool on the roof.

Nikki had chosen this approach for the simple fact that it was the only entrance to the house that wasn't under video surveillance. The owner of the farm, a thirty-year-old, dark-haired Dutchman named Maaravi Meise, had more security on his flower farm than a drug cartel. Nikki assumed this was because, even though there were flowers in the fields, Meise was not actually in the flower business. At best, he was *also* in the flower business. Nikki chose not to investigate – she didn't actually care. She just wanted to get her dad and get the hell out of the country.

However, her chosen entry method, wingsuits, were meant to be deployed in conjunction with parachutes. But parachutes were unwieldy and too easy to spot from the ground. Instead, Nikki had chosen to use an alternative method to soften their landing— the pool. Nikki watched as Val angled her body up, slowing her descent even further. Too much angle and she'd become vertical and gravity would take over. Not enough angle and she'd hit the rooftop at fifty miles an hour and bounce off the water with leg breaking intensity like a skipped stone.

Nikki swung onto her approach vector. From the air things were always so much clearer. The roof was lined with lights focused on the grounds below and ambient light and altitude illuminated the roof clearly. But once she touched down, she knew there would be a period of darkness as her eyes adjusted to being behind the lights. That was the moment of danger. She and Val had debated bringing night-vision goggles. Nikki had been reluctant to pack a giant, clunky, standard issue army pair, which was all they could afford on the black-market, and Val seemed to think night-vision was for sissies. Either way it had seemed sort of silly when it was only going to be for this one moment. But now, as the moment approached, Nikki wondered if maybe they had made the wrong decision. But then, all of her decisions since leaving her teammates, family, and boyfriend seemed worthy of being questioned.

Val disappeared into the darkness beyond the row of roof lights. Nikki checked her watch. If she had timed the jump properly she should be thirty seconds behind Val. Time enough for Val to make the landing and get clear. Nikki angled, spreading her arms and legs, slowing down as much as possible. The roof still seemed to be approaching far too quickly.

Slow. Slow. Slow. Nikki lifted her chin, and clenched her tongue carefully inside her teeth, hoping for a graceful bellyflop that would glide her into the shallow end of the pool. There was a heart stopping moment of impact and the rush of water. She was going to make it. Son of—it's a pool noodle! Ducky! Ducky! It's a ducky. Nikki took the long piece of wet foam and bobbing rubber duck to the face, before feeling them bump over her hair and down her back.

She felt her momentum lessen and she reached for the zippers on her suit. Arriving safely only to drown in the pool would be the definition of a failed plan. She floundered briefly and then found her feet. There was a dim light near the stairs. She sloshed over to them and hauled herself out – stripping out of her suit as she went. Her eyes, not yet adjusted, saw only indistinct blobs of white deck furniture. No alarms seemed to have been triggered. No running feet. Also, no Val.

"Val?" she whispered. There was an annoyed grunt from ahead of her. "Val?"

"Over here," said Val, her voice filled with resignation. "I'm stuck."

"Stuck how?" Nikki inched forward. Hampered by the dragging fabric of her suit.

"I'm not entirely sure," said Val. "I think it's a hammock."

ABOUT THE AUTHOR

Bethany Maines , a native of Tacoma WA, is the author of the Carrie Mae Mystery series and An Unseen Current. When she's not traveling to exotic lands, or kicking some serious butt with her fourth degree black belt in karate, she can be found chasing after her daughter, or glued to the computer working on her next novel.

OTHER WORKS BY BETHANY MAINES

BULLETPROOFMASCARA
A **CARRIE MAE** MYSTERY

COMPACT WITH THE **DEVIL**
A **CARRIE MAE** MYSTERY

SUPPORTING THE **GIRLS**
A **CARRIE MAE** MINI-MYSTERY

POWER OF **ATTORNEY**
A **CARRIE MAE** MINI-MYSTERY

Tales from the City of Destiny

An Unseen Current

Wild Waters

Shark Santoyo Crime Series

Find out more at:
BethanyMaines.com